The Billionaire Is Back

Kayley Loring

Connor Crais

USA TODAY BESTSELLING AUTHOR
Kayley Loring
Connor Crais

This is a work of fiction. Names, characters, businesses, places, events, and incidents are either products of the author's imagination or are used fictitiously. Any resemblance to actual events, locales, or actual persons, living or dead, is entirely coincidental.

No part of this book may be reproduced in any form or by any electronic or mechanical means, including information storage and retrieval systems, without written permission from the author, except for the use of brief quotations in a book review.

The lyrics for "What'll I Do?" by Irving Berlin are in the public domain

Text Copyright © 2023 by Kayley Loring & Connor Crais

All rights reserved

Cover Design: Kari March Designs
Cover Photo: Ren Saliba
Cover Model: Stefano Maderna
Copy Editing & Proofreading: Mandi Andrejka, Inky Pen Editing

Chapter 1

S'more than a Feeling

Twelve Years Ago

C<small>LAIRE</small>

"D<small>O YOU HAVE ANY DARK CHOCOLATE</small>?"

Grady Barber is at my s'more station, staring at my marshmallows, and he wants to know if I have any dark chocolate. His tea-brown eyes are in shadow, but I can still *feel* the glint in them. Half of his face is lit by the bonfire, the other half obscured by darkness. That is so Grady Barber—the golden boy of Beacon Harbor. The part of him we can all see is intense, warm and glowing. But part of him is impossible to know, always a mystery, miles away and years ahead. Dreaming big, setting goals, executing plans.

Wanting more.

"Did you really just ask me that? Really? No, I do not have any dark chocolate. I never have dark chocolate. No one should ever have dark chocolate. Dark chocolate is a bitter, snobby asshole, and it has no business mingling with the likes of marshmallows and graham crackers—on this beach or anywhere."

I'm still a sophomore, so I shouldn't even be at this party. But my brother's graduating, so here I am, in charge of the s'mores because everyone in town knows I do them right. I do all forms of flour confections right as well as chocolate-based sweet treats with crunchy ingredients. Grady knows this because he's in our kitchen eating my cookies and muffins every weekend before his morning runs.

I've set up a table with roasting spears, two different brands of graham crackers, vanilla- and coconut-flavored marshmallows, a now-empty jar of Nutella, a jar of smooth peanut butter, a jar of caramel sauce, bars of Hershey's milk chocolate, squares of white chocolate, a container of coarse sea salt, raspberries, and exactly no dark chocolate.

But Grady wants more than I have to offer.

Grady wants more than this town has to offer.

And he has no idea that I would give him absolutely everything if he would have me. But I'm just his best friend's little sister. And nobody in this town has what he's looking for.

"It was a simple yes-or-no question, Little Sweeney," he says with a gentle smirk that pierces my soul. "I don't need the lecture about how you'd rather eat pegboard—I know how you feel about dark chocolate."

You don't know how I really feel about anything is what I want to say.

He's been calling me Little Sweeney since I was three, I'm told. I just turned sixteen, and I am not little, so every time he calls me that it's bittersweet. Like dark chocolate but better—because literally everything is better than dark chocolate. "Any request for that heinous crime against cocoa is an affront to taste buds in general and me in particular."

"Not a request, just a question." His voice is so calm in response to my rant, it's aggravating. "Here's another: Why is this jar of Nutella empty?"

I roll my eyes at him. I am 100% certain that I am the only person on earth who has ever rolled her eyes at Grady Barber. I am also the only one who calls him Grody Borber because, sadly, that very clever nickname did not catch on. But I am 95% certain that I'm the only victim of his annoying question-asking and advice-giving. It doesn't make me special, it just makes me his best friend's little sister. "That's not a question, that's a passive-aggressive statement with a question mark at the end of it."

"Why's that?"

"Because what you're really saying is that I didn't bring enough Nutella."

"Am I wrong?"

I grunt, very ladylike, in response.

"Supply and demand, Sweeney. You know better than anyone that there's a big demand for Nutella around here. If you're gonna start a bakery business you have to have the right products in stock at all times."

"It's a s'more station at a bonfire, Grody. I'm not catering the mayor's Christmas party."

He laughs. "*That's* your example of a big-deal event? Why not the White House?"

I shrug. "The White House isn't in Beacon Harbor."

He regards me thoughtfully, in the way that only he does. "Well, anyway. Now I'm supposed to have a Nutella-free s'more?" He shakes his head slowly as he drags his fingers through his short, wavy dark brown hair. I swear, he must practice that move in the mirror. "What's that about?" He's being good-natured, as always, but as always, it feels like a tiny dagger to the heart every time I can't provide him with what he's looking for...a skinny body, worldly experience, gluten-free pastries, eyeballs that always face forward.

"*Well, anyway*, if you wanted a high-demand ingredient you should have approached the s'more station earlier in the evening. Robbie just got the last Nutella s'more." I nod in Robbie's direction.

Robbie is holding the perfect s'more that I made for him because he's too big of an idiot to roast a marshmallow and assemble it with other ingredients even when he's sober. Also because, as previously mentioned, I am better at making s'mores than anyone else in this entire county, and that is a known fact. But mostly because Robbie's a drunken buffoon. A drunken buffoon who is currently telling some dumb story to a group of people and waving his hands around. I swear to God, if he drops that perfect s'more I will kick sand into his face.

Grady follows my gaze, casually turns, and saunters over to Robbie and the group. He's wearing dark jeans that already hug his perfect boy butt magnificently, but when he shoves his hands into his front pockets and I watch him walk away from me with the long, graceful stride of a runner, my mouth starts watering at the same time as I get a lump in my throat. Thankfully, a Pink song is blaring from a speaker somewhere, so he doesn't hear me choking on my feelings. It's not even the butt in the jeans that gets to me. It's the back of his neck. The confidence. The way he sees what he wants and goes for it.

It's all something to behold, even though that thing that he wants has never been me.

As soon as people in the group see Grady walking toward them, all eyes are on him. He taps Robbie on the shoulder, gestures toward the s'more, to my s'more stand, and says some things while smiling. That's it. That's all it takes. Robbie hands over the Nutella s'more without resistance and gets a pat on the shoulder. Robbie then salutes him, as if it was his great honor to surrender to him.

Grady takes a bite of my perfect s'more as he walks over to where my brother, Jake, is chatting up multiple girls. He stops in his tracks for a moment as he savors the flavors and textures. The crunch of the graham cracker, the warm hazelnut-chocolate spread blended with the gooey, fire-kissed vanilla marshmallow that tastes like the best childhood memories. He looks over at me and gives me the chef's-kiss fingers. High praise from Grady Barber.

He joins my brother and his entourage, and I can see all the girls suddenly twirling their hair around their fingers and throwing their heads back, laughing loudly. Not that Jake doesn't command his fair share of attention from the ladies, but Grady is on a whole other level. He just focuses on my s'more, though, which is...something.

In the spring I overheard him telling Jake that he

wasn't going to hook up with any local girls for the months leading up to graduation and his imminent departure because he didn't want anyone to get clingy. He got a scholarship to business school at Wharton, and he's doing an internship in New York for the summer. Grady has always had his eye on the prize, and the prize was never in Beacon Harbor, Maine. Everyone has always known this, and everyone has fallen for him anyway.

I realize I'm sighing and staring when I feel my best friend's hand on my shoulder.

"Have a cider, Claire Bear." Vera is one of two other sophomores who was actually invited to this bonfire, and not for brother reasons, like me. People just think Vera's cool, which is why it makes no sense that she's my best friend. The other sophomore here is Grady's brother, Damien, who is equally as cool as Vera, even though they seem to hate each other. "Have two ciders and step away from the s'more station." She hands me a bottle of New England cider and takes a big pull from hers.

"But the s'mores are my responsibility."

She tilts her head as she grins at me. "Are they, though?"

"Of course they are."

"Are they your *priority* at a seniors' bonfire?"

"Obviously. Why else would I be here?"

She glances over at Grady. Not with longing, like most girls glance at him. She glances at him and then back at me to make a silent, horrible point.

I frown at her. "I'm here because my brother paid for the s'mores ingredients and told me I was in charge of them." I stare down at the bottle in my hand, as if it's saying something very important.

"Right. And you wouldn't rather be at home watching *Gilmore Girls* and reading about the history of food coloring."

Dammit, that is exactly what I would rather be doing right now.

Except Grady's here...

I take a sip of cider. I do not handle alcohol well, and Vera knows it. But I still need to fit into the dress my mom bought for me to wear to Jake's grad ceremony tomorrow, so I will drink one bottle of cider instead of eating twenty-seven s'mores, until I no longer dread the days that will follow Grady's migration.

Ten or twenty or forty minutes later, I'm sitting by myself on the sand in front of the bonfire, laughing about a hilarious thought I had a few seconds ago that I no longer remember. Yeah. I'm straight chillin' here by myself on a beach at night, and it's not so bad. Three different guys that I have zero interest in have said "Hey" to me in the past ten or twenty or forty minutes. So, I'm pretty sure that means I'm hot and I could make out with them if I wanted to. If I wanted my brother to punch them in the face, that is. A life without Grady can be very entertaining and fulfilling. That OneRepublic song "Good Life" that the grads have been playing all day, every day is blaring from a boom box somewhere in the distance, and it's so damn poignant I could cry.

"Your brother know you're drinking?" Grady is standing behind me, and I close my eyes because I don't even know if I can handle looking at him right now. Just the sound of his voice is making me all tingly in secret parts of me that I only became aware of because of how they react to *him*.

He's standing next to me now, so I keep staring ahead, into the fire. "My brother know you always ask me questions you already know the answer to and give me advice I've never asked you for?" That's what I think I'm saying anyway. The sounds that actually come out of my mouth are more like *My brutha manumanumanumanah?*

"Sounds like you're on your second bottle."

I raise my second bottle of cider in his general direction and say, "Surprise and demands!" and then I lose my grip on the bottle and somehow lose my balance even though I'm sitting on the ground. And then I roll onto my side, into Grady's leg, and squeeze my eyes shut again, because maybe that will make me disappear?

Seconds later, I'm on my feet because Grady has picked me up. My arm is around his shoulder and his arm is around my waist and I'm pressed up against him. I look up at him and he's looking down at me, and I've never seen him from this angle before. I can feel his sinewy muscles tensing through the Henley shirt and jacket. I can feel him holding his breath. I can see his jaw tighten, his nostrils flare. Even if the sun was shining I don't think I'd be able to read his face right now.

But I swear, the crackling fire is not the source of the heat I feel between us.

This surreal moment stretches into eternity and back again as I realize I am silently begging him to kiss me.

He finally looks away from me, over my shoulder, and

steps back, putting his hands on my shoulder to steady me. "Come on, party animal. Let's walk it off."

"'Kay." I follow him down the beach, away from the crowd, in silence. The sky over the water has gone from purple and pink to cobalt blue. The tide is almost as loud as the music and voices now. Grady is always asking me questions that feel like tests, but I have so many questions for him that I've never asked. I take a deep breath of ocean air and ask him one. "Are you even going to miss this place?"

"Of course I'm going to miss it." He doesn't even have to think about it, and he almost sounds hurt. "I love this town. And the people in it. I just can't do everything I want to do here."

"Get rich, you mean?"

"Yeah."

"What are you going to do with all the money you make?"

"Make more money. And buy my parents a new house."

I guffaw at that. "Your parents would never move out of their house."

"Then I'll pay for a total remodel."

"That's it? You're going to make lots of money and pay for a remodel?"

"No, Sweeney," he says, in a not-at-all-condescending way. "I'm going to do a lot more than that."

"But what if it doesn't make you happy?"

He stops in his tracks for a second, in the same way that he did when he took that first bite of my s'more. I guess no one's ever asked him this before. "I'm already happy, Claire." He isn't being defensive. He's telling the truth.

"Then why do you need more than what you have here?"

He looks away from me, staring out at the lights reflected in the harbor. "I want to see how far I can go. Y'know? Not in terms of distance. I want to see what I'm capable of, what my limits are. Living here limits what I can accomplish. That doesn't mean I hate this town or this life." He looks back at me. "You really can't see yourself ever leaving here?"

"No." I don't have to think about it either. It's true. But the other thing that's true is something I will never say out loud—to Grady or anyone else. That I have this crazy feeling I'd leave with him if he asked me to. Any place, any time. What I say, though, is "I couldn't imagine living more than a few blocks from the water or Main Street or the islands. The puffins and the seals and the whales and the hanging baskets and just...everything. I love everything about this place."

He nods, slowly. I wait for him to ask a question. Any question. Anything to break the silence. All I'm aware of is the maritime air and the sound of his breathing and the twelve or so inches between us.

Suddenly, he's gripping my arms and yanking me toward him as he glares at Robbie, who's seated in a wheelbarrow chariot that's careening toward us, piloted by some other drunk idiot whose name I can never remember. He's wearing a football helmet and holding up one of my marshmallow roasting forks and yelling. They continue on past us as if they didn't even realize they almost ran us over and stabbed us with fork prongs. It's the Robbiest thing he could possibly do, and I'm not even mad at him because it made Grady put his hands on me again.

He finally lets go and shakes it off. Most guys would yell at the drunk idiots, but Grady isn't a yeller. He drags his fingers through his hair. "You okay?"

"Yeah."

"You want to go home?"

"Yeah. I mean, I guess my dad can drive me back in the morning to clean up the s'more station."

"Yeah. I'll give you a ride. Home, I mean. I have a call with the New York investor I'll be working for in the morning, so...not gonna stay up late."

"Well, now who's the party animal?"

He blows out an amused breath. I amuse him. It's something, I guess.

FIFTEEN MINUTES LATER, we're turning onto my street in Grady's 1983 Mercedes that he bought with the money he made from modeling for catalogs. He keeps it impeccably shiny and clean and tuned-up, and it keeps breaking down anyway. His parents give him all kinds of grief about it, but I think this car is hot as hell, and I can't believe I'm in here alone with him tonight. The radio's on a low volume, and we haven't said a word since we got into it. Then "More Than a Feeling" by Boston comes on.

He turns it up and starts bobbing his head and singing along.

I have always felt this song deep in my chest, but ever since last summer, it has meant so much to me I could barely stand listening to it.

There was this one night I stayed up with Grady and my brother when my parents were having an anniversary weekend getaway in Kennebunkport. Jake and Grady let me play *Rock Band* with them on Xbox. I was on vocals, Grady was on drums, Jake was on guitar. We hit all the right notes, and we were flying. We scored over two hundred thousand points and high-fived each other when we finished. I didn't even know I could feel sexy or what sexy would feel like, but I felt sexy. I felt safe and sexy with him even though my brother was there, and I might never feel that way again with anyone else. Ever.

He pulls into the driveway behind Jake's truck. He doesn't turn off the engine, but he does put the car in Park.

He's leaving town next week.

I'll see him at the ceremony tomorrow, but I will never be alone with him again.

I might never see him in person again after tomorrow.

I don't even know if he's going to stay in touch with me. Why would he? We're Facebook friends, but only because I added him and only because of Jake.

My heart feels stuck in my throat.

"Are you crying?"

"No." *Oh my God, I'm crying.* "Shut up." I unfasten my seat belt and wipe away my tears. I can't remember if

I put on mascara or not. I look down and see the black smudges on my fingers. Yup. I did.

"Hey." I feel Grady's fingers on my chin, pulling my face toward him. "What's wrong?"

I shake my head.

Everything.

Everything is wrong.

"Claire?" he whispers.

I swear it doesn't sound like a question so much as an invitation.

It's now or never, I think.

I don't even look him in the eyes, I just lean in, grab his face, and kiss him on the mouth.

Or at least that's what I try to do.

Grady grunts and moves his head to the side. My lips graze his earlobe. And then my mouth lands on the collar of his jacket.

I.

Am.

Mortified.

The song is over.

My life is over.

I feel Grady's hand on my arm yet again, but he's pushing me away this time. "Claire..." he whispers again. This time it's a statement. The beginning and end of a sentence that I don't want to hear.

"Yep." I back into the passenger door, fumbling around for the handle. "Lost my balance."

"Claire. I can't—"

"I know. Thanks for the ride. Good luck tomorrow and, you know, forever. Have fun making money."

I finally free myself from the German-made chamber of humiliation, slam the door shut, and run to my house without looking back.

Grady doesn't follow me.

He won't text me.

Or message me on Facebook.

Why would he?

I'm not even one of the local girls he didn't want getting attached to him.

I'm just not what he's looking for.

Chapter 2

Baby, I Was Bourbon to Run
Twelve Years Later

GRADY

"I'M COMING AFTER YOU, BARBER."

It's not the line so much as the delivery that makes me pause. The Baccarat-crystal tumbler of thirty-six-year-old Pappy Van Winkle doesn't quite make it to my parted lips. It hovers in the air, like a thwarted kiss from a treasured would-be lover. Narrowing my eyes, I take measure of the man sitting behind his desk in this massive corner office.

Harrison Lynch and I have a lot in common. We're the same age. Our cars are German. Our bank accounts are Swiss. If we named the designers of our suits and shoes, it would sound like a meeting of the five families and make you hungry for pasta. His office has nearly the same iconic view of Central Park and Manhattan skyline as mine has a few blocks away. We're both CEOs of wildly successful multinational real-estate development companies.

We're both billionaires.

But the biggest trait we have in common? He cares just as little for all of that as I do. Neither he nor I do it for the money or the status or the material rewards. We enjoy the hunt. We thrive on the chase. We like the fight. For the past few months we've been engaged in a thrilling life-or-death struggle for control of his company.

But now we have one big, shiny new difference separating us.

Harrison Lynch has lost.

I've won.

After seemingly endless rounds of negotiations, his board has agreed to my purchase of his company, Relicteros. My company, Beacon Holdings, will be leveraged to the hilt purchasing all of his stock to make that happen. Buying out Lynch's equity in the company will make him an even richer man. But it will also make him unemployed. There will only be one company, and it will need only one CEO. Me. My strategy has been to win over his board of directors because I don't want this to be a hostile takeover—that's not my style.

And that has bought me a lot of good will at Relicteros.

Except from the man who stands to lose his place as head of the company.

He generally has resting scowl face, but he somehow manages to harden it even more as he glares at me. My resting intense-but-not-too-intense-exceptionally-good-looking face breaks into a half grin. I take my time finishing the thirty-six-thousand-dollar bourbon provided by my host. It is way too early in the morning for whiskey, but it's always the right time for superior aged bourbon that I don't have to pay for.

I didn't come here to gloat. I've come to his office to hear his final plea—like a conquering warlord allowing the vanquished foe the courtesy of relinquishing his sword at my feet before I escort his former army to my more powerful country under my reign of victory.

Okay, that sounds a little like gloating.

"Did you hear me, Barber?" my opponent asks through gritted teeth.

I glance over at my faithful assistant, Alice Strout, who's looking back and forth between us. Like a classy, well-trained German shepherd in a Chanel dress suit, she is fiercely protective of me. She would probably go for his throat, or at least throw her glass of sparkling water into his face, if I gave her the nod.

I savor a sip of bourbon before finally acknowledging Lynch. "That you're coming after me? I did hear you. And I look forward to it. I admire your unshakeable confidence, considering you couldn't beat me when we were on equal footing. Now that your entire board has chosen my offer, I'm finding it pretty hard to see how you're going to do any better than you did before."

I stifle the urge to add *And I drink your bourbon. I DRINK IT UP!* in my best Daniel Plainview from *There Will Be Blood*—which is pretty damn good, in my opinion. But I'll save that for the encore.

Lynch squeezes his glass of bourbon tighter. I'm very concerned he's going to shatter it. I'm not worried about his hand—I'm worried because that priceless bourbon will go to waste. I don't like waste. Of money or time or Pappy Van Winkle.

His assistant places a delicate hand on his shoulder. Miss Lovejoy is her name. She wears her curly hair long and loose. Her flowery dress smells like incense. She seems like the kind of woman who would rather go barefoot than spend a thousand dollars on a pair of shoes, and she is definitely the reason Lynch's desk is covered with crystals. His office has so many potted plants, I have an oxygen high. In other words, she is unlike any other woman in this office building and most of midtown Manhattan. Lynch looks up at her, and they begin a silent conversation with each other, leaning in and mouthing their words. The two of them appear so incongruous, but they clearly have a shorthand, and it looks like a conversation they've had before.

I take another sip of exquisite bourbon and look out over the city. I remember the first time I took in the view of Manhattan from the top of the Empire State Building. I was eighteen, and I thought to myself, *One day, all this will be yours.* I own and control so much more than I did when I first left Beacon Harbor, but every time I close a deal, in the back of my mind, Claire's quiet voice asks, *But what if it doesn't make you happy?* And I tell myself, *It does. For now. But what's next?* And what's next is always *more.* Because *more* keeps you safe. *More* protects what you've worked so hard to earn.

This bourbon will be the extent of my celebration. There will be no dinner at a Michelin-starred restaurant, no night out on the town with a limo full of fashion models, no party. Well, maybe I'll have Alice schedule one for the employees when the deal is official to mark the merging of our companies, but I won't be there. The only upcoming indulgence is a charity gala that Lynch and I have to attend in a few weeks. The Manhattanites for the Ethical Treatment of Houseplants' annual fundraiser. METH. Yeah, the overprivileged elite of Manhattan are unironically going to get dressed up to support METH. Both our boards are going to be in attendance as the society is a pet project of the wife of the most powerful member on Lynch's board, Aston Pembroke. I had marked that as our probable last stand, the place where we could sway the other side one way or another. But my victory has arrived early, so now I'll get to shake hands with the people who made it all possible when I make my appearance there.

I glance over at Alice, who is narrowing her eyes at Lynch and Miss Lovejoy. The two of them are still lost in their own conversation, but Alice is whispering something at them. Now she's wiggling her nose at them. I then start my own silent conversation with my assistant.

What the hell are you doing? my wide eyes asks.

We're winners, Barber. Winners. That woman is clearly a white witch, so I'm casting a spell on them. She wiggles her nose at me. *Like in* Bewitched!

I grew up with Harry Potter! I am not a hundred years old, so I don't get your references! Sit still and behave yourself, I tell her with my hands and eyes.

I glance back at Lynch and his assistant to see if they've noticed Alice waving her index finger around like a wand, but thankfully, they are too caught up in each other.

I don't usually have to worry about Alice being a distraction of any kind. I learned early on in my career to hire assistants who are old enough to be my grandparents. No distractions. Period. In any area of my life. If someone interferes with my business, they aren't going to be a part of my life. Simple as that. *No fuss, no muss,* as my mom would say. I'll chalk up today's behavior to the high stakes of this deal.

I watch Lynch and his assistant silently arguing. There's a familiarity to their manner. Not inappropriate, just...comfortable. The kind of comfort that has eluded me ever since I left Beacon Harbor.

A phone buzzes in one of my pockets. It's my personal phone, the one that's reserved for family and close friends. Which means it rarely rings. Instead of pulling it out, I deftly push the button to silence it through my suit jacket. I'll call back whoever it is after the meeting.

The pantomime ends, and Lynch places his hands on the desk. "So, that's not the only reason I called you here. I also want to know…" He pauses as he clocks his assistant. "I am *demanding* that you be true to your word and take care of our employees. I want to hear that from you."

"Surprise and demands," I murmur. And a dark, firelit memory pulls me from Lynch's tower, back to another time and place that smelled of campfire and chocolate and *her*. Something old and lost—no, not lost—

something absent that I never even had makes my heart ache a little.

No one in this city is Claire Sweeney in firelight.

And no one ever could be.

Claire wasn't an option when we were teenagers, and she never will be.

Why am I even thinking about her right now?

My focus snaps back to this moment, and I see Lynch cock an eyebrow, confused by my private joke. I clear my throat. "Are you saying that if I give you my word not to rip your company apart that you won't come after me?"

"No," he says simply. "I'm going to crush this deal, Barber. *When* I do, I don't want you to accuse me of skulking around and being underhanded or two-faced. When I beat you, I want it on record that I did it head-on." He glances at his assistant again. "But in the miniscule chance that I fail, I need to know, man-to-man, that you will take care of my employees."

In another world, Lynch and I could be friends. We have built up a fair bit of enmity between us in this fight. But this is another trait we have in common. We take care of our own.

"You have my word. I don't want to strip-mine your company. You've built something spectacular with a group of very impressive people." I indicate Miss Lovejoy. She doesn't smile, making it clear whose team she's on. I return my focus to Lynch. "I plan on taking what you've built and bringing it to new heights."

Lynch nods and takes that in. "Good." He finally stops threatening to destroy his rocks glass and takes a sip.

"But it's not going to happen. That's not a threat, it's a promise."

I nod and smile. The momentary detente is over. My nemesis has returned. I finish my drink and place it on his desk with a satisfying thud. "I hear you, Lynch." I rise, buttoning up my jacket. "You've been an immovable object your entire life. Any obstacles in your way have broken against your determination. No one has ever outthought you. Outworked you. Until now. All this time you've wondered if there was a force out there that could beat you, that would show you your limits. You now have your answer. And I promise you it will not change. I, on the other hand, am still in search of that final challenge. Thank you very much for the drink. See you at the gala."

I need not weep for love, I tell myself, *for I have more worlds to conquer.*

Lynch says nothing as he returns to his natural state of glaring and scowling.

"I'll see you out," Miss Lovejoy tells us with icy politeness.

She shows us to the door, and my assistant and I leave without another word.

"Are you actually worried, though?" Alice asks in a low voice as we walk down the hall.

I shake my head. "No. That wasn't bravado. Lynch is smart and capable, and he might throw a couple of minor wrenches but nothing I can't handle. This thing is over."

"Great," Alice says in her usual brassy tone. "Since you're about to own this building, let's talk business. You have a meeting with marketing when we get back. Logistics and R-and-D later this evening—"

"Cancel them," I say as I stab at the button for the elevator.

"What? Why?"

"Whole new ball game. Whatever plans they had to present, they now have to incorporate Relicteros Inc. Are we in a place to do that?"

"I'm gonna go ahead and guess no."

"Right. On top of that, we shouldn't make any big moves until the contract is finalized. So, I want everyone to go back to the drawing board and figure out our next move while we wait for the lawyers to hash everything out."

The elevator doors open, and we step inside. "A holding pattern?" Alice says with a smirk. "What*ever* are you going to do with yourself?"

"That's a great question," I say as the door shuts. My phone buzzes again in my pocket. I forgot about the missed call. I take it out and see that it's a text notification from my mother. Several of them.

MOM: *Grady, please call me ASAP.*
MOM: *This is your mother.*
MOM: *Everything is okay, I just think you deserve to know.*

My stomach lurches as the express elevator descends.

I click her name to call her back, and she answers on the first ring. "Hi, honey," she says. She sounds happy, like she normally does. But there's something off in her tone, and my stomach can't seem to right itself.

"Mom, what's going on?"

"First, I want to preface this by saying that your father is fine. He's fine. Well, now he is. He wasn't, and he's not completely fine at the moment. But if we make some very significant lifestyle changes—and we will—he's going to be just fine."

My heart joins my stomach in feeling off-kilter. It's an iron-clad rule of the universe that too many *fine*s make something not fine at all. "What do you mean? What happened?"

"Your father was having chest pains. He didn't want to, but eventually I *insisted* we take him to the hospital."

Like the flip of a switch, all the missed birthdays and holidays and barbecues and get-togethers that I didn't attend over the years are no longer a testament to my will to win. They are no longer evidence that I had been willing to sacrifice everything to build my empire from nothing, to defeat men like Lynch. Now all those missing memories are an indictment of how much I've lost and what a shit son I've become. When was the last time I was home? Five or six Christmases ago? Has it been longer? I was only in and out for one or two nights. I tried for a while to bring my family to me and we did have a Thanksgiving in my penthouse apartment, but there was a lot of grumbling about traveling, even though I flew them by private jet, and even louder grumbling, both from mouths and stomachs, about how my kitchen at the time wasn't set up for cooking a proper Thanksgiving turkey. They didn't want to come to my world, and I didn't have time to return to theirs.

So I haven't seen anyone in years.

"And? Did you go to the hospital?" I ask.

"Yes, they did a lot of tests, which your father was very uncooperative about and very vocal about not wanting to cooperate—you know how he is—"

The call cuts out near the end of the elevator's descent.

"Shit." I try calling her back.

"What's going on?" Alice asks, sounding very concerned.

"What's the closest car I have in storage near here?"

Instead of asking more questions, Alice goes into uber-assistant mode, which is exactly what I need from her right now. She stares hard at her own phone while I try and fail to reconnect with my mother.

"The Mercedes is still in storage nearby."

"The Mercedes—what Mercedes?" I'm wracking my brain. I've been a BMW guy for a decade...and then it hits me. "You mean the 380?"

Alice nods. "The one from Maine. It's still here in a garage in the city."

"Tell them I'm coming to get it," I say. The elevator doors open, and I rush out onto the street to get a better signal. It finally connects.

"Sorry, Mom. I was in an elevator. What happened? Was it a heart attack?"

"No. No, honey. It turned out to be angina. He has coronary artery disease. They said he doesn't need surgery yet. He's going to *have* to make some changes, but he's going to be fine."

My head is spinning. "When did this happen?"

"A couple of days ago. Your father didn't want to

make a big fuss—you know how he is—and I didn't want to bother you until we knew what was going on. I know how busy you are, dear, but I thought you should know."

Well, there's a big old interesting knot of personal failings to untangle. My father being stubborn and playing everything close to the vest, my mother worrying but not wanting to make waves in my life, and me being so out of touch and unapproachable that my father goes to the hospital with chest pains and I'm not even told immediately.

Everything else fades away.

"I'm coming home," I tell her, slightly out of breath.

"You are?" My mother sounds so surprised and hopeful it breaks my heart. "Oh, Grady, you don't have to do that. Your father will say that I'm being—"

"Mom. I'm coming home."

"Okay. Good. I'm glad. Your father will be too."

"Is he there? Can I talk to him?"

Mom sighs. "No, he's out on the beach with your brother. He's supposed to take regular walks and eat better. He doesn't want to eat better, so he thinks he can just walk constantly and that'll cover for all the garbage he eats."

A smile spreads across my face. Sounds about right. "Okay, I'm heading straight to you. I'll see you soon. Love you."

"Love you too, honey. Drive safe!"

I hang up and make my way toward the garage.

There is a question, one I don't want to answer. If the deal wasn't done, if I was still locked in an epic struggle with Lynch for control of his company, would I go home?

Would I be willing to take a leave of absence and risk losing so that I could go home and see my father? Given how shaken I am right now, I'd like to think the answer is yes. But I honestly don't know. Thankfully the deal is done and I don't have to answer right now if the news of my father's heart disease would be enough to make me stop in my tracks.

Now that I know he's okay and that I'm going home, there are only two questions weighing on me.

What does Claire look like now when her face is lit by firelight?

And will I find out?

Chapter 3

How Sweet It Is? (To Be a Bakery Owner)

CLAIRE

Yay.

It's the dawn of a new day, and I get to turn flour, water, butter, eggs, sugar, and chocolate into delicious treats.

Maybe today is the day my profiteroles will actually turn a profit.

I turn off the alarm on my phone and check for my daily positivity text from Vera.

VERA: Morning, babe. You are a bad ass.

Well, that's just rude. And also incorrect. And most likely a typo.

ME: Really? I'm like 90% sure my ass is my best feature.
VERA: Wait. What?!
VERA: Badass! You are a badass. My eyes aren't awake yet. You are a badass bakery owner!
ME: Honestly, at this point I'd settle for being a marginally okay bakery owner with a great ass.
VERA: You are definitely that. Whatever, it's gonna be a great day! Or at least not a shitty one, probably! See you soon.
ME: <face with tears of joy emoji> Thanks for the poop talk.

I realize, after hitting Send, that my phone autocorrected *pep* to *poop*, which pretty much sums up the trajectory of my career as a small-business owner.

But I needed that laugh. When you get up at four o'clock every day, you have to make your own sunshine. And espresso. Vera is not a natural-born ray of light and she is definitely not a morning person, but she somehow loves me, my coffee drinks, and pastries enough to drag herself out of bed when the nocturnal animals are still out looking for food in the neighborhood.

They say that a bad day baking is better than a good day spent doing anything else. I have found this to be true. Except when I look at my bank balance at the end of the day. But I'm not going to think about that right now. Because maybe today really will be a not-shitty day.

Stretching out in bed, I am tired deep in my bones, but I think positive thoughts before getting up to take a quick shower... *I was so lucky to be given the opportunity to purchase the mom-and-pop bakery that I apprenticed in at the ripe young age of twenty-six. Yes, I took over the lease and bought the name of an existing bakery, but I totally revamped it, so it counts as a new business. I am equally lucky that my parents still own the house that I grew up in and that they didn't turn my old bedroom into a craft room or a sex dungeon so I was able to move back in here a few months ago. New businesses almost always take three years to become profitable. So I still have half a year left to make more than I spend on bills, rent, taxes, Vera's salary, inventory, and loan payments...all of which I am lucky to have! Not making a significant profit doesn't count as failure yet—this is just how new businesses work. Not wasting money on rent for living space is just good business sense at this point in my life and career. And these sheets somehow smell better when Mom does the laundry.*

There.

Now I'm ready for my shower. I definitely won't cry into the warm stream of water just because I'm exhausted and haven't had a vacation in over three years. I certainly won't think about how lame the dating pool is in Beacon Harbor, and I absolutely won't think about the boy I used to fantasize about when I was living in this house as a teenager.

That guy can suck it.

And I have no room in my brain for thoughts of men anyway.

I don't even have time to wash my hair.

"I own and operate a successful bakery business," I mutter as I load up my toothbrush with toothpaste and stare at the affirmations on the bathroom mirror. My mother wrote them for me on neon Post-it notes two weeks ago. She said one of her real-estate clients told her that she manifested her fancy Rhode Island fiancé within one month by doing affirmations. I didn't have the heart to tell my mom that her client has been known for manifesting really great blow jobs ever since junior year, but I mean, maybe the affirmations helped her snag a fiancé too!

"My bakery attracts the perfect clientele," I say around my toothbrush, "who love and appreciate my French pastries and create even more business for me through positive word of mouth." I spit and rinse. "I deserve and attract the love of a wonderful, top-notch man who appreciates my talents and supports my aspirations." I wipe my mouth and apply lip balm. "Also," I add, "I have a great *ass-piration*. And I'm a badass."

Welp. Off to work. I am all affirmed and ready to attack my day.

Just kidding, I need caffeine first.

I tiptoe downstairs so I don't wake up the dogs or my parents—definitely not dwelling on the weirdness of being twenty-eight and living with my mom and dad.

Grabbing an apple and a protein bar from the kitchen, I draw little hearts on the notes my parents left me on the island counter.

We believe in you, honey! Don't forget to take your multivitamin! my mom wrote on her

Helen Sweeney, Licensed Realtor notepaper. Her smiling face and crossed arms exude confidence and small-town charm. But I'm not going to take my multivitamin because I'm a rebel.

My dad left me a printout of the photo he took of a puffin yesterday. He signed it, **The only thing cuter than your muffin is this puffin! —Bob Sweeney, the Birder of Beacon Harbor (aka your dad who is very proud of you, sweetheart)**. I really wish *muffin* wasn't slang for anything. But he's adorable, and the puffin really is cute.

The five-minute drive to my bakery is uneventful. Not even a raccoon sighting, and it's too early to spot any seagulls eating fried clams off the boardwalk. The hanging flower baskets along Main Street are still dimly illuminated by the street lamps, the store windows are all dark, the brick sidewalks are empty.

I stay focused on what's going on around me to distract myself from the shitbox I am currently driving. When the lease on my Prius was up, I could only afford to buy an old Honda that had over three hundred thousand miles on it, had been involved in "at least one accident" according to the description, and smells like soup. But it hasn't broken down yet!

Vera is already unlocking the door to the kitchen when I park. "Turn off your headlights!" she reminds me as I step out of it. I keep forgetting this car doesn't have automatic headlights.

"Got it! Thanks."

Vera holds the door open for me, and that is probably

the last truly helpful thing she'll do here all day, besides keep me and our customers entertained. But that is enough. I switch on the lights and straighten a hand-painted sign that says, **In this bakery, carrot cake counts as a vegetable.** It doesn't go with the rest of the decor in here since I redecorated, but it's been hanging on this wall ever since Buddy and Ruthie opened this place, I was told. So I could hardly take it down.

Vera turns on some music in the kitchen and scrolls Instagram on her phone while I make us espressos. She hands me an apron, puts on her beanie cap over her short hair, which currently features temporary royal-blue chunky highlights, then places my chef beret cap on my head, angling it just so.

And for the next couple of hours, we get to work.

We sanitize the kitchen while singing along to her Motown mix, which means she's horny but not so horny that she's agitated.

Then I preheat the ovens and make dough while Vera wipes down the counters and tables out front. I wiped them down before leaving yesterday, but I learned a long time ago to give her that kind of task. When I let her help me with the actual baking, bad things happen. She handles the social media posts, though, and she's very good at that.

"Hey, we just got an online order!" she calls out.

"Oh yeah? A real one, or an offer from 'Hugh Jorgan' to butter our muffins?"

"It's a real order. A rush order. For this afternoon...for a large custom cake..." she says, mysteriously.

"Amazing. What kind? I hope I have all the ingredients."

"*Absolutely. I have always believed you have all the right ingredients, she said enthusiastically—metaphorically anyway.*" Sometimes Vera narrates instead of talking like a normal person. She enters the kitchen. I look up from the pot as I'm waiting for the mixture to boil so I can add flour for my choux pastry dough. She's staring at me with her eyes wide, clutching the iPad to her chest. Her burgundy-stained lips are clamped shut.

"What?"

"It's an order from Mrs. Barber. For a chocolate cake with Swiss buttercream frosting, no decorations except berries, and lettering that says..." She pauses dramatically. "'Welcome Home, Grady.'"

And suddenly, my ears are ringing and my insides go as cold as the freezer.

But then it all comes rushing back to me. The feelings. The feelings I tried to bury. I took all the humiliation and disappointment from that one time I tried to kiss Grady Barber, and I kneaded it into so much dough. Actual dough for baking, obviously. I think we've established that I seem to have misplaced the recipe for making metaphorical dough.

Baking has been my therapy for twelve years, but I seem to be having a relapse.

The longing, the admiration, the rejection. It's all still there in my bloodstream. I tried so hard to forget about him all through junior and senior year. While I was apprenticing with Buddy and Ruthie, the former owners of this bakery, I tried dating local dudes that I knew would never leave. In the summers, I had fun with out-of-town guys who came through Beacon Harbor. But I'd forget about them within a week. It's not like I lack confidence or that I can't get a date. Even if I had the time or energy to date now, there are no interesting, eligible men in this town. At least not when I compare them to Grady. A lack of high-quality ingredients, shall we say. You could put Chris Kimball in the oven at the perfect temperature for the exact right amount of time and he'd still never rise to husband material.

Not that Grady is husband material—not for anyone who lives in Beacon Harbor anyway.

Why is he back?

How long is he staying?

Does he even remember me?

Is he single?

Does Jake know he's in town?

Am I going to see Grady Barber while he's here?

Why do I care?

Why didn't I wash my hair this morning, dammit?

I realize Vera is still watching me, eyebrows raised, lips clamped shut. "So, I'll let Mrs. Barber know it'll be ready by noon?"

I unclench my jaw, but my mouth can't form words.

"Breathe, honey. Just breathe."

I do that. I breathe. I shake out the tension in my body. And then I say, "Tell Mrs. Barber I'll have the cake ready by noon. She can pick it up between noon and two, when we close. Thank you." And then I remember that I was boiling milk and butter for my choux pastry dough and see that it has reduced to the point of being unusable.

I refrain from glaring at Vera, who could have maybe alerted me to the fact that it was boiling. Instead, I grit out, "Actually, tell her it will be ready for pickup between one and two. And that we're closing at two o'clock sharp."

"You got it, she said as she calmly returned to the front of the store and reminded her friend that she always carries an emergency Xanax in her bag."

"Not necessary!" I yell out, trying to figure out if I can still use this reduced mixture for something. I might just let it cool down a little and pour it into my mouth.

Whatever the problem is, baking is the solution.

Even if the problem is that I haven't forgotten Grady Barber as much as I thought I had.

But yeah. Today is *not* a not-shitty day.

Chapter 4

Bake to the Future

G*RADY*

T*HIS ISN'T A CAR.*

This is a time machine.

That's what I think as I stare at my old Mercedes 380 in the bowels of the dark concrete cave parking structure in New York where she's been housed. She was my first real victory. I set a goal, I worked like crazy, and I got her.

I guess I haven't stopped ever since. I could have gotten rid of her when I got to New York after Wharton. Instead, I did the opposite. I paid way too much to store her here and hired a guy to change the fluids, inflate the tires, and keep the battery charged. I kept thinking that someday I'd sell her. I have more impressive cars, and I don't even have time to drive those.

But looking at this old beauty now, I know I'm never going to do that. Never was.

There's nothing like your first love.

And if you can hold on to her, you never let her go.

I climb into the car and shut the door with a satisfying thud. I sniff the air in here. The car still smells faintly of Cheetos and beer. Shaking my head, I laugh. How is that possible? I am rocketed further back in time as I remember Jake and Robbie drinking and eating, the two of them packed into the back seat. I yelled at them to wait until we got to the beach. As usual, they didn't listen.

"I don't understand the words that are coming out of your mouth right now, Dad! Why would we wait to eat these beautiful, crunchy puffs of corn?!" Jake protested around a mouthful of Cheetos, orange dust drifting down to his shirt and the upholstery.

"Crunchy cuffs of porn!" Robbie nearly busted a gut laughing, an orange cloud of dust spewing from his lips. That guy always acted stoned, but he never was. He was just an idiot who people liked hanging out with.

"Hey." Jake punched Robbie in the arm. "Don't say 'porn' around my sister."

Claire was in the passenger seat next to me, and her eyes did an Olympic-level gymnastics roll. "Actually, Cheetos are made from cornmeal. I read an article about this! The cornmeal gets fed into this machine that causes friction between the cornmeal, and that friction melts the starch and then—"

"Why do you have to make all snacks boring?!" Jake tossed a Cheeto at her face and then quickly retrieved it

and popped it into his mouth after it fell to the floor. He was a class act.

"I wanna hear more about how Cheetos are made," I told her.

And then she smiled up at me.

I GRIN as I remember her grin.

We didn't have anywhere we needed to be.

We had all day to just hang out at the beach.

Back then we had all the time in the world.

Well, I had a lot more going on than most high school students, I suppose, but there were days when I let myself relax.

I inhale again.

There is also something sweet and floral wafting just above and around the young-dude aromas. I rocket through time again.

"ARE YOU WEARING PERFUME?" I asked Claire as she very demurely climbed into the back seat. She'd climbed into my car several times before this. She used to bound over and collapse into the seat the way kids did. But she was starting to move with more self-awareness.

A little grace that she probably didn't even realize she had.

And she smelled a lot like flowers. Pretty ones. The kind you'd buy for a girl you really liked. Up close, she always smelled like vanilla and confectioners' sugar. It was infused in her clothes and hair. Her soul too, I imagined.

"*Yeah, I told her to knock it off with that, but Mom overruled me,*" *Jake complained. He was in the passenger seat that time.*

Claire scoffed. "You're in no position to judge. I've been choking on your Axe body spray for the last year and a half. You think the more you use, the more girls are going to try to rub up on you—have you not figured out how wrong you are yet?"

I remember the look on Jake's face, the sputtering and the stuttering. He didn't have a comeback because that was exactly *what his strategy was.*

I laughed and smiled at her in the rearview mirror. She smiled back. That smile was just as new as the way she moved and how she smelled.

I didn't like any of it.

Or maybe I didn't like how much I liked it.

I SHAKE MY HEAD. Claire didn't always tag along with us. Most of the time she didn't.

But for some reason those memories are the most vivid as I sit behind the wheel of this luxury time capsule.

I start the engine, and she roars to life right away. I pull out of the garage and toward the highway. Alice checks in to ask if she should have anything shipped overnight to my parents' house, and that is the moment I realize I haven't brought anything with me. Not even my laptop. I can access pretty much everything in the cloud, so I tell her to have a new laptop delivered, and then she rolls calls for me. My company might be in a holding pattern, but there are always calls to make. After ten minutes, Alice tells me a MacBook will be delivered to my parents' house tomorrow morning. I have no idea how she'll get it there overnight, but it's not my job to know that kind of thing.

She also reminds me that I have a chauffeur, a helicopter, and a private jet, but I can't think of a better way to get back to Beacon Harbor than this car.

As I get deeper into the drive, the distance between buildings becomes greater and the landscape begins to roll.

The volume gets turned down and my body relaxes.

I didn't even realize how tense my body had been.

I sought out a life in New York because my natural rhythm had always been at a higher RPM than Beacon Harbor's. New York's matched that. Growing up, I had been frustrated that my surroundings didn't move as fast as I wanted them to.

But this feels good now.

Like catching my breath after a long run.

I should call Jake to let him know I'll be in town.

But I'm not going to.

I let out a frustrated breath. It would be weird. I hate that it would be weird, but it would.

I have no idea if it would be a good time to call him or not. Because I have no idea what his or anyone's life is like now. I deactivated my Facebook account after I made my first million because random people started DMing me to ask for money. It's been fun to stroll down memory lane on this drive. But those home movies in my mind end suddenly at the point when I moved to New York.

I've been too busy. Too focused. I've been an amazing CEO. But it's made me a bad son, a bad brother, and a bad friend.

I feel like I should call Claire too. But even if I hadn't fallen off the face of New England once I got to New York, that would still be weird. I never called her when I lived in Beacon Harbor. Doesn't change the fact that I want to hear her voice, though.

The option of calling anyone is taken away from me when my sweet girl finally shows her age and my neglect. The AC dies, and I have to crack open all four windows in the car. The interior is now filled with the roar of wind traveling at highway speeds. My carefully styled billionaire hair that was strategically designed for maximum negotiation intimidation is windblown to shit.

We are in the hot, humid center of early July in the Northeast. I start sweating immediately. Unbuttoning my dress shirt, I strip down to my undershirt. It takes all my training in yoga and jujitsu to do this while driving, but all that practice allows me to accomplish it without crashing or swerving.

I enjoy the drone of the wind drowning out my thoughts. Until my mind starts spinning about all the work I'm not accomplishing. I need music. I glance at the stereo. The second owner of this Mercedes had installed a stereo system that was state of the art—for the 1990s.

My friends all found it hilarious that I had a CD player, so for Christmases and birthdays they would buy me old CDs they found on eBay.

I glance at the stereo again, knowing what I want to listen to.

It can't be in there—can it?

I push the CD button and then hit Play. Mumford & Sons blasts through the speakers, exactly as I was hoping it would. I turn up the volume, and the music overtakes the wind.

Claire gave me this CD the Christmas before I left. We were in the Sweeney kitchen. Alone together, for a moment.

"I THOUGHT *you were only supposed to give me CDs that are ironically nineties." I had received enough Weird Al, Green Day, Nirvana, Pearl Jam, and various ska bands to know the rules.*

Claire furrowed her brow and crossed her arms over her chest. I looked away when she did that. Always. There was so much I couldn't allow myself to see or think about now when it came to Little Sweeney. "Well yeah, it's from the late aughts, not the nineties. But it is ironic. That's new music for young people that sounds old. Kind of like you."

I narrowed my eyes at her. "What do you mean, kind of like me?"

"I mean you have to act young because you have an old soul."

I liked that she thought about my soul. "So, you're saying I'm the Mumford and Sons of high school kids?"

Claire rolled her eyes. Damn was she getting good at that. "Something like that."

"And it's not called the aughts. It's the noughties."

She laughed. "Nobody calls it that."

"Nobody calls it the aughts either. Except actual old people. Plus, the time we grew up being 'naughty' is way more fun, don't you think?"

"So we can talk about how naughty we were to our future kids? I mean...not our kids, like yours and mine... I meant..." She seemed slightly mortified but also a little excited by something.

I was equal parts embarrassed for our terrible joke but also wary of this thing that was crackling between us.

"See? Isn't this something a young person would joke about?" I added quickly.

"No. That's the kind of joke an old person makes to try and sound young."

I nodded and examined the front and the back of the CD case. "You should know. You're the same exact way," I muttered.

I looked back up at her. There was a patch of flour on her cheek. There was always flour on her face or in her hair or on her clothes. Evidence of her passion for baking. I had always pointed it out to her whenever I saw it, and she'd brush it away herself because it didn't seem right for me to touch her like that.

But this time it didn't feel quite right not touching her. In a friendly *you're my best friend's little sister, so this is just me being helpful* kind of way. "Flour on your face," I said quietly. I reached over and gently wiped it from her cheek with my thumb, the way I'd wipe away a tear. I didn't mean to cup her face, but she leaned into my hand. I held it there for just a second. She was Jake's *little sister, and I had always thought of her like my own little sister when we'd been growing up. She was Little Sweeney. But in that moment, I realized I couldn't ignore how things were changing for her. And I knew they could never change for me. I stroked her cheek with my thumb again one more time before pulling my hand away.*

And then Jake or Damien or Robbie or her parents interrupted us, and the memory drifts away.

"Awake my soul!" I scream over the music and wind.

Our music is noughties.

The stereo is nineties.

My car is eighties.

But our souls are even older, Claire's and mine.

I stop a couple of times for gas and snacks along the highway, but I make great time. As I exit off the state route, I can smell the sea. New York is surrounded by ocean water, but it's not the same. New York smells like concrete and people. Like city. I didn't realize how much I missed this smell until the sea salt whips around the inside of my car.

It's around 4:30 when I pull into my parents' driveway. I stare at the house I grew up in. As predicted, they refused to let me buy them a new house. I sent them money for upgrades, but they always claimed the house didn't need it. Right now, I kind of like that it doesn't look much different from how I left it.

My journey back in time is officially complete. I feel a little battered. My voice is hoarse, my skin's sweaty, my heart's aching a little, and my soul is most definitely awake.

But I'm home.

And whatever I've missed, whatever I've failed at, I can make up for it. Because that's what I do. I work hard and I work smart and I get shit done.

I step out of the car, stroll over to the front porch, and try to open my parents' front door. It's locked, and I didn't bring my key. I knock, try the doorbell.

No answer.

I peer into the windows from the porch. Doesn't look like anyone's home.

What the hell? It's not like I was expecting a party but—no one's here?

I text my mom.

ME: Hey, I just pulled up. Where are you guys?

I see dots, and then a text pops up pretty quickly.

MOM: Oh, heavens! I'm sorry honey, we're running late. Can you go to Main Street and pick up the cake? Oh God, it's probably closed by now. Is it closed? It's probably closed.

This is my mother's texting style. She could have said

that out loud or thought it to herself and then typed something else. But that's not how she rolls. Every thought gets typed out.

ME: What's the cake for?
MOM: For your welcome home, silly! I put in the order as soon as I got off the phone with you this morning!
ME: I have to go pick up my own welcome home cake?
MOM: Excuse me, Mr. Fancypants. Too important to pick up a cake? Maybe you can have your butler do it?

I sigh. Even if I wasn't worth a billion dollars, would it be fair of me to think that picking up my own welcome-home cake is weird? I think that's fair. But I guess I can't say because I do, in fact, have a billion dollars.

MOM: We'd get it, but I'm on the beach with your father and brother and they refuse to leave, even though I've reminded them several times that we need to pick up the cake and get home to see you. But the lobster training is taking longer than expected. They're telling me it's in a very precarious place.

I read those last two sentences three times in my head.

I read it out loud: "The lobster training is taking

longer than expected. They're telling me it's in a very precarious place." It wouldn't matter how many times I look at it or say it, I will never understand what that means without guidance. But I don't bother asking.

ME: So Dad's doing okay?
MOM: Yes, he's fine.
ME: Good. Where's the cake?
MOM: Sweet Treats on Main. By the flower shop.
ME: I know where it is. I got it. See you soon.
MOM: See you soon honey. Oh, I just can't wait! I love you!
ME: Love you too.

I climb back into my car. The fact that there is no one waiting here and that I have no idea what she's talking about just confirms what a bad job I've done keeping up with the people I grew up with. I suppose I deserve to pick up my own welcome-home cake. I mean, at least they *got* me a cake.

That's the key to being successful. Don't focus on what you don't have or can't control.

My father is alive, and soon he's going to be well. I'm home. I'm getting cake. The deal is done, and I'll have time to catch up with the people I love and care about.

Life is good.

I pull out of my parents' driveway and make my way toward Sweet Treats, looking forward to saying hi to

Buddy and Ruthie. I wonder if I'll see anyone from high school on Main Street.

As I get closer to the center of town, the buildings huddle closer together, almost like they're jostling each other to get closer to the water. But instead of New York's tall, aggressive, beyond-human-scale buildings that are in a life-or-death struggle for dominance, these buildings look like they're hugging each other rather than throwing elbows.

The town is exactly as I left it, except it looks like it's been Photoshopped to appear brighter and prettier. Maine itself is not a state that's gaining in population, but small coastal towns like Beacon Harbor make enough money from tourists to stay thriving and vibrant.

The money doesn't change it or make it grow into something new. The fact that it's a coastal New England town where tourists come to get away from their hectic lives for a slice of seaside Americana keeps the town in stasis. It is literally the job of this main street to remain as cute as it is for all eternity. Whatever changes that have happened in the last few decades are invisible. I'm sure every business has broadband Wi-Fi and cable or satellite TV. But I'm also sure a snapshot of the streets would look almost the same in 1950 as they do now in the twenty-first century, aside from the make and model of the cars lining them.

I park right outside the bakery, and for a moment, I wonder if I've gone to the wrong address. Now, this place looks completely different. Buddy was an old-school baker with an old-school bakery. It was all velvet drapes and looping cursive writing on the signage and menus. I have very fond memories of coming here as a kid for birthday cakes, cupcakes, all manner of good delicious stuff that no longer touches my body now that I know about nutrition. His storefront is completely transformed and nothing like I remember.

From the street I can see through the giant window that the interior walls are clean and white, the floors and furniture are weathered gray wood. It looks like all the houses at the end of those home-remodeling shows. He must've hired a young person to design it because it looks fresh and new. As I walk into the store, the bell above the door pleasantly announces my entry. It's like walking into an Instagram post. I've gotta say, I'm impressed.

Half the lights are off, and it's eerily quiet. I'm about to say something since the bell didn't do its job, when the stillness is punctured by someone bursting through the swinging doors that connect to the kitchen in the back.

My heart seizes.

Claire. Claire Sweeney is coming toward me.

Those gray-blue eyes lock with mine, and she freezes.

I haven't been going back in time—I've rocketed into the future.

Present-day Claire looks a lot like the Claire from my memory. Her blonde hair is in a ponytail, with little frazzled wisps escaping out the sides. Her skin has a sheen of sweat from working near hot ovens all day, and she's paler than I remember, possibly because she doesn't get out as much as she did when she was a kid. There's a streak of flour on her jaw.

Always a streak of white flour.

I have to will myself not to reach out to wipe it away.

But she also looks very different. She's filled out in all the wonderful ways a woman can fill out. Those slate-blue eyes are still intelligent and alive, but they have this new look of determination, like she's been in a fight for something important and the battle isn't over. It only adds to the life and energy Claire brings to this room.

I find it incredibly attractive.

And I find *that* incredibly wrong.

Claire Sweeney isn't the girl from my memory.

She's all woman now.

She's no longer just pretty. She's beautiful. Beautiful in the way a fond memory is beautiful. Beautiful in the way a pang of longing is beautiful because wanting something makes life worth living. And hot. Fuck me, she's hot. Little Sweeney grew up hot. Like a bonfire that turns into a wildfire.

"Hi," I croak, finding my voice.

"Hi..." she says hesitantly.

"Do you work here?"

Not only do her eyes now show determination, she's only gotten better at rolling them.

"Yes, but I also own the place," she informs me.

My eyebrows rise. "Really? Wow. That's great."

But she clearly doesn't think what I said was great. The fire in Claire's eyes burns hotter, and she folds her arms defensively. In a tone that's about as warm and embracing as an empty house and a welcome-home cake you have to pick up yourself, she says, "Welcome back."

Chapter 5

Can't Buy Me Muffin

C<small>LAIRE</small>

"M<small>Y BAKERY CLOSES AT TWO</small>," I tell Grady, keeping my arms folded in front of my chest to hide two parts of me that have suddenly sprung back to life. I should have kept my apron on. "It is now after four thirty. I stayed late because I thought your mom was coming to pick up the cake she ordered."

"Well, she isn't. I am. Sorry to inconvenience you."

Only Grady Barber can pull off sounding polite and snarky at the same time. "Well...I will get that cake from the kitchen, then."

"Great. Please do."

"I'm going to."

"Fantastic."

I finally sent Vera home at three, even though she very much wanted to stay with me until Mrs. Barber showed up. She claimed she wanted to be here for emotional support, but I know she just wanted to watch me act all weird. She will be disappointed to have missed watching me prove to Grady just how over him I am. I look forward to a time when my nipples get the memo.

"Here I go," I say as I back away from him. "To get your cake." Why am I backing away from him? Because I suddenly feel self-conscious about how tight these jogger pants are around my magnificent cake. Which is ridiculous. Because I do not care if Grady Barber sees my behind and I certainly don't care what he thinks about it. I don't care about that, nor do I care that he didn't even know I bought the bakery. I don't care that I'm all sweaty, and I certainly don't care how freaking handsome he looks with his perfectly tousled hair and his sun-kissed face and forearms.

"I'll be right here, waiting for you to return with it," he says, dragging his fingers through his hair and then resting his hands on his hips.

Same old dragging-the-fingers-through-his-hair move, but the hands-on-the-hips thing is new. I definitely don't care about how damn beautiful his hands are or how expensive that watch must be.

Just as I'm about to turn away from him, I see Crabby approach the front door. Clarence "Crabby" Crawford works at the hardware store, is approximately nine thousand years old, and is a hardcore addict. He's addicted to my chocolate chip cookies. The most basic item on my menu. I used to sell them at the farmers' market before I bought this place, but when I reopened the store they weren't on the menu. Crabby quietly spearheaded an aggressive campaign and petition to get me to sell them here. He could have just asked nicely, but that's not how Crabby rolls.

"You still open?" he steps inside and asks, gruffly.

"Nope."

He narrows his eyes at me, but he's smirking. Helluva smirk on that crabby old face. He cranes his neck and spots the leftovers that are still in the display case. "Liar. Sell me your leftover cookies."

"Ask me nicely."

"No."

"Fine. I have a half dozen leftover chocolate chip."

"I'll take 'em. Don't try to charge me full price."

"Oh, I wouldn't dare."

He eyes Grady, who's smiling at him politely. "You're the billionaire."

"Grady Barber, sir," he says, holding out his hand to shake Crabby's. "I believe you know my father."

Crabby gives him a little nod, a quick firm handshake, and a grunt. "Yeah. Just saw yer folks at the beach." He gives Grady the once-over, lingering at his beautiful leather shoes and fancy pants, which are probably bespoke and Italian. "You on yer way to a fancy party?"

"No, but I'm always ready for one," Grady replies without missing a beat.

Crabby is wearing old paint-stained overalls and work boots. He always looks so out of place here in my attempt at an Instagram-worthy boutique destination. He grunts again and then looks back at me, cocking one of his astonishing eyebrows. "Well? I look like I got all day?"

I shake my head, grinning. He is such a grouch.

"Where were you right before two o'clock? You're the one who's late."

"You're the one standing between me and my cookies."

Grady is watching our back and forth, amused. I bag up the cookies. I didn't box up the leftovers or flip the **Open** sign on the front door yet because I figured I might as well keep the pastries out while I waited for Mrs. Barber. I was expecting more foot traffic, but apparently everyone's at the beach this afternoon.

"That will be three dollars, please," I say to Crabby with all the warmth I can project. "Thank you so much for stopping by, Clarence!" And then I grit out, "I'll get your cake now, Mr. Barber."

I catch a flash of something unexpected in his eyes as I glance at him. His jaw tightens and he rubs the palms of his hands together. "No rush, Ms. Sweeney," he says in a wholly unfamiliar tone that speaks directly to my ovaries.

No rush, but I duck into the kitchen before he can see me blushing. I grip the edge of the counter for support. Why are my knees weak? Why do I feel dizzy? And thirsty?

What. Is. Happening?

Nothing, that's what's happening. I'm probably just dehydrated from stress and from...unwillingly hydrating my panties. Which makes no sense because I've spent the last twelve years willing myself to get over him. Maybe it's not Grady that my body is responding to. Maybe it was the crackling banter with Crabby Crawford. He trimmed his nose and ear hairs, so he looks extra special today.

Or maybe I need to get out of here.

I take three deep breaths, dab some vanilla extract behind my ears, and then carry the cake box out to the retail counter.

Old Man Crawford is still here, eating a cookie and eyeing Grady with suspicion.

Grady is staring into my display case. He points down, tapping his index finger on the glass. "I want your muffin," Grady says in that intense, determined way he used to always say things when he knew what he wanted and declared it so the universe would listen.

"I beg your pardon?"

"Is that carrot cake?"

"Yes."

"You finally perfect your carrot cake recipe?"

I can't believe he remembers I was always working on a carrot cake recipe back then. "Yes. I did. But you can't have that muffin. It's for Mrs. Edelstein."

"Oh. Custom order?"

"No. She just comes in most days for a carrot cake muffin. She hasn't come by yet today."

"But it's after hours."

"And yet I'm still here. Dealing with customers."

"A customer who wants to buy your last muffin."

Crabby clears his throat. "Two customers who want your muffin."

I wrinkle my brow at Crabby. He has never, ever bought a muffin before. "It's not for sale," I tell Grady.

"Really? Is this a pastry library? Can I borrow it for a few minutes, then?"

"First of all, muffins are not considered a pastry.

Muffins are breadstuff. They are classified as quick breads. I meant it's not for sale to *you*."

"I will take that muffin to go," Crabby declares, his mouth full of cookie.

"I will give you all the cash I have in my wallet for that muffin," Grady states, as if that solves everything.

"That will be two dollars, please," I say to Crabby.

He stares down Grady as he hands me two dollars and takes the muffin. "Wanna watch me eat it, Mr. Moneybags?"

"No. I wanna buy it from you. For, let's say..."

"Your big-city money's no good here, Grody Borber!" I exclaim.

Ignoring me, he pulls out a wallet and from there, takes out a crisp hundred-dollar bill. "One hundred dollars."

"Enjoy your carrot cake muffin," Mr. Crawford says, swiping the hundo as he hands him the muffin. He looks at me apologetically. "Need new gutters."

Dammit. I should have just taken all the cash in his wallet. I saw a lot of crisp bills in there.

"Pleasure doing business with you," he says to Crabby, then winks at me.

Crabby grunts in defeat and exits the store without saying goodbye to me.

I just frown at this man. I have no idea why I find him so infuriating, confusing, titillating, and yet somehow comforting. His presence is comforting to me, under all the overwhelming exasperation, because...it's Grady. My brother's best friend. My first crush. The only thing in life that has ever stirred up as much passion in me as baking has.

"Well," I mutter, "that was the dark chocolate of victories."

"It was semisweet," Grady says. But there is no regret in his tone.

I open up the cake box to show him the cake. "If this is to your satisfaction, I will tie it up for you." I really wish I had piped the words *Suck it, Grady!* on there. That would have been a perfect button for this whole conversation. But I didn't. It says **Welcome Home, Grady**. Because I am a professional.

"That looks amazing," he says. "Is it paid for?"

"Yes." I close the box and tie it up aggressively, like I'm binding all of my instincts and feelings.

"You should charge more for your product," he says as he places a twenty-dollar bill in the tip jar. "Supply and demand, remember? If that grumpy guy's coming in for your cookies every day, then he'll pay full price if you ask him to. This is a business, isn't it?"

"Not that it's any of *your* business," I say, sliding the box across the counter, "but this is how all bakeries operate. Baked goods in a bakery are basically worthless if they aren't fresh, so unsold bread is repurposed and sold as bread crumbs and croutons and leftovers are sold at a reduced price at the end of the day. Anything that doesn't get sold by closing time is either donated to the food bank or I give it to friends or take it home. Some days I drop things off at the police station on the way home or I give them to Jake for the rest of the crew at the fire station.

Some things I can sell the next morning at day-old prices."

"Oh, he's still at the fire department? Jake?"

How does he not know that? "Yes, Jake is still a firefighter. It's his calling. Why wouldn't he work there?"

"I'm glad to hear it. I'll be giving him a call. But my point still stands—if Grumpy Gus is coming in every day for your cookies, he'll pay the regular price for them, even at the end of the day."

Now my hands are on my hips. I wish I was wearing five-inch stilettos instead of sneakers so I could be eye to eye with this jerk. "For your information, this bakery is a vital part of the community. It's not all about money. Yes, Crabby usually comes in right before closing time to get the reduced prices. I tried to give my unsold pastries to him for free at first, but he always insists on paying me the day-old prices, and then he hangs around to eat the cookies and chat with me while I'm cleaning up, but he saves a couple of cookies to eat later. He's a widower. He's lonely. He doesn't like going home to an empty house." *Take that, Mr. Big Shot.* I leave out the fact that I bake extra cookies for Clarence. The chocolate chip would almost always sell out otherwise.

"Point still stands. Even more so if he's also paying for the pleasure of your company. Which, in my experience, is worth top dollar." He smirks. "I see you have a number of leftovers." He glances at my unsold madeleines and profiteroles. "When did you take over from Buddy and Ruthie?"

I release the loud, dramatic sigh I've been storing in

my chest for what feels like an eternity. So many questions. Always. "Why are you here, Grady?"

"To pick up my welcome-home cake."

"I know, but why are you back? Now?"

He takes in a deep breath before saying, "My dad had an angina attack. I'm here to help out my parents."

Well, now I feel like an asshole. His dad is friends with my dad. Poor Mr. Barber. I hate hearing this. I sigh again, and everything in me softens. "I'm so sorry. I didn't know."

"He's okay now, I'm told. It wasn't a heart attack, but he needs to take it easy for a while to prevent one."

"Well...it's nice of you to come back and help them out."

"Least I could do," he says, and I can tell he means it. Holding the muffin in one hand, he places his free hand on top of the cake box and then reaches up to gently swipe at my jaw with his thumb. "Got some flour there," he says quietly. "Been driving me nuts this whole time."

And I don't even know why I do it—I don't even think about it—but I lean into his hand. Again. My eyelids flutter closed, and I just want to feel his hand on my face. His beautiful hand.

This time, it's me who pulls away first.

"Welcome home, Grady," I say, and I retreat to the kitchen again without looking back.

I recite a silent affirmation to myself on the fly: *Grady Barber falls head over heels in love with my carrot cake muffin as soon as he takes that first bite of moist-but-dense goodness that is naturally sweetened by finely shredded carrots and perfectly balanced with cozy warmth from a hint of spices; the texture of just the right amount of chopped, toasted walnuts; and the simple yet decadent, unexpectedly tangy cream-cheese-frosting glaze. He will appreciate that there are no raisins because raisins are gross in all baked goods—except for oatmeal cookies.*

Chapter 6

Between a Rock Lobster and a Hard Place

Grady

Claire Sweeney's muffin is delicious.

As I lick the last remnants of the perfect cream-cheese frosting from my fingers, driving back to my parents' place, I am fully aware that I should not be thinking this. Or that I should find it amusing.

But I don't.

I find it exciting.

And I find *that* troubling.

She really has perfected her carrot cake recipe. The walnuts are the exact right addition.

And thank God there aren't any raisins. It has never made sense to me why people add raisins to anything for no good reason, and it never will. It doesn't magically become health food just because you added dried grapes.

Claire's muffin is perfectly moist...

Dammit.

I shake that thought out of my head. I'm *just* thinking about the texture of the muffin she baked. The one I'm allowed to eat. The one I can enjoy without feeling guilt, unless I'm being accountable to my personal trainer—and *screw that guy.*

She did look amazing, even when she was glaring at me harder than Harrison Lynch did. God, was that meeting really just this morning? It already feels like a week ago.

I arrive back at my parents' place and step out of my car, wiping the tiny crumbs from my fingers and wiping the thoughts of Claire Sweeney's muffin from my mind. Claire is the ultimate distraction. She does not align with my goals. Seeing her just now was the opposite of how I felt as I looked out at the view from the top of the Empire State Building: *None of this can ever be yours. Look elsewhere.*

I grab the cake box without any more thoughts of the person who made the cake and pick up the flowers I bought for my mother. My father's truck is back in the driveway, so I know the front door will be unlocked this time.

"Welcome home!" I say sarcastically as I enter.

But no one hears me. My parents are not waiting expectantly in the living room. I only find my brother, Damien, sitting on the couch, rocking out on his guitar.

You'd think he was playing to a big crowd at the Bowery Ballroom in New York with that intensity. But he's just sitting there on a floral sofa, looking cool and just a little bit vulnerable. I've heard Alice use the term *swoony* when speaking in hushed tones to other women, and I guess that's what she'd say about my brother right now.

Swooniness aside, we couldn't be more different. On the outside, Damien and I are a similar height and build. Despite his longish hair and sad eyes, anyone could tell we're brothers. But the similarities are only skin deep. While I have always been type A—for ambition; never stop advancing, never stop accomplishing, my brother is type D—for *Dude, relax. Don't worry so much.*

He doesn't take anything seriously. Never has. Not school, sports, jobs, or girls. Not that those things haven't always come easy for him. Not that he didn't always enjoy those things. He just never did anything beyond enjoying them. The only thing he's taken an interest in is music. He looks up and finally stops playing his guitar, casually resting his forearm and hand on the guitar's body, the way a good boyfriend never stops touching his girlfriend, even when he's talking to someone else at a party. It takes him a moment to snap out of rocker mode to register that I'm here. His only brother. In the family living room. Four years—it's been four Thanksgivings since we've seen each other. He looks like he's in way better shape than the last time I saw him. Because the one and only thing my brother has always taken seriously —and way too seriously at that—is his partying.

"Hey" is all I say. Because that's the only word I speak of Musician.

"Oh, hey," he offers without any enthusiasm.

"It's good to see you?" I didn't mean for that to come out like a question, but there it is.

"Is it?" he replies, raising one dark eyebrow.

"Yeah. It is. You look good."

"Thanks," he says, passive-aggressively plucking at one string of his guitar.

"That a song for your band?"

Damien shrugs. "Nah, I was just messing around. My band broke up."

"Oh. I'm sorry to hear that."

He raises that eyebrow again and speaks in the same flat tone. "Are you?"

Okay, so his little-brother-passive-aggressiveness is in better shape now too.

He tips his chin toward the box in my hand. "What'd you bring me?"

I laugh. "A welcome-home cake."

He finally breaks into a grin as well, and it changes his entire face. "Well, it was a long day at the beach, so I appreciate it."

"Yeah, speaking of—where are Mom and Dad?"

"Busy getting ready for the big barbecue to welcome you home."

"What barbecue?" I groan the tiniest bit as I realize *of course* there's a barbecue. It's summer. This is Beacon Harbor. There is always a barbecue. No wonder the cake is so big. "So they're getting things ready and you're not helping?"

"Hey, *I'm* here whenever they need me..." He waves his hand as if waving away the tension that's been building. "They're arguing about the menu. Dad doesn't want to give up red meat."

"How's he doing?" I ask, suddenly feeling grateful to have a sibling to talk to about this.

"He's fine," he says, in a totally different way than my mom said it and still not at all reassuring. "It was pretty fucking scary when he said he was having chest pains, but he's the same as ever." Damien begins strumming his guitar again.

I'm about to ask him why they were at the beach, but I'm interrupted by the drone of my parents' argument as they enter through the sliding door.

I can hear my dad's deep voice clearly as they pass through the kitchen. "I can't spend all night in front of that grill, smelling the meat that I cook to absolute perfection, and not eat any of it. Sartre was wrong. Hell isn't other people. Hell is watching other people eat your perfectly seared and seasoned meat without being able to enjoy it yourself!"

I hear my mother heave a big, dramatic sigh. "Well, you'd get to find out soon because if you eat that, then you're gonna die and wake up in hell for all eternity!"

"That's garbage, and you know it! My barbecue skills alone get me into Heaven!"

My brother and I share a look, and we can't help laughing. Our faces immediately switch to feigned indifference the minute our mother walks into the room. I can hear our dad opening and closing cupboards in the kitchen.

"Stop doing things!" Mom yells back at him. "You have to relax, remember?! *I* will get the condiments!" Her expression immediately shifts from deep frustration to blinding joy at discovering me in the living room. "Oh, Grady!" She opens her arms wide.

Still holding the things I brought in from the car, I

embrace her in a warm one-armed hug. "Hey, Mom. You look lovely. These are for you." I take the flowers I bought at a rest stop off the top of the cake box and hand them to her. "Sorry they're a little wilted from the heat."

"Oh, that's all right, honey. I'm just so glad to see you. Gosh, don't you look handsome? Hungry. A little tired. But so handsome." She presses a manicured hand to my cheek. Her hands are always manicured, her hair is always in place, her outfits are always pretty and practical. My mother grew up in a wealthy area of Massachusetts, the descendent of a long line of lawyers and doctors and the first females of the state to finish college and get PhDs. That side of the family and the wealthy people she grew up around were very good at adjusting their facial expressions to fit the social scene. Despite looking elegant even when she's pulling her hair out over my dad, she's not like her relatives—her emotions turn on a dime because she feels them so deeply.

"Grady! You're here. Why didn't you tell me he was here?" my dad says to my mom as he enters from the kitchen.

"Oh, for heaven's sake, I just found out myself!" My mother lets go of my face so I can hug my father.

He grew up blue collar, in a family with tumultuous emotions that they wore on their sleeves. He was a sailor —a cook in the navy for some years. He let that go at my mother's behest so they could settle down in one place to raise me and Damien. He obliged and started a fishing-tour business. That wasn't his dream, but he wanted to make my mother happy. He almost lost the business with a couple of bad seasons when the weather just wouldn't cooperate. Damien was too young to know what was going on, but I was old enough to see how much strain it put on my old man and how guilty it made my mother feel.

I made a promise a long time ago that I would never let that happen to this family again.

"Great to see you, Dad."

"'Great to see you,'" he teases, mimicking me. "Who am I? The chairman of the board? Do I look like I'm wearing loafers with no socks?"

Grinning, I try that again. "Hi, Dad." I step back and take him in. He's a couple of inches shorter than Damien and I are, a little rounder in the belly, but we got our good looks from him. He seems healthy too, not at all like he had just had a major heart episode. "You look good," I tell him, probably failing to keep the surprise out of my voice.

"I feel great," he says defensively. "And I would very much like to enjoy this barbecue in your honor. But your mother, as always, wants me to be miserable."

"I want you to live!" she hollers from two feet away.

"Eating the rabbit food those doctors want me to eat is not living!"

Even though they're bickering, I see the little smiles. They can't help themselves. They've been madly in love with each other my whole life. *That* has been my standard my whole life. Maybe it's unfair, but on every first or second date with the women I met in New York—and it never goes much beyond a second date—I can tell that the connection will never be what my mother and father have.

There's only one girl who has ever made me feel that

"Yeah, well, y'know. You're only as good as the lobsters you're given, but I got a couple of good ones. I just gotta make sure not to overwork them—or drop them or step on them or..."

"Boil them?" I say.

"Shhhh!" My dad and brother both shush me at the same time.

"We don't talk about hot water around them," Damien admonishes. "Or melted butter." He takes Clawdia Swiffter from my dad and returns both lobsters to the kitchen. "I won't let anyone cook you guys," he assures the shellfish. "I promise."

"Gotta feed those guys before the guests start showing up," my dad announces. "Nothing but the best for them. Probably gonna have to cook 'em steak after such a long practice."

"Oh, no, you don't," my mother says with a wave of her index finger. She's always wielding that thing like a weapon.

"You would deny those elite athletes the fuel for their bodies to ensure that they become champions?" My father adopts the same tone he would use to reprimand someone for clubbing baby seals or stealing toys from babies.

My mother is completely unfazed as she adopts the tone of a saint explaining her good works. "I'm very concerned for them. I would worry their portions will be a lot smaller than they would be otherwise if *you're* sneaking bites of steak while you're cooking for them."

"They're kidding," my brother explains. "I have to feed them seafood pellets."

"Got it. I'll grill," I say quickly. "You relax, Dad. I'll do it."

"You sure you know how, Mr. Moneybags?" my dad teases. "I know you've learned a lot about business, but you'll never hold a candle to my grilling."

"True. But I did learn a thing or two from a chef named Bobby Flay—perhaps you've heard of him—when he gave me a personal lesson."

"Enh." He waves me off. "That guy's got charm, but I'd beat him in a grill-off, no question."

"No question. But I'm cooking the barbecue tonight," I insist.

"I'll need you boys to help take more chairs outside," my mom says. "Not you, mister," she tells my dad. "You can make the salads."

"Aw, he's gonna make the meat all fancy schmancy," my dad complains.

"I just might," I threaten, pointing a finger at him in the same way my mother does. "If that's what it takes to keep you from eating it."

He frowns and waves me off good-naturedly. "This guy's back for ten minutes and thinks he's running the place."

I get no more resistance and go out back to fire up the grill, happy to see that while they haven't made any renovations to the house, they did have new concrete poured over the patio and they bought a top-of-the-line gas grill. So they used about half of one percent of the money I wired them. Although I guess they also used some of it for the lobster tank.

I wonder if anyone invited the baker to the barbecue, if she'd even show up.

I allow myself exactly thirty seconds to imagine grilling for her and to wonder if she'd find my thick, juicy meat as delicious as I found her muffin.

Chapter 7

Rolling Pin the Deep

C<small>LAIRE</small>

G<small>RADY</small> B<small>ARBER</small>'s face is infuriating.

I hope he stuffed it with my muffin. I wish I could have watched his tea-brown eyes flutter shut and heard him groan as he slowly sank his gleaming white teeth into the generously frosted, evenly browned crust, through the rounded top. I would have gloated as he savored the voluptuous delights of its moist, pillowy interior with his tongue.

I also wish I could stop imagining myself licking cream-cheese frosting off his lips.

And sucking it off of his thumb.

And cleaning it off his abs with my tongue.

God dammit.

I can't believe I leaned into his hand like that when he was wiping flour off my jaw. Like a lonely, attention-starved kitten who secretly wanted him to make out with her and touch her boobs. When really I'm a badass tough cookie who's spent over a decade *not* wanting him to make out with me or touch my boobs.

I thought I'd buried all that longing under so many dates with other guys and so much flour and sugar and eggs and butter that I'd never be able to feel it again.

So I'm doing the only thing I can do—burying it under even more flour and sugar and eggs and butter.

And drinking wine.

And listening to Adele.

It doesn't mean he's still important to me. I got emotionally sideswiped, that's all. By an aggressively handsome billionaire. That fucker came out of nowhere.

Fortunately I had the foresight to make sugar cookie dough last night, so it has been chilling in the fridge and it's nice and firm. I take about half the batch of dough into my hands and massage it. I mold the perfectly smooth, pliable, magical substance into a beautiful, firm mound before slapping it on top of a sheet of parchment paper that I've laid out over the granite countertop. Closing my eyes, I rest the palm of my hand over the rounded dough, gently stroking and savoring the suppleness of it.

I think of nothing but the simple pleasure of creating something delicious from flour, butter, sugar, eggs, baking soda, baking powder, and vanilla extract.

Then I press the heels of my hands into it, to flatten it just a bit, lightly swirling my fingertips across the surface because it feels so good.

I definitely do not visualize anyone's anything while

gently but masterfully manipulating it with my soft but capable hands.

After placing another sheet of parchment paper over the flattened dough, I reach for my rolling pin. Using the perfect amount of pressure, I roll out the dough, changing angles with each pass, ensuring that every inch of it is tended to. I'm careful not to overdo it, of course. *I* want to be a tough cookie, but nobody wants to eat one.

It is incomparably rewarding to be able to create and shape something that is so malleable and forgiving. Something I can consistently understand and control, with exact measurements and timing. And then I get to make it pretty and share it with others. Or eat every last bite myself. Why can't everything in life be this predictable and fulfilling?

When my cookie dough is a quarter-inch thick, I put aside the rolling pin and peel away the top layer of parchment. It's so satisfying, this tiny action.

Now I get to take my cookie cutter and create perfect shapes. Do I reach for the heart-shaped cookie cutter? Nay, I do not. Hearts are too easily broken. I'm going to make perfect circles. Because what goes around comes around.

Except my righteous Adele breakup anthem on Spotify is being repeatedly interrupted by notifications. I can tell it's Vera before I even check my phone because my mom can't type that fast. I don't want to check my phone. I don't want to answer anyone's questions until I've cut out, baked, consumed, and digested my residual teenage feelings.

But I do.

I check my phone.

VERA: Dude.
VERA: Dude. Where are you?
VERA: Crystal told Bailey that she saw Grady coming out of the bakery with a cake box. Why am I not hearing this from you?
VERA: RUOK?
VERA: I can be wherever you are in ten minutes if you need me.
VERA: But first I need to know if GB looks as good as Crystal said he looks. If so, I will stop by the store for a bottle of tequila.

I mean. He looked one-full-glass-of-Pinot-Noir good, not entire-bottle-of-tequila good. Okay, maybe he looked two-to-three-margaritas good, but it's hardly a straight-tequila-on-a-weeknight situation.

ME: Hi! NBD. I am way beyond totally fine.

A split second after I send that message, I regret every word I just typed except *Hi*. Two seconds later, I get an incoming call from Vera. Even though I do not want to talk about this, I answer because she will show up at my door in less than five minutes if I don't.

"I'm fine," I tell her.

"So, he looked great, then."

I attempt to sigh, but it comes out like a huff. I sound like Crabby Crawford. "I didn't say that. All I will say is that he did not have the decency to get meaner and uglier as he got richer."

"Very inconsiderate of him."

"Super dick-ish move. But it was no big deal. I saw him and then he left. That's it."

"You at your parents' house now?"

"Yep."

"You're stress baking, aren't you?"

"No. I'm *therapy* baking."

"To relieve the stress of having so many strong feelings?"

"I don't have *strong* feelings. They're just old feelings." I place my cookie cutter over the surface of flat dough and press down a lot harder than necessary. I silently apologize to my raw cookie baby for being so aggressive with it. That was uncalled for.

"*Riiiight.* With sentimental value. Like that Mumford and Sons CD you refuse to get rid of just in case CDs become a thing again."

"CDs are technically still a thing. Some old cars still have CD players."

"Like *Grady's* old car, you mean."

I hate that she remembers that. "That is not what I meant." Not consciously anyway. I wonder if Grady even remembers I gave him that CD. I shake my head, knowing the answer. Why would he?

I gently cut out another perfect circle of sugar cookie dough and then another.

"Okay," Vera says. "Well, it sounds like you're fine, then."

"I am fine. Super fine." Too many *fine*s are never fine

—I know, I know. Maybe she'll get bored of this conversation and let me get away with it.

"Okay, great, you're super fine. I love that for you! Talk soon." She hangs up. Which is weird. Or maybe I'm the first person in the history of people to convince their nosy best friend that they really are fine.

Adele resumes her singing. I take another sip of wine. After cutting out a dozen perfect circles, I hear a knock at the front door, followed by Vera's voice as she opens the unlocked door. "I knew it. You are never fine when you're listening to 21."

I am so fucking happy to see my friend right now and totally unwilling to let her know this. "Sometimes people just listen to Adele because she's a passionate songstress."

"Right." She drops her shoulder bag onto the floor and reaches for a pinch of uncooked dough. I don't bother slapping her hand because that never stops her. "It was just Grody Borber. It's not like he's an ex."

"Exactly," I say. "He wasn't even my friend, really."

"Right. He was your brother's friend."

"Precisely."

"Someone from your past."

"Yep. *Waaayyyy* deep in the past."

Someone I was never meant to have a future with, I think to myself as I carefully place the cutout dough on the parchment-covered cookie sheet. *Someone who didn't even want to kiss me.* My throat tightens and my nose tingles, but that's not sadness so much as regret.

It's regret that Grady never got to see how hot I looked senior year so that *he* could regret not kissing me. Yes, I had fantasies about him showing up in his

Mercedes to take me to prom, hoping to surprise me and trying to kiss me. But they were revenge fantasies because I walked right past him in my Vera Wang wedding dress and then got into a limo with 1986 Andrew McCarthy. Because my John Hughes era overlapped with my *Gossip Girl* era.

Vera puts a reassuring hand on my shoulder. "Babe. If you want to cry or something, I mean—crying's gross, but I'm here for you."

That makes me laugh. "I don't need to cry. Crying is disgusting."

"Would you like me to list the names of all the guys I can think of who would give anything to date you—worship the ground you walk on every single day—if only you would stop comparing them to He Who Shall Not Be Named?"

I wrinkle my nose. "Do we want guys worshipping the ground we walk on every single day?"

"Okay, that would be annoying, but it's a long list of guys. And not all of them are awful—they live in the tristate area, they own cars, and most of them have jobs and homes of their own!"

I scrunch up my entire face.

"Not helpful?"

"Do you really not have anything better to do right now?"

"I have, like, fourteen other people I could be hanging out with at the moment, but I am *your* person, so I am here for you in whatever way you need me to be here for you." I'm about to tell her I just need her to let me forget about Grady when she pours herself a glass of wine and continues, "Okay, here are two or five ideas, and I'm just spitballing. You let me give you a long overdue makeover—"

"I beg your pardon?"

"—I will do what I can do within a half-hour time period. We're talking blowout; glow up; super casual, slightly slutty outfit that doesn't look like you're trying too hard but also looks like you're making an effort, for a change."

"Ex*cuse* me?"

"Then we 'stop by' the barbecue on our way to some fabulous place, like, I don't know, we'll tell him we're going to hit a club in Portland. You're wearing a crop top, jean shorts, and high-heel sandals. Your lips are so glossy, it looks like you just made out with a stick of butter."

I would honestly just like to do the *make out with a stick of butter* part, but I require clarification on one thing first. "What barbecue?"

"Oh. Did he not tell you about the barbecue?"

"No. He was too busy criticizing me and the way I do business to mention anything else."

"Okay, first of all—how dare he. And I only heard about it from Damien in a group text that I totally forgot I was in because I haven't heard from Damien in forever."

"Oh, really? Don't you go to the beach to watch him play with lobsters?"

"I happen to see him when he's at the beach training his lobsters. And I don't watch him, I advise him when what he's doing is totally wrong and stupid. For his own good." She gulps down the last of the wine in her glass like she's putting out a fire in her throat. "So, do you want to stop by the Barber residence, or do you want to hear my other ideas—one of which involves flying to New York for a rave in Queens that I actually want to go to?"

"Yeah, no." I turn on the oven and set the temperature. "I'm pretty tired."

"Yeah, okay," she says, rinsing out her wine glass. "I'll stop by the barbecue by myself then. Let Grady know you're too busy baking and eating your feelings to swing by and make him regret not marrying or at least fucking you."

Well, *that* hurt. "You sure you aren't trying to convince me to go to that barbecue because you want to see his brother?" Take *that*, Vera.

Her face falls for one millionth of a second before she blows air through her lips and laughs. "Yeah. That's what's up. I have exactly *no* feelings about either brother."

I arch an eyebrow at her. "Same."

She crosses her arms in front of her chest and shrugs. "Good."

I rest my fists on my hips. "Great."

Having a lifelong best friend that you see every single day is good and great because we know each other so well.

It is also annoying and terrible because we know each other so well.

We stare each other down, until we both break into peals of laughter. I throw my arms around her. "You are a bad ass," I tell her. "Thank you for whatever this was. I'm fine."

"You are also a bad ass." She leans into my hug. "And it's okay to not be fine."

I almost tell her about the *flour on the jaw* moment because Vera would get so excited she'd burst into song.

But then I hear the door to the garage slam shut and my mom's heels on the hardwood floor. "Claire?! Claire! Oh, thank God, you're here." My mother is still perfectly coiffed after a full day of encouraging people to either buy or sell or rent properties, but she has the slightest hint of worry on her powdered forehead. "I rushed home as soon as I heard." She places her handbag on the counter and picks up Vera's bag from the floor, also placing it on the counter. "Oh dear, she's stress baking," she says to Vera.

"She's 'fine,'" Vera says with judgy air quotes.

My mother lowers her voice, as if there's anyone besides me and Vera in our house to hear her. "So, we all know about who's back in town?"

"Yeah," Vera says, rubbing my back. "We know. We're super fine."

"Joyce Taylor saw him driving down Main Street in his old car," my mother says to *Vera*.

"Really? I did not receive that information." Vera is way too intrigued.

I start cleaning up the counter, noisily, because apparently I'm not a part of this conversation and apparently I'm passive-aggressively *fine* about everything today.

"My client was wondering if he'd lost all his money and had to move in with his parents too. But I told her about Michael's angina episode."

"Oh no—I didn't hear about that either," Vera says. "Poor Mr. Barber."

It takes me a few seconds to register that my mom already knew about Grady's dad. "Wait, you knew about that?" I ask. "Why didn't you tell me?"

"Well, there was no reason to worry you, dear. But I had no idea Grady would be coming home for this." She reaches out to touch my chin, silently encouraging me to chin up. "You're a gorgeous, talented, successful catch, and you're attracting the perfect mate into your life, right at this moment!" she exclaims affirmatively. "I'll text the Barbers to let them know we already have plans and can't go to the barbecue."

"Wait, *you* were invited too?" I check my phone for an invitation, but nope.

I hear the back door close, my dad's heavy footsteps, and two very happy dogs. "You won't believe who's back!" my dad calls out. "Guess who's back in town!" He walks in, all excited, holding his palms out like an old vaudevillian performer who's about to tell a show stopping joke on stage.

"We know," my mother says with a dismissive wave. "We can't make it to the barbecue."

"Why not?" My dad hangs the leashes and his key ring on the key rack by the centuries-old phone on the wall. He has done this every time he's come home, and he's very proud of the fact that he always knows where the leashes and keys are. "I already told Mike we'd be there."

"Well, you and I can stop by to see Mike some other time," my mom says through gritted teeth as she smooths out his tousled hair. "Claire is too tired to go to a barbecue. Right, Claire? You don't want to go, do you, dear? Look how tired she is."

"She looks fine. That's how she always looks. You look fine, honey. She's a fine specimen," he says, in the same marvelous tone he once used when describing a Steller's sea eagle, so I know he meant it in a good way.

"Thanks, Dad."

"Well, I'm gonna head out, then," Vera tells me. "Since you're fine."

"Yep. Getting finer by the minute. Say hi to Damien for me."

"Not gonna see him! Bye, Sweeneys." She grabs her shoulder bag and disappears from the kitchen.

I hear her say a super chill hi to my brother down the hall. Jake strolls in, carrying a gigantic laundry bag full of dirty clothes. He is grinning from ear to ear, practically jolly. He looks more like an off-duty, totally ripped Santa Claus than a fireman. "You guys will never believe who's in town."

"We know," my dad says. "We're talking about going to the barbecue."

"What's there to talk about? Let's go!" Jake says. My mother takes his laundry bag from him. Jake's been coming by on his nights off whenever he doesn't have a date, and he hasn't been dating much lately. He is perfectly capable of doing his own laundry, at his place or at the station, but Jake Sweeney doesn't like to be alone. "I've got this, Mom. I came by to check out the stove."

"Aww, my angel." She pinches his cheek. "You remembered. But we're not going to the Barbers'," my mother tells him. "I'll put together a flower arrangement for you to take to them."

My mom doesn't want me to go to the Barbers' house because she doesn't want me to get hung up on Grady again. We never, ever talked about it, and my dad and brother certainly had no clue, but I know she saw how I used to stare at Grady. All heart-eyes when he wasn't looking. Back when he used to hang out here. My mother and I didn't talk about why my eyes were swollen pink from crying the morning she had to drag me out of bed to go to Jake and Grady's grad ceremony. She and I both know that Grady Barber still isn't an option. Even if it has nothing to do with the girth of my hips or how skinny my bank account is, it has everything to do with the very different scopes of our ambitions. And the fact that I don't care about him.

"Could everyone clear a path so I can get to the oven, please?" I snap as I pick up my cookie sheet.

My mother pulls my dad and ushers the dogs out of the kitchen. "I'll throw these in the wash and cut some flowers out back."

"What is going on?" my dad mutters, totally lost—the poor guy. "What am I missing?"

Jake steps aside, away from the wall oven, and frowns at me. "You're off work—why are you baking?"

"Because it relaxes me!" I yell as I slide the tray onto the rack and slam the oven door shut.

I set my timer for twelve minutes and refuse to look at my brother's stupid, concerned face.

"Why are you so stressed out right now?"

"I'm not stressed! I just don't know why everyone

decided this area right here in front of the oven was the best place to stand when discussing a barbecue. It's just a barbecue! What's the big deal?"

He crosses over to the built-in gas cooktop at the center of the kitchen island. "Grady's back."

"Yes. I am aware that he's back. Who do you think made the welcome-home cake for him? I've already had the pleasure."

Jake tests the different burners. "Wait, you saw him already?"

"It's the top-right burner. Pilot stopped coming on the other night. Hopefully it's not the gas line," I inform him. Then I casually add, "Yes. Grady came by the bakery to pick up the cake."

Jake doesn't even react to this information about me seeing Grady. In all the years we grew up together, it never, ever occurred to him that I would harbor any kind of girly feelings for his best friend. He tests the top-right burner, and sure enough, it doesn't light up. "Come to the barbecue with me."

"No. Can't you see I'm busy?"

He removes the burner grate, gets level with the countertop as he inspects the burner head. "Busy doing what? Baking cookies? You literally do that all day. Your life is so lame right now, I actually get depressed when I think about it."

That totally derisive comment causes me to snort laugh because the thought of my happy-go-lucky doofus of a brother being depressed at all, much less about me, is hilarious. "Why can't you say something nice to me for once?"

He grabs a spray cleaner and heavy-duty scrub sponge from under the sink. "Okay. I think it would be *nice* for you to go to the Barbers' with me so you can talk to Grady about business stuff. He can help you figure out where you went wrong and fix your shit."

I smack my forehead. "Oh my God. I didn't do anything wrong with the bakery! My shit doesn't need fixing." To say that my brother would run into a burning building for me is not saying much because he would literally do that for anyone—it's his job. He'll even intimidate a douchey tourist dude or five if he catches them hitting on me. But I sometimes wonder if he and Grady swore an oath to criticize everything about me and my life choices back when we were kids. "Why don't *you* ask for his advice?"

"Because I'm not the one living with our parents."

"Oh my God." I cover my face. "Why are you laying into me about this all of a sudden?" It's not all of a sudden. He is always laying into me about this subject. It just feels especially intense because this is the exact opposite of baking and eating sugar cookies. "Maybe I don't want him to know that I'm not making a profit, Jake," I mutter into the palms of my hands.

"Listen," he says. I can hear him scrubbing the pilot-light head and drip pan within an inch of their lives. "You can't be too proud to ask an expert for advice. He's here. I don't know how long he'll be in town for, but this is your chance to get some face time with the most successful person we'll ever know."

I turn away from my brother because my cheeks get warm thinking about getting some face time with that particular person's face. "Grady is not an expert on the bakery business."

"A business is a business, kid." In the reflection of the oven door, I can see Jake rinsing off the sponge, putting the spray cleaner and sponge back under the sink, drying off the drip plate with a paper towel, and replacing the burner grate.

"I'm not a kid. And it's *my* business—it's not any of yours or his." I check my timer, trying not to reveal how proud I am of that incredibly clever, conversation-ending sentence I just uttered. My brother does not congratulate me for being witty, nor does he acknowledge that I am not a kid. I hear the satisfying click of a gas burner lighting up and turn to look. "You fixed it!"

"Yeah." He switches off the burner. "It was all clogged up from dried butter and flour, you dork." He crumples up the paper towel and tosses it at me.

"Oh."

"*Oh*," he mocks. "Little Miss I Didn't Do Anything Wrong. So, what are you gonna do tonight, then?"

"Not that that's any of your business either," I say as I pick up the balled-up paper towel and whip it back at him, "but I'm going to get into the bathtub with a mug of decaf tea and my cookies, listen to some vintage Dolly Parton, and read Mom's old *Glamour* magazines. Be in bed by seven o'clock, cry myself to sleep by eight. Wake up refreshed at four a.m., ready to face another day of my glorious life."

He doesn't blink as he stares at me. "Come to the barbecue with me."

I dry my hands. "No." My timer goes off, and I put on

my oven mitts. I don't even feel like eating anymore. My brother has ruined everything. Everyone has ruined everything just by saying Grady's name over and over. Therefore, Grady has ruined everything.

Except this batch of beautiful, perfect sugar cookies.

"Why don't you take these cookies to the Barbers'?" I say, sweetly. "Give Grady my best."

My cookies and pastries are, literally, the best I have to offer anyone at this point. And sure, it would be gratifying to be there to watch that know-it-all billionaire's tea-brown eyes flutter shut and hear him groan as he sinks his gleaming white teeth into these magnificent, pillowy-yet-firm round tastes of heaven. But I only attend welcome-home barbecues for people who actually want to kiss me.

Chapter 8

A Friend in Knead

GRADY

As I'm marinating, searing, and seasoning, I realize that barbecuing my own welcome-home dinner is a blessing in disguise. People can say hello to me as they get their food, but they have to keep moving to make room for the next in line. A lot of people show up. Cousins of neighbors that I barely remember. People from school and locals from the town. Most are good about not asking me for money. But they are clearly paying extra attention because of who I am and how much I am worth. There are a few local girls who are dressed up way beyond what is appropriate for a barbecue. Of course, I couldn't be less interested in them. There's only one local girl I'm thinking about.

Claire never shows up, though.

Which is probably another blessing in disguise. It's disguised as a barbecuing billionaire who isn't disappointed. On the other hand, I'm the guy who wipes flour from her face. Who's going to wipe delicious animal grease from mine?

I've said hello to a lot of people and cooked a lot of meat, and the party is now in full swing. This certainly isn't an estate, but the backyard is spacious and it feels great to be able to look up and see the sky, unobstructed by skyscrapers. I take a seat in an Adirondack chair by the copper fire pit, trying to relax and take a moment for myself when I hear "What's up, G?" from behind me.

I smile even before turning around. "What's up, Jakey?" I say as I rise.

Jake Sweeney saunters toward me with a big smile on his face, carrying a six-pack and a clear plastic container of cookies. He's wearing a blue Beacon Harbor Fire Department T-shirt that hugs his huge muscular frame. He's got a couple of inches on me—six foot four at least—and outweighs me by about fifty pounds. There isn't a hint of bitterness in his expression even though we haven't been in touch for a few years.

We slap hands and hug.

"It's good to see you, brotha," he says.

"Damn good to see you."

Sitting down by the fire, we each crack open a beer. We tap bottles and then start drinking. We shoot the shit, talk about our lives, how business is going. We talk about the fire department and some of the rescues and major firefights Jake has been in. Then a couple beers in we devolve into *Rick and Morty* impressions.

This right here—this doesn't feel like an "almost." The town, my parents, my brother, and even Claire are *almost* like my memories of them. This doesn't feel like the past has shifted and changed and aged and weathered into something *almost* like I remember. Sitting with my best friend and cracking jokes with him, it feels like it always has with him.

It feels like I never left.

"My sister said she saw you today at the bakery," Jake says and takes a pull of his beer. I don't hear anything extra in his voice. He's just making conversation.

That's been the only thing different about hanging out with him tonight—the fact that my mind never strays too far from thoughts of his little sister. It was never a big problem before. It is a big problem now. Especially as I chew on her impossibly delicious freshly baked sugar cookies.

But seeing Jake is helping me get my head on straight. Because Jake is my guy. He's reliable. Brave. Loyal. Jake Sweeney would not only risk his life pulling me from a burning building, he was also the guy who had my back in the playground, he's the guy who'd find us vintage *Playboy* magazines when we were twelve and the internet controls were firmly in place. He's the guy. My best friend. Still. Even after all these years of me not keeping in touch with him. Which means, at the very least, that I owe it to him not to think about railing his little sister. Or dating her like a gentleman, even. I owe it to him not to have any thoughts I can't follow through on —because I can't be here to be the man she deserves. I will always be too busy and too far away.

I pretend I have to finish swallowing the cookie before responding. "Oh yeah?" It takes every ounce of my self-control and skill at negotiating not to give anything away with those two words. Do not give away that *Oh yeah?* is *Oh yeah, did she say how awesome I am and that the hard time she was giving me was just a cover for how attracted she is to me?* Or *Oh yeah, are you figuring out that I'm really into your little sister and you're going to beat my ass for thinking about her muffin today?*

"Yeah," he says. "What did you think?"

I clear my throat. "Uhhh..."

"Of the bakery?"

"Ahhh." I finish the rest of the cookie and get my shit together. I'm still acting like a horny teenager. This is exactly what I need. Jake Sweeney, paragon of Beacon Harbor. A guy who risks his life to fight fires. My best friend. I'm going to betray him by thinking dirty thoughts about his sister's hips and lips and eyes and tits...?

No. Enough. I'm only here for a little while and then I'm going back to New York, and she'll be here and I'll be there, and that's that.

And if I have to—and I think I might have to—I can dream about her from there.

Where it's safe.

"Place looks great. I thought she did an excellent job refreshing it."

Jake bobs his head, clearly pleased with that. "That's good to hear. If that has your seal of approval... You know how to make money. I don't know why she can't."

I raise an eyebrow. "Business not good?"

"I don't know the exact numbers. Probably wouldn't matter if I did—I don't understand business like you. But I know she's tired and stressed all the time. She had to sell her car and buy a shitbox. She's back home with our parents again. Just doesn't seem to be moving in the right direction."

"Really?" That's all I can think to say. The store does look great. But I suppose that's why Claire's energy was off? I thought maybe it was seeing me. Of course it wasn't seeing me. That's ridiculous. If her business wasn't doing well and she had to stay open late so some asshole could pick up his own welcome-home cake, I suppose that would make anyone stressed out.

Jake clears his throat but doesn't look at me, keeping his gaze on the fire. "I was wondering if maybe..."

I lean in as he hems and haws. "Does she need money?"

He shifts around in the chair. "No. No, nothing like that. Well, probably, but I would never ask you for that. She wouldn't either."

"I know, but whatever you guys need...you know that right?"

He looks me straight in the eye. "I know that. But she wouldn't take it."

"Jake, just tell me how I can help."

He sighs and scratches the back of his head. "I don't know. I don't know how you can help. It's just like I said —I don't know anything about business. But maybe you can take a look at what she's doing. Maybe you can talk to her? I don't know. Give her some advice?"

"I'm not sure if she'll take that any more than she would take a check from me."

Jake laughs and shakes his head. "You're right about that. Stubborn little turd. But as a favor to me, could you try? I'm a little worried she's drowning, and I can't help her with this one. I think you can."

I chug the rest of my beer.

Jake is supposed to be my out. He's fiercely protective of his little sister. He would not be happy if he knew what I'd really like to say to her. And now he's asking me to go to her and help her. I look at him. He's staring into the fire pit, and what I see in his face is sadness. Which is not something I'm used to seeing on that face because Jake Sweeney is one of the happiest guys I've ever known. He's really worried about her. This is him protecting his little sister. He wants her business to succeed, and he has a friend who knows how to succeed in business.

How can I say no to that?

"Yeah, of course, man. I'll see what I can do."

Jake's smile is wide. "Thanks, brotha. I knew I could count on you."

I smile too. It's a more hesitant smile than Jake's, but it feels good to make him happy.

And if I'm being honest with myself, I'm happy too.

I have a reason to go see Claire again.

Chapter 9

A Giant Pain in the Bundt

CLAIRE

THE BILLIONAIRE HASN'T EVEN BEEN BACK for twenty-four hours, and already my whole world has been turned upside down.

Okay, not my whole world and not all the way upside down, but my brain is throbbing inside my skull and everything is out of whack.

I forgot to set my alarm, so I slept in until four thirty and had no time to shower. I got exactly zero positivity texts from Vera. My stupid car smells super-extra like soup this morning because I forgot to crack the windows open when I got home yesterday. Because I was so busy *not* thinking about Grady. Because it was no big deal that I saw him.

I have a hangover—for wine and cookie reasons. Not for Grady reasons. I definitely didn't allow him into my brain while I was taking a bath after my parents went to sleep, and I certainly didn't fantasize about stopping by his stupid barbecue in my prom dress, which still magically fit me, because I was on the way to dinner with present-day Andrew McCarthy. I obviously did not turn up that D'Angelo song while quietly soaping up and diddling myself to thoughts of Grady grabbing me by the arm and leading me to his old bedroom while grumbling about how delicious my muffin and cookies were. And if I came and sobbed at the same time, it was because I was thinking about how hot Andrew McCarthy is now—and an excellent writer too. It was not because I was imagining Grady's head between my legs or his tongue gliding over every inch of my warm, wet skin. It was certainly not because I fantasized about having to cover his mouth with both of my hands to keep him from shouting out how much he loved me while frantically fucking me against the wall of his bedroom, slamming into me so hard that the whole house shook.

I hit the brakes, realizing there's a raccoon hobbling across the street ten feet ahead. "Sorry, buddy!" I call out through the open window. Thank God I didn't hit him, but if I had, it would have been Grady's fault. Because everything is Grady's fault and everything is out of whack this morning.

I'm going to get everything back into whack now.

I am going to do my affirmations for the rest of my drive to the bakery, and once I'm there, in my happy place, I will be able to find my footing again.

"I own and operate a sexy barbery business," I mumble to myself. *Wait, what?* "A successful bakery business. That is what I own and operate. I deserve and attract the love of a wonderful, top-notch man who doesn't criticize or question every single thing I do and every choice I make. Someone who loves Beacon Harbor. Someone who stays in Beacon Harbor. Someone who invests love and passion, not money. Someone who appreciates my tits and supports my ass." *Wait, WHAT?!* "My talent and my assets. Aspirations. Fuck! Someone who *wants* to kiss me. All over. Someone who wants *me*. More than he wants anyone or anything else. And if he could be at least as handsome as that asshole Grady Barber, but preferably even more handsome, that would be really great! Peace on Earth, please keep everyone I love safe and happy and healthy, 'kay thanks bye, amen!"

I turn the corner onto Main Street, with its hanging flower baskets and dim street lamps, feeling like everything is back in the whack. I am an amazing, gorgeous, heat-seeking missile of success on a trajectory of glory. Nothing is going to get in my way.

Except—hello! What have we here? An unfamiliar male-specimen morning jogger in gray sweatpants with a confident stride and a firm, jaunty backside?! Thank you, Universe, I'll take it and have some more!

Except...

Wait...

I recognize the back of that head. And that cocky stride and obnoxious backside.

I recognize the way the rest of the world around him darkens and fades away. The way I'm holding my breath, the way my heart is racing. I recognize the internal hurricane of thoughts and feelings. Excitement because it's him. Melancholy because it's him. A faint, glowing little spark of something that could be hope or joy or anger, depending on how he looks at me or what he says to me, and I don't want him to have that kind of power over my spark. But I also wish I wasn't so damn relieved to discover that the spark is still there inside of me. After all these years of trying to find it again with someone else. At least it's there.

I do not slam on the brakes in order to avoid hitting that particular mammal on the road ahead of me. I have slowed my speed to about one mile per hour and hunched down behind the wheel. I make a very quick, rational decision to quietly and carefully come to a complete stop. Then I calmly put the car into Park in the middle of the street. Reclining the seat back until I'm horizontal, I cover my face—because maybe if I can't see him then he won't see me, and he probably can't even see cars that cost less than sixty thousand dollars anyway. "I am an invisible, successful bakery business owner who is attracting the perfect man for me right now," I whisper into the palms of my hands.

There's a tap on the roof right above me, and it scares the ever-loving shit out of me, but I don't uncover my face, because maybe he'll think I'm dead if I don't move?

"Claire?"

Shit. I forgot to roll up the window. And actually become invisible.

"Sweeney. Are you okay?"

"Why? Do I not seem okay to you?" I reach down to pull on the seat recliner handle, and it sends me straight upright with a jolt. Which is all Grady's fault. Standing there in an old T-shirt and gray sweatpants with his hands all on his hips. Breathing heavily. Being all concerned and judgy.

"You're parked in the middle of Main Street at five a.m."

"So? I'm on my way to work. This is my neighborhood." I turn on the ignition. "I'm supposed to be here. Why are you even up this early?"

He drags his fingers through his hair before kicking his foot up behind himself to stretch his quad muscles. He doesn't even have to rest his hand on my car because he has excellent balance.

This is infuriating to me because I am literally strapped into a car seat right now but I feel like I could fall over at any second.

"I usually get up at five to work out," he says, grunting through his stretch. "But I had trouble sleeping, so I figured I'd get up and go for a run." He raises his arms overhead, bending one elbow and grabbing on to it behind his head with the opposite hand. It causes the fabric of the T-shirt to stretch across his pecs, but I couldn't care less. I only glance up at the bare skin and flexed muscles in his arm because a flock of seagulls are flying by in the distance. He exhales sharply, and I get a waft of minty-fresh breath, which somehow smells more expensive than everyone else's minty-fresh breath. "Wanted to run the route I usually took back when I lived here."

The one that led to my parents' kitchen and my cookies...

He looks around, making sure there's still no one else on the road. He might be about to lean down to talk to me, perhaps about how the town has changed or stayed the same, or he might be about to stretch some other muscle, but I don't have time to wait around to find out.

"Cool. Well, good talk. I've got a business to run."

"Sure. You certainly do." If he feels brushed off, he certainly doesn't appear to be bothered by it. "See ya later, Sweeney."

"I wasn't following you, by the way."

He grins. "'Course you weren't."

"I literally drive this way every morning!"

"Uh-huh." He takes off, jogging down the street again with that cocky stride and obnoxious backside. Like he got the last word. There's no backward glance. He knows where he's going, and he goes there. That's what he's always done.

Not today, mister.

I speed down the road—okay, I can't really call it speeding at a very safe and responsible thirty-five miles per hour, but I pass the billionaire. He can eat my dust. It would have been so cool if I didn't check my rearview mirror to see if he even noticed that I passed him. But I do. And he does.

I am so far out of whack when I pull into my parking space behind the bakery, I can't even see *whack* from here. There are ten partially digested sugar cookies, three glasses of wine, and a billionaire blocking me from the road back to *whack*. But I'll get there. I just need to get my hands on some sugar and flour and eggs and butter and water. And coffee. So much coffee. And absolutely no Grady Barbers.

Vera pulls into the space next to me, like a race-car

driver. I have no idea where she came from—I didn't even see her in the alley. "Turn off your headlights!" she calls out as we both open our car doors.

I turn off my headlights.

She's wearing sunglasses even though the sun hasn't quite risen yet. She looks about as upbeat as I feel as she tries to unlock the back door. "Fucking fuck-ass shit-stick fuck this fuck-hole twat-monkey piece of..." And then she gets the door open and smacks the wall to turn on the lights.

"Have a good night last night, pookie?"

"Stellar, snookums. You?"

"Wondrous. Double espresso?"

"Quadruple."

"Coming right up."

I get to work making us coffee that is even darker than our moods. Vera puts on Nine Inch Nails, which is...troubling. And then I wipe down all the surfaces of this kitchen until I have symbolically cleansed every dehydrated corner of my brain of Grady Barber.

And then I feel fine.

BUT THEN GRADY BARBER shows up in my store as soon as it opens, sets up a brand new laptop at the table by the window, hogs the electrical outlet, asks for the Wi-Fi password, and doesn't leave. He types on his laptop, handsomely. He talks on his phone, wealthily. He keeps ordering coffee. He's treating this like his office, like a mom at a Starbucks, except if he needs a place to do some work outside of his parents' house, he could literally buy an office building. So why is he here? In gray sweatpants and a sexy old T-shirt that stretches across his pecs and highlights his biceps?

I want to complain. I want him to see that I'm frowning at him through the wall. Except he's drawing a crowd. I don't think we've ever had so many customers here at one time. It might be a fire-code violation. But fuck it, I need to make a lot of money, so Grady can get up and Magic Mike on that table for all I care. As long as it sells pastries.

I peek through the horizontal window between my kitchen and the store. There are locals of all ages milling about, trying to chat Grady up, but tourists seem to be curious about him too. A group of four college girls stand next to Grady's table, tossing their *beachy waves* hair over their shoulders and casually glancing at him as they throw their heads back, laughing. God forbid they should eat any of my baked goods and get crumbs stuck to their watermelon-pink lip gloss. Fortunately, there are less annoying people here too. The good kind that eat sugar and gluten. Even Crabby is here, way before closing time, eyeing Grady suspiciously. Which is really the only way to eye him.

"We need more chocolate chip, and we're almost out of apple fritters already," says Vera as she enters the kitchen. She's been gossiping with everyone and seems completely unfazed by the sudden influx.

"Are you pushing the pavlova?"

"Honey. Nobody wants pavlova before lunch. They

ask me what pavlova is, and I can't explain it to them. Grady explained it to Mrs. Doubtfire over there, but she just tried to set him up with her granddaughter." She nods toward an elderly tourist who's wearing stockings and sandals.

I aggressively switch off my food mixer, my chest clenching at the thought of him taking out some lady's granddaughter, but what I say is "Why is he still here?"

"Why do you care?"

"I don't."

"*It certainly seems like you don't,* she muttered sarcastically..."

"I don't! Except I thought he was back in town to help out his parents. So. I don't see him doing that here."

"It's so weird seeing him in Damien's T-shirt" is all my friend says in response, staring out through the window to the front of the store.

"What?"

"That old Stones T-shirt. He used to wear it all the time in high school. Damien, I mean."

"What do you care?" I ask in a singsong voice.

"I don't."

"Certainly seems like you don't. Hey, can you grab me more chocolate chips?"

"Hey, I don't know if you know this, but there are about seven customers out there waiting for someone to take their order," says Grady Barber, who is poking his stupid handsome head into my kitchen.

"Oh, well, let me just get out there and take some orders from some customers, then," Vera says gleefully.

"Hey, Grady, can you be a doll and fetch Claire some chocolate chips? Thanks, doll—you're such a doll."

And she disappears, leaving me alone in my kitchen with the man who throws everything out of whack. He places his shiny new laptop down on the desk near the door.

I frown at him. "Why are you here, Grady?"

"I'm being a doll and fetching you some chocolate chips," he says, walking around the center baker's table toward the wall of metal shelves like he owns the place. It is incredibly easy for him to find the chocolate chips because all of my bins are labeled and alphabetized. "Is it always this busy?" he asks.

"What do you think?" I try to arch an eyebrow at him, but my forehead has been furrowed ever since I saw him walk into the store, and I think it's just going to stay like that forever now.

"And it's just you back here?" he asks as he places the canister of chocolate chips on the counter near me. "This where you want it?"

"Yes, and yes," I huff out. "Thank you," I say, like I'm cursing him. I don't even remember what I was in the middle of making just now. Something with dough. "Why are you here?" I ask again.

"Do you need help with anything?" he asks, as if I didn't just ask him a question that he needs to answer.

Vera enters. "You aren't gonna like this, boss," she says. She calls me boss like once a month, and only when she knows I'm not going to like something. "We just got a special order request for a lemon bundt cake. For Saturday."

"Absolutely not."

Grady crosses his arms and leans against my counter. "Why not?" I can tell he had to stop himself from saying *You aren't exactly in a position to turn down special orders, now, are you, Little Sweeney?*

"She has a strict No Bundt Stuff policy," Vera tells him, straight-faced.

"Vera," I hiss.

"You do!" She shrugs at Grady. "She does."

"I wouldn't call it that," I mutter.

"That's because you're way too anal about bundt stuff."

My cheeks are on fire. The cheeks on my face, I mean. "Vera! Stop."

She skips over to the other side of me and leans in. "Oh, would you like me to put a plug in it?"

I will actually murder you, I mouth to her.

Bring it, she mouths back.

"Well, that's a shame," Grady says, ruefully. "I like big bundts and I cannot lie."

Somewhere in the universe, there is a record scratch.

The whole world goes silent for a few magnificent seconds.

Of all the sentences I never thought I'd hear the golden boy of Beacon Harbor say, that one is at the top of the list, only after *I love you, Claire Sweeney.*

Vera's jaw drops to the floor. And then she tilts her head to look at me, and we both burst out laughing so hard I think we might die.

"You gotta shake that healthy bundt, baby," Vera says to me when she can finally speak again. "I'll deep-six the special order, though. And don't forget we're out of chocolate chip and apple fritters."

I clear my throat and get my head back in the game. "Right. On it." I glance over at Grady, who seems a little embarrassed, which is not a look I'm used to seeing on him. Did we laugh too hard? Does he think we were laughing *at* him and not with him? Why do I care?

"Tell whoever ordered the bundt cake that I make a beautiful lemon layer cake with lemon–cream cheese buttercream."

"You got it, boss." Before going back out front, Vera turns on the Bluetooth speaker for the kitchen, taps at her phone, and blows me a kiss as her Motown playlist starts up. Which means she wants me to be horny, but not so horny that I'm agitated. I'm almost grateful that she didn't cue up the obvious choice—Sir Mix-a-Lot.

So, this is happening. But I have to make two dozen chocolate chip cookies and a small batch of apple fritters, and I don't have time to plan Vera's untimely demise. She should have given me more of a heads-up that we were almost out of chocolate chip and apple fritters, though. And I should have known we would be. But I didn't, and that's Grady's fault. I go to my stove and fill my stock pot with oil for the fritters. I should have asked Vera to bring me more apples from the fridge, and if I'm being honest, she should have known that her job is to do that kind of thing for me when things are this busy. But I can get them.

Crossing to the fridge, I notice that Grady is washing his hands at my sink.

Why is he washing his hands at my sink?

"I'm gonna help you," he tells me. I don't even have to ask.

He helped me once when I had to bake two hundred cupcakes for a bake sale as a freshman. He was actually helpful. And I do need help. So I tell him to peel, core, and dice the Granny Smith apples. I'm so busy getting the cookies into the oven, I don't even think about how I'm swaying my hips and singing along to "This Old Heart of Mine." I barely notice the veins in Grady's hands and forearms as he peels those apples. I have to reach across the counter for a clean spatula and accidentally graze his bicep when I do—but I'm so busy mixing my batter, I don't even care if he thinks I did it on purpose.

And when I check the temperature of my oil in the stock pot, turn around, and walk right into him, I only inhale deeply because he's been stealing all the oxygen in my kitchen. It's not because he smells like a hint of dried-down sweat from his run, a little bit of leftover rich-guy cologne, and fabric softener. Because his mom probably washed that shirt for Damien. Grady doesn't say anything when I look up at him. He just stares down at me, handsomely and wealthily. He stares down at my forehead, my ear lobe, my neck, my mouth. His jaw is clenched and his nostrils are flaring.

There's a flutter in my belly and tightness between my legs, but I drag the back of my hand against the tip of my nose. "Do I have flour all over my face or something?"

He blinks once, as if he didn't realize he was staring, and shakes his head. "No." And then he takes a step back and raises the bowl of diced apples he's holding in one hand.

My throat is constricted, so if he thinks it's rude of me to not thank him when I take the bowl from him, well, that's just too bad. I fold the apples into my batter.

"I couldn't help but notice the container of dark chocolate chips on the shelf," he says as I drop a quarter cup of batter into the hot oil. I can tell he's smirking. "Don't tell me you've changed your mind about dark chocolate."

I lower my voice. "Dark chocolate is exactly as flavorless and terrible as it always has been, but I'm running a business now, and I am trying to attract wealthy asshole tourists. So I do a salted dark chocolate brownie on the weekends."

"That sounds delicious. Noticed you have plenty of Nutella too."

And just like that, my eyes are watering and my nose is all tingly. I'm remembering that night at the beach and the thing that happened later in his car. But I don't have time for watery eyes or a tingly nose or feelings of any kind.

I brush past him to grab a slotted spoon. "Why are you here, Grady?" I ask again.

At the same time, he asks, "Why are you trying to push the pavlova if everyone wants chocolate chip cookies? I'm sure the pavlova are excellent, as are the cookies and everything else you bake—but if nobody is coming in here to order profiteroles or pavlova, then why don't you just make and sell more cookies? It seems like you're trying to introduce elevated products to a client base that isn't looking for that."

"You aren't actually criticizing me in my own kitchen, are you?"

"It was just a question. And an observation. And an explanation of my observation."

"Uh-huh. Well, I'm busy baking things for customers who came here to rub up against a billionaire, so if you're going to be here, at least go back out front where they can see you."

We both look out through the window to the store and see that everyone, including Vera, is watching us.

He gives them a little wave. "I think they can see me just fine."

I whisk my glaze as I wait for the fritter in the oil to turn golden brown. "Okay, but seriously. Why have you been here? For so long?"

He sighs and rubs the back of his neck. "You know..."

And now it's obvious. Of course. "Jake? Right? Jake told you to talk to me?" I roll my eyes.

"He's just trying to help. I'm just trying to help." I'm about to tell him I don't need his help when he holds up his hands and says, "I talked to your suppliers this morning."

I almost laugh at that, but it comes out like a grunt. "How do you even know who my suppliers are?"

"I looked up all the suppliers in the area, figured out prices, distance..."

"Of course you did."

"And now that I've seen how you operate, I've

worked out a plan." He pauses for a beat, tries to present himself as someone who is humble. "I think."

"I have my own plan," I huff out. "I operate just fine. I don't need your help. I don't need *you*." My voice cracks on that last sentence, but he probably doesn't hear it over the music.

"Yeah," says a muffled, gruff old man-voice from the other side of the door. "We don't need you!"

"Crabby!" I can only see the top of his head through the porthole window of the café door.

"Where are my cookies?"

"Give me five minutes! Tell Vera I said you can have a free coffee while you wait!" I call out, exasperated, but that messy wave of white hair and the way he waves me off makes me smile.

I remove the fritter from the pot and place it on a layer of paper towels to drain the oil. This is how I do it. Small batch. If he criticizes me for this too, I'm throwing him out of my kitchen.

When I turn around, Grady is right there again. Staring down at me. Jaw tight. Hands on the hips. "Would you like me to leave, Claire?"

"What do you think?" I look him straight in the eyes. I want to *not want* him to stay, that's what I want. I want to want someone else to be here with me. I want there to be someone—anyone else that I want here with me besides him.

He studies my face. My forehead, my cheek, my earlobe, my neck. He searches my eyes. He stares at my mouth again, his stance getting all rigid. I can't tell if he likes what he sees or if he hates it or if he doesn't like that he likes it. It doesn't do me any good either way. He nods. "Yeah. I'll get out of your way."

He picks up his laptop, and as he is about to press against the swinging door, he says, without looking back, "You have flour on your forehead now."

Chapter 10

Buttered Up

GRADY

I can't get Claire out of my mind.

That's been true ever since I got back. It's been true ever since I moved away from Beacon Harbor. But it's so much worse now. Going to her bakery to figure out her business was probably a mistake. It *was* a mistake. But I learned a lot. I learned that it's a huge turn-on watching her work. I learned that she sways her hips and sings along to Motown music without even realizing it. I learned that my desire to be around Claire is strong. And that my desire to help her is even stronger. She needs my help. Based on what Jake has said and on the numbers I ran, as imperfect and round as they are, she *really* needs it.

I'm a fixer. A grinder. This is what I do. I find a problem and I figure out a strategy and I make that problem go away.

But she's made it clear that she sees *me* as the problem. I have learned over the years in business—maybe the biggest lesson I've learned—is that you can know the spreadsheets and the logic and the strategy like the road home, but it won't matter because humans are emotional creatures. If I press Claire, her resistance would just harden like weeks-old bread.

It's in my nature to want to take control of anything I care about. Anything I want. I suppose that's one of the reasons I've struggled so much with caring about Claire. I see how protective her brother is of her, but if I decide to make her mine, she will be all mine.

Jake wouldn't like that.

Claire definitely wouldn't like it...at first...

It won't happen. It can't. But I never expected her to be so resentful of me. I was doing her a favor by not kissing her that night in my car before graduation. God knows, I wanted to. Surely she knew that. But I was leaving. I would never have been able to give her the time and attention she deserves. Not then and not now. But I can still help her while I'm here. It may not be exactly what either of us wants, but it's something.

However, I've had to let things cool down with Claire. For her sake and for mine and for the sake of my goal—to get her to want me to help her business. I've spent the past few days focusing on the reason I came back to Beacon Harbor in the first place—to help my family. I've been running errands for my mom. When I go running at five in the morning, I make sure to stay away from Main Street and the Sweeneys' neighborhood. I re-grouted the tile in my parents' bathroom. I've taken my dad to his doctor's appointments. I mowed the lawn with the riding mower that Damien isn't allowed to drive. I went to the store to buy groceries, wearing a baseball cap and sunglasses in an attempt to stay incognito. I had my nutritionist come up with a menu that would satisfy both my dad's palate and my mother's concerns.

I've been doing all this while sleeping in my old room. My parents have kept it just as I left it. And it's here, in the bed I slept in as a teenager, that I wake up from a dream about Claire. We were in her kitchen at the bakery. She was wearing an apron—and nothing else. I don't want to leave this dream. But my dick is wide awake and demanding attention, and this family knocks on closed doors without waiting for an answer before opening them.

So I get up out of bed, awkwardly making my way to the bedroom door to lock it.

Then I pull down my boxer briefs, my cock springing free. I'm back in bed. I open the drawer of the bedside table and pull out the lotion I picked up when I was buying groceries. I squeeze my eyes shut. And now I'm back in the bakery kitchen, after closing time, with Claire.

Her blonde hair is up in a ponytail, and her skin glistens all over—but not from sweat. She's covered in melted butter. Why? It's my fantasy—who cares? The front of the apron says **I am *the secret ingredient***. Claire ignores me as she places a large bowl of pink decorating sugar—something I saw in one of her neatly labeled bins—on the big table at the center of the kitchen. I'm leaning against the counter opposite her, rolling up my sleeves.

My cock is straining against my pants. She sashays around the corner of the table, glances up at me, smirking. And then she slowly turns her back to me, leaning forward to grip the edge of the table.

Her bare ass cheeks are round and glorious and slick with butter. I am painfully erect as I close the distance between us, trying to play it cool, but I stroke that glossy skin without hesitation. Gliding my palms down from the sides of her waist, over her ample hips, and around to the front of her thighs. When I reach between her legs, she straightens her arms, pushing up against the table as she presses her sweet ass up against the hard length of my erection.

Little minx.

"Set it free, Mr. Barber," she says in a husky voice. *"What are you waiting for?"*

And I do. I unzip my pants and pull my cock out, caressing the silky, warm flesh of each cheek with the aching tip. She gasps and trembles. I spread the precum around, polishing her already glossy skin with it. And then I let my cock rest in the inviting space between her plump cheeks. She clenches around me. Wiggles around, innocent but so devious. She's driving me crazy in ways I never dared imagine she could.

"Claire... Fuck..."

"Who, me? You don't want to fuck me, do you, Grady? I'm just your best friend's weird little sister."

She angles herself forward so the tip of my cock can find its way to the entrance of her warm, slippery center.

I groan. *"Not here, Little Sweeney. Not now."*

"Bo-ring!" she taunts.

I wrap her ponytail around one fist, reach around her, flatten the palm of my other greased-up hand into the bowl of pink sugar, and I smack her ass. It is so satisfying to hear her catch her breath as her entire body tenses up and then sigh as she relaxes. Now she has a glittering, pink, sugary handprint against one globe of ass cheek.

"Still bored?" I growl, even though I know the answer.

"Nuh-uh," she mutters. It's the most positive response I've gotten out of her yet.

I untie the ribbons at her back, slip the apron off over her head, and she lets it fall to the floor. I grab her by the waist and lift her up onto the worktable, sliding her forward so I can taste and feel that sweet, gritty sugar and slippery butter against my tongue. She gasps and moans. I smack the side of her ass again and grunt as I watch the jiggling flesh. I'm about to bury my face inside of her when she flips around to face me. The front of her body is now coated in sugar. Why? It's my fantasy—who cares?

I lick her all over her quivering body, from her pussy up to her mouth. We finally kiss. Her tongue tastes like maple syrup, and she is so hungry for me. I slowly realize her sweet lips and tongue are taking a journey down the front of me. She drops to her knees and lathers my cock with whipped cream. Then she begins to lick it. Slowly at first, up and down the length before taking all of me into her mouth.

And that is when I explode, my body curling in on itself, here in my bed. I try not to make any noise. Cum shoots up onto my abs and chest instead of into Claire's warm mouth. I sigh heavily, wishing everything I just envisioned could happen. All of it. Except I'd last longer and give her all the pleasure she gave me in return. And then fuck her straight into next week.

Suddenly, there's a *knock–knock–jangle at the door*. The lock on the doorknob, mercifully, holds. "Grady?!" More jangling.

"Just a second, Ma!" I call out, scrambling to clean myself up.

"Why is this door locked?"

"I dunno, must've slipped last night when I closed it." I sound so awkward and young. If I always lied this unconvincingly I'd never make it in business.

She tries jiggling the doorknob again—why? I have no idea. It's my mom. "Will you be around today, sweetheart?"

"Yep!" I ball up the sheet that I just used to wipe cum from myself and hide it under the comforter. I make a mental note to deal with that later. I hop around as I pull on my underwear, reaching for the nearest pair of sweatpants and a T-shirt.

"Would you mind driving Damien to the beach?" she asks through the door. It sounds like her face is pressed right up against it.

Fully dressed, I take a moment to slow my breaths. Somewhat calmer and acting less like I just fucked my hand, I open the door. "Good morning," I say cheerily, casually blocking her from entering the room.

"Well, good morning, sunshine! Can you take him?" she asks again, as if our lives depend on it.

"Sure. That's why I'm here. What's up?"

"I have to be there for your father's appointment, and

Damien says this morning is prime training time—something to do with crustacean circadian rhythms." She waves her hand around dramatically.

"Makes sense. No problem. Hope the appointment goes well."

"Thanks, honey. It's so nice having you here." She gives me a little pat on the cheek as she studies my face.

"What?"

"Nothing," she says innocently. "Just that being home seems to agree with you. You have a nice color to your cheeks."

"Had a good night's sleep," I tell her. Both of us pretending she hasn't raised two sons and lived with men for most of her life. "Let me know if you need anything else." I slowly shut the door.

And now that the adrenaline rush has subsided, I can feel the guilt. Layers of guilt. Guilt for fantasizing about Jake's little sister. Guilt for messing up these sheets. At least there's something I can do about the sheets.

I grab my business phone and text Alice.

ME: Morning. Please have new Frette Egyptian cotton sheet sets sent to my parents' house. For all the beds. Three queen size. Make that six sets of queen size. All white.

Just in case. Because I won't have time to do laundry myself and I sure as hell won't let my mom do it.

ALICE: You got it ;)

The winky-face emoticon tells me she has an idea of why I've requested this, but Alice is paid handsomely to not ask questions.

Unlike my family.

Or maybe not.

My phone buzzes with an incoming call from her. I answer with "Address the packages to me, or my parents will think it's a mistake and send them back."

"I wasn't born yesterday, bossman. I'm calling because I just got a thousand text messages from friends telling me every gossip site in the city is reporting that Harrison Lynch bought an engagement ring at Tiffany's yesterday, but he has not publicly confirmed if he's engaged or who he's engaged to."

I'm stripping the sheets from my bed with one hand when I say, "Interesting."

"I thought you'd think so. Should I be concerned?"

"Should *I* be concerned?"

Alice laughs. *At* me. God, I love her. "I don't think you need to be concerned until we find out if the rumors are true and who the fiancée is. I think it's safe to assume we'll know all by the METH gala."

"Right. Pembroke."

"Mr. Lynch did say he wouldn't give up without a fight. Aston Pembroke is a family man of the highest order. I don't think I've ever seen anyone show so many pictures of his family in the middle of a business meeting before."

"I really didn't want to have to bring a date to that gala," I grumble.

"You can't show up looking like a bachelor if Lynch is

going to show up with a bride-to-be. You want me to round up the usual suspects?"

I sigh and rub my forehead. If there was a socialite left on the planet that I've met and wanted to date, I'd already be dating her. "No. I don't want you to. But go ahead and send me some options."

"You got it. Until then, you'll have some nice new sheets to keep you company." I can hear her stifling a cheeky laugh before she ends the call.

"Why the hell are you stopping here?" Damien asks from the passenger seat of my Mercedes. On his lap are two lobsters that are being carefully transported inside two large plastic spill-proof containers that are lined with frozen liquid gel packs and seaweed. He's got his arms around them, and he's somehow making it look cool. Like all the kids are gonna be carrying around lobsters if they see him like this. "We gotta get to the beach!"

He is so exasperated. I have never seen this guy in a hurry before, but he really wants to get to the beach so he can let his lobsters move around.

And he's going to have to wait another minute. "I thought you said they can stay like that for up to twenty-four hours."

"Yeah, but that's not ideal. I don't want to stress them out."

"Then don't act so stressed." I park in an alley behind Main Street, looking around to make sure nobody's watching before opening up my trunk, pulling out a garbage bag full of bedsheets, and tossing them into a dumpster.

When I start up the engine again, I can hear Damien grinning when he says, "Never mind. Definitely not gonna ask about that."

"Good. Why the big rush to get to the beach this morning? Don't you usually go later in the day?"

"Yeah. But I mean, the weather's been so weird this summer—I want to go when it's nice out. And I just want to get there early so Vera won't be there."

"Oh yeah? Vera from the bakery?" *Claire's Vera*, I almost say. "Is she usually around for lobster practice?" It's embarrassing how much my heart rate picks up just at the mention of someone who's friends with Claire Sweeney.

"Not usually," he says, fidgeting so much it's shaking the car. "Sometimes."

"Interesting."

"Not really. Just annoying." He taps his fingers against the dashboard rhythmically. A lot of nervous energy there. You'd think he was a drummer, not a guitar player. But he's a brilliant guitar player—self-taught, of course. He might be an even better songwriter. But he's never done anything with it. His biggest problem is that he doesn't think his dreams are worth taking seriously. It has always frustrated me a lot more than it ever frustrated him.

"So, no more band, huh?"

I glance over and see him wrinkling his brow. He shrugs his shoulders. He looks out the window.

I guess that's his answer.

"You still playing music?"

"Yeah. Sometimes. At Hair of the Sea Dog. Solo. I get offers to play in Portland sometimes, but..." He gestures toward me, indicating that he can't drive there now.

"You still writing songs?"

"What do you care?"

"If you ever want to come to New York, you can stay with me. Or I can put you up at a hotel. I can make some calls, get you some gigs."

"No, thanks."

All righty, then. Change of tactic. Guess he's not in the mood to be big-brothered. "So. Crustacean circadian rhythms, huh? Tell me about that. You got a strategy?"

Whatever light I snuffed out by being a concerned older sibling has been reignited by the subject of lobsters.

"Yeah, I've got a strategy. I use Clawdia to motivate Crustaceous Clay. Because nothing motivates a guy to do his best like trying to impress a chick. Did you know a male lobster is called a cock and the female is a hen?"

That can't be right. "You don't say. You aren't worried about your guy being distracted by the female? Maybe going off course and chasing her instead of the prize?"

"I mean. If he ends up with her instead of the prize, he still wins."

And that attitude right there is why Damien is an artist and I'm not.

When we get to the beach, I carry one of the lobster containers and follow my brother toward what he calls "the racetrack," but he keeps craning his neck and looking around.

"What are you looking for?"

"Huh? Nobody," he says, still scanning the beach from behind his aviators. Then he stops in his tracks, his jaw dropping open just a little.

I follow his gaze and see a crowd of guys—boys and men—who are casually standing around not far from where Vera is toweling herself off. She's wearing a bikini that's the same shade of blue as the chunky highlights in her hair. And now I know why Damien was in such a rush to get here. He must have gotten tipped off.

Then I realize that if Vera's here, that must mean the bakery is closed today, which means...

Fuck me.

It means *fuck me*.

That is all I'm thinking as I stand in the sand, along with about a dozen other guys, watching Claire emerge from the sea in a bikini. Her wet skin glistens in the late morning sun. There is such a strange dissonance between my memories of her as a girl and this woman I'm watching now. She is even more gorgeous than she was in my fantasy a couple of hours earlier. I can't tell if she's even aware of being the center of so much male attention, but I am positive that she will be the star of at least a dozen fantasies later today.

And that makes my skin heat up so much I'm afraid I'm going to cook whichever lobster is in this container I'm holding.

Claire has paused in her journey from the water's edge to adjust her bikini bottom at the hip. This movement causes her tits to press together, and there is a chorus of sighs that is louder than the waves. I want to kick sand in the faces of every guy who's gawking at her, but then I might accidentally get sand in my own eyes and not be able to see her body anymore, so—not worth it.

It's like she's walking in slow motion. She is walking way too slowly. Now I'm starting to think she's totally aware of all the eyes on her and is putting on a show. If Jake were here, he'd throw a towel at her while simultaneously shoving those guys' faces into the sand. So I give the plastic bin to Damien, who's still staring at Vera. Before he even starts complaining, I'm picking up the beach towel that's in a big bag next to where Vera is standing, and I storm over to Claire, wrapping the towel around her bare shoulders.

"What the hell?!" She is totally taken aback.

"All right, show's over!" I call out to the perverts who are throwing their arms up in the air in frustration.

"Grady?!"

"It's what your brother would do," I explain, realizing my arm is around her shoulder and one hand is clinging to her arm over the towel.

She stares up at me with so much confusion in her pretty gray-blue eyes.

I let go of her and drag my fingers through my hair. "You should dry off."

"Is that what I should do?" she says in a husky voice that's a little too reminiscent of the one she used in my filthy head earlier.

I clear my throat, nod, and walk back to Damien, who appears to be having an argument with Vera.

"It's too early for them to be racing!" she's saying as

she waves her arms around, still wearing nothing but a bikini.

Damien continues to make it look cool to hold large plastic containers with live lobsters and seaweed in them. "They're my lobsters. It's my training schedule," he says calmly, through gritted teeth. His attention is so focused on her face that it is painfully obvious to me how hard he has to work to not look at her body.

"Don't you want to win?" she taunts. "Or are you just going to half-ass this too?"

"Oh, I'm whole-assing it, Vera. My entire ass is going into this. It's nothin' but my ass."

"Well, Clawdia and I are going to beat your whole ass today." She grabs the handles of the top container and gently lifts it up.

"You won't. But bring it."

"Consider it brung, D-man," she says as she turns her back to him and calls out to Claire. "Claire Bear! I'll be at the racetrack! You coming?"

I STAND NEXT to the lobster racetrack with my arms crossed, staring down the beach at Claire, who has stubbornly decided that she will not be joining us over here and also decided not to cover up her amazing voluptuous bikini-clad body.

I'm certainly glad she hasn't brought that amazing voluptuous bikini-clad body over here, but I am not pleased to see it on display for all those other men to drool over.

"How much longer do we have to be here?" I ask Damien.

"We literally just got here," he reminds me.

Vera has thrown on a T-shirt and shorts. She and Damien each remove a lobster from a container—how they can tell which is which, I don't know and will never care.

This setup is pretty impressive, though. There's a big plexiglass racetrack on a covered stage. Each saltwater-filled lane is one level, so it looks like a big clear staircase. Each uncovered step is about two feet wide and ten feet long. There's a big tub filled with saltwater nearby. Vera and my brother place the lobsters in there—I guess so they can warm up? But you know, not get too warm, or else they'd start to cook.

I can't fucking believe I'm even here for this, but Damien seems really into it, and the sea breeze *is* relaxing.

I take a moment to check my phone and find that Alice has already texted me five options for dates to the gala. I quickly check the Instagram links she's sent me and scan through their pedigrees. Maybe if I was in my office in Manhattan right now they would seem more appealing to me. But standing here, on a beach in my hometown, next to some live lobsters...these women just don't seem real to me.

"Oh, hello, everyone!" The loud, relentlessly positive, slightly out-of-breath voice belongs to Stacy Hutchinson, the very fit middle-aged mayor of Beacon Harbor. She

The Billionaire Is Back

must be out for a lunchtime jog. She gives us all a double wave while trotting over, off the paved walkway. "Grady. Vera. Damien."

We all acknowledge her as she stops in front of me, jogging in place. She checks her fitness watch before staring intently into my eyes. God, she's intense. "Grady Barber. I can't tell you how happy I am to see you. Have you had time to read my emails?"

Mayor Stacy has been emailing me at 8:01 on the dot every morning since my return. Most of the messages have been requests for various appearances around town, some of them philanthropic events, but she has repeatedly invited me to give a speech at the end-of-summer Shellibration.

Suddenly, Claire is dressed and standing right next to me, beaming at the mayor. "Mayor Stacy! Hi. Did you get the email I sent you last week? The one with the link to the Dropbox folder? With the sketches for the cake designs? It's all part of my pitch. I was wondering because I updated some of the designs yesterday. I just want to make sure you see the most recent versions."

Wow. I've never seen Claire Sweeney so hungry for approval. She always did have a weird thing about the mayor of Beacon Harbor. Why doesn't she care this much about *my* approval? Am I jealous of the mayor now? Or am I picturing Claire being hungry for my approval in a totally different circumstance? Yeah. Filing that away for later.

"Yes, Claire Sweeney, hello! I did get your email. I haven't had a chance to look at the sketches yet." She turns to me again, still jogging in place. "So, did you get my follow-up messages, Grady?"

Claire looks so disappointed, it kind of hurts my heart.

"Yes, Stacy, I read them. I haven't had time to respond yet."

The mayor places two fingertips on the side of her neck to check her pulse while asking me, "And do you know yet if you'll be here at the end of the summer?"

I can feel Claire watching me, quietly asking the same question.

"Well," I say to Stacy, "as I said in my initial response, I do not know yet. It depends on how things go with my dad's recovery."

Stacy's constantly active hands wave away any concern. "Of course, of course. Totally understand. Obviously I wish your dad a speedy and thorough recovery, but I also, of course, hope you stay a while. You're a very important person in this town!"

Claire scoffs at that and then covers it by faking a coughing fit.

Stacy raises her open hand up in the air as she beams at me.

I'm not sure if I'm supposed to high-five her or not.

She smiles even broader and nods vehemently, while giving me the thumbs-up with her other hand.

So, I slap her five.

"Boom! I love that Big *D* Energy!"

I stare at her blankly. Claire starts choking again.

"*D* for *Dynamo!*" Stacy explains and then raises both fists in the air, like Rocky at the top of the steps of the Philadelphia Museum. "The prodigal son returns!"

"For a visit, yes."

"Grady Barber. I am excited. I am grateful. On behalf of the entire town of Beacon Harbor, I would just like to say that we would be overjoyed if your worldly wisdom and successful energy would grace our festival! It's inspiring! Am I right?!" she asks around, as if she were surrounded by a group of sycophants. She isn't.

Claire just frowns at me.

If it were any other politician who was buttering me up like a lobster, I would have rolled my eyes and walked away by now. But Stacy Hutchinson is so damn earnest in her enthusiasm. I can't help but smile. "Right, well, we'll just have to see how it goes."

"Well, you know who'll be here at the end of the summer, just like she's been here at the end of every summer and attended every Shellibration since she was a baby?" Claire asks. "Me. I will. And I would really love to bake a very large cake for you, Mayor. So, if there's anything in particular you're looking for..."

"I don't know yet, Claire, but you're definitely still in the running." Mayor Stacy picks up her pace and runs in place instead of jogging.

Claire pretends to find that hilarious. "Running! Great. That is...great."

"Stacy, tell you what," I say. "If Sweet Treats on Main is selected as the official baker for the end-of-summer Shellibration, I will be here to give the speech. Even if I have to come back to do it."

Mayor Stacy claps her hands three times and jumps

up and down, more like a high school cheerleader than a fiftysomething public servant. "You will? Yay!"

"You will?" Claire asks, with more skepticism than excitement.

"I will," I assure them. "Call my office in New York and tell Alice to put it in my calendar."

"I will do that as soon as I return to my office, in approximately fourteen minutes," Mayor Stacy declares, shaking my hand again. "This will be perfect!" she calls out as she jogs away. "Perfect! I mean, you did make the very generous donation that paid for our lobster racetrack and state-of-the-art lobster retirement habitat, after all!"

"Right," I say, as if I knew that. "Exactly."

I catch sight of my brother, who's shaking his head. I read his lips. *Of course you did,* he's saying.

I shrug. "It was an anonymous donation," I tell him.

He does not look pleased. I get it. This was supposed to be his thing. He can't escape the long shadow of the billionaire older brother. Well. I'll just have to remind him that I can't play any instruments. That should level the playing field.

"What do you think you're doing?" Claire asks me, her arms crossed in front of her chest. As usual.

"Making a deal."

"Here's the deal, Grady." She faces me, planting her feet and squaring her shoulders. "I don't know how to make this any clearer—I don't need or want your help."

Well, that's cute.

I was gentle before. I went easy on her because I was unsure of how or if I should help her. But I know she needs me. She just won't admit it. And now I know I can help her get something that she willingly admits to wanting. You don't get to be as good as I am in business without having a little wolf in you.

"Too bad, Little Sweeney. You need my help. And I want to give it to you," I growl.

The growl surprises both of us, and neither of us know what to do with it.

But Claire is a tough cookie. Her brow furrows. Her jaw sets. Her eyes narrow.

It's hot as fuck.

But she isn't any closer to relenting.

I look over at Damien and Vera. They're both holding their contestants over their lanes, giving them pep talks as they're about to lower them into the water. I quickly assess my brother's body language. He doesn't look happy or confident.

"Tell you what," I say to Claire. "Let's leave it up to fate. If Crustaceous Clay wins this practice race, I'll still give the speech at the Shellibration, but I'll leave you and your bakery alone. You won't hear from me for the rest of my time here. But if Clawdia Swiffter wins, you will let me help your business."

Claire's brow softens slightly, but her eyes remain narrowed and her jaw is still tight. "Damien. How fast is Crustaceous Clay?" she asks without taking her eyes off of mine.

"The fastest ever," he replies without hesitation.

"You're on, Grody Borber," she says quietly. "Get ready for some Big D Energy. D for *Defeated*."

Sassypants.

"Three, two, one, go!" Claire yells out.

Damien and Vera release their lobsters, and Claire and I get up closer to the track.

Claire joins Damien in cheering on Crustaceous.

Honestly, the whole thing takes a really long time.

Lobsters are not fast.

They're sort of swimming forward, but this is just the slowest fucking race I have ever seen. Still, my heart is pounding in my chest and it feels like there's a lot on the line here. I don't have too much to worry about, though. Clawdia easily beats Crustaceous. My brother is too proud to let on that he's crushed by defeat, but I see it. Vera sees it too and places a reassuring arm around his shoulder. Which is unexpected.

But the strangest reaction of all is Claire's. She just lost the bet. She has to let me help her. And I don't find any trace of disappointment on her pretty face.

Chapter 11
No S'More Mr. Nice Guy

CLAIRE

I STAND AT THE DOCK, arms crossed, watching Grady rig his family's sailboat. I tried to help him because I do know my way around a boat, but he insists I stay on the dock and let him do it. The sailboat is called *High & Tight*. Because Barber. Which is cute. Grady bought it for his parents for Christmas a few years ago. Which is also cute.

Know what isn't cute? Since I lost the lobster bet, Grady Barber *ordered* me to meet him here at 5:30 sharp. I'm a little annoyed about losing—and very annoyed that he is now ordering me to do things. My traitorous lady parts, however, were just delighted. They tried telling him that if he would like to continue doing that, they would enthusiastically support it. I told my lady parts to shut it.

This is why I'm keeping my arms crossed over my chest.

Forever.

I'm only here because I want to show this guy how over him I am, even if it was weirdly sweet and sort of hot that he threw a towel over me at the beach today. If he wants to be a good friend to Jake by trying to help me out, well, I'll let him think he's being a good friend to Jake. But I'm going to prove to both of us that I don't need anything he has to offer. *So, bring it, Barber. Watch me resist every single part of you. I've got all night to make you regret not wanting me.*

Still, my very rational brain is in agreement with the rest of me on one thing—it is not unpleasant to watch him work. This has always been my favorite view of Grady, and it has nothing to do with the way his dark jeans showcase his butt or how perfectly his navy-and-cream merino-wool sweater fits his torso. It's when his attention is laser focused on a task. His face is never more beautiful than when his mind is wrapped up in whatever he's doing. His body moves with incredible grace and ease as he makes his way back and forth across the vessel. The veins in his forearms bulge as he prepares the sails for hoisting, stows our backpacks, and coils line. Gotta hand it to him—the guy can tie a good knot.

I watch as his fingers deftly coil the rope to create a loop. An opening. Two thick strong fingers penetrate the loop to hold it open while he thrusts the ends of the rope into the opening. He slips his thumb and forefinger farther down the rope, looping it again and doubling back, penetrating the opening again. And again. Before his big strong hands with knuckles that are like knots themselves pull everything tight, the opening tightening like a vice around the length filling it.

"Okay, Sweeney," he says in a tone that makes me snap to attention and then immediately resent it. "Time to raise the sails. All aboard," he orders. Again.

See? Isn't that nice? my lady parts whisper.

"Shut it."

"What was that?" Grady asks. His dark brows are furrowed, but the corner of his mouth quirks upward.

Shit, I said that out loud. I shake my head. "Nothing. Help me up," I order. Grady smiles that damn smile of his and obeys, pulling me up and helping me onto the deck, over the lifeline, and directly into his chest. He grips my arm until he's sure I'm steady.

"You good?" He stares down at me without moving.

I glance up at him, trying to read the expression on his face. His jaw is so tense, you'd think he was holding on to me for dear life. But he isn't. It seems like he's torn between wanting to hang on and push me away. He almost looks guilty? I nod and step aside, carefully shuffling over to the cockpit in the sexiest manner possible. Wishing I had answered, *Yeah, I'm amazing. Have you really not figured that out yet? Too bad because, like the one we're standing on is about to, that ship has sailed.* But it's more important not to fall over right now.

"Put on your sweater," he commands.

When I step into the cockpit, I notice he has folded the thick sweater I brought and laid it out on the seat. I put on the sweater. Not because he told me to, because I remember how chilly it can get out on the water once the sun starts to set.

When I turn around, he's right behind me, holding up a life jacket. "Put this on too," he grunts.

"Aw, man." That is not hot. "Are *you* going to wear one?"

"Yes. Put it on," he orders.

I wrinkle my nose—that is the only fuss I make, but he shoves my arms through the arm holes and slips the life jacket on me. Then he zips it up and fastens the plastic buckles. If he noticed the nipples beneath my sweater trying to wave at him to save them, he ignored them.

Once he confirms that the life jacket is snug on my torso, he's off to hoist the mainsail.

"You still remember how to sail?" I ask, simply because I don't want him to know how much the part of me from the neck down enjoyed what he just did to me.

"I have a sailboat in New York" is his reply.

"Of course you do." I stop rolling my eyes midroll because I feel like such a Little Sweeney when I eye-roll him, and I need him to know that I'm not Little Sweeney anymore. "I mean, why bother sailing? You can afford to just have any island moved closer to shore for you."

"I can. But it would take too long," he deadpans. "And I enjoy sailing, Little Sweeney."

I press my lips into a straight line and blink at him slowly, but he's too busy putting on his life jacket to notice. So, I take the opportunity to apply ChapStick. Not because I am anticipating the use of my lips beyond frowning and snarling at him, because we're going sailing and there will be wind.

As we set sail, Grady coils more lines and sets them up neatly, ready to use.

We say nothing at all for the next half hour or so as we glide toward the horizon. The waves aren't too choppy, and it's not too windy. There's enough of a breeze to keep him from having to use the engine. The clouds are fluffy and huge. The sunset tonight is going to be gorgeous. Or it might rain—you just never know this summer. I notice that as we get farther from land, away from my bakery and my shitbox car and my old bedroom in my parents' house, my body relaxes. My breaths are deeper and slower. My shoulders don't feel tight. I hadn't realized just how tense my body was until it started to relax.

It has been entirely too long since I've been out on the water. I've spent more time outside and by the water today than I have all year, I think. Which is impossible to believe. I used to go hiking or boating, or both, every week. What have I been doing with my free time for the past couple of years?

Sleeping. And therapy baking. And learning how to be a better baker. And forgetting about the billionaire who wouldn't kiss me.

But then we get even farther away from land. There is nothing and no one else around. "Why are we out this far?" I finally ask Grady without hiding the suspicion in my voice.

He continues steering and staring ahead. "I just want

us to get away from everything. Somewhere no one can watch us or bother us."

Uh-huh. So that's why he looked guilty earlier. *Maybe he's going to murder us!* my lady parts deduce. Except they're turned on. What the hell, lady parts? That is neither exciting nor sexy. *You're wrong,* my heart pleads. *Maybe you've been wrong all these years! Maybe he's super, super obsessed with you! So obsessed he has to kill you to make you his forever!* My heart swoons. I mean, what the fuck, heart? Is it romantic? Sure. Would I begrudgingly admit that it would be gratifying to learn that Grady had thought about me at all, even if it was because he had some master plan to make my soul his forever? Okay, yeah. I would. Begrudgingly.

But I have to work. I have bills to pay and mouths to feed. I don't have time to get murdered. Not even by the golden boy of Beacon Harbor. "Are you going to kill me?"

"What?" He finally looks over at me. "Is that what you've been worried about?"

"Girls always have to worry about this. All the time."

"Well, if I didn't come back with you, I think people would have some questions. Jake, for starters."

"So you're saying it would be a bad plan."

"Yes."

"Which means you've thought of a better one."

He laughs. I made Grady Barber laugh. It's something. He grins at me, the golden skin around his eyes wrinkling. "No!"

"How would you do it? I want to know."

He shakes his head, still smiling. His teeth are so perfect, they make all other teeth look like rotted wood. I don't have a teeth thing, but those teeth are hot, and it makes me mad.

"I have absolutely no desire to kill you. I want you to relax. Will you just relax? Now!"

I sigh. Not because I want to relax. Not because he told me to. Because of course he isn't obsessed with me enough to want to murder me. God forbid he should spend even one minute of his busy, important life thinking about how he'd kill Claire Sweeney.

"Now you just look mad," he says, exasperated. "Why are you mad?"

"I'm not mad, I'm just annoyed! I'm so sorry my face isn't doing what you want it to do!" I cannot stop my eyes from rolling now. What else are they supposed to do? Fill with tears? That's not going to happen.

"Your face is..." He seems to be fumbling around trying to find the right word, which is not something I've ever seen Grady do before. "Fine" is what he lands on.

Which is *wonderful*.

"I'm so pleased to hear that you think my face is fine!" I scoff.

"Will you just— The water's getting choppy, so I have to concentrate. Just sit there, quietly, and think about what kind of future you want. Okay?"

"What is that? Some kind of punishment?"

"No, Claire." Now *he's* annoyed with *me*. "I need you to figure out what you want for your business so I can help you achieve it."

Well, that's not annoying at all. "Okay!" I huff.

He shakes his head and gives all of his attention to

aerodynamics and hydrodynamics, propelling us forward across the water, preventing us from capsizing.

Like a bossy dick.

I stare up at the sky. At the water. I look back at Beacon Harbor and then toward the horizon. I try to look pretty, deep in thought—and totally not attracted to Grady, in case his attention drifts back over to me.

It never does, which is fine because I get completely caught up in thinking about my bakery. Remembering why I wanted to own my own bakery in the first place. Daring to dream big, if only for this assignment. Suddenly, I'm aware of Grady's movements. He's slowing the boat down, getting ready to drop anchor near a secluded island. We must be more than ten miles from Beacon Harbor. This is one of those islands that's sparsely inhabited. Various parts of me perk up again. My heart is racing. And then I remember my dad bringing me here to look for puffins when I was a kid.

"I haven't been here in years," I say, marveling.

"I figured we could build a fire and just, you know, talk."

I still have a fair amount of resentment toward Grady. A lot of frustration. But that does sound nice.

He rows us to shore in the dinghy, leads me through a majestic, ancient forest of spruce and balsam-fir trees, carpeted in moss. He keeps picking up dry twigs, sticks, and loose moss from the ground. I do too, even though he doesn't ask me to. Then we're out the other side, to a beach that faces west so we can watch the sun set. He sets to building a fire inside a metal fire pit on the sand. All of this as if he's been doing it every weekend for his entire life instead of being a fancy rich guy in New York or God knows where.

"Let me do it," he barks.

I realize I'm absentmindedly rearranging some twigs in the fire pit. "Fine."

I sit on a big rock and watch him work, like I watched him rig the sailboat. I'm just not used to not doing things. I'm not saying I want to get used to this, but I'm also not saying that I am not enjoying this. If my nose is tingly and I'm tearing up, that has nothing to do with the fact that Grady is building a fire for us on a secluded beach that he has sailed us to so we can talk about my bakery while the sun sets. It has everything to do with the fact that I'm trying to remember the last time I just sat still and watched as someone else did something for my benefit. I was probably four or five. Plenty of people have attempted to do things for my benefit since then—I may have just forgotten that I don't *have* to work in order to be appreciated.

But that is not something I'm going to think about while sitting on a beach, alone with a handsome billionaire.

Or maybe we aren't alone?

Grady and I both startle at the sound of a young woman's squeal as it echoes around the rocks and across the water. It's quickly followed by joyful laughter and a young man's chuckle. We look back toward the entrance to the forest and see a young couple. They're teenagers, maybe college students. A guy and a girl that I don't recognize. He is carrying her over his shoulder and then lets her slide down the front of him. They kiss and then hold hands, unaware of our presence. Probably unaware that anyone else exists in the world. Images dance through my mind. They aren't memories of anything that actually happened. They're daydreams I used to have when I was in my mid-teens of me and Grady. I imagined us at that age, holding hands as we went on day trips.

I'm so glad I mostly forgot about those childish daydreams.

The adorable couple slows their pace as they realize they aren't alone in their love bubble. Grady concentrates on stoking the fire, probably worried they'll recognize him, but I make eye contact with them. I see no recognition in either of their expressions—of Grady or myself. The girl smiles at me and the guy gives me a friendly nod.

"Hey," he says.

"Hey," I say, trying to sound like I hang out with gorgeous billionaires on beaches all the time.

Grady politely acknowledges them.

"We'll get out of your hair—don't worry," the guy says. I'm about to explain that the quiet, annoyingly handsome man and I aren't a couple, when he asks, "You want a couple of beers?" He removes the backpack from his shoulders and pulls out a six-pack.

Grady shakes his head, but I say, "Yeah, that'd be great!"

I unzip my backpack. "You guys want chocolate?"

The girl nods enthusiastically, "Yes, please."

"Come by Sweet Treats on Main if you're in Beacon Harbor," I tell them as I share a bar of the artisan milk chocolate I order from Canada. "This is the kind of chocolate I use." Boom. I just did some marketing. *And I* got beer. Do I really need anyone's help with my business? I think not.

"Oh, cool!" she says, politely feigning excitement. I don't even shudder or grimace when she asks if I sell keto options. And then she giggles because her boyfriend's hand slides down to her butt, and they leave, to do what couples do.

Somehow I feel even more aware of being alone with Grady than I did before we had company.

I hold out a can of beer to Grady. "You always carry around premium chocolate?" he asks, as if he already knows the answer.

"Obviously." I crack open my beer and take a sip. "Actually, I brought more than just chocolate." I reach for my backpack again. "In case of campfire emergency." I kneel down in the sand, and then I pull out a box of graham crackers, a bag of marshmallows, skewers, aluminum foil, and bars of Hershey's chocolate. Because I've sampled hundreds of kinds of chocolate, but Hershey's plain milk chocolate is the best, and I mean the *only*, chocolate that should ever be used in s'mores. I will die on that eleven-percent-cacao hill.

I arrange all of my ingredients in front of me before looking up at Grady, fully expecting him to be shaking his head at me like I'm nuts.

Instead, his gaze has gone soft as he stares at my impromptu s'mores station. He cracks open his beer. "Surprise and demands," he mumbles. At least that's what it sounds like.

"Huh?"

"Nothing." He joins me in taking a seat on the sand,

sitting on his butt, his feet flat on the ground, arms wrapped around his bent legs as he holds the beer can with both hands. He looks so good as he takes a sip of beer and stares at the fire that I forget why I'm mad at him for a minute.

We're back to being silent in each other's company again. I like it. I can't help but wonder if he's ever this comfortable being quiet with anyone back in New York. I wonder if he's still happy. I wonder if he's dating anyone, if he's ever been in love, and I also don't want to know.

"So...what do you want, Claire?" he finally asks. "Tell me." Okay, he's back to ordering me around.

I gulp down half my can of beer and then fix him with my gaze. *I want you, you big, beautiful, clueless man. Even when I don't want you, I want you. Good luck helping me with that.* "What do you mean?" God, I hope he can't hear the lump that has formed in my throat.

"What's your goal for Sweet Treats on Main? I have some ideas, but it really just comes down to what you ultimately want. What did you originally want when you bought the business from Buddy and Ruthie?"

I'm on my knees in the sand, roasting a marshmallow at the end of a skewer, and I wait until it's perfectly, evenly toasted before answering him. Then I place the squishy golden-brown marshmallow on top of the square of chocolate that I've already assembled on half a graham cracker. Grady puts down his beer and reaches out to take the handle of the skewer from me so I can top off my campfire delicacy with the other half of the cracker. I sandwich everything together just enough so the marshmallow starts to ooze over the edges but not so much that it drips. Grady slowly pulls the tip of the skewer out from the marshmallow, and I can barely deal with how intimate and sensual this simple act feels. Fortunately, the flush in my cheeks can be explained by the fire and the sky that's already starting to turn pink and purple.

"Thanks," I say, taking the skewer from him and handing over the s'more. "I love Beacon Harbor," I state. "And I loved the idea of owning Sweet Treats because it's always been such an important part of Main Street. Everyone who's grown up in our town has memories of getting cakes and pastries from there."

He nods in agreement and then takes a bite of my s'more. His eyelids flutter shut in slow motion, and he emits a guttural sound that is so gratifying. I wait for him to finish chewing and swallowing before continuing my answer. He doesn't have to tell me how good and perfect this thing is that I just made. I know it's good and perfect. I know what I'm good at, and he's hardly even gotten a taste of it.

"I apprenticed there, you know? I was so honored that they gave me an exclusive offer for their business. Buddy and Ruthie taught me everything I needed to know about how to run their bakery. Their recipes as well as the lease and licenses and permits and everything in the kitchen and storefront were included in the LLC transfer." I toast another marshmallow. "I wanted to honor what they'd built and what they meant to the town. I wanted to give the new generation of Beacon Harbor and the tourists the same kinds of memories I had. But I wanted to update the business and make it my own. Buddy and Ruthie were so generous when I worked for them, but I realized pretty quickly that they weren't open to my ideas. And that was fine. They were very old-school, as you know. I mean, they were profitable based on word of mouth alone. But they didn't do any marketing. They hadn't updated their menu or equipment or decor in over twenty years. I wanted to bring it into the twenty-first century. And I needed money."

"So, you got a loan?"

"I got a lump-sum small-business loan from the bank. Jake and Vera and my parents and I remodeled as much as we could to keep costs down. The large appliances are the same ones that Buddy and Ruthie used."

"And the other equipment?"

"I sold what they had and got new mixers. Anything for the counter, I bought new."

He sucks melted marshmallow and chocolate from his thumb and then asks, "Why'd you get a seven-quart mixer?"

I shrug. "I make small batches and it's just me doing the baking, so..." I can tell he's struggling to refrain from saying something, so I wrap things up. "And I did what I could to make it look like a destination bakery. You know. Instagram-worthy. To attract tourists and people like me, who grew up seeing pretty pictures on the internet and watching the Food Network. Traded half of the original menu for French pastries that I taught myself to make, putting my own spin on things. And you know. The rest is history." I squish my s'more together and shove as much of it into my mouth as possible so I don't have to talk about money.

Grady nods, waits for me to finish chewing. "That's all wonderful, Claire."

His eyes are glassy by firelight. My name on his lips is a tiny song. That was the least judgmental he's ever sounded. It feels good.

I swallow and take a deep breath. "But?" I want him to get the rest of that sentence over with.

He doesn't throw me a cocky grin, he just looks so thoughtful and serious. "But I'm wondering if you wanted to make it your own or if you wanted to make it what you thought other people were looking for."

Well, shit.

"Because," he continues, "what you're doing isn't exactly in support of that. Is it? The renovations you've made to the storefront are beautiful. Your pastries and muffins, obviously, are incredible, on top of being photogenic. But what Beacon Harbor traffics in and what Main Street sells and what it sounded like you wanted to sell is nostalgia. Do you want your bakery to look and feel shiny and new, like an Instagram post, or do you want it to look like a Polaroid? Because tourists will pay top dollar for that. That's why they drive out here from Boston and Providence and Connecticut. And you know it's what the locals want...right?"

The damn smoke from the fire is making my eyes watery, but it's like I can finally see clearly for the first time in years.

Dammit.

He's right. And I'm not even mad about it or annoyed. I'm grateful. He finally said the thing that no one in my life would say. "Yeah. You have a plan, I suppose?"

He rubs his hands together and nods. "We can talk about the numbers later, but I think you need to think of your business as elastic. You have your everyday baking for the locals. Your grumpy hardware-store employees and your families who are on their way home from the beach. That's your bread and butter, no pun intended. And I know there are weekend tourists for most of the year, but you need to take the profit you'll make from the day-to-day business and use it to expand for the summer tourist season and special events."

"Like the cake for the end-of-summer Shellibration," I say.

"Exactly."

"Thank you for that, by the way. I'm sorry I didn't thank you before."

He shrugs. "It seemed weirdly important to you."

"It is important to me. In a not-weird way." I polish off the rest of my s'more. I don't know what it is about this one in particular that makes it so perfect and delicious. Maybe it's Grady's fire. Maybe it's the pink-and-purple clouds in the west. Maybe it's that it's been so damn long since I've made s'mores... "Why has it been so long since I've made s'mores?" I ask myself out loud. I know the answer, of course. Because it's been so long since I've been around a fire pit. But I could make them in the oven. "I can make s'mores the centerpiece of my new campaign," I state, as if I'm pitching it at a board meeting.

"Exactly!" he says excitedly.

"I can make chocolate chip–s'more cookie bars!"

"Yes. Amazing."

"All kinds of variations. I could make them with peanut butter. Pretzels. Butterscotch. And it would be so easy—just in a sheet pan." I am actually getting turned on thinking about this.

"I love it," he says, and I can tell he means it. "I mean, you can still make your profiteroles—just call them cream puffs."

God dammit, he does have a point.

Is it my imagination, or is he sitting a little bit closer to me now than he was ten minutes ago?

"I guess I should be grateful you won the lobster-race bet. What would you have done if you'd lost?" I give a little shrug. "Just not help me?"

"I wasn't going to lose," he says matter-of-factly.

I roll my eyes but can't help my smile. " I know you're good, Grody Borber, but you're not *control the fates* good."

His turn to give a little shrug. "I don't control fate. And I don't know anything about lobsters. But I do know human body language. And if Crustaceous Clay was actually as fast as my brother says he is, my brother wouldn't have looked so tense."

So smart. So shrewd. So Grady.

"Well, I have a little secret for you."

"Oh yeah?"

"Yeah. I may have been okay with you winning. I may have wanted you to win. That's why I asked Damien which lobster to bet on and not Vera."

Grady's beautiful face breaks from a grin to a laugh. Hope blooms in my chest, sprinkled with joy, and it isn't even dusted with anything bittersweet. I feel more at ease than I have in ages. I'm so excited and grateful, I want to throw my arms around Grady and hug him. But we were never huggers, he and I. Not of each other anyway.

"I'm really excited about what comes next," I say.

"I'm excited to help you get there. I think it's going to be amazing." He wrinkles his brow and leans in toward me a little. "You have a little chocolate, right...here." He touches the tip of his index finger against the corner of his own mouth as he stares at the corner of my mouth.

"Where?" I ask, refraining from sending the tip of my tongue out on a search for it.

"Here." He reaches out to slowly wipe away the melted chocolate from my cheek, and my face involuntarily nestles into the palm of his hand again.

I look up at him. It's a tiny, bold move, but the sugar and fat and alcohol are sailing through my bloodstream in an intoxicating, dreamy blend. Or maybe it's just Grady's sunset-and-firelit face that's making me feel tipsy. My billionaire baking advisor. I want so badly to let myself want him again. I lick my lips, and it feels like our heads are being pulled into each other's gravitational orbit.

I'm so excited, I'm actually buzzing.

Or is that the sound of a phone vibrating?

Grady's face stops an inch from mine. He pulls back. And just like that, the moment is broken.

He clears his throat and pulls out his phone.

How does he even get reception out here? He probably has a special billionaire cell phone with billionaire cell-phone service. He probably has his own personal satellite trained on him wherever he goes.

Glancing down at the caller ID, he exhales and mutters, "I have to take this." Not a trace of apology in his tone. He actually sounds relieved as he gets up and walks away.

Of course he walks away.

I'm the quirky small-town baker, and he's the golden-boy billionaire whose dreams are too big for a small town.

Nothing's really changed since high school. He will always, always pull back and then leave. So I just have to stop leaning in to kiss him. He only wants to get his mouth on my sweet treats. My head, my heart, and my lady parts all nod in agreement as I empty the rest of both beer cans into my mouth.

Chapter 12

Fake It till You Bake It

GRADY

I HAVE a personal trainer back in New York who's a total dick. I pay him a lot to push me hard, and he got my resting heart rate down to forty-five beats per minute. That's the resting heart rate of a professional athlete. I have never once broken a sweat in a high-stakes negotiation or board meeting. I once jumped onto the tracks at Penn Station to pick up an old lady's purse when she dropped it, about twenty seconds before a train pulled up. Then I dusted myself off and finished typing a text message.

But right now my heart is racing.

I walk into the darkness of the woods where the air is cooler. My skin is warm—not from the fire; it's from the heat that Claire and I were generating. It would have been so easy to kiss her. So easy to cross that line, those final few inches that have been separating us. Unbridgeable for over a decade, even when she's right in front of me.

I can confirm that Claire is even more beautiful by firelight now than ever.

And I know I would feel even more guilty kissing her tonight than I would have that night before I graduated.

I sigh heavily as I redial the missed call from my assistant.

"Can you hear me?" Alice yells in my ear.

"Yes. I'm on an island right now. Can you hear me?"

"Yes! I will never understand why people have any interest in visiting places where there's spotty cell-phone coverage. I may be ancient, but I'm used to Wi-Fi and I'm used to good cell-phone service, and when I croak, I want to be buried in concrete with my iPad and all of my cell phones."

"That's why I didn't bring you, Mrs. Strout. I promise to keep you in cities for as long as you work for me."

"Bless your heart. I have an update for you. Stand in a spot where you know you'll hear me so I don't have to repeat it."

"Done. Go ahead."

"I've been dialed in with my whisper network all day, and I have it on good authority from a dozen friends and forty friends of friends that Mr. Harrison Lynch is indeed engaged and the woman he's engaged to...is Emma Lovejoy."

"His assistant." God dammit, he means business. I'm standing alone at the edge of the woods on a secluded island in New England, but suddenly I feel like I'm back in the jungle of Manhattan and Lynch has got me by the throat.

I will not lose this deal because of an engagement that is clearly fake.

"You should have let me cast a spell on them."

"You were just wiggling your nose."

"It might have worked!"

"So he's playing hardball. She's someone he really knows."

"Someone Aston Pembroke already knows from the office," she reminds me.

"Someone who filled his office with houseplants. Someone unlike anyone else who'll be at the METH gala. Someone Pembroke's wife would probably like."

Shit.

He's good.

But I'm better.

I need to fight fire with fire.

"Do you really think Aston and the board would reconsider your acquisition just because Lynch appears to be settling down?"

"Stranger things have happened. The cold hard numbers don't run the humans, the emotional humans run the numbers. Unfortunately. Yeah, Aston just might get the board to reconsider."

"Well, that blows," Alice huffs. "Have you had time to peruse the selections I sent you?"

"Yeah. They won't work for this. I have someone else in mind," I say as I look down toward the beach.

I need someone that I have a real connection with. Like Lynch seemed to have with his assistant—only better. I need someone that I care about. Someone who, deep down, underneath all the sass and flour and sugar and frustration with me, cares about me too. Enough to close a deal I've been tirelessly working on for months.

"I can't tell you how surprised and pleased I am to hear this. Anyone I know?"

"No. But she's perfect." *She just doesn't know it.*

"Well, let me know if there's anything you need me to do. Send flowers? Cast a love spell?"

I might need all the help I can get.

I end the call with Alice and watch Claire from a distance. Framed by the cove and a stunning pink-and-purple sunset, she's hugging herself and staring out at the water. I can't see her face, but I can tell by her rigid posture that I'd be in for a fight if I bring this up right now.

She would never accept a gift of capital from me. I'm fairly certain she wouldn't agree to come to New York with me to pretend to be my girlfriend. But trading one for the other? I am determined to get her on board with that when the moment is right.

We need each other. For our respective businesses. I may have brought her out here so we could be alone. I may have built that campfire so I could see her face illuminated by firelight again.

But I'm not going to play with fire—not where Jake's little sister is concerned.

This would be strictly business.

Claire's body stiffens even more when she sees me approaching. The mood has shifted for both of us, but so has the air. It's gotten more humid and breezy. We don't even need to say anything to acknowledge that we need to get back on the boat. I snuff out the fire, and we leave the teenagers to repopulate the island.

I row us back to the *High & Tight* and then set course for the mainland. The sound of the wind and the waves lapping against the side of the boat makes this an inopportune time to broach the subject. You never want to *begin* the negotiations by shouting. So I take this time to consider how to handle this.

Having locked horns with Lynch these past few months, I'm used to projecting strength. To reveal absolutely no weakness. But Claire would feel the mismatch. I'm older, bigger, richer. Apparently I'm a potential murderer when she's alone with me. I will have all lines prepared and proceed with her as slowly as I approach the dock, assessing every nuance, gently course correcting. And then I will secure everything properly and lock it down.

Once I've got my vessel gliding gently up to the side of the dock, slow and steady into its slip, I say to Claire, "I need your help."

Without hesitation, she hops onto the dock and holds out her hands. "Toss me the spring line," she calls out.

That was not what I meant, but I toss her the spring line anyway and let her help me moor the boat.

I stow the life jackets, grab both our backpacks, hop onto the dock, and say, "Thank you."

"You're welcome. Thanks for letting me help you."

This is actually going better than expected. "You're welcome." We nod at the few people we pass by on the dock. The clouds are rolling in fast, so everyone's prepping for a storm. "Actually," I continue as we stroll toward the parking lot, "I need your help with something else."

"Oh, really?" She looks confused and intrigued, which is better than closed-off and annoyed. "With what? A baking problem?"

"Well, not exactly." I've got my serious business face on, and she doesn't appear to hate it. "I need your help," I repeat, "and if you're going to make the changes we've discussed to your bakery, you're going to have to renovate. Again. Which means you'll need another infusion of cash. Which I have."

"I'm not taking your money."

"Hear me out," I say, raising my hand.

She's walking alongside me, but it does not go unnoticed that she stares at my hand.

So I keep gesticulating with it. "I'll help you with your bakery, and while it's being renovated—by hired professionals, not by you and your family—I need you to come to New York with me."

She stops in her tracks and folds her arms across her chest. "Why do you need me in New York?"

Here we go. "I need a date to a gala event."

She scoffs. "You need a date? As in you can't get a date, so you want to pay *me* thousands of dollars in renovation costs to go on a date with you?" Her words echo across the harbor.

I shush her. "No," I say, then lower my voice. "Not exactly. This is an important gala event, and I can give you the details later, but I need to attend it with someone that I have a significant connection with."

She blinks. "Go on."

"I need to make the host, who is a key figure in a very big deal that I've been working on for months, believe that I am in a serious relationship. I don't just need a date. I need you to pretend to be my girlfriend. Temporarily. Strictly business. Only until all the contracts are signed and the deal is officially closed."

Claire blinks again. Once. Twice. I watch as ten different emotions dance across her face. I only understand and recognize half of them, but I definitely see hope in there. But it all ends with teary-eyed anger as her jaw sets and she storms away from me.

"Claire. What?" I catch up with her just as we reach the edge of the thankfully empty marina parking lot.

"Thanks so much for the business consultation, Mr. Barber. I will take everything under advisement." She starts stabbing at the air as she picks up her pace. "I will leverage and synergize and strategize underperforming workflow practices—"

"Okay, I never used any of those words."

"But I am not interested in being your pretend girlfriend to close your very important business deal," she hisses. She stops by her car that really is a shitbox, fiddles with the key, finally gets herself in the driver's seat, and slams the door.

"Claire." I stand beside her car, just like I did when I found her parked in the middle of Main Street.

She puts the key into the ignition, turns it, but nothing happens.

She left her window cracked open, so I'm able to

speak to her without raising my voice. "I think you left your headlights on."

"*Yes!* I left my headlights on because Vera wasn't here to remind me to turn them off!"

She thrusts the car door open, nearly hitting me, slams it shut again, and storms away from me again.

"Where are you going?"

"Home," she replies curtly without bothering to look back at me. She is so stubborn, I don't doubt that she's willing to walk over a mile just to get away from me. She doesn't seem to notice or care that it has started to drizzle.

I get in my car and follow slowly behind her. Rolling down my window and pulling up alongside her, I say, "Claire. It's starting to rain. Get in. Come on, let's talk about this."

"I don't want to do any of those things," she says without looking at me. "Leave me alone."

I rub a hand over my face, sighing. Give me cold, hard numbers any day. Emotional humans are a pain in the ass. Especially the pretty ones that I care about. "Get in the car, Claire."

"Stop ordering me around!"

She leaves the parking lot and turns onto the sidewalk. The raindrops are getting bigger. I turn on the windshield wipers and lower the passenger-side window, traveling about half a mile per hour. "Get out of the rain!"

"Leave me alone."

"No. We need each other, Claire."

"No, we don't. We've both lived our lives without each other just fine for twelve years. You've lived it out there with God knows who. I've lived it here with the people I actually need, who actually stay to help me. Vera, for one. Vera, who would have reminded me to turn off my damn headlights if she were here."

"You need to fire Vera," I blurt out. It's not like the negotiation was going well anyway, so it's time to throw in a monkey wrench.

Claire stops, turns, and glares at me. Her blonde hair has gone from frizzy to plastered around her beautiful, furious face. "What did you just say?!"

"Listen, I like Vera. She's a great friend to you. She's a very smart and capable woman. But she is not the person to help you achieve what you want to achieve. You have to put the right people in the right positions if you want your organization or the people you care about to thrive."

I watch her process this for about three seconds—and almost acknowledge it—before rejecting the idea, everything I represent, and walking away again.

Shit.

I smack my palm against the dashboard. Does she not realize how desperate so many people are for my advice and money? I need to leverage and synergize and strategize and... My attention lands on the CD player. Yes. That is what I need.

I press Play and turn up the volume.

The first song on the Mumford & Sons CD that Claire gave me so many years ago plays. "Sigh No More." She's still stomping in the rain and I'm still driving alongside her, but her pace slows. *I'm sorry,* they sing. *You know me,* they sing. It's what I'd say myself, but she wouldn't believe it.

She stops walking, her shoulders trembling and

hunched over as she lowers her backpack to the ground and covers her face.

She's crying.

I park, jump out of the car, and run around to her, placing my hands on her shoulders. She tries to shrug them off, keeping her face covered. "Claire," I say softly. "Just get in the car. Please."

She sniffles.

They don't teach you how to handle this kind of thing at Wharton. There's no crying in multimillion-dollar business negotiations. Of course, this isn't just business. This is Claire.

"Please," I repeat as I open the passenger door and hold my arm out to her.

She picks up her backpack and wordlessly slips into my car.

I gently shut the door and jog around to the driver's side. I turn down the volume on the stereo and roll up the windows. She rests her elbow against the door and her head against her fist, staring ahead. Tears fall down her already-wet cheeks, but she remains silent and it's breaking my heart.

"I'm gonna pull over somewhere so we can talk, okay?"

She doesn't answer, but she doesn't get out of the car and storm off either.

I drive a couple of blocks and pull into the empty parking lot behind a home goods store that's closed. There aren't any street lamps nearby and no houses facing it, so it feels private. Especially in the pouring rain. After turning off the engine, I unbuckle my seat belt and turn to face her. "Talk to me, Claire. What's wrong?"

She blows out a breath, laughing and shaking her head, but she unbuckles her seat belt too. "You tell me. You make me feel like I'm not enough," she says, so quietly I can barely hear her over the sound of the rain on the roof of the car.

But I hear it. I feel it. "Why?"

She shakes her head again, looking out the passenger-side window into the dark, wet, empty parking lot.

"Talk to me."

She sniffs. "I can't believe you still have this CD."

"Of course I do."

She wipes away her tears.

"Keep talking."

"Stop ordering."

"No."

She huffs and then laughs. "Fine." She takes in a deep, jagged breath. "And I know I'm responsible for how I feel, blah, blah. I'm not blaming you. Positive thoughts, blah, blah." She waves her hand dismissively, and it's so cute, but I'm taking this very seriously. "When you're not here..." She exhales. "I'm enough. I mean, things aren't exactly going the way I want them to—yet—obviously. But I love my life. I do. I love my family. I love my friends. I love myself. I love my bakery. I love baking. I love this town, and I'm building the life that I've always wanted. Here. And that's enough. But when you're around..." She shakes her head again and looks away.

I curl my index finger under her chin and gently turn her face toward me.

The tears are falling again.

I wipe them away this time.

"Please don't make me say this out loud."

I wipe away another tear. "Okay. You don't have to if you don't want to."

"Fine," she says defiantly, as I knew she would. I can tell she has to force the words to come out, but she finally says with a trembling voice, "When you're around, I feel like I don't deserve to be kissed."

"That's not how I feel about you," I tell her without hesitation. As I cradle her face with one hand, I caress the damp skin of her cheek with my thumb. "Not even close."

"Don't lie to me because you feel sorry for me. You didn't want to kiss me back then. You were relieved that you didn't have to kiss me tonight. I'm not worthy of being your girlfriend. Only a temporary *fake* one." With the word *fake*, her quivering voice takes on an angry tone again.

"You're wrong, Claire," I say softly.

"I'm not, and you know it."

I'm still cupping her face, but she keeps glancing away.

"Look at me."

She won't.

"Claire."

Still, her eyes won't meet mine.

So stubborn.

I cradle her face with both hands and turn it toward me, leaning in, forcing her to see me. Really see me, the way only she can. "I wanted to kiss you. On the island.

Twelve years ago. Now. I didn't kiss you...not because I didn't want to—because I knew I couldn't."

Her wet eyelashes flutter.

She sees me and hears me now.

"You're my best friend's little sister, Claire. It's my job to protect you. Even if it's from me and how badly I want you. But believe me, Claire, I never stopped thinking about you."

Chapter 13

S'more than Words

CLAIRE

I LIKE LISTS, and I don't usually like surprises, but I always make it a point to remember the good surprises. Here are the top three favorite surprising moments in my life so far:

1. That time in middle school when I came home crying because Shithead Shawn had peed on every single cupcake I'd made for the bake sale, and then Jake and Grady found him at the park and beat the crap out of him.
2. The time Jake, who had just graduated from the fire academy, pulled over on the side of the freeway to help deliver a total stranger's baby.

3. I don't remember what the third thing is now, and it doesn't matter because it just got bumped off the list.

With one sentence, Grady has rewritten the last twelve years of my existence.

And I believe that sentence. He doesn't need a fake girlfriend that badly, and he couldn't possibly feel so sorry for me that he would say something that startling. Also, it's Grady. He wouldn't lie to me.

But I need to make sure I heard him correctly.

"Say that last part again..."

It doesn't make him laugh like I thought it would. In fact, he's staring at my parted lips so intently, I'm not sure if he's even listening. He shifts around in his seat when I bite my lower lip.

Still cupping my face, he says, "I never stopped thinking about you, Claire. Not that night after I dropped you off. Not during the graduation ceremony the next day. Not in college..."

"Not in New York?" I prod because his eyelids have grown heavy and I don't think he's got much talk left in him, but I really need to know.

He barely shakes his head. "I think on some level I was always comparing the women I met to you," he says, just loud enough that I can hear it over the percussive beat of the rain on the roof right above us. "And none of them measured up. I think you're special and beautiful. By firelight. In any light. I wanted to kiss you. It was never about not wanting you." He almost sounds defeated when he declares this. "Because I do."

The rain is a heavy beaded curtain all around us. It's coming down so hard and loud outside, but that's nothing compared to the thudding of our hearts and our heavy breaths, as if finally telling each other the truth took physical effort. What is it about this damn Mercedes that makes me so emotional? I can't tell if I'm sad or if I've reached some new level of joy and relief, but I can't stop crying. Heaving chest, tears pouring down my face, sobbing from deep in my lungs.

"Shhhh, shhh, shhhh, baby girl," he whispers into my ear. He presses a kiss to my temple. He kisses my cheek. He brushes the wet strands of hair from my eyes, kisses my forehead, caresses my cheeks and my jaw, and I go limp from all the comfort he's giving me. I still can't stop crying, but I am definitely not sad.

Maybe I passed out back there on the sidewalk and this is all a dream. If it is, then I'd better make the most of it before I wake up. I force myself to catch my breath and pull it together and look Grady straight in the eyes. "If you're planning on waiting another twelve years before really kissing me, you're going to need a new strategy."

Again, he doesn't laugh. He has the same expression I used to see on his face at the start of a race at track meets. If I have to be the one to fire that starter pistol, then I will. I pull my damp sweater over my head. When I toss it aside, he cups the back of my head with one hand, leans in, and kisses me with all the force of a man who's been trying not to want me for over a decade.

His lips are soft and warm like his soothing words and caresses a minute ago. His stubble is rough and grating like every conversation I've had with him since he's been back. His tongue, though. Grady's tongue is advising my tongue of things that I've never truly experienced before, but I completely understand them between my legs. Beautiful, life-altering, filthy things, and every inch of me is dying to learn more. He kisses me with his determined hands and his sharp exhales and the protective strength of his entire upper body. One moment I feel claimed by his mouth, the next I'm silently being asked by his hooded eyes if this is okay.

It is.

It is the most okay thing that has ever happened to my face. If this is what it would have been like if he'd actually kissed me when we were teenagers, then a lot of pastry-loving people in this town would have been out of luck. I would have followed him anywhere if he'd kissed me like this when I was a girl.

Good thing I know better now.

Inner sixteen-year-old me may be whimpering and trembling and succumbing to his very masculine passion because this is so much more than she'd ever allowed herself to imagine experiencing on these tan leather bucket seats.

But twenty-eight-year-old me has visualized a lot of very specific scenarios, and she has a few sexy tricks up her sleeve.

A tiny high-pitched song escapes from my throat as I suck on his tongue. I frantically nibble on his bottom lip, dipping in to kiss him deeply and then teasing him by pulling back when he wants more. I tug at his sweater, and he helps me pull it off over his head. Then I push him back into the driver's seat, and with one swift motion, he slides the seat back so I have room to straddle him.

Whatever emotional turmoil brought us here has dissipated, turned into steam, and fogged up the windows.

Do grown-ups make out in cars in parking lots? I don't know, but fuck it. It's raining and this has been a crazy day and I need a happy ending to the sad story I've been telling myself about Grady ever since I was in high school.

I slide my hand up Grady's thigh to feel how hard he is. He's hard. Jesus, he's hard. I glance up at him. His jaw is clenched, and he gives me this look, like, *Now do you get it, Claire?*

I want to. I want to get it. I start to unbuckle his belt, but he grabs my wrists and shakes his head, just once, definitively.

Not here, he says with his face.

Aw, come on, I say with the palm of my hand.

Not. Here. He repeats it with his grip on my wrists.

But I'm really good at it, I tell him with a pout.

Rain check, he insists with his flared nostrils.

Even though no one could possibly see inside unless they pointed a flashlight at us, he is a Forbes-listed billionaire, and I guess he draws the line at public hand jobs.

Fair enough.

I'm just the town baker—what do I care if I get caught riding a boy in a car?

I climb over the center console and lower myself onto his lap. The ceiling is low and these jeans are tight, but I can still get 'er done. I bear down and rock back and forth. Not with the urgency of an inexperienced, sexed-up virgin—with the control of a fit, curvy woman who knows exactly what kind of effect she has on men and just found out that Grady Barber is not, in fact, the only man she's ever met who's immune to her charms.

But then I grind down on him because he's so firm and my entire body is engorged and his hands are slowly sliding up the sides of my waist under my shirt, and holy shit, he's hot. He's gorgeous and sexy and he wants me and I want his hands and mouth on my everything right now. I start to lift up my Henley, but he pulls it back down to my waist.

I reach down between his legs again, but once again, he grabs my wrists. I dip down to lick him from his chin to his lips, capture his lower lip between my teeth, kiss him furiously, and try to unbutton his shirt. He grabs my wrists again and raises my arms up over my head, flattening my hands against the fabric headliner. He exhales warm breath over my covered nipple as his hands glide down the sides of me, and it sends shudders and warmth all through me. His fingertips flirt with my skin, skating across my belly, just under my shirt. Slow, soft circles and waves with a gentle touch that electrifies all my nerve endings.

I'm so used to being groped by men who are in a race against time, but this is something else entirely. It doesn't feel like he's exploring my body either. He's just making me feel good. Reassuring me. Carefully acquainting himself with the landscape of my physical being, the way I lovingly inhale and gaze at and fondle a piece of freshly baked bread before putting it into my mouth and savoring it. I'm not even naked, but I feel seen and so alive. Like I'm rising beneath his touch.

"Beautiful girl," he whispers into my neck, his breath and lips and stubble grazing my skin, light as a feather. Never in my fantasies did I imagine Grady could bring me to the brink by breathing on me and delicately tracing figure eights on my skin. Then he reaches around to massage my butt with both hands, vigorously, releasing so much tension that I didn't know I was holding there. My head drops back with a loud moan. What is he doing to me? I go limp and then tense up again, clenching and rocking against his hard length enough to make him groan.

"Claire..."

I go for his belt buckle again.

He grabs my wrists again, this time bending my arms and holding them behind my back. He bites the side of my boob and flicks at both erect nipples with the tip of his tongue, through the fabric of my shirt. My insides feel like they're going to explode, and I think I'm losing my mind.

He lets go of my wrists, unbuttons and unzips my jeans.

I would do so many things to and with and for him, but if he wants to take care of me right now, then my body promises not to resist him for the rest of the night.

He hooks his fingers through the belt loops of my jeans. I grip the headrest behind him and raise my ass up so he can yank the waistband down to the tops of my thighs. He takes a moment to investigate my cotton panties as he strokes the flesh of my round hips appreciatively. Kneading me like dough. It's probably too dark for him to see the pastel cupcakes that are printed on my undies, but he seems to like them anyway. Then he slips a hand inside my bikini briefs, between my legs, and sucks in a breath when he feels how slippery it is down there. "Jesus."

"I know."

He squeezes my butt cheek with the other hand and swirls his fingers around in the silky pool of my arousal. "Fucking hell," he groans.

"I know."

He massages my clit in a circular motion with his flattened hand, but I'm so wet, there's no friction. He taps at my pleasure center, makes a V with his index and middle fingers, strokes up and down the sides of it. Soon, those two fingers slide up inside me with ease. I eagerly clench and release around him. He glides in and out, slow and steady, reaching up to caress my face with his other hand. My cheekbone, my jaw. I tilt my chin down and take his thumb in my mouth, nibbling and sucking on it like it's giving me life. The guttural sound he makes is so satisfying.

I want to see his face, but I can't open my eyes. I am so far gone, so deep inside my own body, and so connected to Grady even though I wish there was more of him inside of me. He removes his thumb from my mouth, and I feel his lips on mine. His tongue penetrates my mouth to the same rhythm as his fingers down there. Then he curls his index and middle fingers toward himself. Finding my supercharged G-spot, he strokes it, picking up speed, applying the perfect amount of pressure to yield rolling waves of pleasure through my belly, radiating outward. I feel full and ripe. And I feel deeply, deeply connected to him and to my body and to the truth of being wanted.

Then he extends his fingers and penetrates a deeper part of me that I didn't even know existed. I gasp. He thrusts. Every nerve ending sparks, every muscle in my body spasms.

I don't recognize the sound of my voice when I chant my gratitude and praise, but Grady takes it as a signal to change things up. He wraps one arm around me, pressing his torso against mine as close as possible, presses the heel of his hand against my clit, and holds his fingers still. I grind against his hand as he rocks his pelvis upward. He's just letting me ride his hand because he knows it's all I need right now. I hug his neck so tight, rocking back and forth and making happy, surprised animal sounds until my whole body suddenly tenses up and I don't even exist anymore.

Everything has been erased.

There was never any rejection or heartache, and Grady never left.

The stillness as he holds me close and waits for me to have my release is the only thing that's real.

It isn't until I heave a sigh and rest my cheek on his shoulder that he places both of his warm hands on my back.

I never consciously uttered any positive affirmations about getting fingerbanged in a car by my high school crush after he finally admitted to liking me, but I feel very supported by the Universe right now.

I kiss Grady on the cheek and then assemble myself in the passenger seat.

The raindrops and windshield wipers provide the soundtrack to the drive back to my parents' house. The silence between us isn't heavy. A little tired, maybe, but sated. Like coming home from a long day at the beach.

He pulls up in front of the driveway and doesn't turn off the engine. I wait until I see him turn to face me, in my peripheral vision, before looking at him. We both smile, warmly.

"Well..." I say, shrugging. "Good night."

He nods once. "Good night."

I'm glad he doesn't walk me to the house, but I do feel his eyes on me as I hurry up the path and porch steps. I open the front door and turn to give him a cute little wave before going inside. Thankfully, my parents are already upstairs. I lean back against the door and cover my face.

That was, in so many ways, more fulfilling than baking therapy. But I do feel like I just binge ate a fresh batch of cookies. Dopey. Content. Tired. Gratified. Trying not to think about the consequences. Finding it difficult to walk quickly.

But I do feel like I can move forward now. Slowly. Because I can still feel Grady's fingers inside me.

Chapter 14

Don't Take Dough for an Answer

Grady

I WAKE UP EARLY, covered in new Frette Egyptian cotton sheets. This morning, instead of wishing I could stay asleep to prolong a sex dream, I'm eager to start my day, trying to remember every detail of what actually happened last night because it doesn't seem real. The sweet, musky scent that lingers on my fingertips confirms that it did, in fact, happen.

And it was fucking great.

I've never been big on affirmations. There was a cultish part of business school that was all about verbalizing the things you want to make them manifest. All that *Secret* nonsense. I don't know if I've ever said it out loud before: "I want Claire Sweeney. I've wanted her for years." I say it in the mirror around my toothbrush. The words come out muffled and distorted, but they make it clear. The thought that I've had since I was eighteen, the feeling I've hidden in my heart, and the lust I've hidden much lower was always a secret.

The very first time I said the words out loud was in the car last night.

To Claire.

Saying it out loud set it free and made it real.

And I don't just want her because of how tight and warm and wet her pussy felt around my fingers. It's not just because of the way she kissed me like I was her first and last meal. It's because I realized how hard I've gotten. I'm not talking about how hard she made me last night, which was very, very hard. I mean being a New Yorker has made me a hard person. Being in business has hardened me. Little by little. Everyone I've learned from and done business with and dated ever since I left Beacon Harbor—they've all been putting on fronts. I've spent my whole adult life dealing with a version of people that was fabricated for boardrooms and trendy restaurants. Claire was real and vulnerable and honest. It was a gift that no one else could have given me. And I want to keep giving back to her.

I want Claire Sweeney.

Now, here's the problem. You don't get to where I am by being super chill about not getting what you want. You don't get to where I am by being indifferent about your goals. There are smarter people in the world. More skilled. More capable. Not many, but enough. What sets me apart is when I decide I want something, I don't rest until I have it.

I want Claire.

I'm up before anyone else in the house today. I set out

the flax muffins, hard-boiled eggs, and overnight oats that my dad will refuse to eat, check on the lobsters in their tanks—why? I have no idea. I guess I'm invested in their well-being now. Then I leave a note for my parents, telling them I'm heading out to "run some errands" but I'm reachable by phone.

I find jumper cables in the trunk of my dad's truck and don't think twice about foregoing my morning run, about not checking my emails or the news. Because as soon as I climb into my car and shut the door, the atmosphere is thick with Claire's fragrance. Her shampoo, her perfume, and her arousal. Floral, earthy, honeyed, warm. I fill my lungs with these gorgeous, sexy molecules as I turn the ignition and try to remember why I had ever convinced myself I can't have her.

She's my best friend's little sister, yes. I am a man of honor, yes. But it's the memory of my father, looking at stacks of bills with wet, glassy eyes, that has always driven me. Away from Beacon Harbor, away from Claire. My mother's supportive hand was always on his shoulder, and I know he never regretted his choice to give up the life he had planned for her. But even as a child, I knew that my dad's home and his business were slipping away. I saw how vulnerable it made him, how weak and ashamed he felt.

That was never going to happen to me.

I was never going to feel that powerless.

Little Sweeney and the guy who had always planned to leave the small town she loved so much? That never made sense.

Young, hungry business student who barely had time

to make it home to Thanksgiving or Christmas with his family, trying to date a girl who was trying to figure out her life but already knew it wouldn't be in the big city? It didn't make sense.

A Wharton-grad CEO scrambling for capital, working eighty hours a week, with a girl who wanted to start her own bakery business over three hundred miles away? It just didn't make sense.

But a billionaire who can marshal the resources to order anything he wants from around the world and have it delivered to his or her doorstep? Who can charter private jets or fly by helicopter over traffic to bridge the miles between himself and the girl he can't stop thinking about?

That could make sense.

I can make that make sense.

I can make those two worlds come together.

I have that kind of power. And I'm going to use it.

I pull up and park at the curb in front of the Sweeney house. It hasn't been long since I dropped Claire off right here. Flipping down the sun shade, I check my reflection and comb my fingers through my hair. I don't have a date or a meeting, but I do have the increased heart rate that I've come to associate with Claire Sweeney. I gather up the jumper cables into one hand, holding it like a bouquet.

Fuck.

I should have brought her an actual bouquet.

I'm so used to letting Alice take care of that kind of thing. I get out of the car and scan the front yards nearby to see if there are any flowers I can pick. But then I remember I'm Grady Barber. I have a big deal that I need to close. There's a key player whose wife is obsessed with houseplants. I can't have pictures circulating of me stealing flowers from some old lady's garden. I nod at the middle-aged man who's walking his dog. I don't recognize him, but I can tell he recognizes me. There's a woman out adjusting the sprinkler on her lawn, watching me.

Everyone in town will be talking about how the billionaire showed up at the Sweeney house with jumper cables by this afternoon.

And I'm glad.

Let 'em talk about me and Claire.

I knock on the front door, ready to woo the fuck out of the woman I finger fucked in my car last night.

Claire opens the door, dressed in a tight little T-shirt and sweatpants, her hair up in a ponytail, blue eyes the color of the morning sky, mouth already forming a grin, and I just want to kiss her again.

"Is that an Armani suit?" First thing out of her mouth. I caught her catching her breath, but her tone is sassy and I'd expect nothing less.

I confidently smooth down the front of my shirt so she can get a good look at my hand. In case she's forgotten what it did to her last night. And it's not like I wore a tie and a pocket square. I wanted to look good, and this was the second-nicest suit Alice had delivered. "It's Emporio Armani. Calm down."

"I'll try." She's blushing now, staring at my hand, but she smirks. "Are those jumper cables?"

I hold them out to her. "For you."

"They're beautiful," she coos, taking them from me

and cradling them in one arm like a beauty queen. "Thank you."

I rest my hands against the door frame and lean in, hovering a foot from her pretty face, and we just grin at each other for a minute. God dammit, I want to take her for another ride and make out with her in another parking lot. But we've got things to discuss first. Then I'll make out with her wherever I want. "We need to talk. About last night."

Her face falls, and I realize she probably thinks I'm going to tell her last night was a mistake.

"Grady, I—"

"No, I mean—"

"Is that Grady Barber?!" I look over Claire's shoulder to see her mom, all chipper and meticulously coiffed for so early in the morning.

"Mrs. Sweeney. Lovely to see you."

Claire steps aside so I can shake hands with her mother.

"Oh, Grady. I still want you to call me Helen. Give me a hug, silly." She takes me in a warm embrace. I spent so much time at this house growing up that Helen was basically my second mom. This is another homecoming.

"It's really good to see you, Helen."

"Well, my goodness, don't you look handsome in that suit. Why are you standing on the porch? Jake isn't here," she informs me. "But he should be coming by any minute."

"Oh, great." Ignoring the twinge of guilt at Jake's name, I tell her, "I actually came by to give Claire a ride." I hastily add, "Back to her car."

Mrs. Sweeney looks confused.

"Grady gave me a ride in a parking lot last night," Claire explains and then realizes what she just said. "*From* a parking lot. My car battery died. After he took me sailing and didn't murder me."

Helen looks even more confused now. Two dogs come bounding down the stairs, and suddenly there's a face in my crotch, but it isn't Claire's. Which is a good thing, I guess, because her mom is standing right behind her.

"Oh, you went sailing? You didn't tell me. Dudley! No!"

Dudley the golden retriever is not taking no for an answer. *I can smell Claire on you!* he's thinking.

"Dudley, no!" Claire takes Dudley by the collar and pulls him away from my junk.

A smaller dog is still sniffing around my ankle, which I'm pretty sure is a part of me that didn't touch any parts of her last night.

"Yeah, Grady's giving me the business. *Advice.* He's giving me advice about my business."

"Well, that's so kind of you, Grady. Who *wouldn't* want you to give them the business?"

"Mom!"

"Advice. The business advice. From a billionaire. Come in, Grady. Join us for breakfast."

"Don't you have to get to work?" I ask Claire, really wanting to get her alone. I just need five minutes to talk with her in private so I can blow her mind.

"I'm closed on Tuesdays," she says. "I thought you knew everything about my business."

"I guess there's still a lot I want to learn about your business."

She doesn't smirk like I thought she would. "You can come in. I just made coffee. And I just pulled some scones out of the oven, if you're interested."

"Oh, Grady! You have to try Claire's scone. If you want to know what heaven tastes like, just split one open when it's warm and butter it up," her mother gushes.

Claire slaps her forehead.

I clear my throat. "Sounds good." I pick up the furry little dog and bring him inside.

"That reminds me, Grady," Mrs. Sweeney says as she leads the way back to the kitchen, "I was just thinking about you yesterday, actually. I have a new commercial listing, in case you're looking for a local real estate investment."

"Mom!"

"Well, he might be interested, Miss Huffypants."

"I'm interested, Helen. Thanks for thinking of me." I will plunk down a few hundred thousand if that'll keep Claire and Jake's mom in my good graces.

I put the dog down on the linoleum floor. "Sweet dog. Havanese?"

"Shih tzu!" Mrs. Sweeney says, pulling a carton of eggs out of the fridge. "His name's Magnum. After the PI. Not the condoms."

"Mom!"

Her mom shrugs. "Do you still like Spanish omelets, Grady?"

"I actually don't eat breakfast most days now, but thank you."

"Oh, the fasting thing." Mrs. Sweeney regales me and Claire about a client of hers who lost ten pounds doing intermittent fasting at first and then gained back twenty but then lost ten.

I notice a Post-it on the counter that says, **The universe has your back, Claire Bear! Success and your soulmate are on the way!**

Interesting.

While Claire pours me a cup of coffee and her mom's back is to us, I mouth, *We need to talk. In private.* I signal back and forth between us. *About* us.

She nods and hands me the coffee, just as the big dog starts nuzzling my crotch again. I put the mug down on the island counter and crouch down to give Dudley some much-needed attention. I guess Mrs. Sweeney thinks I can't see her from this angle because she widens her eyes at her daughter, mouthing, *Are you and Grady...?* She bumps the sides of her wrists together repeatedly, like they did on *Friends*, but I don't think it means what she thinks it means. Claire waves her mom away.

"You know what, the dogs need to go outside. Why don't we..." Claire grabs a scone while ushering the dogs and me toward the back door.

"How many eggs do you want, Claire?!"

"Zero!"

"You need your protein!" her mom calls out.

We walk to the center of the lawn, the dogs running around us, and I finally say, "So, you do need your protein—she's right. But about last night..."

Her mouth is still full of flaky, buttery scone when she replies, "Yes?"

"I had some sense that maybe I should apologize. But I'm not sorry about what happened. I don't think it was a mistake."

"Neither do I," she states matter-of-factly.

It's crazy how relieved I am to hear her say that. "Good. I'm glad. Because I—"

"Grady Barber!" I hear from above. I look up to find Claire and Jake's dad waving at me from a second-story window.

"Good morning, Mr. Sweeney."

"Still callin' me Mr. Sweeney." He laughs. "I'm Bob! Hey, look at that suit, will ya?! Got any stock tips for a guy who's hoping to retire early?"

"I am so sorry," Claire says under her breath.

"That depends, Mr. Sweeney," I call out, not too loudly in case some neighbors are still asleep.

"I'm Bob!" He chuckles. "Mr. Bob!" We've had this back and forth since I was a kid.

"I'd want a clear picture of your net worth and assets and liabilities, and your risk tolerance, before giving any real advice, Mr. Bob, since it's a relatively short time horizon. But if you don't already have a good real estate investment, that's something to consider adding to your portfolio."

"Hey," Mr. Sweeney says. "I think I know a gal who could hook me up with some options."

"I think you do too, sir." I chuckle.

"Dad! Are you peeing right now?"

I suddenly realize that her father is indeed speaking to us from their second-story bathroom.

"Just finished, honey!" He holds up both hands to wave. "Post-flush, pre-wash!"

"*Daaaaaaaaaaad!*" Claire makes the word six syllables long and coasts up and down several octaves.

"Well, it's great to see you, Bob. Feel free to email me if you need more specific advice."

"Will do, young man!" He gives me the thumbs-up. "We havin' scones today, Claire Bear?"

"On the counter! Mom's making eggs." She turns back to me. "I guess you can drive me to get my car and we'll talk on the way."

"Great. Let's do that."

She lets the dogs back into the house, grabs my wrist, and pulls me in the direction of the driveway. But as we round the house, we find Jake climbing out of his truck.

"Hey. What up, G?"

And now I feel guilty, like I should apologize. Speaking to Jake about all of this was at the top of my mental to-do list before I went to sleep last night, but then I woke up thinking about Claire and my car led me here.

"How'd you know I'd be here, Mr. Fancypants?" he asks, taking a big bite out of a big donut as he pulls a big box of donuts from the passenger seat of his truck.

I calmly button up my suit jacket, realizing I must have subconsciously decided there was less of a chance Jake would beat the shit out of me if I was wearing a nice suit. I shrug. "It's my job to know things, Jakey."

"Well, it's my job to fix things. Ma wants me to look

at the boiler. Come on." He leads the way to the side entrance to the basement.

Her mouth full of scone, Claire says to her brother as he walks past her, "Good morning to you too, asshat."

"Good morning to you, asshole," he says, mouth full of donut. "You make scones?"

"On the kitchen counter."

I'll be right back, I mouth to Claire.

Claire grimaces. *I hope so,* she mouths back, giving me the thumbs-up just like her dad did.

She's so cute, I think to myself as I descend the cement stairs to the basement with my big, hulking best friend. I suddenly get a strong sense of what Claire was talking about on the boat last night—this dark, dank basement would be the perfect place to kill the man who made out with your sister.

Jake takes a seat in a folding chair and grabs another donut. "Want one?"

I shake my head. "You going to work on the boiler?"

"Nah. There's nothing wrong with it. My mom worries too much. What's up? You wanna hang out?"

"No." I take a deep breath. "There's something I have to tell you. And ask you. And explain."

"Shoot," my best friend of forever says generously, without a hint of suspicion, as he admires the jelly in his donut.

I'm not Catholic, but I mentally cross myself. "I have feelings for your sister."

Jake stops chewing. His eye twitches. His nostrils flare. He clenches a fist. "What kind of feelings?"

"Real feelings. Romantic feelings."

Jake begins chewing again, his donut and my words. Finally, he asks, "How long have you had these real, romantic feelings?"

"A long time. But I never acted on them. Out of respect for you. For her. I knew she wouldn't want to leave Beacon Harbor, and I knew I needed to be in New York."

"So what's changed?"

Nothing. Everything. "Your sister is great, Jake. Really great. I've been spending some time with her since I got back—you know, because of her bakery—and I just can't deny it anymore."

Jake studies my face, harder than I've ever seen him study anything. He reads me for longer than I've ever seen him spend time on a book. Without blinking, he asks, "She feel the same way?"

"I think so."

Jake polishes off the donut, brushes off the sugar from his fingers, and stands up from the chair to his full height. He is a large man and this is a small, dark space. He stares me down. His expression is inscrutable. I can feel my heart thumping inside my chest. I have never, ever known Jake to be this quiet. I'm pretty sure he wouldn't give me a beatdown. But I saw him intimidate a lot of guys who were hitting on Claire in high school, so I'd say there's a fifty-fifty chance my suit and I make it out of here unscathed.

But I'd take a beating for Claire.

Jake raises his hand, and I don't flinch. He scratches his chin and then holds his big, meaty hand out to me.

I take it.

"Thanks for telling me," he says. "I guess if I wanted her to be with anyone it would be my billionaire best friend."

"Thanks, Jake."

He places his other hand on my shoulder and grips my hand tighter. Not quite a viselike grip, but we both know he could break all the bones in my hand right now if he wanted to. "Just make sure you do right by her," he says, his voice deeper than usual.

"I will. I promise. I'm gonna go find her. You coming up?"

"Nah. I want Ma to think I'm making a real effort down here." He takes an apple fritter from the box and settles back down onto the folding chair.

I go through the door to the rec room in the basement and get hit with a flash memory of me, Jake, and Claire playing *Rock Band* down here one night when their parents were away.

The chorus of "More Than a Feeling" is the triumphant soundtrack in my head as I bound up the stairs. This is it. I always get a rush like this. I can always feel it in my gut when a deal is coming together, and it feels like the deal of a lifetime is coming together now. Combing my fingers through my hair, I enter the kitchen, ready for the next part of my life to start.

Claire is leaning against the counter, picking at another scone. Her mom is speaking to her, voice barely above a whisper, looking very concerned about something. I can't hear what she's saying, and neither can her dad, who is doing squats while eating an omelet at the kitchen table.

I pick up the jumper cables that Claire left on the little desk by the door. "Should we head out?"

Claire glances over her shoulder at me and sighs. I can't tell what the sigh means. It's nothing like her sighs from last night. "I need to get something from my room," she says. Giving her mom a look that I also don't understand, she brings her scone with her, and I follow her up to the second floor, leaving the jumper cables in the foyer.

It is surreal, going up these stairs with Claire to her old room, when I spent so much of my youth in Jake's room down the hall. I don't think I ever set foot inside her bedroom, even when she was little. That door with the stickers and the **Do Not Enter Unless You're Holding a Cake** sign was a boundary I wouldn't cross.

But I'm crossing it now. There are more old magazine tear-out photos of Food Network stars pinned to these walls than posters of singers or actors. And a calendar with a headshot and recipe from a popular baking show host for this year. But really, there are more pictures of the guy who used to host *Cupcake Wars* than I'm comfortable with.

She shuts the door behind me. We both take a deep breath at the same time. Look at each other. Laugh.

And then I take a step toward her, cup her beautiful, sweet face in my hands, and kiss her. Because it no longer makes sense not kissing her and we have a lot of time to make up for. She doesn't lean into it right away, but she doesn't pull back either. I keep kissing her. Everything I was planning to tell her can be declared with the caress of my lips, the sweep of my tongue. A revelation told to her mouth instead of her ears. She emits one of those sighs from last night, I hear the half-eaten scone hit the floor, and her fingers are in my hair. Her tongue tastes like sugar and butter and my fantasy, my history, and my future all at once.

Quietly groaning, I reach down to grab her ass and hoist her up. She wraps her legs around my waist, gasping and whispering my name and the words "God dammit" as I back her up against the wall. Some part of my brain retains a vague memory of Claire's family being in the house with us, but most of me just wants to claim her body right here and now. I'll spend the rest of my life earning her heart and soul.

I press my lips against the soft skin of her cheek, her jaw, her neck. She tilts her head to the side, exposing it to me, surrendering herself to my passion. But then she jerks her head up. Her whole body stiffens. I feel her hands pressing against my chest.

"Grady. Grady." She's breathless, but her hushed voice gives me pause. "We're here to talk," she reminds me.

"Right." I hold her waist as she lowers her feet to the floor and step away from her, adjusting my pants and jacket. Licking my lips, I rest my hands on my hips and launch into it, since we might get interrupted again. "Like I said last night, I've had real reasons for holding back my feelings about you. But after last night, I realize those reasons are like anything else that has ever stood in the way of what I want. The obstacles aren't what matter. It's what I want that matters. I want you, Claire."

She catches her breath and stares at my mouth as I

speak, as if she can't believe the words she's hearing are actually coming out of there.

I cup her face in my hands again, stroke her cheekbones with my thumbs. "I want to be with you and make you happy. I don't want to fake anything with you. What we have is real. I want you to come to New York with me —as my girlfriend. For real."

I can feel her trembling. Her eyes finally meet mine. The only thing she could possibly see in them is how much I care about her. My Little Sweeney. She takes in a deep, shaky breath, opens her pretty, swollen lips, and says firmly... "No."

Chapter 15

I Bet You Think This Scone Is about You

CLAIRE

I FINALLY HAVE Grady Barber in my bedroom, and I said the word *no* to him.

After he kissed me.

It doesn't feel good.

This isn't revenge.

It isn't a joke.

It isn't me playing hard to get.

This is self-preservation.

When I woke up this morning I felt better than I had in years. Maybe ever. Affirmations are nice and all, but sometimes a girl just needs a good fingering by a hot billionaire to feel validated.

The problem is I was convinced that after last night I could not live without Grady Barber. It felt like we were in love. It felt like I always thought it would feel, with the person I always secretly wanted to feel it with. I didn't want it to stop. I would have followed him anywhere if he'd asked me to. Just like when I was a teenager, all the way up until that moment when he rejected me. But I'm not a teenager. I'm a grown-up with an unprofitable business who lives with her parents and won't give up on that business or herself.

And while my ovaries may have been dancing and singing *This will be! An everlasting love!* ever since he first kissed me in the car, my brain—that wise, old Professor McGonagall—sent them to their room when I got out of bed and docked ten points from House Hornymuff. This is my life. Real life.

Last night was a dream come true for me, but every single thing I told myself for the past twelve years about why it could never work between me and Grady, they're still true too. He is who he is and I am who I am. I don't want to leave Beacon Harbor, and Grady will always choose his ambitions over everything and everyone here. I don't take it personally anymore—it's just who he is.

That sucks, but reminding myself of this is what's keeping me sane. It's what's keeping me from trying to engulf Grady with my labia. It's what will keep my heart from splitting in two when he leaves again.

I just want to kiss his beautiful, surprised, confused face again.

But I'm not going to because if I do, I will never stop.

"What?" he exhales. "Did you just say no?"

"No, thank you."

He glances down at the floor. "Is this because I made you drop your scone?" His lips curl into a grin, but I hear the quiver in his voice. I see the uncertainty in his tea-brown eyes.

I pick up my scone. If he weren't here, I would totally still eat it. Not the part where the tiny carpet fibers are stuck to the butter, but the rest of it. I place it on top of my desk and prepare to lay things out for both of us. Because I need to hear it too.

"No."

"Did you hear what I just said to you? I want you, Claire. For real. Do you not believe me?"

I take his hand in mine. Which is a mistake because now I want to place it on my boob. "I believe you. Please stop saying it. Or never stop saying it—no, don't say it again. I love hearing it way too much."

He places his hand over mine, and it feels so good, I can't touch him.

"Nope." I take three steps back. "Can't." I drag my fingers through my hair. "Please don't think that this is easy for me, seeing you standing there, looking all earnest, in a suit, telling me you want me to be your girlfriend and then me saying no to you." I shake my head and start pacing back and forth.

"This is really hard. I'm not negotiating—it's a hard no. You don't get up before the sun, measuring and cutting and mixing and rolling and kneading for hours and hours only to have all your work literally gobbled up and then get up and do it all over again the next day without being disciplined."

I stop in front of him and hold my finger up for emphasis, which might be another mistake. "You have given me a great gift. And I'm not just talking about, you know..." I slide my hands into my pockets, shrugging. "That thing you did last night. I mean telling me how you feel, wanting me. I know how hard it is for you to say all of this. I'm not taking it for granted. But I can't take the life I've built for myself for granted either. I am worthy," I say, trying not to sound too much like I'm reciting something my mom wrote on a Post-it note. "Not just of you and your affection and attention. Of my dreams. And while I did dream of being with you for years, Grady—you have no idea how much—I have other dreams too. And those dreams live here." I point to the ground with both hands. "Not here in this room—in this town."

He sighs and rubs his forehead. "I know that, Claire..."

"Are you going to move back to Beacon Harbor?"

He pauses for half a second before answering, and in that half second I envision an entire life for us. "No."

Fuck.

I cross my arms in front of my chest. It's my go-to stance, but all my arms want to do is wrap around his waist and let him hold me for a few hours while caressing my hair and telling me how much he wants me. But *I'm* in charge of these arms. They're staying right where they are. In front of my chest. In Beacon Harbor.

"Well, I'm not willing to move to New York," I say, and it definitely sounds like I mean it.

Grady sighs again. This must be some advanced negotiating technique they teach at Wharton because I am losing my resolve. And then he places those magnificent hands of his on his hips, and I'm hearing the intro to "Empire State of Mind" in my head.

"I understand," he says. "I'm not asking you to do that. But people with far fewer resources than I have manage all kinds of long-distance arrangements. I don't know exactly what it will look like yet, but we can figure it out together." He looks me straight in the eyes. "I want to. I *need* to."

God, he's good.

But I'm better.

I have to be.

"That's not what I want. It's definitely not what I need." I stop short of telling him my heart can't handle only having half of him. I don't know this for a fact, but it sounds like a recipe for disaster to me.

He looks like I just knocked the wind out of him.

Did I just crush him?

I place my hands on either side of his head because I don't want to hurt him. I couldn't possibly have that kind of power, could I? It must be that he's afraid of losing that big deal.

He instinctively pulls me to him, hands on my waist, and it takes all the strength I have left to push him away again.

Clearing my throat, I straighten myself up and get back on track. "But I will help you with your business deal. I will go to New York with you to attend this gala. As your *pretend* girlfriend. I will do this in return for the *loan* you will be giving me so that I can renovate my bakery." I punctuate that sentence with one firm nod. My face and body language scream *professionalism*. My lady parts are screaming something else entirely, but they were not invited to this meeting.

The shrewdness returns to Grady's expression. His posture projects all the confidence a man can have without being cocky. His eyes narrow. "I'm giving you the money for the renovations, Claire. You don't have to pay me back."

God, I really don't want to take on any more debt. "We can discuss the details later." I place my hands on my hips, just like he did earlier. "But I need you to understand that me going to New York as your date is just about business. My business and yours. It is *strictly* business."

All tension vanishes from his face and body. His beautiful hands slide into the pockets of his fancy pants. The hint of a grin forms. You'd think it would make me feel relaxed as well. Instead, it's slightly terrifying. And more than a little sexy. This is the Grady Barber who always gets what he wants and knows it.

"We have a deal," he says evenly.

"Good," I say, trying to sound like the confident businesswoman that I know I could be.

I may not get whatever I want in life, but all of a sudden I'm getting more than I ever thought possible.

He extends his hand, and we shake on it.

But he doesn't let go.

He leans in.

I can't stop myself from tilting my chin up so I can stare into his damned beautiful eyes.

"I want you to know that I'm coming after you," he whispers.

My mouth goes dry and I'm finding it difficult to swallow. "Excuse me?" I squeak.

"I'm going to seduce you, Sweeney. *When* I do, I don't want you to accuse me of skulking around and being underhanded or two-faced." He brushes a strand of hair from my forehead. "When I make you mine, I want you to know that I did it head-on."

Meep!

He continues. "I want you to know that so you're not confused." He's doing an excellent job of ignoring how sweaty my hand has become. "I'm coming after you, Claire. *Billionaire* is just a word to you. But you really don't understand what it means." His mouth is kissing distance from mine, and Christ Almighty, he is fucking my ears so hard with this speech. "You really think you can travel with me to New York, experience everything I have to offer you—more than you could ever imagine—and *resist* me?" He practically growls that last part.

Does he growl like that in business meetings?

Is that another thing he learned at Wharton?

My panties are soaked, my insides are trembling, but I decorate my face with a slow and steady smirk like I'm piping icing onto a badass lady-boss cake. Like I eat growly New York billionaires for breakfast and still have room for two more scones and my mom's omelet.

"Well, I've given you my demands. Good luck surprising me, cowboy."

Chapter 16

Money for Muffin (but the Chick Ain't Free)

Claire

Grady is supposed to pick me up soon to take me to the airport. I have packed, repacked, and triple-checked the contents of my luggage. I have deep-conditioned, face-masked, showered, and accidentally over-shaved my private parts because I ignored Vera's reminders to make a waxing appointment. Why would I get a bikini wax if I'm not going to be exposing my private lady-business areas to my fake boyfriend during our strictly business trip?

The shaving part was just standard grooming procedure. The Full Monty shave was truly an accident. I was nervous and distracted because I haven't flown anywhere in years. I haven't had a vacation in years. Not that this is a real vacation. It's a real business trip with billionaire benefits, like private jets and who knows what else.

I am filled with equal parts excitement and dread as I

anticipate what moves Grady will try to pull. I must stay strong. That would be much easier to do if I had the support of my best friend. Vera hasn't been answering my texts. She's been cagey since last night, and I don't even bother texting her before I leave because I'm sure she's asleep. And she should be. There's no reason for her to get up before the sun today.

The bakery is now closed for renovations for a whole week, so she can sleep in. Grady and this magical Alice lady managed to book an amazing interior designer and a remodeling contractor so fast, he made me promise I wouldn't ask how much he's paying for them. Crabby Crawford staged a public protest, standing on an apple crate outside my storefront. He tried to start a petition to keep me from closing. But when I got him to settle down, I explained to Crabby that the front of the bakery will be more comfortable when the renovations are done and that I'll be selling s'mores and more cookies. In general, I assured him, I'll be applying my innovative talents to more comforting and relatable treats. I helped the old fella down off the apple crate, in a way that wasn't emasculating, and he gave me a sweet little pat on the back. Then he warned me that Mr. Suit is all wrong for me. *You don't have to tell* me, I said.

My phone finally buzzes with a text notification, but it's not Vera.

JAKE: Hey. Have fun in NYC.
JAKE: But, you know, not too much fun. Or go

ahead and have too much fun, but I don't wanna hear about it. Ever.
ME: Trust me, I will not have too much fun. I'm only pretending to be Grady's girlfriend so he can close a business deal. This is just a business thing. I'm helping him because he's helping me. With the bakery.
JAKE: What are you talking about? He told me he has feelings for you.
ME: He did?! When?
JAKE: A few days ago. When he was at the house that morning.
ME: Why didn't you tell me?
JAKE: Why would I? I figured he'd tell you that he had feelings.
ME: He did. I mean why didn't you tell me he told you about it?!
JAKE: Because I'm not a teenage girl named Stephanie.
ME: Who is Stephanie?
JAKE: I don't know! This is why I don't talk to you about girl stuff!
ME: Oh my God why are you like this?!
JAKE: Why are YOU like THAT?! Why can't you just be happy? What, my billionaire best friend isn't good enough for you? Are you holding out for Elon Musk to take you to Mars? New York isn't exotic enough?
ME: Oh my God. I can't with you right now. I have to get ready to go.

JAKE: I can't with you either.
ME: I love you. Don't die in a fire.
JAKE: Whatever, nutjob. Love you. Don't die in a plane crash.

It doesn't change things, knowing that Grady told my brother he had feelings for me. If anything, it just strengthens my resolve. Because Christ on a graham cracker, that is so fucking sweet and if I allow my brain to accept how fucking sweet it is, I will fall madly in love with someone I can't really be with, and lives will be ruined. Mine and Crabby's—and that poor guy's already lost a wife.

After spritzing myself with a little business perfume, I pick up my bags. My dad dashes out from his bedroom as soon as he hears me in the hallway, closely followed by Magnum and Dudley. "Let me get that for you, honey."

"I got it, Dad."

"No, I got it." He wrests the suitcase from my fingers and takes the carry-on bag from me as well.

"Oh, he's here!" my mom calls out from the foyer. "Oh, good, it's a limo! I'm so excited for you, Claire Bear. It's just like *Pretty Woman*! Except for the hooker part. You're happy, right? You're fine. We aren't worried about anything, are we?"

I try not to trip over the dogs as I slowly make my way down the stairs behind my dad, who is struggling to carry both bags. "Let me take one of those bags, Dad."

"I got it, honey!"

"Oh, there's Grady getting out of the car," my mom

announces, peering out the window beside the door. "My goodness, does that young man look good in a suit! You two will look wonderful together, Claire. You do."

I could have done without the excessively reassuring tone in her voice. "Okay, good. I'm not worried and I'm kind of excited, I guess, but this is just a business trip. For both of us. We're just pretending to be in a relationship because Grady wants to impress someone on the board of some company he's trying to buy. It's fake."

"The company?" my dad asks, setting the bags down.

"What? No, the company isn't fake. Our relationship is. I mean, that's a secret."

My mother wrinkles her usually very smooth forehead. "Your relationship is a secret, or the feelings are?"

I give my dad a hug. "Huh? I mean I'm not really his girlfriend. We're just pretending."

"But your feelings are real, and that's a secret," my mother says, half statement, half question.

"No, our real feelings are strictly business. The relationship is fake—it's a...bake relationship. There will be no kissing on the mouth. So, it is kind of like *Pretty Woman*. Except that I don't need to be saved. I'm allowing him to help me because I do not have the liquid cash flow to spend on a remodel, but I'm also helping him in return."

My mom narrows her eyes at me. "You do know that Vivian and Edward made love several times and then got together at the end of that movie, right?"

"Well, I've only seen clips because John Hughes didn't write or direct that one, but why don't we just say that this is nothing at all like *Pretty Woman* and leave it at that." I give my mom a quick hug and then lunge for the front door.

I'm dragging my bags out onto the porch just as Grady strolls up the path, and gosh darn it, I don't know if that suit is Emporio, Giorgio, or Groucho Armani, but that boy looks fine. My tummy does somersaults when he removes his aviators and gives my parents an earnest, boyfriend-y wave.

The limo driver hustles over to pick up my suitcases.

"Hi!" I say, holding out my hand to shake his. "I'm Claire."

"Jim," he tells me. "A pleasure."

"Very nice to meet you." I pump his hand up and down. "How's traffic?"

"So far so good. Should make it to the airport on time." He carries my bags to the limo.

Now I have to deal with Grady, who is grinning at me handsomely.

"You're late," I say.

"You're stunning."

I giggle and roll my eyes because I'm just wearing jeans and a blouse, but I mean, my hair *is* very shiny today. "You're forgiven."

We stare at each other for a minute, both notice that Mrs. Bowden is watching us as she pretends to dust around her front door frame. I also note that she's got her earbuds in. She's probably talking to one of her friends about us.

Grady leans in and says in a hushed voice, "Permission to pretend to hug my fake girlfriend? So the neighbors won't question the nature of our affiliation."

"Permission granted." I hold my breath because if he smells as good as he looks, I will start humping him before we reach the driveway.

I hold my arms out and come in for a hug-plane landing, but the bastard's hands slip around my waist and then slide up my back.

"Which airport are we flying out of?" I ask, trying to make polite conversation.

"Jetport in Portland," he says, holding me close. "We have time."

"I feel like we've hugged for long enough now, don't you?"

"Your neighbor is still watching us."

"She has arthritis in her knees. She moves very slowly. We'll be here all day if we wait for her to get back inside her house."

He still doesn't let go of me.

"Don't we have to get there early to go through security or something?" I ask, and dammit, now I have to breathe, and he smells like a cinnamon roll that got left out in the snow and then got warmed up again by the fire in a billionaire lumberjack's cabin. I hug him tighter and groan a little. To make the hug appear really authentic.

"Actually, TSA requires all owners of private jets to pat down their guests. If I'm not satisfied with my preliminary inspection I have the authority to strip-search you."

"Oh, for the love of cream puffs."

"Fine, I'll let go of you." He smiles and cups my cheek, stroking my cheekbone with the pad of his thumb.

I am ninety percent certain there wasn't any flour on my face because I checked ten times. "Flour?" I ask.

He shakes his head. "No, I just wanted to touch your face."

I WAS PREPARED for Grady to try to seduce me in the back of the limo during the hour-long ride to Portland, but he didn't. He was preoccupied with business calls and emails, so I tried texting Vera again, since I saw that she replied to some people's comments on the bakery's IG post from yesterday. I'm glad to know she's probably alive, but I still get no reply. I thought Grady would attempt to initiate me into the mile high club on the plane, but the pilot and attendant are about ten feet away from us, and it's only a fifty-minute flight. I have a mimosa, watch an episode of *Friends*, and then I have another mimosa.

By the time we land—and I know for sure that we aren't going to crash—I am almost relaxed. Or at least this is what I think I remember it feels like to be relaxed. I give the flight attendant, Judy, a hug and give my compliments to the pilot, thanking both of them for making this such a pleasant experience.

Grady shakes both of their hands, tells them to say hi to their family members, each of whom he seems to know by name. Which is sweet. He has been a perfect gentleman with me as well ever since I told him I want to keep this arrangement strictly professional. Which is annoying. But also perfect because it gives me a reason to be annoyed with him. Which is relaxing because it feels familiar.

He holds my hand as we take the steps down from the jet to the tarmac in some special part of LaGuardia Airport. "Welcome to New York," he says.

I'm too nervous about tripping to gaze around, so I fix my attention on the two Lincoln Town Cars that are parked nearby.

"The air doesn't smell as good as it does in Beacon Harbor," I mutter.

I catch his expression out of the corner of my eye, and you'd think I just slapped him.

"But I bet the people here smell great," I offer.

He forces a smile. "Some of them." He leads me toward one of the cars.

A chauffeur who looks kind of like the one we had in Maine but not quite gets out, tips his hat at me, picks up my luggage, and puts it in the trunk of one of the cars, but not the one he just got out of.

Grady takes my hand in his and slowly licks his lips.

Here we go, I think to myself. *He's going to make his move in the back seat of the town car with "New York, New York" playing on the stereo or something. I can't wait to not fall for it.*

"Well," he exhales. "I have back-to-back meetings, so I'll be at the office, and then I'll see you for dinner tonight." He raises the back of my hand to his lips. "I hope you have a great day, Claire."

"What? You're leaving me? I'm going to be on my own all day?"

He smirks. "I will not be escorting you around town today, no." Letting my hand slip from his, he goes around to the side of the town car. "That doesn't mean I'm leaving you alone." He opens the door to the back seat, and out pops Vera.

My best friend Vera.

The one who hasn't been replying to my texts.

She is squealing.

I am squealing.

We're both jumping up and down.

We hug and continue jumping and squealing.

I pull away from her, still holding her hands. "When did you get here?!"

"Last night. Your *boyfriend* flew me here early in that jet because he knows I'm a night owl. I saw some bands in Brooklyn, went to a rave in Queens, ended up at an after-party for some Kristen Stewart movie premiere, and then I went for an early breakfast with some randos on the roof deck of a hotel in Times Square."

An elderly lady clears her throat. She looks like Cruella de Vil but slightly friendlier.

Behind her, Grady is watching me, amused.

"Claire," the lady in the Chanel outfit says, "I am Alice Strout." She holds out a silver credit-card holder. "This is for you."

"Oh, hi. It's so nice to finally meet you. Thank you." I take the card holder from her and flip it open. Inside is a shiny black American Express card with my name on it.

"This is a secondary card for Grady's account. You are now authorized to use it. You may use it for any and all of your expenses."

"Today, you mean?"

Alice glances over her shoulder at Grady, who coolly shakes his head.

"Whenever," she says. "Wherever. If you have any trouble using it, you call me." She holds out her hand, and I give her my phone. "I am programming my numbers under *Alice* and all of Grady's numbers under *Grady*. Ted, your driver, is listed under *New York Driver*. You call me if you or your friend need anything." She squints at Vera, suppressing a grin, as she returns my phone to me.

Vera bumps her hip against Alice's. "Alice and I have already met," she says. "Alice is the shit."

"You stay out of trouble," Alice says to Vera. Then she winks at her. "But if you get into trouble, you call me." She hands me an envelope. "Here's some per diem cash too. If you need more, you call me."

I take a peek inside the envelope and try not to gulp too loudly. I could have paid an entire month's rent and all my bills with this back when I had my own apartment. "This will do for today, I think."

I give Alice a hug, which I guess she wasn't expecting because she says "Oh, shit" under her breath. "Okay." She gives me a pat on the back. "Okay. Enjoy your stay, my dears. Ted will take you wherever you want to go. He has been instructed to return you to Grady's penthouse by six, Claire. Your bags will be there waiting for you."

"Where are you staying?" I ask Vera.

"I'm heading back to Beacon Harbor tonight," she says, "but Alice hooked me up with a flight back, right, Alice?"

Alice gives her a nod and retreats to the back seat of

the other Lincoln Town Car, muttering to Grady that they have a meeting in forty minutes.

I just stare at him from about six feet away, shaking my head.

I feel my best friend's hand against my back, pushing me toward him. "Say thank you and goodbye to your boyfriend so we can all get going."

I go over to my not-real boyfriend and give him a real hug this time. The kind of hug a grateful fake girlfriend gives a really generous guy with an assistant who's thought of everything. "Thank you," I say. "For everything. Have a good day."

"You too," he says, waiting for me to pull away first. "I look forward to seeing you tonight."

I nod. "As do I." And then I curtsy because it feels like the right thing to do.

"Use that credit card," he says. "For anything you want. I mean it. Anything."

I'm about to tell him I really only want a hot dog from a street vendor and to eat a donut on the park bench in Washington Square Park where Rory found Jess in that episode of *Gilmore Girls*. But he'd just tell me they shot it on a studio set in LA, and anyway, Vera calls out before I can say anything.

"Question! Hi. What if, say, one or both of us purchases items that are too cumbersome to carry to or from this lovely car or a fine airplane? Is there an alternative manner of transporting said items home to Beacon Harbor?"

"Why are you talking like a cartoon rich lady?" I ask her.

"Allow me to rephrase. Are you going to pay for my shit to be shipped home or not?"

"Consider all of your shit shipped home and paid for," Grady tells her, all straight-faced and rich-like. "If you want something shipped directly from the store, just put someone on the phone with Alice and she'll take care of it."

"Fuckin' A," Vera says. "And let's say your lovely girlfriend's best friend in the entire world wanted to get simultaneous appointments at a very popular hair salon and/or a table at a very popular restaurant on Spring Street. How would she go about securing those?"

"Text Alice the details immediately, and if necessary, I'll put in a call myself."

"*She offered him a grateful smile as she nodded calmly and thought to herself that Grady really was the best of the Barber brothers,*" Vera narrates.

"Damn right I am. Tell everyone."

I WAS a little nervous about walking into this trendy East Village hair salon, knowing that Grady had put in a call to the owner and said that I was his girlfriend. Even with the two-mimosa buzz I had going and the natural high of being in New York with my BFF, I was apprehensive about the potential derisive looks and condescending under-the-breath comments. But it turns out this salon is super chill. It also turns out people are really nice to you when Grady Barber has already tipped them ahead of time and his assistant had a case of champagne sent over to thank them for squeezing us in.

Vera instructs my stylist to give me "a quick gloss and a blowout," while she gets some teal added to her faded blue color.

I don't even recognize my own hair when Hudson is done with me. I thought it was shiny when I left my parents' house this morning, but now I look like an actress who's playing a small-town baker in a major Hollywood movie.

"You look sensational," Hudson tells me, and I have to agree with him. "If I had any interest in boning women, I would be extremely interested in boning you. But I just want to bone your boyfriend even more now."

"You and me both, Hudson." That was remarkably convincing of me. "I'll email you my white chocolate–macadamia nut cookie recipe, but you have to promise to use brown sugar along with granulated—and don't forget the cornstarch, or else it won't be chewy enough." I give Hudson a hug, even though I can already tell he's not going to bother with the brown sugar or the cornstarch.

Vera is grinning like a maniac while texting someone as we walk out onto Seventh Street, and I almost bump into a man who looks like Stanley Tucci. I excitedly turn to Vera, and without even looking up, she says, "That was not Stanley Tucci."

"But he was—"

"It's not him."

While it may be true that I have thought four other well-dressed bald middle-aged men with black-rimmed glasses were Stanley Tucci since we started walking around Manhattan, I really do think that one was him. "Who have you been texting all this time?"

"What? No one. Not *all* this time. I've just been telling Damien how awesome his brother is because it drives him nuts."

"Interesting."

"Nope. Let's head this way down to Spring Street for lunch and carbo-load for the shopping marathon." She takes my phone from me, orders me to look at my phone like I "want to suck it senseless," and then texts whatever picture she just took to Grady.

I'm about to complain and ask how to unsend it, until I see how hot I look and decide it's not my fault if Grady's getting mixed messages. I am literally not the one sending them. When we're seated at Balthazar and I'm looking at the fantastic French menu instead of the five celebrities that Vera informs me are also here, I get a text notification and calmly check my phone.

GRADY: Wow. You look amazing.
ME: Thank you, but Vera forced me to pose like that and then sent it to you without asking me first. Sorry to bother you!
ME: But thanks for getting us the appointments and the lunch reservation!
ME: See you for dinner!
GRADY: See you for our dinner date.
ME: <neutral face emoji> I have to go out again tonight?
GRADY: <laughing face emoji> Just be at my

place at six. I have to head into another meeting now. Have fun.

I'm not sure if I should be pretending to be his girlfriend in our text messages, just in case someone sees his phone, so I send him a smiling-face emoji and then tuck my phone into a pocket.

When I look up at Vera, she is staring down at her phone and swiping through pictures. "I want you to see something," she says. Holding her phone up, she shows me a candid photo of myself, taken when I was texting just now. "Do you see how happy you are?" She keeps swiping. I am smiling like a lunatic in these pics.

"I'm just so happy to be here with you! We never get to have lunch like this."

She frowns at me. She doesn't even roll her eyes, she just puts her phone down and fixes me with a hard stare. "What is wrong with you?"

"*She asked as she pretended not to be freaking out about Meg Ryan, who was in the same room as her,*" I say, brilliantly mimicking Vera's quirky habit.

"No, *you're* the one who's pretending. Why?"

I look back down at the menu. "Because Grady wants to impress someone on the board of a company he's trying to buy."

"No. That's not the part you're faking." She takes my menu away from me. "Stop staring at that. You and I both know you're going to order the smoked-salmon hors d'oeuvres because you want to check out their homemade brioche and the strip steak because what you really want is the pomme frites that come with it, even though you could just order a side of fries."

She is exactly right, dammit. Now I'm frowning back at her.

"So look me in the eyes and tell me why you're pretending you aren't in love with Grady and that this isn't exactly what you've always wanted ever since we were kids."

I can't look her in the eyes. I can't see anything clearly all of a sudden because my eyes are filling with tears. I blow out a long, shaky breath, deflating until I'm shaped like a croissant. God, I wish I could throw myself into making croissants right now. I would love to learn how to make a perfect croissant.

"Hey." Vera's arm is outstretched across the small table, palm up, gesturing for me to give her my hand. "Talk to me. For real."

I give her one hand to hold and wipe away tears with the other one. It does somehow feel safer to talk about old feelings with an old friend when we're in a new place together. "He told me he has feelings for me. He told me he never forgot me after he moved away. He even told Jake he has feelings for me."

Vera squeezes my hand. "Wow. That's amazing."

I nod. "I still can't believe it."

"I do—I believe it. I saw the way he was looking at you this morning. I saw the way you used to look at each other in high school. You're scared, aren't you?"

"Good afternoon, ladies." Our waiter appears out of nowhere. "Have you had a chance to look at the menu?"

Vera doesn't let go of my hand. She orders for both of us and asks for nonalcoholic cranberry mojitos because she knows that if I drink any more alcohol, I'll want to take a nap instead of shop after we eat. She also asks for some Kleenex or paper towels so I can blow my snotty nose.

"Absolutely—coming right up." The waiter leaves us.

"Keep talking," she says, giving me a little squeeze.

It takes me a moment to be able to say it out loud. "Yes, I'm scared. Of course I'm scared. It's Grady."

"Exactly. It's Grady. Why can't you just be happy and enjoy this?"

"Because I don't want to leave Beacon Harbor."

"Who says you'll have to?"

"Grady. He told me he'd never move back."

"He did? He literally said that?"

"Yes. I think." Did he? "But I mean, of course he wouldn't. I remember him talking about moving to New York when he was twelve. It's all he ever wanted."

"Well, would it be the worst thing in the world if you moved here?"

"How can you even ask me that?"

A busboy brings a little unopened packet of tissues to the table and leaves as quickly and discreetly as he came.

Vera shrugs. "I mean, I love Beacon Harbor too, but if I fell in love with someone who didn't live there, I'd at least consider moving. I'd miss you, but I'd consider it."

I shake my head. "It's a part of me. All of it. Main Street and the beaches and the sunsets."

"And how often have you gotten the chance to enjoy those things in the past few years?"

"Well, the bakery is even more a part of me. *That*

bakery." I take a deep breath, and after exhaling, I finally tell her. "You remember that seniors' bonfire? The night before Jake and Grady graduated?"

"The first year you set up a s'mores station, yeah."

"Exactly. Grady drove me home that night, and I thought we had a connection. It really felt like he liked me and I was a little bit drunk, so I tried to kiss him. And he pulled away. And it's not that big of a deal now—I know it isn't—but back then it was humiliating and it hurt because right before I tried to kiss him, I knew that I would have done anything he asked of me. That's how much I wanted him. I would have dropped out of school and moved with him when he went to Wharton. I would have dropped everything for a boy I hadn't even kissed.

"But he didn't want me, or at least that's what I thought, and so I built a life for myself in Beacon Harbor. I came up with new dreams and plans and goals that had nothing to do with him. And it's all centered around my skills and my hometown. Not Grady. I filled that part of myself that would have dropped everything for him with all the things I care about that have nothing to do with him. Because no matter how much I kiss him, no matter how much he tries to help me, and no matter how much we might care about each other," I lower my voice because I will always be as discreet as that busboy was with the tissues, "Grady Barber will always care about his ambitions more than he cares about anything or anyone else. And I tried to convince myself for twelve years that that made him a selfish asshole. But he isn't an asshole. He isn't selfish. His dreams are just too big for Beacon Harbor.

"He might come back for his family or for Jake or for me. But he will always, always leave. He isn't leaving the people behind—that's the thing that I've realized. He's just always moving toward something that no one else can give him. He will always want more. Even when he has me. So I know he would keep leaving me even if I followed him here. Or anywhere. It's just who he is. And I don't want to be left again. Not by him."

The waiter brings our drinks to the table.

I sigh, clink glasses with Vera, who I am just now realizing has never been this silent in my presence for the entire time I've known her, aside from when she was asleep.

"Well, shit," she finally mutters.

"But..." I take a sip of my virgin mojito before continuing. "This is all pretty great. I'll enjoy it while I'm here. I mean, the last time I took anything even resembling a vacation was..."

"That time you drove out to Bangor to pick me up from the hospital in the middle of the night after I cut my hand on a broken bottle at a concert?"

I laugh, and a tiny little snot bubble forms under one of my nostrils. I hope Meg Ryan saw it. "Yeah. It was a nice drive. But this is definitely nicer."

We hardly talk for the rest of the delicious meal. Surrounded by the hustle and bustle of the excellent waitstaff and all the other patrons at tables that are very close to each other, it's easy to just take in the ambiance. Plus, I've just said all the things I've never wanted to say out loud and survived it, and that has made me very, very hungry. As if I've finally digested something that's been stored inside of me for over a decade. We forgo dessert, though, because Vera informs me that Dominique Ansel's world-famous bakery is within walking distance from here, and if the line to get in is too long, she reminds me that I can order online and have it delivered to Grady's place while I'm here.

"And," she says, leaning in even closer after the waiter has brought the check, "promise me you'll try to focus on the good stuff while you're here, okay? One fun step at a time. Okay?"

I suppose. I suppose instead of putting up more walls to protect myself from Grady, I can concentrate on all the fun things that are pushing up against those walls. Or try to, at least, for Vera's sake. "Sure. I'll take one fun step at a time."

"Good." She grabs my hand as soon as I've signed for lunch. "Come on. Let's go spend some more of your not-boyfriend's money!"

I take some really fun steps as she leads me out of the restaurant, trying to embarrass her, but she struts like Beyoncé all the way down the block and I pretend not to know her. But I do know her. And she knows me. And I have to admit, so does Grady.

Chapter 17

Sixteen Love Handles

CLAIRE

WHEN TED PULLS UP in front of Grady's building on Park Avenue, I hug Vera for at least ninety seconds, thanking her and telling her I love her fourteen times before she finally kicks me out of the back seat.

"I'm not the one who flew us both out here, remember?" she says. "He's the one you should be thanking."

I give Ted a hug and thank him too and then introduce myself to the doorman. Hector carries the two shopping bags that Ted handed him inside. He uses the house phone to call Grady, ushers me through a beautiful, glossy Art Deco lobby to an elevator, and then escorts me up to the seventeenth floor. I am dying to ask him how many other women he's escorted up to Grady's penthouse, but I don't. Because I don't really want to know.

The elevator doors open onto a private landing. "After you, Miss Sweeney," he says. "Mr. Barber is in his home office. He asked me to bring your bags up and show you to the living room."

"Oh, cool, thanks!" I step off the elevator, and then he opens a door to a big, open sun-filled gallery. High ceilings, lovely old parquet wood floors, and a sweeping staircase. Tall windows, a glass door to a terrace off to the side. "Holy shit," I mutter. I guess I always pictured Grady in a dark, masculine loft. This is elegant. And huge. "Um. Should I take my shoes off?"

"Entirely up to you, miss. Mr. Barber does not require it."

"Cool, cool, cool." *Stop acting like a sitcom nerd and start acting like the girlfriend of a billionaire.*

"Right this way to the living room," Hector says. "May I leave these bags here in the gallery?"

"Why, yes, absolutely."

He places my department store bags on a long console table that looks like a more expensive version of one that I had been eyeing on the Wayfair website before I had to move back in with my parents.

Wow is what my inner sitcom nerd thinks to herself as she takes in the somewhat imposing architecture of the living room. *Just wow.* The decor is understated yet confident, inviting and somewhat comfortable. I love all the furniture and the art. It actually feels good to be in here. And now I'm starting to tear up again because this place reminds me of Grady. It has a beautiful and impressive design, but what's inside is familiar and welcoming and maybe just a little too structured for my tastes...but it's not off-putting.

"It's just lovely" is what I say out loud.

"It's pleasant, isn't it? Mr. Barber will be joining you shortly. His housekeeper has gone home for the day, but he did say to make yourself comfortable. Is there anything else I can do for you?"

"No, thank you. I'll just wait here. For my boyfriend."

"Very good, miss. Have a wonderful evening." Hector turns to go.

"Oh, hang on! Hang on!" I rifle through my handbag and pull out one of the fifty-dollar bills Alice gave me, to offer as a tip. "Here you go. Thank you."

You'd think Hector must get tips like this all the time in this building, but his eyes widen. "Thank you very much, Miss Sweeney. You let me know what else I can do for you. Enjoy your stay."

"You too!"

Hector smiles as he goes, in a way that doesn't make me feel ridiculous.

I decide to take off my shoes and leave them near the entrance to this room. Partly because my feet are killing me and partly because the rug looks really soft. I wander over to examine the huge painting that's hanging over the fireplace, flanked by picture windows that look out over the city on either side. It's an oil painting of a purple-and-pink sunset over the ocean, and I don't know why I didn't realize it upon first glance but it's the view from one of the beaches at Beacon Harbor. The senior bonfire beach. Exactly how it lives in my memory from that night.

God dammit, Grady Barber, why can't you just be an unsentimental dick?

Suddenly exhausted from the effort of resisting him, I collapse onto the leather sofa. The leather is buttery soft, the cushions have exactly the right amount of give to be comfy without ruining your posture. While I will continue to resist falling in love or making love with Grady, I will not resist the urge to lie face down on this sofa and attempt to hug the seat cushion. I don't even care if anyone sees me doing this. If Grady walks in right now, he'll get a great view of my booty in these jeans that are just a little too tight for me. Serving up cake for the man of the house. Least I could do, I suppose.

I hear soft chuckling from the entrance to the living room. "Ready for dinner, I see."

"I'm hungry, so I can rally," I say as articulately as possible with one side of my face smushed into the sofa. I roll onto my back, stretching my arms and legs out, giving him a nice view of my muffin top now. "I can be ready in a few minutes."

He strolls over, one hand in a pocket, one hanging casually by his side. His tie and suit jacket are off, his dress shirt is untucked, sleeves rolled up, exposing his forearms. My stomach dips as I imagine that six o'clock shadow chafing the skin of my inner thighs.

Squeezing everything tight and tamping everything down, I bolt upright. "Hi. So. Nice place. Who did that painting?"

"I commissioned it from a local artist. Gave her a photo and told her the colors I wanted."

"Local here or in Beacon Harbor?"

"Here. I was too busy to make it back home much once I could afford to commission a painting. I used to keep the photo in my room at Wharton." His wistful expression tugs at my heartstrings. Then he snaps out of it. "Why are there two shopping bags from a discount department store out there when I gave you carte blanche with my black card?"

"Hey. They didn't discount things anywhere near as much as I was expecting. Three hundred dollars for a T-shirt?! No, thank you. But I did buy a couple of very pretty brand-name dress options for the gala."

"Yeah? Great. Can't wait to see them. Want a quick tour of my apartment? We have a few minutes to kill before dinner."

"Do I need to change?" I ask, combing my fingers through my surprisingly silky hair.

"Never." He holds his hands out to help me up.

I can't tear my eyes away from his, but I do let go of him as soon as I'm standing. Busying my hands by pulling down my camisole and blouse, I ask, "Have a good day at work?"

"Yes. I was more excited to come home today than I usually am, though."

Well, that's just way too adorable to dwell on.

"So, this is the living room," he says. "That's the west-facing terrace, with views of the park. Great place to enjoy coffee in the morning. The formal dining room is through those doors." He leads me back through the gallery to the staircase, picking up my shopping bags on the way. "Over there is the library. I'll show you that later, but that's where you'll find the bar and the south-facing terrace."

"And will I find books in the library?"

"You will find many books in there. Half of them are books on business and economy, biographies I've read, travel and art books. The other half are fiction and history books that I hope to read one day when I retire."

"And when will that be? The day after never?"

I can't see his face, but I can feel something in the range of sadness when he says, "Something like that. You can also take the elevator up, by the way. But I like the stairs."

Going up this staircase feels operatic, but it would feel all wrong to walk down it if you aren't wearing a ball gown and a tiara, I'd imagine. We arrive at the second floor, welcomed by another evening sun–filled gallery and hallways that lead off in two directions.

"There are closets and an entrance to a wraparound terrace down that way," he says, nodding in one direction as he leads me in another. "I had Hector leave your bags in my room for optics, but you can make yourself comfortable in this room, which is right next door." He opens the door to a bedroom the size of my former apartment. "Marble en suite bathroom," he continues, placing the shopping bags on the dresser. "This thermostat controls the temperature of your room, so you can set it to your liking." He casually nods in the direction of another door at the far end of the room. "That door leads to the master bedroom, but you can lock it."

This room is so simple and pretty, I can hardly stand it. It's not exactly feminine, but the wall paint is bright white, the linens are pure white, and the sheer drapes let in such lovely light.

"I love it, Grady. Thank you."

He's still staring at the adjoining door to his room when he says, "Wanna see the view from the roof?"

"But of course." I realize I'm barefoot. "Oh, do I need shoes?"

"Nah. Rosario sweeps up there daily."

He leads me up a narrow staircase to his private rooftop terrace, and while it is the exact opposite of being led down a narrow staircase to a dark basement, there is some quiet chatter in a part of my brain and from certain other parts of me who are still somehow worried or excited about being murdered by a sexy billionaire.

Stepping out onto the terrace, I gasp and my heart starts racing, same as when I saw Dominique Ansel's bakery. There are trellis-covered stone walls, long box planters all along the edge of it. Beyond the ledge is a view of the treetops of Central Park, high-rises and skyscrapers and the rooftops of so many apartment buildings for so many miles. I can't even remember the last time I was this high up, aside from when we flew here this morning. I'm so used to being at sea level. I can feel my feet on the tiled floor, but I don't feel grounded. Despite how inviting Grady has made it, *I* am clearly not made for the penthouse.

I get a little dizzy and start to sway a little, but Grady reaches out to steady me.

"You okay?"

"Uh-huh. A little overwhelmed, I guess. It's a very nice view."

"Come sit down." He takes my hand and pulls me over to a white canvas–covered love seat with a teak frame. It faces away from the city view so we can only look at each other or the faded slate tiles or the wall across from us.

I stare down at Grady's hand, which is still holding mine. I do love his hands. I don't want them touching anyone else. "So, have you always lived here by yourself?"

"Yeah."

"It's nice."

"Yeah. Do you really like it?"

"I mean, yeah, it's incredible. It's very, very large."

"Well, it only has three bedrooms."

"I was just going to say, but I mean, if your family comes to visit, Damien could sleep in the library, I guess, along with around twelve other people because I bet it's huge."

"Nah. I think he'd be more comfortable in the butler's pantry. That would be closer to the kitchen, which is where we'd have to set up his lobster tanks."

"Oh yeah, I haven't seen the kitchen yet."

He grins. "Saved that for last because I know you won't want to leave it." He glances down, biting his lip.

I realize I've been absentmindedly stroking his index finger. Here I was, anxiously waiting for Grady to make a move, meanwhile I'm giving his hand a hand job. "Oops." I let go and stand up, clasping my hands behind my back.

He slowly stands and adjusts his pants. "Your hands are really sending mixed messages, Claire."

"Sorry."

I really am.

Clearing his throat, he says nothing as we take the elevator back down to the first floor. I can't believe he has his own private elevator. He brings me through the living room again and the dining room, which is tasteful—and appears unused. "This is the butler's pantry," he says sheepishly. "But I don't have a butler."

I guffaw and open my mouth to make a joke, but then I walk into the kitchen and my jaw drops. I want to slap his face because this is the most amazing kitchen I have ever been in. Top-of-the-line appliances—six-burner Wolf range, Sub-Zero refrigerator, wine refrigerators, a center island, a separate eating nook, and gorgeous molding around the domed ceiling. Everything is sparkling clean and so well organized. It's wonderful, but it's also surprisingly charming. I am gobsmacked. My gob is completely smacked.

"You like it?" he asks, smoothing his hand over the marble countertop, and I detect the slightest twinge of nervousness. He really wants me to like it.

I feel like Daisy Buchanan when Jay Gatsby is showing her his mansion, except I'm not a rich girl he's trying to impress. I'm just the girl from back home with flour on her face. I'm tearing up again. "I love it, Grady." I laugh. Maybe he'll think I'm crying because I'm happy. "I really do. I'm so proud of you," I blurt out, and I don't realize it's true until I've heard myself say it, but I am.

A landline rings. Grady checks his watch and then picks up the phone. "Yes? ...Thank you, Hector. Send them up." He grins at me, takes my hand, and leads me back out to the gallery.

As the elevator dings, Grady opens the doors to the landing, and eight delivery men walk through, carrying big bags of food. He directs them to leave it all on the console table and tips them. I inspect all the bags. Dinner from Chinese, sushi, Italian, and Mexican restaurants.

Cookies from Levain, éclairs and macarons from Dominique Ansel, ciabatta from a family-run Italian bakery in Brooklyn that I may have mentioned wanting to visit, and cupcakes from Magnolia.

All of it.

I will eat all of it.

And okay, yes, I want to slap my own face for being so stubborn about resisting Grady. But we'll both be so stuffed after we finish all of this, we won't be able to do anything physical anyway, surely. I can't stop shaking my head in disbelief.

Grady disappears down another hallway and then returns holding a covered tray. He presents it to me. "I figured you'd be too tired to go out tonight. Open it," he says, nodding at the silver catering tray.

There's a one percent chance the head of his last dinner date is under that dome and a ninety percent chance that I'll just laugh it off because I can't wait to eat those éclairs. Instead of a severed head, I find a bouquet of John Hughes Blu-rays. Cue "If You Were Here" by the Thompson Twins. I look over my shoulder, just in case there's some other woman standing behind me that this was all meant for. But there isn't. There's just me. I'm the woman.

This.

Now, *this* is a move.

We take the food and the movies to the library, eat on the floor, and watch *Sixteen Candles*, followed by *Planes, Trains and Automobiles* on a projector screen. When the sun goes down, he lights candles and uses an app on his phone to close the drapes. It is the most low-key decadent thing that I never knew I needed to experience. I have never been this aroused and frustrated while watching a John Candy movie, but Grady is giving me a foot massage, and by the end credits, I'm thinking we should name all of our kids after John Hughes characters.

"This has been really wonderful, Grady. Thank you."

"You're very welcome," he says, still looking at the screen. A less skilled negotiator would make his pitch now, try to sell me on the whole *real relationship* thing at this perfect moment at the end of a perfect day. But he doesn't. He simply continues to rub my feet and watch the end credits.

He makes *me* bring it up.

"But I still can't be with you. Not for real."

"Why not?"

"Because as wonderful as this is, it's not sustainable. This is a lovely vacation for me, but—"

"You're wrong."

"I'm not," I say forcefully. Well, as forcefully as I can after ingesting seven thousand calories while having my feet kneaded like dough by a handsome billionaire.

"You are." He finally lets go of my feet and turns to face me, his warm brown eyes intense and wide open. "This is not unfeasible. This could be your life, Claire. This could be our life. I can fly us anywhere, anytime. I can bring Vera here. Your family. Mine. I can take us back to Beacon Harbor. We can't be there all the time, every day, obviously. We can work up to this. You can get your bakery to where you need it to be, to where it runs itself—which is possible—and until then, I'll come visit you whenever I can. But I can absolutely make this sustainable. I can give this to you, Claire. I want to."

He reads my face and the solitary tear that falls down my cheek. Sighing, he wipes the tear away. He knows better than to keep pressing. He stands up and holds his hands out to help me up again. That I will allow him to do.

He insists I leave everything in here for Rosario to clean up in the morning, which is almost as difficult for me to do as turning down Grady's other offers. However, moving is very difficult right now, so I agree to leave the dishes and empty takeout containers where they are. He does me a kindness by letting us take the elevator to the second floor this time.

"I'm guessing you don't want to unpack your bags right now, but there's room for your things in this walk-in closet." He indicates the sliding doors to the right of a short hallway that has closets on either side. This closet hallway leads to his bedroom. He brings my bags into the walk-in closet, leaves them at my feet, and then starts unbuttoning his shirt. "Well, I guess this is good night," he says, as if he didn't just promise me the world a couple of minutes ago. "I don't have to be at the office until eleven tomorrow, so I hope to see you after I get up."

"Great. Cool, cool, cool. I'll probably take a bath or something," I say, also unbuttoning my shirt.

"Great. There are Epsom salts in a container in your bathroom."

"Wonderful." I wait for him to lean in to kiss me.

He doesn't.

He removes his shirt, smiles at me, and walks away, into his bedroom.

I unzip my suitcase and pull out five pairs of panties and my cosmetic bag. When I'm trying to find my pj's, Grady saunters past the door, shirtless, in navy blue pajama pants, brushing his teeth. He must exfoliate with crushed gemstones and massage truffle oil into his skin every day to get that smooth. His abs are sculpted and beautiful, but it's his chest that I can't stop staring at. He has the perfect amount of dark hair covering his pecs, and I just want to be sandwiched between him and that leather sofa for, like, five minutes while inhaling his sexy armpits.

But I won't.

He winks at me.

And then shuts his bedroom door.

And that just might be Grady's most brilliant move of the day.

Not making a move at all.

I shuffle out of the walk-in closet to the room next to it. The entire time I'm in the guest-room tub, I watch the door to the bathroom, which has remained unlocked, waiting for it to open.

It doesn't.

I guess you need a lot of discipline in order to become a billionaire if you weren't born into wealth.

Good for him.

But I still think you need just as much discipline, or more, to make a living as a baker.

So here we are. The billionaire and the baker. *Not* having sex with each other.

Good for us.

Wrapped up in the luxurious hotel bathrobe that was provided for me, I cross the guest room and quietly press my ear against the adjoining door. I listen. For what, I don't know. The sound of Grady jerking it to thoughts of me, perhaps. Some light, inconsolable weeping because he can't have me? But all I hear is the tapping of laptop keys.

I let my robe drop to the floor and climb into bed. The sheets are exquisite. They feel as smooth as Grady's skin looks.

I'm exhausted.

I'm glad I don't have to have sex with him tonight. I really am. I need to rest up so I'll have the energy to resist whatever perfect thing he'll say or do for me tomorrow.

Chapter 18

Beauty & the Yeast

C<small>LAIRE</small>

I WAKE up alone in my guest bed, exactly as naked and frustrated as I was when I went to sleep last night. But wow, did I sleep soundly. This was the first time I went to bed without setting an alarm in I don't even know how many years. Stretching, I don't even recite any affirmations this morning because the past twenty-four hours have been one long affirmation.

I check my phone and find pictures and a video from the interior designer at my bakery. I'm ashamed to admit I didn't even think to check in with the team all day yesterday, but things seem to be progressing smoothly. Grady has already sent a thumbs-up emoji response. I reply with a paragraph of praise and thanks, even though all they've done so far is cleared everything out of the store and started painting. I can't believe things are getting done without me. I really can't believe I'm letting other people take care of things for me, but it feels pretty great.

The door to Grady's room is wide open when I casually wander into the closet hallway, barefoot in my donut-and-coffee pajama pants and a tank top, with my hair in low pigtails that drape over the front of my shoulders and absolutely no makeup on. This is my boss-lady way of signaling to Grady that I'm not trying to seduce him while accidentally-on-purpose looking like a manga college girl who's daring him to seduce me.

He is not in the master bedroom area. I quickly glance around the space, which is a mistake because there is something so very alluring about it. Three of the walls are bright white like the ones in the guest room, so the morning light bounces off of them, but the wall behind the king-size bed is painted slate gray to match the duvet. The pure white sheets look so luxurious, and the headboard is a cognac leather wall cushion that hangs from a sturdy steel bar. I hightail it out of there as soon as I envision my head banging against that soft leather because nope—not happening.

I hear faint chamber music emanating from the first floor as I take the stairs down. I'm sure there are a number of ways to reach the kitchen from the gallery, but I go through the living room and dining room the way Grady took me yesterday so I don't get lost. As soon as I'm in the dining room I can smell the most incredible coffee. I mean, I make great coffee, but this aroma is otherworldly. I wonder if the housekeeper makes it for him every morning. Pausing in the doorway of the butler's pantry, I spy something that just makes me angry.

Grady is frying bacon and cutting up cherry tomatoes. He's still wearing those navy blue pajama pants and he's still shirtless. His back is to me, so I can watch his muscles tense and release as he flips the bacon and slices into the tomatoes. I can admire the back of his neck and how perfectly groomed his hair is. Even the backs of his earlobes are sexy, dammit.

The air is filled with Bach's Violin Concerto, the scents of freshly brewed medium roast and bacon, and I'm angry because I am going to lose my damn heart to this man. It was always only a matter of time. *It might as well be him* is what Vera would tell me.

Okay, okay is what I would say to her.

Just not yet.

I mean, his coffee might not taste as good as it smells.

I step inside the kitchen just as he's transferring the contents of the frying pan and the cutting board to a large dish. Then he tears up the bacon into smaller pieces. I lean back against one of the counters, squeezing my thighs together, curling my toes. I can feel the heat emanating from the nearby oven, and I notice a mixing bowl that's covered with Saran Wrap.

He's letting a yeast dough rise. Shit. He's going to bake something. Maybe it will be terrible and I won't have any respect for him. That would be great.

He turns to look at me and gives me a good once-over while sucking bacon grease off his thumb. "You look hot," he says—not like he's coming on to me, like he's stating a fact.

"Thank you." It's the first time I have ever responded

to that sentence with a thank-you, but I'll take that compliment from Grady.

"Coffee?" he asks while washing his hands.

God, I love a man who keeps his hands clean.

"Please."

He pours it into a perfect white coffee cup that's already on the counter. I walk over to take it from him. "Perfect timing," he says as I take my first sip. "The dough has risen."

"Fuck me, that's good," I blurt out.

He laughs. "The beans are from Mount Kilimanjaro."

"I love the chocolate notes."

"I thought you might."

"What are you making? That better not all be for me. I thought you don't eat breakfast."

"Only on very special occasions."

"What's the very special occasion?" I ask, trying not to smile too brightly. It's me. It better be me. "That you're cooking?"

"Oh, no. I love to cook. And bake."

"Oh, *really*?"

"Yeah, really. It relaxes me. That and sailing. No, the special occasion is that I'm wearing you down," he says as he removes the plastic wrap from the mixing bowl.

I guffaw, perhaps a little too vehemently. "You aren't wearing me down."

"Yeah," he says as he washes and dries his hands again, "I am." He uses one hand to gently deflate the expanded dough inside the bowl. "And you're glad I am too."

"No. No to all of that. I wouldn't want you to gain an ounce of body fat in vain. Maybe I should eat all of this."

"Oh, I'm gonna eat it, Claire." He pours the dough out onto the marble countertop, where it's already lightly floured, and then folds it over and over into itself until it's rounded. Picking it up, he molds the dough into a smooth ball. "And I'm going to enjoy it." He pinches out a couple of air pockets and then slaps the dough ball back onto the counter. I wince and shudder every time his palm makes contact with it. "And so are you." He keeps watching me as he spanks that smooth, round ball of dough, and I keep feeling it.

I feel it, but I'm not going to let on that my butt cheeks are tingling in anticipation and that there is a tiny orgasmic fireworks show going on in my lower belly.

He uses his hands and knuckles to press and massage the dough, stretching it out and shaping it into a rough rectangle before finally using a big rolling pin to flatten it out just a bit more.

He's making pizza dough.

Oh, yeast almighty, he's making a breakfast pizza.

I'm dead.

He rolls the dough back over the pin and lays it out onto a cookie sheet that's sprinkled with cornmeal, using his hands to stretch it out, covering the entire surface of the tray. He grabs a bottle of olive oil, drizzles it all over, then layers mozzarella and freshly grated parmesan cheese, tops that with bacon and tomatoes, then cracks half a dozen eggs over all of that. Sprinkles of salt and pepper over everything, he washes his hands yet again, and then the pizza goes into the oven.

I am salivating for so many reasons, and I've forgotten to drink the rest of my coffee because watching Grady do anything is always thrilling, but this is the first time I will get to eat the thing that he's made with his beautiful, bare hands.

He sets a timer for fifteen minutes and starts cleaning up. I immediately start to help him, but I get a look that tells me to stop without him even having to order me to stop doing things. I'm getting better at letting him do things for me. I'm not great at it yet, but I am getting better.

When he's done cleaning up, he takes my coffee cup from me, dumps the cold coffee into the sink, and pours me a fresh cup. "You put up a good fight, Little Sweeney," he offers generously.

I'm about to protest, but the timer goes off, and I just want to sink my teeth into that pizza. Dear God, I am starving for it. He lets it cool for a minute before cutting into it. Then we eat directly from the tray, standing over the counter.

I groan without shame. This is, admittedly, even more satisfying than eating my own therapy bakes. Grady Barber made me a breakfast pizza from scratch. It's gonna be all downhill from here.

"What is this, like, five hundred calories a slice?" I ask without apprehension.

"About that, yeah." He helps himself to a second slice. "We'll have a couple of days to work it off after the gala." He smirks at me as he takes a bite, somehow managing to avoid coming off as salacious while speaking in a tone that implies I will be hitting my head against that leather wall cushion at some point.

"Oh God, I shouldn't eat too much," I say, pouting. "I won't be able to fit into either of the dresses I got for tonight."

"You'll be fine," he assures me. Then he checks the time and tells me I have to go get dressed in ten minutes because Ted's picking me up in half an hour. He refuses to tell me where Ted is taking me, but he does throw on a T-shirt and sweatpants to escort me down to the sidewalk after I've changed.

"I'll meet you back here before we head to the gala," he says as he opens the door to the back seat of the town car. "Enjoy your day."

"You really aren't telling me where I'm going? Am I dressed okay?" I'm wearing another version of what I wore yesterday—jeans and a blouse.

"You're perfect. And no, I'm not telling you, but you're going to love it." He curls his index finger under my chin and tilts it up, planting a quick goodbye kiss on my lips.

I forget that I didn't want him to kiss me while we were here. Then I remember that we're in public and that we're pretending to be a real couple. So, I wrap my arms around his neck and pull him down for a thank-you kiss. I thank him for the coffee with my lips. I thank him for the breakfast pizza with my tongue. And then I tug at his lower lip, gently, with my teeth, to punish him for being so damned shirtless earlier.

"See you tonight, boyfriend!" I say, loud enough so half the block can hear.

The Billionaire Is Back

We did some good business this morning.

I'M STILL all dreamy and grinning like an idiot when Ted pulls up in front of a location that looks like a warehouse. It's painted black and there are no signs telling me where we are, but this is one of those neighborhoods with an industrial vibe. The kind you always see in *Law & Order* crime scenes. Standing in front of a big metal door is a large man in a suit who's wearing dark sunglasses, a headset, and a don't-fuck-with-me frown. Ted opens the car door for me and pulls me out, promising that this is indeed the correct address. He gives my name to the scary guy, and I'm ushered inside before I even have a chance to introduce myself.

I'm led down brightly lit hallways, past even more security people and people who are dressed in black, also with headsets, who are dashing about while staring at iPads and clipboards. Finally, we arrive at a black soundstage that's flooded with blinding lights. I can make out camera equipment and chairs along the perimeter.

It's a TV studio.

What am I doing here?

Then I see the rows of brightly painted counters. Prep stations with sinks, stove tops, and ovens.

Gasp.

This is the set of *The Grand English Baking Show, American Edition.*

I cover my mouth to muffle a squeal even before I

notice the stout, snow-white-haired man approaching me. He is strong like a proper pint of Guinness, and his piercing blue eyes bore into me, daring me to impress him. It is Peter Broadway, and I may or may not have professionally peed my pants a tiny bit.

"Mornin'," he says with a perfunctory nod. His hands are in the pockets of his jeans and he moves slowly, but he still manages to give the impression that he's in a hurry and doesn't have time for this.

"I have your calendar," I squeak, finally managing to meet his Siberian-husky gaze.

"Right. Let's get to work, shall we?"

I refrain from telling him how much I love his accent and how often I used to imitate it just to drive Vera nuts. "Work?" I follow him over to one of the prep stations.

"I'm a very busy man, Miss Sweeney. Which is why your boyfriend had to pay me so much money to teach you this master class."

"Master class..." I echo. And I have to give Grady credit. I am more terrified of baking for Peter fucking Broadway than I am of the fact that Peter fucking Broadway referring to Grady as my boyfriend feels so right and so good. I calmly roll up my sleeves. "A master class in what, exactly?"

"Depends. What do you need the most help with?"

Turning a profit. Delegating. Succumbing to my brother's billionaire best friend. "Oh, gosh, let's see. Well, I'm always trying to perfect my buttercream. It's so hard to get the texture just right and the flavor not too sweet but sweet enough. Making sure it doesn't melt in the heat while not hardening in open air."

Peter looks very uninterested in teaching me the secret to mastering buttercream.

"Italian buttercream, especially..." I add.

His eyebrow quirks a tiny bit with mild interest.

"Also, I'd love to perfect my cake-stacking technique."

Peter is bored again.

"But I'd really just love to make a perfect croissant."

And that lights him up. "Now you're talking."

I clap my hands and jump up and down.

"But we don't have time. The dough needs to rest and rise for at least eight hours. What else you got?"

"Victoria sponge cake," I say without missing a beat. "With whipped cream in the middle. I've never been able to get my sponge cakes spongy enough."

"Yes. Good. An easy bake that's easy to mess up. It's all in the way you cream the butter and sugar together at the start."

I just want to listen to him say *buttah* over and over. This day is tied with yesterday for the best day ever. And the day that ended with Grady fingering me in his car. And the next morning when he came to my parents' house. And hopefully tomorrow.

Peter rests his hands against the edge of the counter. "We'll need a good raspberry jam for the filling. Softened butter." He stares at me.

I stare back at him, waiting for him to snap his fingers so the baking elves or production assistants will appear with all the ingredients.

"Well, go on," he urges.

"I didn't bring anything with me."

"Check the fridge."

I do that. I check the nearby fridge. It is so well stocked, I nearly pee my pants again. "Oh, it's in here!" I gleefully assemble all my equipment, tools, and ingredients, preheat the oven, rushing around as if I'm a contestant. But I'm not. I just don't want Peter Broadway to get mad at me. Or maybe I do?

He instructs me as I beat the softened butter, margarine, and sugar in a bowl with a hand-held electric whisk and tells me the exact moment that I should start adding the eggs. He incorporates the flour for me, hand mixing it with a spatula. I always get creative and lose myself in my bakes, but his confidence and expertise is inspiring.

By the time I'm spreading the jam and whipped cream on top of my golden, bouncy cake base, I feel ready to host my own show. We enjoy a slice of the finished cake with a cuppa tea, and he tells me he still has a couple of hours for me. He'd like me to bake something for him. "What's your best?"

"It's simple," I say.

"Simple is good. But simple is harder. Every element must be perfect."

"It's a s'more," I tell him, and I can't say it without smiling because s'mores remind me of Grady.

An appreciative grin spreads across his face. "Make it."

I make it. I make graham crackers from scratch and have to get over the disappointment of not being able to make my marshmallow from scratch because I'd need at least four hours for it to set. But I do explain to him, in great detail, how I'd be making them for him if I had the time. My graham crackers come out with the perfect amount of crunch.

I have to ask him to send someone out for a bar of Hershey's chocolate, but I have zero remorse about it. At least they have a butane torch that I can use to toast my store-bought marshmallows, but I caramelize those buggers to perfection. My finished product is aesthetically pleasing, but I can just tell from looking at it that it's delicious. I know my s'mores.

I watch Peter Broadway bite into it as if in slow motion. I hear the crunch of the cracker. I marvel as the marshmallow and chocolate melt into each other without oozing over the edge in a mess of goo. I hold my breath as he chews and swallows.

"The textures and flavors are all different, but they complement each other perfectly," he says. He finishes the whole thing, wipes his fingers on a napkin, and then extends his hand.

To me.

It is the highest compliment anyone can receive from Peter Broadway—a handshake after he's tasted your bake.

And I get one.

I get a Peter Broadway handshake.

Because I'm good enough.

I RETURN to Grady's penthouse on cloud nine.

I usually do fifty times as much work on any given day at the bakery, but this was so intense, I'm going to need a nap before putting on a slightly discounted designer evening gown for the gala event. The dress code is formal, and we must wear clothes that are green and/or black. I'm skeptical that I can pull off green, but since this executive's charity is for houseplants, I'm determined to wear a green dress. The apartment is empty when I take the elevator all the way up to the second floor, ready to collapse onto the guest bed.

But I can't do a belly flop onto the mattress because I find a huge black box waiting for me there. It has a big jade-green bow and a notecard with my name on it. At this point, I wouldn't be surprised if Molly Ringwald climbs out of this box and helps me do my hair and makeup for the event.

What I don't expect is to start tearing up as soon as I see Grady's handwriting instead of his assistant's.

Claire,

I hope the master class with Peter Broadway was instructive. I also hope it proved to you that all the hard work you've done, the countless hours and days and years of sweat equity you've put into becoming the best possible baker you can be has put you in a place where you can stand next to the best bakers in the world. As a peer.

I hope Peter made you feel like you belong.
Because you do.

And if he didn't make you feel that way, I will crush him.

Inside this box is something I had designed for you. I commissioned it a week ago, before you'd even agreed to come with me, and then I asked your best friend for your size and approximate measurements. My point is not that I knew with certainty that you would come with me—my point is that I wanted you to know with certainty how beautiful you are. That you will be the most beautiful girl in the ballroom, just as I have, truly, always known you were the most beautiful girl in the room, on the beach, in town.

You deserve to be here as much as I do.

You are world class.

All my best,
Grady

PS: I will just say right now, in case you didn't know, that Vera Wang does indeed design non-wedding gowns. That's not what this is. So calm down.

PPS: There are three pairs of shoes and a jewelry box inside the large black box, so don't throw out the box when you see the dress.

PPPS: Seriously, calm down.

Calm down, my ass.

I pull the cover off the box, tear through the gold tissue paper, and pull out the most beautiful French tulle gown I have ever seen. The fabric is a pale cobalt green, like watercolor, with an ombré effect. There's an elastic waistband, and the material is so light and airy that it will drape beautifully even though I'm pretty sure my waistline has expanded by a few inches since yesterday morning.

I'm going to look as good as I feel tonight.

In a Vera freaking Wang dress!

Grady has won.

Which is still a little terrifying because if he's won, that means I'm going to lose. I'm going to lose control. I'm going to lose my mind and my heart. I'm going to be lost. Lost in his eyes, his confidence, his kindness and strength. Just as I lose myself in his kisses and his promises and his passion for me.

But if I take one fun step at a time, maybe I'll find myself in him too.

Chapter 19

You Had Me at Marshmallow

Grady

"Okay, I have to wrap this up. How about a compromise? Dad gets grilled chicken instead of steak for dinner. No barbecue sauce, no fries, extra helping of broccoli, but with grated cheese on top. Fair?" I should not have called to check up on my parents right before the gala.

"Absolutely not," my dad grumbles at the same time as my mother sighs and says, "Fair."

"This isn't living," he complains. "A steak-free life is a fate worse than death."

"Well, call me selfish, Michael, but I would still rather see you suffer through a somewhat-low-cholesterol dinner than live without you."

"Well, call me masochistic, but I'd still rather suffer through your loving guilt trips and a meal of flavorless white meat than drop dead of a heart attack."

"Did you hear that, Grady? That right there was the sweetest thing your father has said to me all day."

"Oh, here we go..." my father says with an audible grin.

I could hang up right now and they would just keep bickering through their phones even though they're in the same room. But they didn't raise me to hang up on people. That's a little-brother move. "Sounds good. Listen, it's time for us to head out. Text me if you need anything, and have a wonderful night."

Now I hang up on them.

I can hear the clicking of high heels against the hardwood floor upstairs. I stride over to the mirror in the gallery to make sure I look as sharp as I did fifteen minutes ago in my bespoke dark green tuxedo jacket with black silk lapel, white shirt, black bow tie and pants. It's certainly not my favorite color combination for a tux, but I am definitely pulling it off.

Casually leaning against the handrail at the bottom of the staircase, I await my date.

I'm sure I've appeared calm, cool, and collected on the outside every time I've been around Claire. But I was a boiling cauldron of desire and longing for her on the inside. I've just perfected my resting sexy I-don't-care face over the years.

The churning of emotion and passion inside me intensifies when she appears on the stairs above me. I thought that evening gown I had made for her and the diamond jewelry were beautiful when I first saw them, but they only serve to enhance Claire's beauty now that she's wearing them. Her hair is up, her skin is glowing, the plunging neckline and sway of the dress somehow highlight her curves without putting them on display. There's a mischievous grace in her expression and the way she's moving, like a girl playing dress-up, but she is all woman underneath that dress. All my years of sexy-I-don't-care-face training have not prepared me for this moment. She is taking my breath away.

She looks like all the money I have *and* all the really important things in life you can't buy with it.

She has paused her descent to allow me to gape up at her. Her incandescent smile tells me that she knows exactly how good she looks, and that makes me even happier than the fact that I get to be the man by her side tonight. Lifting the skirt of her dress again, she keeps her chin up as her blue eyes remain fixed on the stairs the rest of the way down. Jake and I always hogged the TV in their family room when I slept over, so I never watched any girly movies with Claire when we were growing up. But I bet she's watched about a hundred scenes in films and TV shows where the heroine descended a staircase in a gown before attending a gala event. I am determined to make this night so much more memorable for her than anything she's ever streamed on Netflix.

"Hi," she says, two steps up from me.

"Hi," I manage to say. "You look..." My gaze unapologetically sweeps up and down her gorgeous form and back to her pretty face. "Stunning."

She blushes, and I don't know how it's possible but she's even more intoxicating. "Thank you," she says, genuinely. "For everything," she adds, touching her diamond necklace.

"You're welcome." I grin, trying to gather myself. This is going to be a long night if I can't get myself under control. "Shall we?" I offer her my arm.

She raises an index finger. "Just one sec." She gives me her little handbag to hold, kicks off her heels, lifts up her skirt, skips down the rest of the stairs, and twirls around the gallery, humming and giggling.

I've already enjoyed being with Claire more than I ever did with all the other women I ever dated here combined, and this evening has barely begun.

Exhaling, she says, "Okie doke," as she slips her feet back into her shoes and retrieves her handbag from me. "Had to."

"Loved it." I offer my arm again, and she takes it.

We exit my building and step inside my limo like a king and queen. She might still think we're pretending to be a couple tonight, but we capture the attention of everyone who's passing by, and we will own the charity gala event. It's a short drive to the Plaza from my place, but Ted has been instructed to drive around the park first.

Claire is quiet for a couple of minutes, staring out the tinted window, and I let her get in whatever zone she needs to be in. "So. What do I need to do tonight?" she finally asks.

"Just be you." I smile.

She rolls her eyes, and damn, I love it. *It.* I love *it.* The way she rolls her eyes. That's what I love.

"It would be helpful to have a little more information."

"Fair enough. Aston Pembroke is chairman of Harrison Lynch's board. Lynch's company is the one I'm trying to acquire. I need a majority of the board to sign off on the deal, but they follow Aston's lead. I have Aston on board, so the board is on board, as it were. I need your help to make sure it stays that way. And the way we're going to get to Aston is through his wife. They're a very traditional family, and they're both hosting tonight's fundraising event."

"Right. And we win them over by pretending we're a couple."

"That's right," I say. "Or by actually being a couple, if you'd prefer."

She doesn't even blink at that. "I gotta be honest—I'm a little nervous."

I look at her, really take her in. "I'm not. They're going to love you. Besides, you faced down Peter Broadway today. You can take on the world."

That gets a grin out of her.

"I got a handshake," she informs me, bursting with pride.

"Not surprised at all, Little Sweeney." I suppose she was expecting me to be, but I'm not in the least. I take her hand in mine. "I want to hear all about it."

She spends the rest of the limo ride telling me all about the master class that I spent a ridiculous amount of money on—an amount I would have gladly tripled, given how elated she is.

"I had to use store-bought marshmallows, though," she says, pouting. She's pretending to be complaining, but I know how much it really pissed her off that she didn't have time to make her own marshmallows for Peter Broadway. And I love it.

It.

I love *it*.

We arrive at the Plaza Hotel, and I have to ask Claire, without sarcasm, if she's ever posed for photographers on a red carpet before—because she is a natural. She's poised, confident, smiling calmly.

"I'm thinking about the s'mores I made today," she tells me in a hushed tone. "And wondering if I should sell s'mores brownies. Vera sent me a picture of Crabby Crawford sitting outside the bakery, looking all lost. I think he'd love a brownie version."

It's not weird that I'm jealous because she's standing next to me thinking about a nine-hundred-year-old man back home.

A photographer calls out asking who designed Claire's dress, and she yells, "Vera freaking Wang!"

I love it.

I got Vera freaking Wang to design that dress for her, so Grumpy Gus can suck it.

When we enter the foyer to the grand ballroom, it's like walking into a greenhouse. The air is more humid because the room is filled with potted plants. We're accosted by oxygen and Alice Strout. She looks as though she was squeezed into her dress. She once told me she's been a size zero her whole adult life, so this gown must be a size negative two. There's an enormous green silk flower on one of her shoulders, perched there like a parrot, and I can't stop staring at it as she leads us to our table inside the ballroom.

"Arrgh, matey," she says, squinting at me.

"You look lovely, Alice. Are they already here?" I don't need to explain to her who "they" are.

She gives a curt nod as we take our seats. "They are. The assistant looks fabulous, but *you* look sensational, honey," she tells Claire.

"Anything I need to know?" I ask her.

She hands me a small, folded piece of paper. "Here's some *break glass in case of emergency* information if you need it. I did a little digging." She winks at me, and her extra-long fake eyelashes stick together for a second.

I'm about to open it, but the appetizers are already being served and Mrs. Pembroke is welcomed to the stage to give a speech, so I slip it into my pocket.

We sit through an hour of small talk and fine dining, speeches from botanists and plant psychologists beseeching us to show more concern for our ferns. Pleading for reciprocity in our relationship with houseplants—it is a scientific fact that human interaction with plants is therapeutic and enhances our health and well-being, so we must, in return, relieve undue stress upon our indoor vegetation. And then there's a rare exotic-houseplant auction, and I bid eight thousand dollars on a monstera something or other that I'll have delivered to my office. Finally, the lighting changes and a band takes the stage, signaling that we can start milling about and dancing. Signaling that I can finally present my out-of-this-world, down-to-earth, small-town date to the Pembrokes.

I stand up and scan the room, immediately clocking Lynch and Miss Lovejoy as they are getting up from another table. Lynch already has me in his stare. With a nod, I silently comment on how lovely Miss Lovejoy looks and how great they look together.

And how absolutely full of shit he is.

Lynch glances over at Claire and back at me. He nods, indicating that Claire also looks lovely and that we look great together.

And that he knows I am completely full of shit too.

We raise our glasses to each other from across the room and polish them off. We both spot Aston Pembroke and his wife at the same time. I lock eyes with Lynch once more.

Game on.

I place my hand at the small of Claire's back. He places his hand at the small of Emma Lovejoy's. We gently guide our partners toward the Pembrokes.

"What is happening?" Claire asks through a broad smile.

"The Pembrokes are over there," I murmur. "Lynch and his date are over there." I indicate our competitors with a tilt of my head.

Claire marks them.

It's like a couples' luxury speed-walking race as the four of us arrive at the finish line at the exact same time.

"Oh, hello there, Grady," Aston says, shaking my hand vigorously.

First. He greets me and shakes my hand first. I smirk at Lynch as Aston greets him second.

Is this a trivial win? A petty battle? Absolutely.

But when you're world conquerors like Lynch and I are, fighting multimillion-dollar wars every year, really all you have left to enjoy is the frivolous.

I almost feel bad for Lynch as I watch him struggle to turn his usual frown upside down. Aston doesn't seem to notice, but there's another somewhat terrifying battle going on between Lynch's forced grin and his furrowed brow.

Aston holds up his hands, pretending to separate us. "Now, now, gentlemen, please remember—this is a peaceful function for charity."

Lynch and I chuckle at his lame joke. *Oh, we know.* We aren't going to fight each other directly. Our weapons are the amazing women on our arms.

Lynch gives Mrs. Pembroke a peck on the cheek. "Genevieve," he croons. "Mind if I *plant* a kiss on your cheek?"

She laughs heartily at that stupid punny joke that I was planning to make. Dammit. My delivery would have been a lot smoother.

"I think you've already met my assistant, Emma, but not...as my fiancée." Lynch, I must admit, presents Emma with a charming flourish.

Emma does a weird bow-curtsy thing before taking Mrs. Pembroke's hand. I notice Lynch holding her arm to steady her. She might be a bit tipsy. "So wonderful to see you again, Mrs. Pembroke."

"Oh, please, call me Genevieve." She admires the engagement ring. "I just think it's so lovely that you two have finally given in to your very obvious affections toward one another. I just adore workplace romances. I suppose they're frowned upon nowadays—in real life anyway. But that's how I met Aston, you know." She clasps Emma's hand, and they share a warm, knowing smile. "I was his secretary back when he had a three-man company in a one-room office. We know how much help these boys need and we know exactly how to help them, don't we, dear?"

I refuse to meet Lynch's smug gaze.

He may think he's currently winning, that Claire and I are a third-rate, third-wheel couple next to the sham workplace relationship that is LynchJoy. But I know better.

I clear my throat. "Mrs. Pembroke, I'd like to introduce you to my girlfriend, Claire Sweeney, from Beacon Harbor. Claire, this is Aston and Genevieve Pembroke, our hosts for the evening."

"It's a great pleasure to meet you," Claire says, shaking their hands, and you just have to believe her because she's so sincere. "Thank you for a lovely evening."

"Pleasure, my girl," Aston says. "Pleasure."

"Oh my, what a lovely gown," says Genevieve. "Sorry—he said you're from Beacon Harbor? Is that a subsidiary of Beacon Holdings?"

I have to hand it to Claire. I can sense her entire body clenching, but she continues to smile angelically. "Not exactly. Beacon Harbor, Maine. It's the coastal town that Grady and I grew up in."

"That's why I named my company Beacon Holdings." I smile at Claire. "To bring a piece of home with me."

Claire smiles back at me, then looks at Genevieve. "I own a bakery there."

"Oh, a bakery! How wonderful. I love Maine. Well,

I'm so glad you beautiful young people could come out to support Manhattanites for the Ethical Treatment of Houseplants."

We all mutter our undying support for her weird charity.

"You know, I've always felt a deep connection with plants," Emma Lovejoy tells our hosts. "Oh, that's such a pretty dress!" she gasps, suddenly distracted by Claire's gown. "It reminds me of a trailing golden pothos that I grew up with—you know, with the variegated leaves? But sadly, she is no longer with us. I took her with me to college, and she was senselessly killed by Anthrax." She shakes her head, continuing. "The band. My roommate insisted on listening to thrash metal music very loudly, without her headphones, and all that negative energy and distressful sound vibrations slowly murdered all of my plants, no matter how much Bach and Chopin I played for them when she wasn't around."

Both Claire and Genevieve reach out to give Emma's arm a little squeeze, offering their condolences, while we men covertly check each other's reactions.

Yeah, we all think this is horseshit.

"Well, that's why I love METH," Claire says. "I mean, this is why we need it. I'm so happy to be a big new supporter of METH."

I swear, I hear a record scratch. Only hipsters in Brooklyn have record players anymore, and the band is still playing on the stage, but I swear I heard one.

Mrs. Pembroke sputters, then begins mouthing *Meth, meth, meth* over and over again to herself, as if she's never realized what her foundation's acronym is.

Aston Pembroke squeezes his eyes shut and massages his temples, as if he's been fearing this moment would come, but his plan is clearly to avoid talking about it.

So, I help him out there. "Well, Lynch. What are your plans for life after you leave the company?" It's a classic sales tactic—move past the sale as if it's already done. Because it is.

"Not sure yet," Lynch replies coolly. "Nothing to speak of."

"Oh, except that you're getting married, of course," Genevieve reminds him.

Lynch wraps his arm around Emma. "Oh, of course. In terms of my personal life—*our*—personal life, we are planning a wedding. A big one. Huge, in fact."

Emma's eyes widen excitedly at this news. "We are?!"

"We are hoping you will do us the honor of attending," he says to Aston and his wife.

"Oh, of course, of course," Genevieve coos. "I do love a big wedding. Our daughter is having one soon. Have you set a date?"

"Soon," Lynch mumbles.

This is not going well for me. I realize Claire's hand is in my pocket, and as much as I like how it feels, this is not the time. Then I realize she's pulled out the piece of paper that Alice gave me earlier, handing it to me. She gives me a little wink.

I surreptitiously unfold the note, and we both read it. **LynchJoy = *Green Card Marriage*** is all it says.

I fold the paper and put it back into my pocket.

That makes sense.

But that also means Emma must be facing deportation, and as much as I would love to reveal Harrison Lynch as a felon, his assistant is a nice person. I share a meaningful look with Claire, who gives me the tiniest shake of her head. I mirror it. Not going there.

"I mean, it does have to be fairly soon," Emma is saying, "but we'll have to make sure we pick a date when there aren't any retrogrades. Venus, especially, but also Mercury or Mars."

I watch as Lynch tries to silence her with his expression, but that adorable little silent-movie pantomime I watched them engage in back at his office happened when Miss Lovejoy wasn't under the influence of alcohol. Or astrological retrogrades.

"And of course, we wouldn't want a wandering moon or a hard Neptune in either of our charts either," she continues.

Aston stares at the floor. His wife clears her throat. She must have a hard Neptune stuck in there or something. "Of course." She frowns.

"Well, what about you two lovebirds?" Lynch says, trying to turn the glaring spotlight away from his kooky fiancée. "How long have you known each other?"

Claire takes my hand and looks up at me. "I've known Grady for as long as I've known myself," she says. "He's my brother's best friend. It's a brother's-best-friend romance," she tells Mrs. Pembroke. "We grew up together."

The woman touches her heart. "Ohhhhh, how sweet."

"And how convenient that you've found love all of a

sudden," Lynch says cynically. "Just in time for this event."

"Oh, but I saw it in the tarot reading I did, when—" Emma starts to say before Lynch silences her by planting an awkwardly timed but very effective kiss on her mouth.

They both look a little flustered when he finally pulls away, and I almost believe that kiss as much as everyone else seems to, including Emma. Until Lynch looks at Mrs. Pembroke and says, "Actually, I didn't want to mention it earlier, but Emma and I will be starting a family as soon as possible. I want as many little Lynches running around as we can swing it."

Genevieve is eating this up and completely ignoring how surprised Emma is by this declaration. "Oh my goodness, how delightful. Isn't that just marvelous, Aston—did you hear that? They're starting a family."

"I heard, darling," Aston says, wrapping his arm around her waist. "I heard."

"That's why I want her to be my wife and the mother of my children ASAP," Lynch says, hammering that final nail in the coffin of my deal. "When you know, you know."

A direct shot at Team Glaire Bweeney. Or Crady Swarber. Whatever. Just because we don't have a good ship name that doesn't make us less awesome. Maybe Lynch's relationship with his assistant is real, maybe it isn't. But he's doing the thing. Genevieve is not going to want her husband to dethrone a man who's about to marry and start a family. I'm screwed.

"Well, I love Grady. I've loved him my whole life, and I'd wait for him forever."

All eyes are now on Claire Sweeney, including my own, wider than they've been all night. She doesn't look at me, she just squeezes my hand, staring down at it.

"I can tell you the exact moment I knew it too," she continues. "I was seven years old. Grady and Jake—my older brother, Robbie, and Grady's brother Damien were playing with their Nerf guns around the house. They didn't usually let me play, but for some reason this time they did. Of course, the teams were Jake, Robbie, and Grady versus Damien and me, so we didn't stand a chance, being the younger siblings. I took a lot of Nerf darts to the face that day. But it was fun being included. And Grady never shot me. Not once. He showed his little brother no mercy, but he'd catch up to me and point the Nerf gun at me, and somehow I'd always be able to dodge it. Because he would never pull the trigger as quickly when it was pointed in my direction.

"At some point I fell and twisted my ankle, running around the side of the house trying to get away. I fell on the grass, and Grady had me dead to rights. But instead of shooting me, he put his Nerf gun down and carried me into the house, yelling at my brother not to shoot me or he'd kick his ass. Being held in his arms and looking up at him as he carried me into the house—that's when I knew. That's when I felt it. Even being seven years old, I knew it was love that I felt for him. And that feeling has never gone away. Even when Grady did."

There is a long moment of silence after she finishes.

"That's such a wonderful story, my dear," Genevieve manages to say, even though she's all choked up and teary eyed.

And it is. It truly is.

Claire finally looks up at me. That doesn't make it any easier for me to speak. "Well, it was a pleasure seeing you, Aston, Mrs. Pembroke. Miss Lovejoy. Lynch. I think my girlfriend and I are going to go dance now." I offer them all a smile.

As I lead Claire to the dance floor, I glance back and see that Lynch and Lovejoy are now engaged in one of their silent-movie conversations again, but this one is clearly an argument. Emma storms off, and Lynch follows after her, calling out her name. He doesn't even say goodbye to the Pembrokes.

Poor guy.

He didn't necessarily lose.

But he certainly didn't win.

And all I needed tonight was to come out with a tie.

I feel like I've ended up with much more than that.

So much more.

Now on the dance floor, I snake one arm around Claire's waist and hold her hand in mine. There are a lot of old couples around us, slow dancing to "I'll Be Seeing You." Can I imagine dancing with Claire like this when we're old and gray? Yeah, I can. But right now, we're young and vibrant and there is so much we still have to discover about each other.

"You were wonderful," I tell her. I have never meant anything more in my life, and those words aren't nearly enough.

She grins. "Did you like my story?"

"It was perfect. I remember that day. And I don't remember being that chivalrous."

She rolls her eyes and laughs. "You weren't. You shot me to pieces."

"What? I don't remember *that*."

"Seriously? You don't remember what you were like with Nerf guns? You would calculate the rate of fire for every possible weapon and only choose the one that had the highest fire-to-reload ratios."

"I actually shot Nerf darts at you?"

"Oh, yes. I know you're disciplined, but you were a nine-year-old boy. You did not have the discipline to *not* shoot a person with a Nerf gun as many times as possible. Any person, including a girl."

"Well. I can't help it if I like to win. But I do remember carrying you into the house. And telling Jake not to shoot you."

"Yeah, well, you'd already pummeled me enough times at that point." She gives a little shrug of her shoulders. "But that part was true."

I lock eyes with her. I have always loved how honest she is. I can always see it in her eyes. "And the other part?"

She hesitates. The answer that is waiting on her lips is difficult to say out loud, as difficult as it was for me to ask that question.

That day of the Nerf gun war comes back to me. And I do remember shooting her. A lot. And now I remember why. I was becoming strangely protective of her, and to cover for that, as any nine-year-old boy would do, I went in the opposite direction. No way would Jake know, no way would Claire know how much I cared about her if I shot the shit out of her with my Nerf machine gun. But when I saw her hurt, that pretense went away. I had to scoop her up into my arms and carry her to safety. That feeling never went away. It's only deepened and expanded.

"Claire, I..." I begin to say, but I can't finish.

Neither one of us can say out loud what we feel, so we let our lips end our unfinished sentences. I cradle her face in my hands, and we kiss. Deeply. A little too intensely for a public dance floor, surrounded by New York's wealthiest plant lovers, but with the beckoning of her lips and tongue, she's trying to tell me that she meant what she said. She fell in love with me—and never stopped. And with my lips and tongue, I'm trying to say that I feel the same way.

I've never stopped wanting to carry her home.

We break our kiss, and I stare at her, both of us breathing heavily, no longer swaying to the music.

"Let's get out of here."

Chapter 20

Multiple S'moregasms

Claire

When we reach the second floor of the penthouse and the elevator doors open, I know even before Grady puts his arm around me that he's going to pick me up and carry me to his bedroom. I'm holding my Prada heels in my hands, but I let them drop to the floor when he lifts me up. He is such a damn cheeseball, I'm not even going to roll my eyes at him because I was really hoping in my heart of hearts that he would carry me like this.

This is it. It's happening, and I'm letting it happen. This thing that I've wanted for half of my life and resisted for the other half of it is finally happening. As promised, Grady has worn me down with classy determination, bacon-y shirtlessness, thoughtful gifty-ness, and sexy smellitude. God, his cologne has been making me want to rub up on him all night. He smells like he spilled vanilla extract on a leather sofa and then took a nap on it while burning incense and snuggling with a damp cedar log.

I am going to give in to all of it.

But I won't pretend that I'm not nervous and slightly terrified.

I take a deep, shaky breath, and begin to visualize... *I'm by myself making s'mores, all by myself, middle of the night, in my bakery kitchen. There are so many different recipes I'm going to try. I will take my time and relieve so much stress.*

"Claire. You're thinking too much," he states very plainly as he crosses the threshold into his bedroom. A few weeks ago, I would have taken it as a reprimand, but I hear the amused concern in his voice now.

"Yup. Let's do this."

He sets me down near the bed. I stand to face him. Tilting my chin up, he grazes his lips against mine, so softly. So lovingly. I melt into him like marshmallow and chocolate melt into each other when sandwiched between two crispy graham crackers.

Snickers. I'm placing sliced bars of Snickers on top of a graham cracker. Now I'm piercing my homemade marshmallow with a skewer and slowly roasting it over my portable grill that is just for marshmallow roasting.

"Beautiful girl..."

Oh, dear lord, he's letting my hair down. Removing the bobby pins and hair tie from my hair, so carefully, as if they aren't easily replaceable. He could literally buy the companies that make them, but he's transferring them to the palm of one hand and then placing them on top of the nearest bedside table as if he were holding a baby bird. If he's going to be that precious with me, I will not be able to endure it. I will not. My knees almost give out at the thought of it. I take a step back to lean against the wall for support.

Salted caramel. I'm so laid back I'm just using store-bought items this time. Because sometimes your schedule doesn't allow for homemade marshmallows and graham crackers and you just have to chill. But high-quality sea salt is a must.

"So beautiful..."

He runs his hands through my hair as he kisses me. Not quite frantic, but not as controlled as he usually is. He pulls away from me for a second, taking off his jacket and tossing it aside. He already removed his bow tie in the limo. He tossed it aside on the back seat, but I leaned over him to pick it up, carefully folded it, and placed it in his jacket pocket. I don't know if he's in love with me, but the look he had in his eyes when I did that —if that isn't love, then I don't think I could handle what is.

He pulls away from me for a second, and my insides quiver when I see that look in his eyes again.

Nutella. I'm spreading one tablespoon of Nutella over a graham cracker. Good old-fashioned milk-chocolate Hershey square over that. Coconut-flavored marshmallow this time...

He gently turns me to face the wall. "You're mentally baking right now, aren't you?"

I try to laugh seductively, but I sound like I'm trying to lift a washing machine. "Technically I was mentally assembling a confection."

"Claire...put your hands against the wall and keep your head in the game," he orders.

We're back to ordering again.

My girly bits are not sad about this.

I put my hands against the wall.

Grady gathers my hair and places it over my left shoulder. Then he drags his fingertips from the nape of my neck, down to my back, and unzips my gown past my waist. It wasn't tight, but I exhale loudly because...I am not wearing a bra—this is it. He's going to see me naked. The lighting in here is dim. Almost like firelight. But he'll be able to see my everything.

"Hands off the wall and turn around," he says.

Waffle cookies. I'm using waffle cookies instead of graham crackers. And warming up strawberries in a pot...

"You need me to turn off the lights?" he asks in a kind voice as he pulls the delicate dress straps down my arms.

"No. You should see what you're getting yourself into." I release a tiny, nervous laugh. "Literally."

"Turn to face me, Claire." He sounds so serious. Did he not get my joke?

I slowly turn toward him. After mentally putting away the s'mores, I look up at him. His eyes are getting hooded. Already. He's holding himself so still, but I can hear him breathing. I place my hands over his, guiding them down as he holds the straps of my dress, watching him watch as my breasts are revealed. I tug at the skirt and wiggle around so the gown falls in a beautiful green heap around my ankles.

Grady's jaw is so tight. His fingers are still stretched out, hovering an inch from my arms, as he stares at my very hard nipples. My hands are trembling, so I hide them behind my back, crossing them at the wrists. He traces the scalloped edge of my black lace panties—the nicest ones I own. He massages my hips, smooths his palms up the sides of my waist. His hands only skim past my breasts, flirting with my nipples as he cups my face and presses his lips to mine. "God, I don't know if I would have survived tonight if I couldn't make you mine, Claire."

"You can. I'm yours."

Bowing his head, he whispers to my neck, "Finally, finally."

Taking my hand, he leads me to the end of the bed and sits me down. He starts to unbutton his shirt, never looking away from me. I'm about mouth level with the most magnificent bulge in the nicest pants my face has ever been this close to. I bite my lower lip as my gaze travels up to his handsome, intent face.

"Wait..." I cover his hands with mine. "Wait. Can I?" I sit up on my knees and unbutton the rest of his shirt, exposing his toned chest. The sparse hairs are dark and softer than they look. His golden-tan skin is so smooth and taut. I'm used to touching soft, powdery, creamy things when I'm baking. But the men I've touched didn't feel anything like this. Grady is smooth and firm and strong and refined. Not like he's a statue of a perfect specimen. His body is warm and inviting. His rosy-brown nipples are pretty, and his abs are further evidence of his discipline.

Grady stands with his arms at his sides as I admire and inspect and explore him. When his hands form fists,

I know it's time for me to move on. I unbuckle his belt, undo his pants. He impatiently lowers and steps out of them, kicks off his shoes, but he lets me do the honor of removing his fitted black boxer briefs. I know there probably aren't really angels singing, but I do hear them.

Grady's cock is long and thick and so erect. This cock is used to being seated at the head of the table. This cock has built an empire. This cock is ready to make a deal. I look up at him, smiling. I'm really just so proud of him. I don't know how better to show him than by cupping his balls, licking up the underside of his shaft, and flicking at the most sensitive part of the head with the tip of my tongue.

He runs his fingers through my hair as he groans. One swift move and I'm flat on my back on the mattress. "You're done working for today," he grunts. "Got it?"

I blow out a long, raggedy breath, frowning at him as he removes his socks.

He laughs quietly, shaking his head. "Will you let me make you feel good now, Claire?" he asks, hovering over me.

"Yes." I mean it this time. I am his. I am his, I am his, I am his. "Yes!" I loop my arms around his neck and kiss him, so long and deep. Longer and deeper than I've ever kissed anyone. I am kissing my resistance goodbye and welcoming him inside of me. "Mmmm, Grady..."

"Yeah?" He is so deliciously breathless.

"Huh?" I nibble on his lower lip, catching it between my teeth, licking him across his stubbly jaw over to his earlobe.

"You said my name."

"I did?" I ask dreamily. "*Gradyyyyy...*" I twirl my tongue and flick at his earlobe, and it makes him groan. Grady Barber has sexy earlobes that taste good. Grady Barber has sexy everything, and I'm going to let him make me feel good with all of his sexy things.

I plant a kiss on his cheek and then sink back into the mattress, fisting the duvet with both hands.

He slowly pulls down my panties—slowly, slowly. "Well, well, well," he muses. "What have we here?"

I mumble an explanation about accidental travel shaving as my eyelids flutter shut. My whole body is fluttering when he blows a warm breath over my very naked strictly lady business.

"To be clear, I am not complaining." He pulls my panties down my legs, kissing me on one thigh, just above the other knee, slipping them over my feet.

I squeeze my thighs together, wriggling around. All of my energy has gathered just below my belly button, and all of the feelings I have for Grady are flowing from the center of me in the form of warm wetness. Ready to greet him there. *Welcome, welcome. I'm ready, I'm ready, I'm ready.*

"Actually, I am complaining. I hate knowing that this was happening down here and I had no idea."

I feel Grady's lips raining kisses across my lower abdomen. Where he is flat with curved ridges and built for business, I am supple and rounded and made for pleasure. His tongue sweeps up the skin of my belly like he's a rebellious teenager licking the frosting off a birthday cake. I get more and more toned in the area between my belly button and my breasts. He kisses his way up and up, moaning as he savors the soft cushion of my breast and swirls his tongue around my nipple, sucking it into his mouth. I cry out because I've wanted this for so long. Wanted his mouth on me there, his hands roaming every curve, his stubble gently scraping my skin all over.

My whole body is quivering. I'm aching for him between my legs, arching my back, trying to feed myself to him. I am the sweet treat he is savoring, and I want him to consume me. "*Gradyyyy.*" I reach up over my head and find a horizontal bar to hold on to just above the mattress.

"Your skin is sweet," he says. "Did you know that?" He licks me and kisses me all over my chest. So much desire for me. For *me*. "Did you know you taste good, Claire?"

I grip the metal bar a little tighter, my arms stretched out straight. I could float away or melt into the mattress, but I don't want to go anywhere. He grunts and flips me over onto my stomach. I reach for the bar again, looking up at the leather headboard. I wish there was a mirror there so I could see Grady staring down at my ass as he squeezes it.

"This. Ass." He nips at it, explores the vast landscape of my right butt cheek with his mouth. "I dream about this ass—did you know that?"

"I'd always hoped."

He strokes and kneads the fleshiest part of me with both hands. The rumble from deep inside his throat sounds like an engine revving. A really sexy, powerful engine that really likes my butt. I start to get a *little bit* nervous again, but he carefully moves me onto my back again and spreads my legs apart.

"Hot" is all he says. A one-word sentence that is music to my ears. He pushes my legs up so they're bent on either side of him, massages my inner thighs with his hands, and then strokes up my center with his tongue, just once. That sends a jolt through me.

My whole body has been teased for so long, it seems, and I'm so close, it would be cruel of him to flirt with me down there, and *oh, Hallelujah*, he's going for it. Sliding his hands under my ass, he grips me firmly and lavishes long, luscious laps and swirls on my clit and then dives right in with his tongue. Grady Barber is fucking me with his tongue and holding me in place while I buck around, screaming.

I love him. Oh God, I love him, I love him, I love him, I love him.

It's too much. All of his strength and focus and determination is focused on making me come and I guess this is what crazy feels like, but I never ever want him to stop doing this to me—ever, ever.

Eyes closed, the image I keep seeing is his boat. His family's sailboat. Grady at the helm, the waves crashing against it. Am I the waves crashing against the boat or the boat he's fearlessly steering to shore? I don't know, but there are waves and there is tossing and upheaval, and there is Grady, creating the unrest and anchoring me at the same time.

I'm still aware of Grady down there, his tongue between my legs, as the waves subside and the final currents of electricity punctuate all that pleasure.

Finally, I'm still and everything disappears, until I hear Grady saying my name.

I feel him kissing his way up my belly and chest. He kisses me where my shoulder meets my neck and then whispers my name into my ear, and I answer him back with "I love you." I kiss him all over his face. "I love you, I love you, I love you." I kiss his smiling lips that are giving my sweet scent back to me. "I love you, and not just because you just did that to me. I've never not loved you. You don't have to say anything—just fuck me right now, okay?"

He lowers his head, laughing quietly. "I love you too, Little Sweeney. *For real* for real. And I will fuck you right now." He kisses my cheek and says "Hang on" as he starts to reach for the drawer of his bedside table.

"No, come inside me," I whisper. "Please. Please, please, please."

"Really?"

"I'm good. I took my pill this morning." I reach for him, sitting up to cradle his face in my hands again. "It's okay, right?" I kiss his cheek, his jaw, his chin, his mouth. My fingertips find his cock again, gently pleading with it.

Moaning into my mouth, he lays me down again and braces himself over me, notching himself at my entrance. "Jesus," he whispers when he gets a preview of the warm wetness that awaits him. "Claire."

"I love you. Don't be gentle."

"You are so perfect," he groans, and he pushes himself inside of me.

And everything feels full and warm and right. "I love you, Grady." I will keep telling him this until I remember why I was so afraid of it.

"God, you don't even know..." His thrusts are swift and graceful, like his runner's strides. "So good."

"I love you." I curl my arms under his armpits, hooking them around his shoulders, and hold on for dear, sweet, sexy life.

He picks up the pace, finding a rhythm that is both vigorous and beautiful. It's exactly how I imagined Grady fucks—but ten times sexier because his grunts and groans are growing louder and more urgent.

"Oh my God, I love you!" My neck arches back, and I let the part of me that doesn't know how to speak English take over. I rock my hips and tell him how much my body loves his body with sighs and moans and screams. His pace slows for a moment, and I know it's because he's enjoying the sensation of me coming on his cock. He is probably watching me, and I don't even care what my face is doing because my face covers my brain and my brain is not the star of this show.

This time, my body is the captain and the boat and the waves and all the stars. I wrap my legs around his, scrape my fingernails down his back. His hot skin is slick with sweat, and I did this to him.

Grady's thrusts and breaths get sharper.

I want him to come inside of me more than I have ever wanted anything. I have never done yoga in my life, but I will myself to become flexible for him. I bend one leg, and he knows exactly what to do. He hoists it up so I can rest it against his shoulder, and I am so tight around him now, we both cry out.

His voice hits a falsetto note when he empties himself into me, hot and intense and so Grady Barber.

I love him, I love him, I love him.

It's the only thing that's real.

When he collapses on top of me, it is the best feeling. Not better than all the feelings I just had, but one of the top ten best feelings. He is spent. Grady's body is exhausted from fucking me. I'm too tired to turn or lift my head the tiniest bit to kiss his arm or shoulder, but I'm kissing him with my heart. Our hearts beat against each other, and he's still inside of me, and we did this to each other.

"I love you," he whispers on an exhale.

"Yes."

GRADY HAS a mini fridge in his master bathroom. That is why he is able to bring us crystal tumblers filled with ice water without leaving me alone in his bed for more than a minute. We gulp down the cold water. He takes the glass from me and places it on the bedside table. Then he joins me under the sheets.

He props up his elbow on a pillow, rests his head against his fist, and stares at me intently. I mirror him, but with one hand, I stroke up the side of his thigh and find his magnificent penis again. I watch his nostrils flare, his jaw tense. I watch his beautiful, dark eyelashes flutter, and then I see him take in a breath, and everything relaxes. Everything except his penis. And his testicles.

"Let's do this," he says. "Let me make this your every day."

"Can this be my every night too?"

He grins. There's some kind of sadness lurking in his eyes, but he's grinning. "You in my bed every night, Claire. Let's make this work."

"You are such a good salesman I'm not even going to make a joke about—"

"Just say yes, Claire."

"Yes." I laugh. "Yes. Let's make this work." He has grown so hard in my hand already. "I believe we can make anything work now. I really do."

"Me too, baby." He leans in closer so I can kiss him.

I have no concept of time anymore. "What time does our flight leave? It's tomorrow, right?"

"Flight? We aren't flying back. That's not good enough when my girl needs more of a break."

My girl. I'm Grady's girl. I am quite sure that I could take him in my arms and fly us both home right now. "Oh yeah? You think a private jet isn't good enough for me?"

"Nah. I have a much better idea."

Chapter 21

Pat Her Cake, Pat Her Cake, Baker's Man

GRADY

I WAKE up suspended between dream and reality. I can't quite remember the dream, but it doesn't matter. There's no way it was better than the reality of my life.

I have Claire.

We're together. For real. Or we were together, at least. I feel around next to me on the bed. Opening my eyes, I discover that she's no longer here.

Earlier, we enjoyed a five-course meal on this yacht that belongs to one of my friends. I'm renting it from him, paying for everything, including the crew. We're taking three luxurious days to get back to Beacon Harbor on a fully staffed, fully stocked pleasure vessel that was designed for elegant, off-the-chain parties. But the only non-crew passengers for this voyage are Claire and me. I'm going to get so much shit from Jake when he sees how extravagant this boat is.

But he can't complain that I'm not treating his sister right. I sit up, realizing I'm still wearing my dress pants, white oxford dress shirt, and tie. Claire and I had decided to get fancy for our last big vacation dinner. She couldn't stop chatting with the chef and our servers. She may never get used to being the one getting served, and I will always find that charming. But she's getting better at enjoying herself. It was her idea for us to lean into our food comas and take a little nap. I liked how decadent that sounded. Now I'm wondering if she ever really fell asleep. She's been so open and warm and relaxed since our last night in New York. But it seems as though the closer we get to Beacon Harbor, the more tense she's getting.

"Claire?"

No answer. She isn't anywhere to be found in the owner's suite. Where is she?

My anger cuts through the fog of sleep. Why am I pissed? Because while I can't remember my dream, I know it was about Claire and I know it was a good one. Because I've woken up with a raging hard on that I want to share with my girl. And she should be here, right next to me, languid and moaning when I press myself against her.

Instead she's gone.

This is a 263-foot mega yacht. It's late, and I don't want to ask the crew to locate my missing girlfriend, so now I have multiple luxury rooms and decks to search while subduing my nap wood—the bar, the screening room, the beach club, the indoor pool, the outdoor pool, the jacuzzi, the gym...

I scrape a hand over my face. Wait a minute. I don't need to search the ship. I know exactly where she is.

I make my way down to the galley on the aft deck and find her exactly where I thought I would. The spacious, completely stainless steel commercial-design kitchen is basically coated with flour and sugar and butter. There are bowls and mixing spoons and all manner of baking accouterments out everywhere. It's like walking into a mad baking scientist's lair.

"Claire. What are you doing?"

She doesn't look over at me, but she does pause for a moment before going back to frantically mixing and measuring. "You're a billionaire CEO of a major company, about to be in charge of a company twice the size of the one you were running. I have absolute faith that you'll be able to figure out what it is I'm doing."

I place my hands in my pockets and take deep breaths, attempting to calm down. Not only because of what she just said. Not only because she's wearing a tank top, little sleep shorts, and an apron. *And* she's a little bit sweaty. *And* there's that damn streak of flour on her face. I was horny as hell when I woke up, and she's literally not making anything less hard for me or on me.

"Yes, I see that you're baking. I see that you aren't doing it to help you relax. I see that you're not resting on this last night of our vacation. Claire, we're on a luxury yacht and things are about to get pretty stressful when we get back on shore, so this is our last chance to relax. Together. I know this kitchen is the shit, but the hardcore I-run-a-bakery-and-it-might-as-well-be-five-a.m.-in-Beacon-Harbor kind of baking? That can wait."

"I am relaxed! This is fun for me," she hyperventilates.

I scoff, shaking my head. *This woman.* "Yeah, you sound super chill, babe. Claire... *Claire...*" She doesn't give me her attention and she doesn't stop moving. She never stops moving. She never stops *doing*. I stride toward her, entering her space and forcing her to look up at me. "Listen, you're going to be busier than usual for a while when we get back. So let's not waste our last hours here. I want you calm and well rested for your reopening."

"I am!" She checks the temperature of one of the ovens. "I will be." She stirs something in a pot on one of the burners. "But I need to be at the top of my game so I can start strong!"

She tries to reach for another pot and another wooden spoon, but I gently grab her wrists. "You will be. But I'm telling you right now that you need to relax." She tries to move again, but my grip on her gets a little tighter.

Her jaw sets, and her steel-blue eyes finally fix on mine. "Excuse me? Do you think because you're my boyfriend you can just order me around and tell me what to do?"

"No. I can order you around and tell you what to do because for the time being this is my yacht—"

"This is not your yacht. You're borrowing it from—"

"And I am the captain."

She rolls her eyes. There it is. "And what does that make me—Tom Hanks? Grady, if you don't let me go, a lot of things are going to burn."

I make an adjustment, holding on to both of her

wrists with one hand while I turn off all of the ovens and burners.

She gasps in frustration. "Grady! You're ruining my—"

"I don't care. You are going to relax."

There's fire in her eyes now. And God damn if it isn't just as delicious as anything she could ever bake. But there's more than just the annoyance that I'm interrupting her. She is actually annoyed with *me*. And I'm actually annoyed with *her*. Is this our first fight as boyfriend and girlfriend?

My breathing is heavy as we stare into each other's eyes, both of us obstinate. There's also some sort of frustration underneath there. The kind that can be worked out the fun way.

I kiss her. Hard. Because I just can't not kiss her anymore. She kisses me back, letting her frustration press against my lips and thrust against my tongue. She's been taste testing whatever she's been making, and although our mouths are at war, hers tastes like heaven.

She suddenly breaks the kiss, straightens her apron, and attempts to go back to work.

Oh, no you don't, young lady.

I cup her face and force her mouth back to mine. I begin untying her apron, and she tries to stop me. She pulls away from me again.

I pull her back to me, a little rough. "You are going to listen to me, Little Sweeney."

The heat in her eyes intensifies, now with the added ingredients of lust and excitement. I loosen my necktie and yank it off without breaking eye contact with her.

The sudden movement causes her to blink, but her sexy mask of anger remains in place. I wrap the tie around her wrists, and she makes a couple of attempts to pull away but they're half-hearted. It doesn't take long before I have her hands tied together in front of her.

"Are you going to behave now?"

"No" is her simple reply.

I turn her around and place her hands on the counter. Now I feel like I'm back in a dream. *My* dream. My fantasy. There's a mixing bowl filled with smooth pink frosting on the counter right in front of her. I pull down her little sleep shorts, leaving her insanely tiny thong in place. I set my hand in the frosting, coating it, and then I smack her ass. It makes a satisfying crack, the sound bouncing off the stainless steel all around us. It leaves an equally satisfying handprint of frosting and elicits an even more satisfying moan from Claire.

"If you're going to be a brat..." *Spank.* "I'm going to treat you..." *Spank, spank.* "Like a brat." *Spank, spank, spank.*

I drop to my knees behind her, and I am in my dream. My beautiful Claire's soft skin is covered in butter and sugar, and she's all mine. But I'm wide awake. I proceed to lick all the buttercream frosting from the surface of her sweet, pink ass cheek. Every last dollop. I taste vanilla, rose water, a little lavender, a hint of salt. I am even more turned on by how fucking subtle and delicate and perfect she made the flavor and texture of this frosting. *That's my girl.* When I've licked her clean, she's groaning and trembling from squeezing her thighs together so tight. Her torso is flat against the counter, arms straight out in front of her, and she's trying to press her sex into my face.

"Not yet," I tell her. I grab her ponytail and raise her up to stand.

She sways a little. I turn her around to face me so I can see how heavy her eyelids are. But the tension isn't completely drained from her face. Yet.

I take out my phone to call the captain. "Terrence, I need the halls clear."

"Right away, sir. They're down in the crew quarters. Consider it done."

I give Claire a look—*Did you hear that? That's how everyone else on this ship responds to my commands.*

Claire's eyes widen slightly, just for a second, but she continues to look divinely, cock-hardeningly petulant. I remove my belt from my pants, and now her eyes get really wide. I place the belt next to her ass, but I'm not going to use it the way she thinks. Instead, I bend down and wrap it around her ankles three times. When I feel it's secure enough, I hoist her over my shoulder and carry her back to our room.

"Grady," she hisses. "Someone will see us."

"No, they won't. You heard me—I ordered for the hallways to be cleared, and they will be cleared. Because, as you're about to find out, I get what I want." I reach up to spank her ass over my shoulder. "In the way that I want it." *Spank.* I take the stairs up to the deck and set her down for a moment by the railing, looking out over the ocean. Loose strands of her hair blow in the ocean breeze. She is gorgeous in the moonlight, and she looks ready to be buttered.

And there's that damn streak of flour on her cheek.

I lick that flour from her cheek. It's mixed with sugar. My lips travel to her ear. "No one—I repeat, *no one* gets to see you like this but me." I can feel her shiver, and I know it's not from the ocean wind, which is still warm this time of year.

I hoist her over my shoulder again and bring her to our bedroom. I throw her down onto the bed, watch her bounce, and grab three more neckties from my closet. Claire manages to get up and hops away, pretending to try to escape. We both grin, a little drunk on our game. But her tits are bouncing under her tank top as she hops around, and it makes my already throbbing erection painful and it's not funny. I grab her and toss her back onto the bed. Then I work to secure each of her wrists to the bed posts. I remove my belt from her ankles, and then I slide her panties down her legs. But she's still wearing the tank top, and her arms are tied up.

Sorry, tank top.

I grab hold of the ribbed cotton fabric, and Claire lets out a yelp as I tear it apart with my bare hands. It hangs lifelessly from her shoulders, but her tits are exposed and she is, for all intents and purposes, completely and gloriously naked. She can't hide how happy she is about it either. We are so far beyond hiding our desire for each other now. Years of trying to repress our feelings has resulted in a lot of...release. Tension and release. Rinse and repeat. This will never get old.

"Thanks a lot," she mutters, trying to frown. "I really liked this tank top."

"Not as much as I liked it."

I use the two remaining ties on each leg, binding her ankles to the bed posts so she's spread eagle on the mattress. She never stops squirming. It's more from arousal than fighting it, I can tell. When I'm done, we're both panting heavily.

I give her another command: "Now struggle." And she does. *That* she complies with. She tests the strength of the Italian silk and my knot-tying skills. I guess those neckties weren't just made to make me look good. They can also hold my feisty baker in place. God, I love her soft curves, the way her delicate flesh feels beneath my hard body. But seeing how toned she is when her muscles are straining, the little droplets of sweat covering her flushed, ripe, naked body—that does something to me.

This woman does something to me.

Hearing the growl she elicits from deep in my soul, she goes still, watching me stare down at her. I watch her marvel at how the bulge in my pants expands. She bites her lower lip and wriggles around again. Her arousal is dripping down the inside of her thighs, but I want more. "I wouldn't exactly say I'm relaxed now, Captain," she finally grunts out.

"I'm about to fix that." I remove my shirt and dress pants, leaving my boxer briefs on for now. If I free my cock I won't be able to keep it out of her. And I have plans. Extensive plans. I watch her take in my naked torso. She licks her swollen lips. I climb on top of her, caging her in with my body. Hovering over her, I wait for her to arch up as high as she can, trying to reach my lips, pulling away until she can't bear the distance between us, and then I kiss her hard, aggressively entering her mouth with my tongue when, really, I want so badly to enter her body with my aching cock. Hard and fast. Over and over.

But not yet.

I work my way down, kissing her neck, lavishing attention on her breasts, which makes her writhe in her bonds. I kiss my way down to her soft belly, her round hips. "These hips drive me crazy, you know that?"

She huffs and squirms around. "Good."

That gets her a little smack on the side of her ass. "You like driving me crazy?"

"Sometimes." She tries to lift her head up to make eye contact with me, immediately dropping it back down.

I nip and suck at the luscious, satiny cushion of her inner thighs. "Why's that?"

She whimpers in response.

I lick and then blow warm breath onto her skin, just below her center. I wait for the trembling to subside before saying, "Use your words, Claire."

"Because you drive me crazy. And I like knowing I can make you feel that way too."

"Is that why you shave your pussy? Huh? To drive me wild?"

"That was just a happy accident," she claims haughtily. But her voice is strained. Her vocal cords, like the rest of her, are tense and yearning for release.

"Happy indeed." I crawl up to whisper in her ear. "I want to hear you beg for it." I press my hard length, still trapped inside the boxer briefs, against her wet pussy.

Claire's moans turn a little desperate. "Please, Grady. I need you inside me."

"Good," I say, pressing a kiss to her damp forehead.

"You're finally starting to listen." Her face is still pouty, but there's a beautiful anguish there. "But not yet. I need you nice and ready for my cock." I position myself down between her legs again.

"Trust me, I'm beyond ready," she whines, pulling at the ties.

"Oh, no. Trust me, you're not," I whisper against her pussy.

Her whole body shudders, and it's magnificent.

One quick taste of her and I'm a goner. Nothing she could ever mix together in a kitchen will ever taste as good as her sweet nectar. If she ever figures out how much control she really has over me, body and mind, I'll be in so much trouble. So for now, I will savor the pretense of controlling her body. "You feel how wet you are for me?" I flick at her clit with the tip of my tongue. "Do you?"

"Yes."

"You want me to make you even wetter?"

She shakes her head vehemently but whimpers, "Yeah."

I swirl my tongue around her clit, lick up her center. She is so engorged and sensitive. The slightest touch gives her a jolt. I scoop her ass up in my hands, squeezing both cheeks hard and tilting her pelvis up so I can bury my face between her legs. Jesus, I could live in this place. There is no company on earth that I could buy that would make me feel as powerful and satisfied as I do making Claire come when I fuck her with my tongue.

I hear a muffled symphony of groans and *Oh my Gods*, my name screamed out in rapturous agony.

She bucks and twitches and convulses.

When she suddenly relaxes, I suck on her clit and hold there as she clenches up, suspended in time, finally letting her ride out her orgasm. This is not a tension borne of work or shame or money troubles or expectations. This kind of tension is created from trying to contain the bliss that's flooding her body. Bliss that I made her feel. It subsides and she collapses, and the moment I've been trying to get her to give in to finally arrives. She goes completely limp. Even if she wasn't tied down, she wouldn't be able to move.

Claire Sweeney is now relaxed.

Of course, I myself am still rock hard and so horny I'm pissed off. So, for not listening to me for so long, for making me wait to make her truly mine, I won't be taking any pity on her. I quickly remove my boxer briefs and notch myself at her entrance.

She struggles to open her eyes, smiling up at me dreamily.

I hold myself there, ready to drive into her as soon as she says the magic word.

She pulls at her bonds, trying to lift herself up to kiss me. "Please," she whispers.

And I thrust inside her. She is insanely wet and deliciously tight, my Little Sweeney. I don't take it slow. I begin pistoning into her relentlessly. With her legs tied down, her hips remain still and I can get very deep, very quickly.

We're grunting and moaning in unison.

"You're going to come again." It's not a question.

"Yes," she says on an exhale.

"Come for me, baby." It's an order. "Come for me."

And this time, there's no delay in her obedience. She releases another full-throated cry of ecstasy, and I follow immediately, spilling myself inside her.

Emptied out and spent, I collapse next to her, placing a gentle hand on her breast and kissing her shoulder. She hums and gives me a cute little wiggle, her wrists and ankles still bound.

She takes a full, deep breath. "Okay, I guess relaxing until we get home is the right idea."

We both laugh. A sated, relaxed, deeply happy laugh of two people whose waking hours are the stuff dreams are made on.

She turns her head toward me. "Are you going to untie me?"

I pinch her pink nipple.

"Grady!"

I climb on top of her again, my face hovering inches above hers. I stroke her cheek, wiping away the soft exhaustion like sleep from her eyes. "I'm not done with you yet." I kiss her, soft and slow, so she can taste her sweet self on my tongue, and then hard and deep, so she understands that I can't get enough of her. "And I promise I never will be."

Chapter 22

Sweeter than Friction

CLAIRE

As I survey our local townie bar, the Hair of the Sea Dog, through the tranquil lens of my freshly fucked haze, I notice there are fewer pairs of eyes pretending not to stare at us tonight.

Grady and I have been back for a few days now, and we didn't make any official announcements to anyone in town. I mean, I feel like I have a neon flashing *My Boyfriend Tied Me to the Bedposts While I Was Naked!* sign over my head all the time now. But as for us being a couple, when we go anywhere we just act like boyfriend and girlfriend, holding hands and hugging, and then we let Ye Olde Beacon Harbor Rumor Mill do its work.

Of course, we told our families that we're really together. Jake is cautiously optimistic. My mom is cautiously ecstatic. My dad is still just really confused.

"Fantastic s'morples, honey," he says, mouth full of a s'more sample.

"*Daaaad!* Leave some for the other customers! I can make them for you anytime." I crane my neck to see if there are any left on the tray at the counter.

"Sorry, honey. This is the last one I eat tonight—promise." My dad gestures toward my little marketing setup at the bar. "But while I was over there, telling people how delicious your goodies are, I handed out twenty flyers for the reopening"—he raises his voice—"that your *boyfriend* Grady Barber has been helping you with!" He gives me an exaggerated wink, which would not have been helpful if we actually were still pretending.

"Dad." I lean in to explain things to him for the fifth time. "We really are together now. Privately and publicly. As a couple."

"Yes. You are. And you're really pulling it off." I get a Bob Sweeney thumbs-up.

Grady's parents stop arguing about whether or not his dad can order onion rings long enough to come over and compliment me on my s'more samples. It is so amazing to be here with our family and friends and half the town. And I'm not just saying that because I'm so relaxed even days after being tied up by my billionaire boyfriend.

We're all here to see Damien play for the first time in ages. As much as I'd like to think that people are excited about me and Grady being together, all the energy in the building is focused on Damien tonight. A lot of people in Beacon Harbor have missed hearing him play live.

"Bweeney" is already old news to the general population.

My *boyfriend* Grady Barber is texting someone on his phone. He's been preoccupied all night. His plan worked and the deal is going to go through. Now he has to leverage and finance and synergize or whatever it is he needs to do to combine his Fortune 500 company with Lynch's. So, we've both been busy ever since we got back, just as he said we would be. But tonight he's compromising for me. For *us*. He's text swiping with one hand while holding my hand with the other.

We're making this work. In the real-relationship-y, not-strictly-business sense.

Vera enters the bar with Damien, who's carrying his guitar. She's picking lint off his T-shirt and telling him what songs he should sing, and I need everyone around me to shut up so I can eavesdrop on their conversation. Vera is insisting he do a song called "Unsaid." Damien refuses. She pleads with him in a heartfelt, genuine way that is so unlike her that it's surprising to both me and Damien. He relents. Then Vera tells him not to do "Tangled" because it will just bring the whole bar down. There is eye-rolling and nose-flaring and he tells her he has to go set up on stage, but I just want them to make out, and then I want Vera to come over here so I can girl-talk her face off before the show starts.

"Break a leg, Damien!" I call out. He laughs and shakes his head at me. I guess that's just for theater people. "Knock 'em dead, tiger!" I give him the double thumbs-up because apparently I've turned into my dad.

Grady glances up from his phone. "Gonna sound awesome, D."

Jake walks over, and I catch him shooting Grady a dark look. What is *that* about? "Hey, G." My brother's voice sounds deeper than usual.

"What's up, Jakey?" Grady doesn't even look up from his phone.

"We're gonna go get the girls some drinks. That's what's up." Jake isn't asking.

Grady registers his tone and finally gives him his full attention. "Absolutely." He squeezes my hand as he stands. "You're getting a chardonnay," he tells me.

"Oh yeah?"

"Yeah. It's going to help you relax."

I wrinkle my nose. "You don't know me...yeah, it will."

"I know you, Claire Sweeney," he says with that frustratingly charming grin of his. "I know you." He kisses me, and God, it feels so good to just lean into it. No resistance. No pretense. I watch him walk over to the counter with my brother, and by that I mean I gape at his marvelous butt, and it doesn't even make me mad that he's so much more fit and toned than I am.

Vera finally quits yammering at Damien while he tests his mic and comes over to take a seat in the chair I've been saving for her. "That guy is so frustrating," she huffs.

I give her thigh a little squeeze, so happy to see her. The only time we've spent together since I got back has been at the bakery, and there's always been a construction crew and designer around. "I want to hear all about how frustrated you are," I say. "But first, I have to tell you about something that happened on the yacht with his brother." I give her a slow wink because, again, I've turned into Bob Sweeney. "It's not the kind of thing I could tell you in a text or a phone call."

"Oh, why yes, please do tell me that kind of thing."

I whisper into her ear about the spanking and the tying up and the surprising relaxing effect it had on me.

"He *what?!*" she yells out, glancing over at Grady with her mouth open.

I cover my face.

"Did you like it?!" she stage whispers.

I nod, totally unashamed by how much I liked it but a little embarrassed that Mrs. Barber is walking by.

"Oh, goodness. What did my boy do now?" she asks, rubbing my back.

"Oh, goodness! He is just so considerate. It's so many things. Nothing I can— He does so many amazing things to me."

"*For* you," Vera says under her breath.

"*For* me. So many sweet things are done for me. By your son."

"Aww, that does sound like him. Mike and I are thrilled he's finally locked you down." She gives me a little wink before rejoining her husband and my parents.

"I guess the handcuffs are next," Vera says somewhat quietly before busting a gut laughing.

"That is the last time I tell you about my sex life," I hiss.

"Yeah, well, you'll probably be gagged too, so you

won't be able to tell me anything!" She's turning red from laughing so hard.

I'm probably turning red from trying so hard not to laugh. "Why don't you tell me why it was so important for Damien to play 'Unsaid.'"

That gets her to stop laughing immediately.

She sighs as she glances over at him on stage and then pulls out her phone. "I've just missed hearing him sing. I miss that boy's voice." She opens up her camera app. "But don't tell the boy because he's impossible on a good day." She starts taking pictures of Damien and then informs me, "This is just for his IG. I told him I'd take pics for him."

"Uh-huh."

"I will be deleting them from my phone once I send them to him," she assures me.

I'm about to press Vera on that, since finding happiness with Grady is like being stricken with a glorious, benevolent disease—I want to spread this wonderful illness to my best friend so we can marry brothers, become legally related, and have babies that are cousins. But I catch sight of Crabby Crabberson entering the Sea Dog in a full flannel pajamas set, his messy old-man hair flopping around as he rubs his eyes. Oh no. Is he sleepwalking? He spots me and trudges over, stopping abruptly in front of me and resting his wrinkly old fists on his narrow hips.

"Clarence? Are you okay? Did you just wake up?"

"Yes. I set an alarm. No one should be up at this hour."

"At nine p.m.?" Vera says. She's not even trying to be snarky—she sounds genuinely bewildered.

Crabby ignores her. "Since your establishment has been closed," he says to me, "I have been unable to make contact with you. I figured you'd be here tonight to enjoy some rock 'n' roll music."

I don't say anything—because I don't know what to say to that. I wait for whatever it is Crabby braved the streets at this ungodly hour in his pajamas to tell me.

"I'm willing to forgive you for the disruption to my daily routine and to continue giving patronage to your establishment..." He holds up a knobby index finger. "I can accept that you've made changes to the store. But I do not want the menu changed."

"Well, that is actually the point of the changes, Clarence. Everything was too shiny and new. We're going to go back a little to the old ways and the old style—remember?"

Hearing that seems to make Crabby the happiest I've ever seen him. Something resembling a smile etches its way across his craggy face. *"Yeaaahhh.* That's what I'm talkin' about." He snaps his fingers. They don't make a sound, but he snaps them. "The old's got style." He does some sort of weird old-timey shuffle dance toward me and takes my hand. "The old's always got style." He raises my hand to his dry, old lips to kiss it.

Oh, Crabby. If only you were a hundred and fifty years younger.

"C'mere." I lead him over to the bar to where I set up the sample tray, chalkboard sign, and flyers. "Try one of my s'mores. It's not hot anymore, obviously, but it's still pretty good. This is the kind of thing I'll be selling more of when we reopen."

He takes a bite of my s'more sample, and it sort of looks like he's going to cry. "We used to make s'mores when we went camping." He sniffs. "My Rosie and me."

I put my hand on his bony arm. "I would love to hear more about Rosie sometime." I give him a flyer. "Come to the reopening. This flyer is a coupon for twenty percent off."

He swipes it from me. "I will take this flyer as a memento, but I will pay half price at the end of the day as usual."

"I don't know if there will be anything left on that day."

"Well, I like to live on the edge. We'll just have to see."

Jake and Grady come over, carrying drinks. Grady hands me my chardonnay.

Crabby extends his hand to Grady, who shakes it with a bemused grin.

"I suppose, in this situation, the better man lost. But as long as you treat her right and don't screw up my bakery, I will allow it."

"Very gracious of you, Mr. Crawford."

Jake places a strong, insistent hand on Grady's shoulder. "Oh, he'll treat her right."

Grady, as ever, is unfazed by the warnings. "Absolutely. You staying to hear some music, Clarence?"

"Absolutely not!" Crabby yells, returning to his natural crotchety state and leaving in a huff before the devil's music can assault him.

Laughing, we return to our table and sit back down with Vera and our parents.

Grady raises his glass. "I propose a toast." We all raise our glasses. "This is a great town with a great history. This group of people has a great history and great memories. But let's drink to the future. I'm really looking forward to it." Grady keeps his eyes totally and completely on me, and it makes me shiver—in the good way.

As soon as he takes a sip and puts down his drink, he looks down at his phone and frowns.

"What is it?" I ask.

"It's Alice. I have to call her. I'll be right back." He gives me a quick kiss and exits.

The house music fades out. Damien returns to the stage, watching his brother walk out the door just as he walks into the spotlight. As he picks up his guitar and steps up to the mic, we all cheer so loudly for him—surely that makes up for Grady's temporary absence.

"Nice to see you again, Sea Dog people," Damien says into the mic. "Thanks for coming out." He combs his fingers through his hair. Just like Grady always does, but different.

There's more cheering. There are so many women here swooning over him, but Vera is just grinning as she watches him up there. Not smirking. Grinning. A full-on happy smile as Damien plays the opening chords of "Unsaid."

I glance over at Jake, who's staring at the door, looking less than pleased. I'll have to figure that out. I thought we had his blessing. But as the alcohol courses through my body, I realize how happy I am. I'm in Beacon Harbor, enjoying some free time with my friends and family, with a bright future for my business and an even brighter one for my love life.

Those damn affirmations worked.

I have everything I want.

As soon as Grady gets back.

Chapter 23

It's All or Muffin

GRADY

I EXIT the Sea Dog to find a quieter spot down the block so I can call Alice. Before I even tap on her contact name in my phone, I hear, "You didn't say anything about that video I sent you."

I turn to find Jake right on my heels, not looking very happy. "What?"

"You never even commented on the video I sent you."

I put my phone down. Now, Jake Sweeney is a big guy. A strong man. A very cool dude by anyone's definition. But if this guy isn't happy with you, he will pout like a toddler. He has been so moody since we got to the bar, but I have no idea what's up with him. "What video?"

"The old fisherman guy who fell off the pier."

"Now, y'all did that on purpose!" I call out, like the guy in the video.

Jake laughs in spite of his clear frustration with me. "Ya did that on purpose!" he echoes.

"I saw it. Bill is a legend."

"You didn't reply. I didn't even get a Like reaction so I knew you saw it."

"I'm sorry, Jakey. I meant to respond later, but the day just got away from me. Thank you for sending it. I laughed."

Jake sighs and puts his hands on his hips. He shakes his head. He is clearly disgusted by me and searching for the proper way to articulate it.

As always, it's up to me to get a Sweeney to open up about feelings. "This isn't about fisherman fails. What's going on?"

"What's going on is you said you would take care of Claire."

"I did. I am. I love her, Jake. I've told her so."

"Yeah, I know. Good. Great." He holds his hand up, like he doesn't want to hear it. "I get it. But that's not the same thing as taking care of her."

"What do you mean?"

"I mean you've been on that thing all night." He points at my phone so aggressively that I take a step back. "And right now she's in there all alone."

"Well, she's not alone. She's sitting with her best friend and our parents and about a hundred other people, listening to Damien sing a song. She knows I stepped out to make a phone call."

"You've barely said two words to her since we got here."

"That is definitely not true."

"Okay, look, I haven't counted exactly how many words. But you're just not *here*, man. And I know you gave her a lot of shit and bought her a lot of shit and did all these really nice things that only a rich guy can do, but I don't care about that. I want the guy who says he's going to take care of my sister to give her the attention she deserves."

I let out a long, slow breath. I'd say that I can't believe that I'm hearing this from Jake and not Claire, but this doesn't really surprise me at all. "Jake, I shouldn't even be out tonight. I should be working. Making calls. Sending emails. Reading reports and dictating memos to my assistant. You have no idea how busy a CEO is. It is nonstop responding to input, making decisions, communicating with people, and getting shit done. It only slowed down for a little while because the deal was on hold and I came home to help Dad, but things are getting crazy again."

"Does she know that?"

"Yeah. We've talked about it. We know it's going to be a challenge, but we're up for it because we love each other."

I can tell Jake isn't satisfied by that answer but he doesn't know quite how to respond to it. Someone goes into the bar, and the sounds of Damien's guitar, cheering, and applause slip through the door. We both look toward the Sea Dog.

"Listen, I gotta make this call. I want you to keep sending me ridiculous videos, and I want to laugh about them with you. I want to get in there and sit next to Claire and hang out with you and Vera and our parents and listen to my brother play. Believe me, that's what I want to do, but there are a lot of other things that I *have* to do too. Okay?"

Suddenly, Jake gets that look, like he's about to turn on the fire hose and I'm about to get blasted with all the words he's been trying to find for the past half hour. "No, not okay. I do get it, y'know, Mr. Big-Shot Billionaire. I know you work hard for the big money. We all get it. But that doesn't mean you don't have to work hard for the other things in life too. Including my sister. I'm glad you told her you love her. I've scared off a lot of guys who tried to get into her pants because I knew they weren't good enough for her and I knew they wouldn't treat her right. You? You're good enough. But treating her right, taking care of her—that means going all in. This is all or nothing, bro. So you need to do me a solid. You think about whether or not you're capable of going all in for Claire. If you want out, I need you to get out now. Because the longer you wait, the worse it's gonna get." He turns to walk away from me. "See you inside."

Well played, dude. Well played.

Taking up any more time trying to convince him of my intentions would be a poor use of that limited resource. I need to show him that I'm all in. Actually, I need to show Claire. And I can do that after I call my assistant back.

She answers on the first ring. "Sorry to bother you so late, Mr. Barber."

"I miss the days when you used to ask me to call you so you could tell me something good."

"When did I ever do that?" Alice scoffs.

"What's going on?"

"Harrison Lynch is like a giant, grouchy, extremely well-dressed, handsome cockroach. With big hands. We just can't seem to snuff him out."

"What's he up to this time?"

"Well, all was well and good. Your plan worked. But maybe a little too well. You know the financials on this deal were always very complicated. We were going to have to take on a lot of leverage to make the numbers work."

"I am well aware of the numbers, Alice. Get to the point."

"Yes, well, you being you and your consistent demonstration of how disciplined you are is what allowed us to make that sale. But now Lynch is telling the board you falling in love has made you a spendthrift. Extravagant gifts, very expensive unique experiences."

"And a mega yacht," I finish for her.

"And a super-duper yacht."

I let out a billion-dollar sigh. "What's his play?"

"Lynch has requested another meeting of the board, and he has been granted one. He's going to make the case that the person they originally made the deal with isn't focused on Relicteros and its employees anymore."

I have to bite the inside of my cheek. This is the first time Lynch has really gotten too close for comfort. I am not sure I am the same man now that I was before Claire gave herself to me. I would give Claire the world. I didn't mean to let the world I was trying to build for myself slip away because of it. I didn't mean to give Lynch the winning hand. "When's the board meeting?"

"August twenty-seventh."

"That son of a bitch," I murmur. I know my assistant well enough that I can sense her nodding on the other end of the line.

Lynch set the meeting for August twenty-seventh.

August twenty-seventh is the reopening of Claire's bakery.

And we both know that is not a coincidence.

"Do you want me to try to move it?" Alice asks.

I shake my head even though she can't see me. "That would just prove his point. Get them to make it as early in the morning as possible."

"You got it. Do you know how you want to defend it?"

"I'm not going to. That would be accepting Lynch's frame, which I'm not interested in doing. It's go time, Alice. All the work that was on hold—the calls with every department head...I want to meet with them tomorrow morning. Late morning. In person. It's time to show them what we would do when we take ownership of their company. It's time to show them how we get things done."

"You got it, boss. I'll arrange for the private jet to leave from Portland at nine a.m. Does that work?"

"Yes. Thank you, Alice. Good night."

"Good night."

I turn off my phone and put it in my pocket, telling myself I won't take it out again until Damien's show is over. Another burst of live music pulls my attention to the Sea Dog's entrance. Claire—my beautiful, wonderful, deserves-my-full-attention girlfriend—is coming toward me.

"Hey," she says on an exhale. "I was just checking on you." She's hesitant, as if expecting me to wave her away because I have to make another call or leave.

"Hey." I open my arms wide as an invitation for her to come to me. She does, and I wrap her in a tight hug, kissing the top of her head.

This. It's little things like this that I had flashes of when I'd imagine being with Claire. Moments of comfort and familiarity that I knew I could never have with the women I met in New York. I kiss the top of her head again because once is never enough.

"Everything okay?" she asks, her voice muffled by our embrace.

"Yeah. No. Sort of."

She pulls back and looks up at me, concerned. "What's going on?"

I contemplate not telling her. Dealing with all this later. But Claire knows me too well. She's intensely scanning my face and reading me like I'm a recipe for chocolate fondant.

"Just tell me, Grady. This is only going to work if we're up-front about everything. We don't really have time to do it any other way."

Oh my, how my girl has grown. "You're right. But after this, I'd really like to forget about it and just hold your hand and listen to my brother play music."

"And that is what you shall do. What's going on?"

I fill her in on Lynch's new plan and the whole situation. She listens intently. "When is the board meeting?"

I wince.

I can tell she understands immediately.

She swears under her breath, and I can see how disappointed she is.

I place my hands on her shoulders. "But I'm having Alice set the meeting as early as possible. I'm gonna go in there, crush Lynch...again. For the last time, I swear. And then I'm going to get on my private jet—or possibly commission some sort of Iron Man suit—so I can get back here as fast as I possibly can. I probably won't make the very beginning of the opening, but I will do everything in my power to be there."

Her face changes from sad to resigned to hopeful. I watch her beautiful mouth form a smile. "Well. We knew this was going to be part of it. Part of you there, part of me here."

"Yeah. This is part of it." She nods and turns away from me, but I grab her hand and pull her back. "But there's a part that we haven't talked about yet..."

"If you're referring to butt stuff, I'd rather not discuss that when our parents are within shouting distance."

I arch an eyebrow. "Is that up for discussion?"

She laughs. "Not really."

I have to shake my head to get my brain back on track. I take both of her hands in mine. "What I was actually thinking about is..."

"I'm listening..."

Someone opens the door to the bar again, and I spot my parents inside. Sitting together, my dad's arm around my mom's shoulder. *Things are fine for them now*, I remind myself. *I'm not going to lose anything if I have Claire.*

"I was thinking I should rent a house in Beacon Harbor. Or buy one if the right one's available. Obviously your mom would be the one to ask about that."

She blinks once and waits for me to continue.

"And I was thinking we should both move into that house. Together. So we'll have more time together when I can be here."

She blinks twice, as if she can't quite believe what she just heard.

"That is, unless you'd prefer to stay in your room at your parents' house. And before you answer—yes, you can bring your Peter Broadway calendar and all of your little Post-it notes with you."

"To clarify—you're talking about keeping your kickass penthouse in New York, right? That would still be your home base, but you'd rent or own property here, and I would live there all the time?"

"Correct."

She twists her lips to one side, pondering my idea. "You know I get up before dawn, right?"

"You know that's when I usually go for my runs, right?"

"You know I'm going to have to bake at home sometimes, right? Even when you don't want me to?"

"I promise I'll only tie you to the bedposts when you ask me to."

She narrows her eyes at me. "We should go back inside. I'll think about it and get back to you."

"Really?"

She laughs. "Just kidding. Of course I want you to get a house here so I can move in with you!" She jumps up, wrapping her arms around my neck.

I grab her sweet ass and hold her so tight while she wraps her legs around my waist and squeals.

"I'm gonna get us a house with the perfect kitchen," I tell her.

"I'm gonna bake you perfect carrot cake muffins every day."

I make a mental note to find a local personal trainer and then forget it immediately when Claire's lips find mine as I carry her back to the Hair of the Sea Dog.

This. It's moments like this that I tried so hard not to envision for years. Now I can't stop.

"I love you," I tell her in between sweet kisses.

"Not as much as you're gonna love waking up to my muffin," she whispers.

This.

Chapter 24

Ladyfinger in the Streets, Tart in the Sheets

CLAIRE

I'VE BEEN COOKING and rearranging furniture and dec-organizing ever since I got home from the bakery at two thirty.

"Home" is now a five-bedroom house by the water. My mom found us this property the day after Damien's show at the bar. It had been on the market and empty for half a year because of the 2.5-million-dollar asking price. Helen Sweeney was able to get us a lease with the option to own that same week. And by "us," I mean Grady. My name isn't on the lease, but my panties are in the drawers. My KitchenAid mixer is on the counter. All of my baking tools have moved from my parents' house to this massive kitchen. I'm sleeping on the finest sheets I've slept on since Grady's penthouse.

Oh, and when we moved in there was a brand new Prius in the driveway. He didn't want me getting stranded anywhere in case I forgot to turn off the headlights. I already miss that soupy old shitbox.

Just kidding—I hated that thing.

I don't know how I got here. How did I start this summer in my parents' house with a small business that was hemorrhaging money and no romantic prospects whatsoever? And all of a sudden, I have a renovated bakery, an actual business plan; I'm the dessert caterer of the Beacon Harbor Shellibration; and I'm living with the man I've secretly loved my whole life—in our hometown. Living in a four-thousand-square-foot house! With so many rooms. There wasn't a lot of inventory to choose from, and Grady wanted the best. The best happens to be the biggest. There are five bedrooms as well as the home office and guest house.

This is the kind of house you raise a family in.

Does Grady want kids? Am I ready for that? I mean, I didn't think I was emotionally ready to handle having his penis inside of me a couple of weeks ago, but now I don't like it when his penis isn't inside of me. I am definitely open to possibilities. Or maybe I'm just horny.

We may be moving too fast, but we're making up for lost time, and I can't wait to see him again. I can't believe we went twelve years without seeing each other at all. Now we text each other every couple of hours if our schedules allow it. But this will be the first time he comes home from a trip to find me here in his house. This will be the first time we get to spend a night at home together, just the two of us. I've been looking forward to dinner on the patio, drinks down by the water, followed by binge-watching a few episodes of something or other and then bath time in the deluxe jacuzzi tub before bed—all of the above with Grady.

It has been an hour and a half since he sent me a text from his private jet in Portland, so he could be back any minute. My heart starts racing even before I run to the kitchen to check on my roast chicken. We may not be pretending anymore, but all afternoon it's felt like we're playing house—and I love it more than I ever dreamed I would. We could be living in his parents' garage and I'd still feel all my nerve endings vibrating at the thought of him coming home to me.

Just as I'm checking the meat thermometer, I hear the front door opening, and I actually squeal and hop up and down.

"Honey, I'm home!" Grady calls out from the foyer.

I am so giddy and impatient to see him that I don't even check my hair or remove my stupid apron that says ***I COOK AS GOOD AS I LOOK*** before sprinting to greet him.

He's carefully placing all of his bags on the floor, but as soon as he realizes I'm coming at him, he braces himself, holds out his arms, and twirls me around when I leap up into them. He stops spinning, lowers me to the ground, and we both let out a long, loud sigh as we hold each other tight. The rush of seeing and smelling and touching him after missing him for three days is like nothing I've ever known. It's even more thrilling and comforting than curling up in front of a fire with a brand new recipe book while drinking wine and listening to Taylor Swift.

We finally pull apart enough to kiss each other. He

tastes like espresso and scotch and dark chocolate, and I'm not even mad about the dark chocolate. I have so much I want to say to him that it comes out like, "I *misloved* you so much it's so good to hope you're hungry!"

I squeeze my eyes shut and wait for him to tell me he's made a terrible mistake and will need me to move out by tomorrow. But he doesn't.

He puts his hands on my face. "Open your eyes."

I do. He looks so concerned, it's almost comical.

He inspects my retinas, holds a finger up. "Follow my finger."

My gaze follows his finger as he moves it in sweeping motions in front of my face. "I didn't have a stroke—I'm just too excited to speak," I tell him.

He cracks a smile, his eyes sparkling. "I know. I'm just messing with you."

I give him a playful shove.

He hugs me again, and I bury my face in his chest. "I missed you so much, baby." He kisses me softly on the top of my head. "I've never missed anything as much as I missed holding you and sleeping next to you and waking up with you and making you come in person instead of over the phone. Although I very much enjoyed the video-call sex."

I think my heart and all my bones *and* my panties just melted. I just shake my head. I still can't speak properly. The man had a secure video-call app developed for his own personal use, and I never thought I could be so turned on by talk of end-to-end encryption.

He inhales deeply, arms still wrapped around me. "God, it smells incredible. What are you making?"

I manage to hold my head up to say, "I've been cooking—not baking, so it doesn't count as work."

He starts to pull me toward the kitchen. "You went overboard cooking for me, didn't you?"

I hold on to his arm with both hands to try to stop him from going to the kitchen. "It's not overboard—it's just a few simple dishes!"

He kneels down, lifts me up, and pulls me over his shoulder, gripping my arm and carrying me into the kitchen the way I've seen my brother demonstrate how he'd save women from a flaming building at a party. But I do not want to think about my brother right now. "I've had some filthy fantasies about you in an apron, by the way. You weren't wearing sweatpants, but I am not complaining." He gives me a pat on the bum. "Jesus," he exclaims when he sees the counters. "How many people are you cooking for?!"

I slide down the front of him and launch into a wildly defensive response. "Just us—it's just roast chicken with roasted vegetables and sauteed potatoes and a chilled shrimp salad—which was super quick and easy to make, and now I can boil the fresh linguine to eat with the lobster I got on the way home. That's not a lot—I didn't even make dessert!"

He just shakes his head as he takes off his suit jacket, grinning at me. "I would fly halfway around the world every other day if I had to so I could come home to you."

I would rather he didn't leave town at all, but I keep that to myself because I know he meant that as a high compliment. I remove my apron and take his jacket from him. "Can I get you a drink? Also, I lied. I made dessert, but it's a no-bake lemon cheesecake that I made yesterday, so that doesn't count."

He looks down at his watch. "Shit. I have a Zoom meeting in two minutes."

"Oh. So I shouldn't boil the pasta yet."

He returns to the front hall to get his laptop briefcase. "Yeah, no. It's a quick meeting, but this is the only time we could find to connect. I'll be done in half an hour. Forty-five minutes, tops. Then you'll have my full attention, I promise."

I pout. I don't mean to, but I pout.

He glances over at me as he passes by on his way to his home office and does a double take. "Babe, I'm slammed. I'm sorry—I have to talk to this guy."

And he disappears before I can tell him I understand.

I do.

I understand.

It's really something that he came back to be with me for two whole days. I go back into the kitchen to check the timer. My chicken still has twenty minutes in the oven. Everything else is prepped. I might as well be productive...

I hear the deep rumble of Grady's voice from his office and feel it vibrating between my legs.

Laundry?

I think I'll do some laundry. I amble over to the laundry room. My sweatpants are feeling...so dirty all of a sudden. So I remove them and drop them into a laundry basket. My socks need to be washed too. I pick up a tea towel and toss that into the basket as I pass through the kitchen. I'm such a good girlfriend, I would be remiss if I didn't do Grady's laundry too. Since he's *sooooo* busy. He still has everything at his penthouse in New York, so he doesn't travel home with a bag full of dirty clothes like most people. But still.

Grady is staring intently at his giant computer monitor when I quietly swing into the room. His sleeves are rolled up just below his elbows, his shirt is untucked, and I find myself wishing I could crawl under his desk to take him into my mouth because that's how hot he looks. He's concentrating on some shared screen, probably, clenching his jaw while a man pitches him something, and now I want to do laundry even more than I did a minute ago. Now I want to do his laundry so hard.

"No. That's a strategy they've tried before," he says to his very-important-Zoom-meeting person. "Three or four years ago. Why they stopped it, I'm not sure, but we'll have access to their internals soon, so we can..." He stops mid-sentence when he finally notices me wandering around in my tiny little tank top and panties, resting a basket on my hip like a maid in a porno.

I point to the basket, silently asking him if he has any laundry to do.

He licks his lips. I watch his Adam's apple bob as he swallows, doing a full, appreciative sweep up and down my body. Finally, he shakes his head. I am very pleased to see him struggle to hide the desire from showing on his face. Because I'll bet it's showing in his pants.

He turns his attention back to the monitor and clears his throat. "Sorry about that. As I was saying..."

While he's saying whatever he's saying, I turn around and slowly bend over to place the laundry basket on the floor and pick up a whole armful of nothing. It's not my fault if he can see my panty-clad ass. He should be paying more attention to his Zoom meeting.

"Erickson, could you excuse me for a minute, please? I will be right back." I turn to face him as he's swiping at the trackpad. I assume, or hope, that he's turning off the camera and microphone. Then he gets up, strides over to me, takes me by the shoulders and walks me backward until my back is against the wall. "What are you doing?" he growls.

I blink up at him, innocently. "Laundry. You're welcome."

He grips my arms as he stares down at my hard nipples through the thin fabric of my tank top. His nostrils flare. "You think it's funny to make me hard while I'm in a meeting?" His voice is so deep I don't even hear it with my ears—he's speaking directly to my reproductive system.

I reach for the hard length in front of me and stroke his balls and shaft through his pants. "I don't think it's funny at all."

He groans as he presses his hot erection into my hand. "Claire..." he whispers. He's trying to sound forceful, but we both know who has all the power right now. "I have to get back to the..." He struggles to find the word he was looking for, and that's my cue to unbuckle his belt as quickly as possible.

"Me. You have to get back to *me*, Mr. Barber."

"Multi...billion dollar...fuck."

My hand slips inside his underwear, his pants drop around his ankles, and his head falls back.

"Grady. You're so hard." He is. So hard. I'm actually concerned.

He grabs my ass and then hikes my leg up so I can wrap it around the back of his. "You like making me this hard in the middle of a meeting?"

"Yes." I make a circle with my thumb and index finger, stroking up and down his shaft, oh so delicately, twisting when I get back up to the most sensitive part. And then I grip him hard with my whole hand, squeeze and release, squeeze and release.

"Yeah? You like having control of my cock when I'm trying to work?"

"No. I think it's rude of you to work when I'm trying to make you hard."

Well, that does it.

I feel Grady's entire body clench up before I get a swift spank to my left cheek. He pulls my hand out from his boxer briefs and spins me around to face the wall. Gripping my wrists above my head with one hand, he tugs my panties down with the other.

"You want my cock that badly, huh?"

"Yeah. I missed it." I feel the hot tip at my entrance. Flattening my palms against the wall, I push away and press back into him.

He takes a fistful of my ponytail, gives it a firm tug, grips my hip, and then pushes into me, moaning. I am so wet and swollen, but either he's gotten bigger or I've gotten tighter since the last time he was inside of me. The sting of his thrusts are startling and exquisite, and I cry out every time.

"I missed...every...part of you," he grits out with each penetration. "But I...could have...waited."

I reach down to take his hand from my hip and slide it up, holding it against my breast. What I mean by that is *no, you couldn't have*, but I'm breathing too hard to say it out loud. I push back against him, and his thrusts become more frantic. His trousers are still around his ankles and his belt buckle keeps jingling. He grabs me by my waist and pulls me into him every time he plunges into me. I am an ecstatic, lustful goddess. He is panting and wild, and he sounds more desperate than I ever imagined he could be.

I feel so much love for him because I made him feel this way. I made Grady lose control, and I want to give him everything in return. I chant his name, over and over, like a prayer, until he slams into me with an intense shudder, releasing everything into me as he howls. So much rage and sadness and strength and vulnerability in one sound.

I'm still leaning against the wall, and he's bracing himself against it too, draped around me, heaving behind me. He rests his cheek against my shoulder. I don't even know how much time has passed, but that was a glorious, unpredicted fuck tornado, and I do not even care if my roast chicken has dried out.

"Baby," I whisper, staying as still as possible until he pulls out and I feel his hot cum spill down the inside of my thigh.

I used to watch him run races in high school. It was

so beautiful, the way he'd arch his neck back and pace around with his hands on his hips, catching his breath after a sprint. He's not doing that now. He's still bracing himself against the wall. Not completely spent, but also nothing like the intensely focused businessman who was staring at his computer monitor a few minutes ago.

He drops his forehead to the back of my neck and wraps his arms around my waist. "Jesus," he lets out on an exhale. "What are you doing to me?" It's a real question that he's asking. More to himself than to me. I wish he didn't sound so apprehensive, or I'd tell him that was just the appetizer.

I no longer feel him touching me. I pull my panties up and grab the tea towel from the laundry basket, handing it to him. "It's not dirty," I tell him.

"Thank you." He's about as disheveled as I've ever seen him. But just as beautiful as he always was after running a race.

"I love you." I stand on my tiptoes to kiss his cheek while he's cleaning himself up.

"I love you," he says. A statement. "But I need you to leave so I can pull myself together." He isn't cold, but he is very matter-of-fact.

"Okay." I refrain from saying I'm sorry—because I'm not. We both needed a good fuck tornado. I'm confident that Erickson will understand.

He tosses the towel back into the laundry basket and pulls up his underwear and pants. Even the way he puts clothes *on* is sexy.

"Did you want me to bring you a clean pair of—"

"No, I'm good. C'mere." He jerks his head while buckling his belt.

I approach him like a classy grown-up who totally didn't just walk in here in her underwear during his Zoom meeting. A classy grown-up who still has his semen dripping down her leg.

He holds my chin and leans down to give me a quick kiss on the lips. "That was hot."

"It was, wasn't it?"

He tucks in his shirt and combs his fingers through his hair. "Get outta here. Start boiling the linguine in twenty minutes." He gives me a pat on the bum as I walk away. "Close the door behind yourself."

"Yes, sir!"

Twenty-three minutes later, I hear Grady call out from his office, "Claire Sweeney. Can you come in here for a minute, please?"

Dammit, the linguine needs two more minutes. "Two minutes!"

I get no response.

Fine. If he's moping, he'll understand once he swirls my perfectly al dente noodles around his fork and tastes my lemon butter sauce.

After draining the linguine and coating it in sauce, I remove my apron and return to his office—fully dressed in jeans and a T-shirt.

He's sitting in his desk chair, which is facing the window, his back to the desk and the door.

I rap on the doorframe. "What's up? Dinner's ready."

"Miss Sweeney..."

"Mr. Barber..."

"I've been expecting you..." He continues staring out the window as he talks, like a Bond villain.

"Yeah, well. I live here. How was your meeting?"

He spins around in his chair dramatically. In his hand is a Nerf gun. It's pointed at me.

I hold up my hands. "I come in peace."

"Oh, Little Sweeney. That is not how you come." He shoots me with a foam dart. Straight to the heart. He hasn't changed at all. "Meeting went fine. I told Erickson I had to help you unload things from the car."

I snicker. "More like I helped *you* unload."

Grady doesn't laugh. He puts the gun down on his desk and pats his lap. "Get over here."

I do. I go over to him and sit on his lap. "Like I said, dinner is ready."

"And I can't wait to eat it." He rubs my back and my thigh, gazing at me thoughtfully.

"What's up?"

"I just want to make sure I say this the right way..."

Oh, here we go. He's going to kick me to the curb.

"I love you. I love living with you so far. But this is a huge merger... I hope you take it for the compliment that it is that you drive me crazy and you made me lose my mind today, and it would not be okay for me to screw up a multibillion-dollar business because I can't keep my hands off of you. So that can't happen again. Not when I tell you I'm working. Okay?"

I nod. "Okay." I guess if he's going to reject my future attempts at seducing him in his home office, then that's the way to do it. I stand up, reach for the Nerf gun, and point it at his heart.

He holds up his hands. "And what do you need from me?"

"I need you to eat dinner with me on the patio, have a drink with me by the water, and then watch three episodes of a show of my choice with me—while snuggling."

He grimaces.

I shoot him in the chest.

"Okay," he says, grinning and clutching at his heart. "You got me."

And I think I really do.

Chapter 25

Bloomed to Fail

CLAIRE

THIS DOESN'T FEEL RIGHT.

I roll the tiny ball of marshmallow between my thumb and forefinger. This will not melt properly. This is not s'more-worthy.

"I'm thinking maybe Damien should start with something fun. Something loud to bring the energy. Would that be too distracting?" Vera pontificates.

I ignore her. I'm not doing half as good a job as she's doing ignoring me while she goes over Damien's set list for this morning. At least she's doing a good job at something.

It's a week before my grand reopening. We're doing a trial run today. It's an invite-only preview event for family and friends to try some of my new and old favorites on the revamped nostalgic Sweet Treats on Main menu.

Normally I'd do this three days before the official reopening, but it's also operating as a goodbye party of sorts for Grady. He has to go back to New York tomorrow morning. He'll only be gone for a week before making a quick trip home for the reopening event, but it's balls to the wall with the merger now, so he won't be able to make it to Beacon Harbor very often for a while. With my business starting up again, I won't have much time to visit him. And I certainly don't have a staff in place that I can hand things off to if I ever do need a break...

But I don't have time to think about that now.

Because my guests will start arriving in forty-five minutes, and something isn't right.

I taste the marshmallow. Nope. Something is definitely off.

"Or maybe I'll just have him strum something mellow. He's so good at melancholy. I don't know what he has to be sad about when he looks like that, but..." Vera mumbles and shakes her head at no one. Since apparently it's just her alone with her thoughts of Damien back here.

This was the *one* task I delegated to Vera that involved a recipe because it's incredibly simple, but it had to be made properly yesterday so it could set overnight. I don't have time to make more marshmallows now. They're a key ingredient in a third of my menu, and I do not want to serve store-bought marshmallows. So I'm giving them a light dusting of powdered sugar in the hopes that it will solve all my problems.

"But I don't want to start off on a sad note. Maybe a

love song? Like one where love works out, not one of the mopey ones about the end of a relationship."

I cut a small piece of the marshmallow I just dusted with powdered sugar, but it's not even a clean slice because the texture's all wrong. I take a bite. Nope.

Now it's a poorly bloomed gelatin marshmallow covered in sweet white powder.

"No, I think we need upbeat energy. I'll tell Damien to—"

I slam my knife down on the counter. "Will you stop?! I'm opening a bakery, not a concert hall."

She looks shocked.

I am shocked. "Vera. I'm so sorry—"

Vera holds up her hands. I try to talk again, but she insists with her hands that I should remain quiet. She approaches me, her arms open wide, and takes me into a giant hug. "No. Claire Bear. I'm sorry. That guy makes me crazy even when he isn't around. I'm here. I'm here for you. What's going on?"

"What's going on is the gelatin must not have bloomed properly before you mixed the rest of the ingredients. I have cookies that need to go in the oven. I have to put the finishing touches on three cakes. The products need to be in the display cases before the doors open. I don't know if the coffee is ready. I can't even make a clean cut with this knife. I need to know that if I have to use store-bought marshmallows for my s'mores that I have enough of them, that I have the right flavors—and if I don't, then I need you to run out and buy some for me immediately, and I shouldn't have to ask you to do that because you're my assistant but you're not assisting me." I finally take a breath. "I thought we streamlined this process. I'm doing more simple recipes because it's supposed to make everything easier and better, but you're obsessing over my boyfriend's brother—which, yes, I do very much want you to hook up with him, just not until after I have successfully reopened my bakery."

Vera has been nodding, arms crossed over her chest, as if I'm making some very good points. The chunky blue highlights in her hair have faded to an almost gray color, but I'm going to have all gray hairs a week from now at this rate.

"*'I see,' she said as she carefully mulled over the best way to phrase this to her best friend and boss...*"

"They'll be here in forty minutes, Vera! I don't have time for documentary narration!"

"Yeah. I fucked up. I didn't wait for the gelatin to absorb—"

"Bloom."

"Bloom. I rushed the process. I'm sorry."

"You should have told me yesterday so I could have made more."

"I should have. Yes. Also, I sharpened one of your knives, like you asked. But it wasn't that one."

I huff out a breath. "Well, you have to put it in the right place."

"I know. I know!" she says, rushing to find the knife that I should be cutting with. She finds it and presents it to me.

"What are you giving me the handle for?! Just stab me with it and put me out of my misery!"

Vera gives me a look. She's done being Sympathetic

Employee Vera. She tells me with a Best Friend Vera look that I'm being a ridiculous, spazzy drama queen.

"Honey, this is why we do a dry run. It's a rehearsal. We will make adjustments based on what we learn today." She tries a piece of the marshmallow and moans into her own mouth. "This is *divine*. What are you talking about?"

"It's not divine. It's satisfactory. It's the wrong consistency, it won't melt properly, it's not s'more-worthy. It certainly isn't handshake-worthy! I want everything to be perfect!"

"Babe. It's just friends and family today. We all love and support you. Everyone who's going to be here today is going to be here for the reopening too."

"Not everyone," I murmur as I stomp over to my shelves to find my bags of marshmallows—which Vera should be doing.

"Ohhhh," she says, as if she's finally remembered how to speak the best-friend language we've been speaking to each other since we were kids.

"I mean, I want everyone to be impressed, but he funded this whole renovation and I just want to get everything right."

"Claire. He's going to love all of it. And more importantly, he loves *you*."

As if on cue, my cell phone rings and it's Grady. If he's calling to tell me he can't make it today, I will lose it. I answer hesitantly, "Hi."

"Hey, babe. I'm out back." Suddenly, my heart is racing for a different reason. I head over to the back door to unlock it, but he stops me with his tone. "Don't open it yet. I have company."

"Company? What do you—"

"He means me, cupcake!" Crabby is always yelling, but his attempt at sounding more masculine than Grady throws him into a coughing fit.

"I'm putting you on speakerphone," Grady says.

"Crabby, we aren't open yet."

"Yeah, well, what's this dingus doing here, then?!"

"This dingus was invited by his girlfriend," I hear Grady explain calmly. "The owner of this fine establishment."

"This is discrimination!"

"How am I discriminating against you, Crabby?" I ask, grinning and shaking my head.

"You don't like old people. Or bald people. Or short people. Or old, short, bald people. I want your cookies, and you won't let me have them! I've got my apple box in the trunk of my car! I will take it out front, stand on it, and start a petition if you don't let me in now so I can get the first taste of your new chocolate chip cookies!"

Vera and I share a look and laugh. "Gosh. I don't know if you chose the right guy, Claire Bear," she mumbles. "That one's got some big ol' rum balls on him."

"Clarence, I thought we cleared this up at the Sea Dog the other week."

"Pah! That was before I found out you shacked up with Mr. Suit."

Oh boy.

"Claire..." I can tell Grady's phone is pressed up against his ear again.

"Yeah?"

"Remember that year my brother and I were trick-or-treating? We got to your house, and Damien threatened to steal all the candy from the bowl inside your front door. And I told you not to open the door..."

I know exactly what he's talking about. Grady was a vampire that year. I don't have time to think about how badly I wanted him to take a bite out of me, but I know what he wants me to do.

"I remember."

"Say when..." Grady says. His voice sounds younger, and I can hear his grin through the phone.

I dash over to the kitchen door. "Now!" I unlock the door and pull it open.

Grady sprints toward me from the parking lot, his long strides graceful and beautiful. Crabby Crawford, shockingly, is right on his heels. His feet barely leave the ground. He's speed walking. His already wrinkled face is all screwed up in concentration, and he's muttering something fierce.

Grady glides through the screen door and the wooden one. I close and lock it right behind him. We rush back to the counter so we don't have to deal with the angry old man who's banging on everything he can bang on out there. We laugh and hold each other. A lock of hair falls over his forehead, the way it used to when he ran races in high school. Only this time I get to give in to my desire and move it out of the way with my fingers. Just like he can now wipe the flour from my face.

"Hey," he whispers.

"Hey."

He presses his lips to mine, and suddenly things don't feel as bad as they did five minutes ago.

"How are things going in here?" Grady asks, looking around.

"Try this," Vera says, offering him a piece of marshmallow on a fork.

Grady's beautiful lips wrap around my marshmallow, and he swallows. "That is delicious."

I know Grady well enough to know that he means it, that he's not just being nice. But I know myself well enough to know that *delicious* isn't good enough. I want it to be perfect.

"Well, try telling her that. This is the best marshmallow I've ever tasted. I followed her recipe almost exactly, and she thinks it's a *disaster*," Vera says, throwing that last word in my direction.

Grady places his hands on my shoulders and deftly turns me away from Vera. He encourages me to look up into his eyes. "This isn't going how you wanted it to go?" I shake my head. He nods. "That's the point of today. It's not about getting everything exactly right. It's to run through, observe, and then make adjustments."

"That's what I said..." Vera sings out from behind me.

"Have you figured out what you need to do?" His question is laced with meaning.

A meaning that Vera would not understand.

"Yeah. I know what I need to do. I just can't do it yet."

"Okay. You'll figure it out. I believe in you. Now get 'er done."

This might be Grady's greatest gift that he's given

me. Not the money, even though the money is great. Not the sex. Okay, maybe the sex. But tied with that gift is that easy, winning way he has. When I was awkward and nervous and didn't believe in myself, I always wanted just a taste of that. Just to try it on for a little bit, like one of those ancient stories when someone finds a magic cloak and gets to become something they aren't for a day.

"What can I do to help?"

I have a running list in my head of things I need help with. Enjoying his warm embrace was comforting and helpful. But he's not going to be here the morning of the opening. He won't be here for so many mornings. So I don't want to get used to relying on him.

I just want to appreciate him when he's here.

I tighten my apron straps.

"Why don't you get the coffee set up out front? I got this."

Chapter 26

Recipe for Disaster: The Shellfish Edition

GRADY

It seems like only yesterday I was picking up my own welcome-home cake at this bakery and seeing my best friend's little sister for the first time in over a decade. Now I'm here again, greeting our family and friends in the capacity of Claire's boyfriend so that they can say goodbye-for-now to me and celebrate the renovation that I funded. Or, if they're over the age of two hundred and fifty, they're here to eat free cookies and give me the ol' stink eye while eagerly awaiting my departure so they can put their ancient moves on my live-in girlfriend.

Grumpy Gus, or Nasty Neville, or Crabby Clawfoot —whatever his name is—has been staring me down from the corner of the room ever since I let him in. I push the serving cart over to him. "May I offer you some coffee or tea, Mr. Crawford?" I ask in my most butler-y tone. "A mimosa, perhaps?"

"Pah! You think I was born yesterday? I'm not gonna fill up on coffee so there's no room for cookies. Keep it movin', hot shot."

"Very well, sir." I keep *movin'* the cart and serve a few more gracious attendees before making my way to the other corner of the front-of-house area. I have my business phone in my back pocket and it's been vibrating with email and text notifications ever since I got here, but I've refrained from checking it whenever I'm around Claire. I take it out so I can set it to Silent, but there's a text from Alice telling me to check an email chain ASAP so the IT team can get an answer. Scanning the email convo, I type up a quick reply, and now I'm done thinking about work for the next hour.

But I am not done thinking about creatures with hard shells. Damien has brought his lobsters because my mom has to drop him and my dad off at the beach for a training session after this. So that's fun. I've got two lobsters in one corner and a crab in the other. But I'm more worried about the friction between my brother and Vera creating so much heat they'll boil his prize racers.

"What—you're just going to ignore the set list I spent an hour working on this morning?" She frowns at him, holding up an open Moleskine notebook that he refuses to look at.

"Not that you asked, but I already know what I'll be playing, and it's based on the emotional needs of Muhammad Lobbee."

Vera stares at him, incredulous.

"Who the hell is Muhammad Lobbee?" I ask before she can form the words.

"*Crustaceous Clay* was the wrong moniker for him. My boy deserves the name of a champion."

I'm the first to admit that I don't understand much about women, but I do know that if my brother didn't have the face and hair and body and musical talent that he has, Vera would have kneed him in the balls by now.

Damien starts strumming the opening chords of "Eye of the Tiger," and while I appreciate that Claire herself is a fighter and that we're here to cheer her on... "No," I tell him. "Absolutely not. You are here to play quiet, pleasant café music, and that's it." I refrain from telling him I will throw his guitar into the street and drive over it ten times if he doesn't because I want this day to be as stress-free as possible for my girl.

Well...I glance over at Vera, who's telling Damien she told him so instead of helping Claire... I mean, I don't want it to be any more stressful than it already has been.

I'm about to go check on her when I see Crabby sneak into the kitchen. *Oh, hell no.* But my mom blocks me from heading back there with a teary hug.

"Oh, honey. I've gotten used to having you around, and now I'm going to miss you again." She sniffles.

"I promise I won't be a stranger, Mom. I'll be back to visit whenever I can. It's just going to be a—"

"A really busy period for a while," she finishes for me. "I know, I know." She gives me a little pat on the cheek. "That won't make me miss you any less."

"Well, I'll be checking in to make sure you and Chef Gordon are keeping Dad in line," I say as I pat my dad's shrinking belly. "You look ten times better than you did when I first got back."

"Yep. I've lost an inch and a half from my waist—and all the joy of grilling and eating," he mutters. "But thanks for bringing Chef Gordon into our lives, son. I had no idea there were so many different kinds of lettuce."

I stick around to listen to my mom lovingly berate my dad for being ungrateful while also somewhat agreeing with him in a way that makes me feel appreciated for my efforts.

But Claire is the only one who has my attention as soon as she makes her grand entrance from the kitchen—in her brand-new chef jacket with a redesigned logo that says **Little Sweeney's Sweet Treats on Main**, to match the new sign out front. I swear, she is just as radiant as she was when she descended the stairs in that Vera Wang gown in New York. She sets a cake down on the counter and looks so happy. I didn't know it could feel this good to make another person happy, but if I can take any credit for that smile, I'm as proud as I've ever been about any of the accomplishments I'm famous for.

Damien segues into an acoustic version of "Pour Some Sugar on Me," which is funny. I guess. And the focus of the room shifts to Claire and the amazing treats she's made for us. Jake removes her little baker's beret, puts her in a brotherly headlock, and gives her a noogie.

There's a good solid ten minutes of chaos-free celebration, love, and support in the room until we hear an officious rap at the front door. We all turn to find a studious little man with black-rimmed glasses and a clipboard who's making a constipated face as he tries to peer inside.

Claire graciously unlocks and opens the door, while I

stand right behind her. "Hi. I'm so sorry, but this is a private party. We aren't open."

"Good," the man says, pushing his glasses up the bridge of his nose. "Otherwise I'd have to shut you down."

Claire blinks once. "I'm sorry—who are you?"

With the flick of a wrist and two fingers, he presents his business card. "Preston Bellwether. From the health department. I'm the new inspector. I have an appointment with Claire Swoony."

"Sweeney," she corrects.

"Yes. The appointment is for right now."

Claire stares down at the card, at the man, back to the card again. "Okay, well, I'm Claire Sweeney, and I thought our appointment was on Tuesday."

"*Ohhhh, shiiiiiit,*" Vera whispers from behind us.

Claire and I both look back at her best friend, and there is absolutely no confusion about the source of the confusion now. "Mr. Bellwether—can I call you Preston?"

"No."

"I'm so sorry, but my assistant didn't inform me about this schedule change. Is it possible to—"

"No. I have to go out of town in two days. For one week. And I don't work tomorrow."

"But we're scheduled to open in a week, Preston," Vera says, as if she isn't the one who screwed this up.

"Well then, it sounds like we need to do the inspection now, doesn't it?"

I place a reassuring hand on Claire's tense shoulder

when she says cheerily, "Yes. Well. Come on in! The more the merrier."

The inspector steps inside. "Not if you're over capacity, it isn't."

"Well, we aren't. Would you like some coffee? S'mores? Cookies? Cake?"

"Are these live lobsters?" he asks, staring into the two open containers on the table behind my brother.

"They aren't just alive," Damien replies, without irony. "They're truly living—on the razor's edge." He punctuates that with a sweet guitar riff.

"You can't have live lobsters on display here. This bakery isn't rated for crustaceans."

"So, there are bakeries that *are* rated for crustaceans?" Vera asks with more curiosity than sass.

Claire shoots her a look.

"Those aren't just lobsters," my dad calls out. "They're hardshell precision racing machines," he adds, unhelpfully.

"But more importantly, they won't be here when the bakery is open for business," I assure Mr. Bellwether. "Maybe we should move on. I can guarantee you they won't be a problem."

"And you are?"

Is he kidding? "Grady Barber, sir," I inform him, offering my hand to shake. "I'm Claire's boyfriend."

It feels good to say it out loud, but Claire adds, "Grady Barber is one of my investors. In this bakery."

"Ah." Preston absorbs the information but gives no indication that my name or any of it means anything to him.

When he turns his attention to one of the food displays, Claire and I share a look and a shrug.

Helen and Bob Sweeney swoop in to distract our unexpected guest with talk of real estate and puffins, but they don't hold his attention for long because Jake bursts out of the restroom holding up a toilet handle.

"John's broken!" he announces.

"Aw, poor John," Mr. Sweeney jokes.

He is met with an epic eye roll from his wife, the likes of which Claire could only aspire to.

The love in this room really is overwhelming. The help and support from ninety percent of the people here is less than underwhelming. It is not the least bit whelming.

"Jake?! What did you do?!" Claire removes her beret herself this time and swipes at him with it.

"It just came off in my hand," he protests. "It's not a big deal. I'll grab my toolbox from the truck and fix it."

"Are you a licensed plumber?" Preston asks.

"No, I'm a firefighter."

"Is the toilet on fire?"

"Nah, I didn't have chili for breakfast today." Jake surveys everyone in the room, expecting laughter, applause, and a rim shot.

Honestly, it's tough for me to refrain from laughing. But I do. Because I'm here to support Claire, not her brother.

"I will get a licensed plumber here to fix this immediately," Claire tells the inspector as he makes notes on his clipboard.

"On a weekend? In this town? Unlikely," he says, shaking his head.

"Listen, I will fly someone in from the other side of the state if I have to, but it will be fixed by the end of day. Can we move this along?"

Preston looks up at me, vaguely confused by my sudden alpha-billionaire voice, which I only use in Beacon Harbor if I'm telling my girlfriend what to do in the bedroom or if I'm telling clipboard-carrying bureaucrats who's boss.

We're interrupted by another knock at the front door. I hold Claire's hand. I can see by her posture and expression that she's spiraling a little bit, and Vera is not being her usual World's Best BFF self. She's in Terrible Employee mode.

When we cautiously turn to look, we find the mayor outside the front door, chipper as ever, jogging in place, alternately waving enthusiastically and giving Claire the thumbs-up. Claire is not nearly as eager to speak to her as she was the last time we saw her at the beach, but we head over to let her in. Before reaching the door, Crabby appears out of nowhere, unlocks the door, and pokes his head out to say, "We aren't open, Mayor. This here event is for VIPs only. And you're not one of them."

To Stacy's credit, her permasmile doesn't falter for a second. "Oh, of course! I just wanted to say hello and offer my congratulations!" she calls out to us.

I block Crabby so Claire can greet the mayor. "Stacy, I'm so glad you could make it—I hope you got the invitation for the grand reopening. This one's for friends and family, and Clarence, and the health inspector, but we all think of you as a friend, of course."

Stacy enters, still jogging lightly in place. "Oh, Preston is here? Fantastic. Or terrible. It can sometimes be terrible. I hope it's fantastic."

"It's not," Preston remarks as he adjusts his tie.

My girl's massaging her temples, and the vibe in here is not festive. I signal to Damien to start playing guitar again. "Hey, these s'mores aren't going to eat themselves, everyone!" I call out to the guests. "Have s'more!" I give Stacy my full attention for a moment because I have a feeling I'm going to need a favor. "Stacy, can I interest you in a mimosa?"

She finally stands somewhat still. "Well, why not? I could use a little vitamin C and sugar to power up the run home."

"I'll need to see your kitchen now," Preston tells Claire.

"Yes, right this way." She gestures toward the door to the kitchen. "I'm confident you'll find everything in order back there, Mr. Bellwether."

I give her a little pat on the butt, letting her know that everything is in order back there too. And then I give her shoulder a little squeeze to let her know that I have her back. Reminding her that I'm here. Silently assuring her that I'm prepared to take care of anything she needs me to take care of before I leave.

Except...

"Raccoon," Preston says as soon as he enters the kitchen.

"What?" Claire looks around and covers her mouth,

muffling a long string of swear words that I've never heard her utter before—and honestly, I never even heard her brother say those things that time he stepped on a nail when we were in high school.

"You can't have a raccoon in here," he reprimands, as if she were harboring a fugitive.

There is indeed a large raccoon shuffling around, trying to find a place to hide. Worse yet, there is evidence of its attempts at eating anything it could get its weird little hands on. The back door to the alley is open, and the screen door isn't shut all the way.

"I have no idea how this happened," Claire says, her voice trembling. "That door was closed the last time I was in here."

The inspector is so busy scribbling notes and aggressively making Xs on his clipboard, he doesn't seem to need an explanation or to inspect anything further.

"What happened? Did Mark get in here?" Crabby says from behind me. "Outta my way, Suit." Crabby pushes past me, taking charge. "How'd you get in here, you little son of a gun?" he says to the raccoon in the corner. "Come on, buddy. Out ya get." He gestures for the raccoon to follow him, which it does, and leads him out the back door, pulling the screen door shut behind him. "Well, here's your problem right here," Crabby tells Claire. "The screen door doesn't automatically latch shut."

"Is *that* the problem?" I ask.

Ignoring me, Crabby continues. "Yeah, I can grab what you need from the hardware store in ten minutes and fix this for ya." He sniffs. "No big deal. I got this."

One look at Claire's watery eyes and I'm ready to throw the old man into the alley too. "Crabby. How did this happen?"

"Aw, that's just Mark," he explains with a dismissive wave. "I've been leaving one of Claire's cookies out for him on my back porch for the past few years, every evening. We both want the best. Nothin' wrong with that. But when the bakery was closed and you were both off gallivantin' around New York City, we had to make do without the best. So I tried leaving out store-bought snacks, but Mark wasn't havin' it." He rests his bony fingers on his bony hips, shaking his head. "So, he followed me here this morning, and I tossed him a few cookies earlier. He's just lonely and hungry—you know how it is. Yep. Guess the screen door didn't shut all the way. Or this other door. So...I can fix that. No worries."

Claire is holding her head in her hands, speechless.

"I'd just like to point out that this was not my fault," Vera mumbles. I didn't even notice her come in.

I shoot her a look that sends her back out front, tell Crabby to follow Mark out the back door, and then stay by Claire's side while the inspector lists off the series of violations and forms that need to be filled out before her bakery can reopen.

When Claire and I are left alone in her kitchen, she is still holding her head in her hands, still unable to speak.

"Babe, I'm going to take care of this. Okay?"

She just looks at me, shaking her head.

I take her in my arms. "Claire, I am going to take care of this. You are going to reopen in a week. Do you trust me?"

She sniffles and nods.

"Good." I kiss the top of her head and go back out front to pull Mayor Stacy aside. We both cross our arms in front of our chests and lean in. "Mayor," I say in a hushed voice, "let's say that inspection didn't go the way we'd hoped it would."

"Okay."

"And let's say that I'll say that everything will be fixed. Every *t* crossed, every *i* dotted. Before the end of day, no matter the cost."

"Yes, let's say that." She nods, stroking her chin.

"Let's also say that in order to get Preston Bellwether back here tomorrow for a follow-up inspection, I'd be happy to make a sizable donation to the library to make sure that happens. Double what you've been asking for. Can we say those things?"

She shifts her weight back and forth from one restless foot to another. "We can definitely say those things."

"Good. Then let us say those things." I sound vaguely like a priest saying a prayer, but I suppose I am answering two prayers at once—Claire's silent one and the mayor's very persistent one that she's been emailing me about for a month.

After sending Stacy off to finish her jog and do my bidding, I thank everyone for coming and ask them to leave. Including Vera, whose job is now to help Damien carry the lobsters back to my mom's car. I don't let anyone say goodbye to Claire because I don't want them to see how distraught she is. I would make everyone sign nondisclosure agreements, but these are our friends and family, so I just have to trust that they know not to mention anything other than how delicious Claire's treats tasted and how perfect the new decor is.

I fire off some texts to Alice, telling her to send a licensed plumber, a handyman, and a cleaning crew over here as soon as possible, no matter the cost. Then I roll my sleeves up as I enter the kitchen because I know how much Claire likes to see my veiny forearms. Also because I need to help her clean up this mess, which she has already started doing on her own.

"I guess there's no point in trying to get a plumber or a handyman here this week if the only health inspector in town is going to be out of town" is all she says, tossing muffins and cupcakes into a garbage bag because they might have raccoon germs on them. She pauses for a second, rubbing her temples. "And I can't push the reopening day either. Vera has been promoting it all over social media—it would just confuse people."

"Then there is a point, and he will be back to reinspect tomorrow," I inform her as I pick up a broom. "And you will reopen in a week. I am taking care of it. And so is Alice."

She slouches. "Grady...how much is that going to cost you?"

"A fortune," I say with a grin.

"I'm so sorry."

I lean the broom against a counter and take her into my arms again. "Don't be. That's what money is for, Claire. It's always been a number for me, sort of keeping score for something I wanted to accomplish. Now I get to use it to make sure you get to accomplish what you want too. What you made today was amazing. People love the new menu. So we had a few minor violations. And one major raccoon." I shrug, but it gets a little laugh out of her.

She sighs. "I can't believe I just froze like that today. That's so unlike me." She looks up at me as she steps away. "I don't know what I would have done if you hadn't been here."

"Well, I was here."

"I wish you'd be here for the opening."

"Me too. But I'm only going to miss the beginning. I'll be here before you close."

"Promise?" The way she's looking at me, holding that big garbage bag, she seems so young and vulnerable.

I wish I could promise her that. I wish I could promise her everything. But I can't. "I will do everything within my power to be here as soon as I can on opening day. And as you know, I am extremely powerful."

That doesn't get me another laugh, but I do get another hug.

I made a commitment to my company and all of my employees and all of Lynch's employees that this transition will be as fluid as possible. I made a commitment to helping Claire achieve her dream. I can't falter. I can't stop moving. I will protect what I've built and do everything I can not to let anyone down. For now, that's the only promise I can make.

Chapter 27

Apps for Dessert

GRADY

"Hang on one second, babe. I just have to reply to this email, and then you will have my full attention." I quickly type up an email on my laptop without looking over at my desktop monitor first because I don't have to look at the screen to know that my beautiful, beloved virtual dinner date is frowning at me. I don't enjoy making Claire wait, unless it's part of a carefully planned edging technique that I can eventually pay off—in person. But I really do have to respond to this email ASAP. And then she really will have my full attention.

That's what being a CEO is, for the most part. Choosing who and what will get my attention, when. Making decisions. Calculating risk. Is this something that I can fix if things devolve, or do I need to find a solution now before it becomes a bigger problem?

I am confident that I can still turn things around for us tonight, so the email gets answered, and then I close the laptop. I've been eating dinner at my desk in my home office, and Claire and I were having a very pleasant long-distance dinner date via my private video-call app for all of fifteen minutes before my phone started blowing up. "You were saying? How did the *Gilmore Girls* reunion end—did the old guy finally start wearing his baseball cap the right way?"

If there wasn't an iPad, a computer screen, and about three hundred fifty miles between us, I would be wiping ice water from my face right now.

"His name is Luke, and he is not an old guy! You know what, I'm done eating. You're obviously too busy for this. And it's fine, so let's just call it a night." She dabs at her luscious lips and then balls up her napkin and tosses it at the iPad camera.

"Oh, is it *fine*, Little Sweeney? I know his name is Luke. It's Luke Danes. I know that because I once made the mistake of asking you what you liked so much about that show, and you listed off about fifty reasons in a ranty monologue."

Her expression softens a little. "You remember that?"

"There isn't anything about you that's forgettable, Claire. Except for your obsession with that Jess guy. I had to block that from my memory."

She grins. "I was just trying to make you jealous. I'm happy to hear that it worked."

As I'm turning my business phone over so I can't see the notifications, I spot a text from Alice. I said I'd give

Claire my full attention, but Alice wouldn't text me after eight if it wasn't important. So I read the text. And then I type my reply.

"Okay, well, I have to do laundry, so..."

"Claire. Do not end this call."

She gets up from her stool at the kitchen counter and takes her dishes over to the sink. "It's fine!" she calls out. I can't see her anymore.

"I am putting the phone away now. Come on. We haven't had dessert yet...Claire."

She returns to stand in front of the iPad on the counter. "I have to wash some things before I leave for the bakery tomorrow morning. I'm tired anyway, so..."

"You brought laundry from the bakery home? Why didn't you have the laundry service I set up for you take it?"

She waves her hands around, trying to dismiss me, but I will not be dismissed. "I'm talking about clothes that I wear around the house."

"That's what the housekeeper is for. That's why I hired all of these people, Claire, so you have more free time."

"I'm not comfortable letting other people launder my panties, okay? Maybe I never will be."

Christ. Just hearing her talk about her panties, even laundering them, does something to me. I am so in love. "Babe. I have a very important question to ask you."

She's pouting. She's pouting in that way that only girlfriends who know you're crazy about them pout. "What?"

"Did you charge that thing I got for you before I left, and did you download the app and then bind the device to it?"

She crosses her arms at her chest and tries to frown. She's wearing an old, worn-out T-shirt from our high school that she's cropped. It hugs her tits and bares her midriff, and I can't see all of her and it is very frustrating. "That's three questions. Yes, I charged it and I paired it with the app."

"Binded it. It's called device binding."

"That's ridiculous."

"I didn't make it up. Go get it."

"I have to do my laundry."

"You will do your laundry. First, you will place the device where it belongs, then you will do whatever you need to do with your hands, and I will ensure that you feel good while doing it."

"But you don't want to use the video-chat feature that's in the app, and I don't want to carry around my iPad."

"I have a solution for that."

"Oh, really? So do I. You could come home."

"Claire. You know I can't come home yet. Do you want to argue about this now, or do you want to argue with me while you're doing laundry and I'm controlling your pleasure?"

"Those are my options?"

I must look like I'm about to pick up my monitor and throw it out the window.

"Fine! I will go upstairs and get it. I'll text you when

it's in place." She ends the video call before I can tell her that I want to watch her put it in place.

I'm just mad that I didn't think to have someone develop a smart-control app *and* a remote-control wearable panty vibrator sooner so I don't have to rely on commercial technology. But my tech guy will have a prototype ready next week. And fortunately, I did have a top-notch security system installed as soon as we took possession of the house.

I have never been so eager to open a home-security app. I pull it up on my iPad instead of my personal phone. So I have a bigger screen to look at, but also because I'll have to use the app on my phone to control something else. As I carry it over to the sofa in my home office, I marvel at how quickly I have access to every camera on the inside and outside of the house in Beacon Harbor. *Our* house. Impatiently, I scan through the different screens, passing through the living room, the kitchen, the dining room, until I can see the master bedroom. *Our* bedroom. The light is on in the adjoining bathroom.

There's a microphone icon on the screen. I tap it and lean in closer to the mic on my iPad. "Claire. You in the bathroom?"

She cautiously pokes her head out of the bathroom door and scans the room for me. She looks like a cat who just heard her person's voice. So. Cute.

"I'm not there. Wish I were. I'm watching you on the security system now."

She arches her eyebrows as she looks up at the small camera that's installed on the ceiling. "Wait, what?" She walks out holding the small pink silicone vibrator in the palm of her hand, the way she'd hold up a cupcake or a muffin. As she figures out what's happening, though, her hands form fists. "Are you kidding me?"

Before she can wind herself up, I jump in: "I will only ever do this when you're at home if you say it's okay first. After this, that is. Is this okay?"

I can see on her pretty face and in her posture that she's intrigued and turned on by the thought of me watching her like this. And she should be. I love to look at her almost as much as I love to hear the things that come out of her mouth and eat the things that come out of her oven. Which is almost as much as I love to eat her—never mind.

She angles herself to face the camera directly. "Yes. It's okay."

"Good. Thank you. I'd like to watch you put that vibrator in place against your clit. May I do that?"

"Yes. You may." She unzips her jeans and wiggles out of them far enough to expose her panties and the tops of her thighs.

Now I can see her whole body. I can't see it up close, but I can see her belly and her hips. I can see the way that old T-shirt hugs her tits. My dick is already hard. I grab it, over my pants. Most of my conscious brain is focused on my girlfriend as she slides the vibe inside the front of her panties. Part of my brain is seriously considering investing most of my money into developing a portal that can get me back to my girl so I can be the one slipping my hand between her legs. Or sticking my face in there.

Claire is concentrating so hard as she makes adjustments, wiggling the thing around. Like this is an exact science. Like she's measuring out ingredients. Finally, she slips her hand out, squeezing her thighs together. "The apparatus has been properly placed, your highness," Claire says, smirking up at the camera.

"Aw, babe. You don't have to call me *your highness*. *Sir* will do just fine."

She guffaws at that.

"Now, get out your phone and open the app. You have to send me an invitation so I can control the device for you."

"Right." She pulls her jeans back up and then pulls the phone out from the back pocket. She zips and buttons up her jeans before opening up the pleasure app.

"What are you doing?"

"If I have tight jeans on it'll stay pressed up against me and I can use my hands for other things," she explains as she swipes at her phone.

I accept the invitation to control her device faster than I've ever accepted any invitation to anything in my life. With one hand. My other hand is undoing my own pants. "I'm going to start slow," I tell her. I tap the Smooth Operator Mode button. A quick and steady vibration.

She immediately jumps and lets out a yelp. "Oh!" She covers her mouth and giggles. "It tickles."

"Tickles, huh?" That will never do.

"But I like it. Leave it." She takes a seat at the edge of the bed and leans forward a bit, closing her eyes and smiling dreamily. Then she rocks back and forth, side to side.

Oh, baby. "Good?"

"Yeah." She squeezes her knees together, wiggles around.

"Those jeans are coming off later."

"We'll see," she says, so quietly I can barely hear her.

I touch the button to turn the vibrator off. I'm rewarded by her attention snapping back to the camera with a pout. "Hey!"

"The jeans will be coming off later. I want to see your ass, and I want to see you touching yourself."

She bites her bottom lip, and her expression reads equal parts annoyed, frustrated, and excited by that. "Fine," she huffs. "You're the boss."

"God, I love you," I say as I fist my dick.

"I love you too...sir."

I am so turned on by her telling me I'm the boss and calling me *sir* that I almost forget to use the app. I tap the button called Pants Rocket in Sight, After-Work Delight. If I weren't so fucking horny right now, I would be laughing so hard.

Claire lets out another little yelp in surprise.

"Tell me how that feels."

"It's a rhythmic tapping, but a vibrating tap."

I switch it to Good Vibrations and cycle back and forth between that and the tapping one. "You remember that night in my car?"

Her eyes are closed. She's swaying a little. "Of course I do." She casually strokes her belly and then sticks her hand up her shirt to cup her breast. She grins as she opens her eyes, forcing herself to stare at the camera. "Are you touching yourself now too?"

"'Course I am. Pretending it's your hand instead of mine."

"Am I stroking you nice and slow like I usually do in the beginning, or am I pumping you hard and fast the way you do it in the shower?" She massages her breast.

"Somewhere in between." I groan. "Let me see your beautiful tits, baby."

She smirks, that flirty, bratty little smirk. I may have the controls, but she has all the power right now, and she knows it. She flashes her tits at me and then hops up. "How was that?"

I am gritting my teeth. That was evil. "Never mind. Get back to work. Do your laundry." I punctuate that order with a vibrating punctuation mark. Smooth Operator again.

Her eyes flutter shut again, again she sways a little. She lifts up her T-shirt with one hand and circles her nipple with the fingertips of the other.

Good girl.

Then she walks out of view.

Bad girl. Very bad. "Hey. I can't see you."

I swipe through the camera views until I find the stairwell. She's holding on to the railing, stepping slowly. Instead of punishing her by turning the thing off again, I switch it to Beast Mode.

Claire screams, her spine goes straight as an arrow, and she grips onto the railing with both hands. "What is that?!"

"Karma. Keep moving."

I take it back to tapping. She shakes her head and giggles as she walks the rest of the way down the stairs.

"Where are you going?"

"I put the...the whatsit...the laundry in the...the laundry room already," she barely manages to say. I swipe to the living room camera. There she is. Holding on to the wall for support. "Do that vigorous one again," she says with a whiny voice I've never heard from her before. "Please."

"We'll work back up to that if you're a good girl."

She frowns up at the camera and then stomps across the room, through the dining room, to the kitchen and into the laundry room. I catch up with her through the security cameras. She's tossing panties and sweatpants and pajamas into the washing machine.

I try out Rock Me Ima Deus Mode.

Seriously, who came up with these names?

Claire looks like she is hit with a jolt of electricity. A jolt that she likes very much. She cries out and then moans.

"You like that?"

"Yeah."

"You stay in view so I can see you."

She rubs her lips together, nodding, eyes closed, gripping the edge of the washing machine.

"You need to add the detergent now."

She sighs and nods, reaches for the detergent, pours some into the dispenser drawer, slams it shut, and jabs at the control buttons.

"Okay. Now get back to the living room."

I switch it back to Smooth Operator Mode. She gasps and does as I tell her to do.

I'm there in the living room, watching her, before she arrives. "Stop right there."

She does.

"Get on your hands and knees."

She slowly lowers herself to a kneeling position on the rug, facing the camera. Then she angles herself away from the camera more when she gets onto her hands and knees, so I can see the curve of her amazing round ass. Her thighs and knees are locked together as she rocks her hips front and back, back and forth, side to side.

"Does that feel good, baby?" I'm gripping my cock harder, stroking with more intensity. If this were a setting, it would be Rub It.

"So good," she moans.

"You want more?"

"Yes. Please," she says, a satisfying desperation creeping into her voice.

I spend more than a few seconds on Yes, Daddy. I'm having trouble working the app given how hard I'm pumping my dick. I'm matching her Yes, Daddy with a Yes, Ma'am.

She whimpers.

God, I love it when she whimpers like that.

Fuck, I miss touching her.

God dammit, I miss that ass.

She loses the table pose and lowers herself onto her back, bending her legs and rocking her pelvis.

I can't find my voice at the moment, or I'd reprimand her for moving without me telling her to. So I turn it up to Fast and Furious. She cries out. Pressing one hand against the crotch of her jeans and tilting her pelvis up, she massages her breast with the other, vigorously. "Grady," she pleads. The vibration of her voice ups my dick pulling to Friction Impossible: Rogue Nutting.

"Take off your pants," I growl.

"Noooo," she whines.

I turn the vibrator off.

"No!" she yells. She yanks down her jeans, protesting with her face. I can see her panties now. I can see the outline of that thing beneath the fabric. Precum is leaking from my dick. I turn the vibe back on, and she cries out.

"Hold it in place with your hand," I command. She does, and the pleasure intensifies again. "Show me your tits with the other hand." She smooths her hand up her belly and then exposes her pert, hard nipples.

"That's my girl."

I'm so close. She's panting and seems unable to form words. I've never been able to watch her when she's like this before. Not with a full view of her. She is even sexier than I imagined, and it's driving me wild.

"When I'm with you again you're going to put that thing back into your panties, you're going to get on your knees, and you're going to suck my cock while I control all the pleasure your pussy feels." I can't even believe what I'm saying. I don't talk like this. "You want that, baby girl?"

"Yes! I want that so badly," she wails. "I miss you so much, Grady. I will suck the living daylights out of you when you get home!"

Jee.

Zus.

Christ.

I hit Beast Mode again for Claire and increase the fucking of my own hand to level ten—The Terminator.

I force my eyes to stay open for as long as possible until we both come, various electronic devices bringing us to absolute ecstasy together.

Hundreds of miles away, across the vast distance of our responsibilities, we actually come at the exact same time.

I wait until Claire has gone limp before turning off her device.

I hear nothing except our heavy breathing for a while.

Rolling her head around lazily, she drags her fingers through her hair and finally says, "Holy shit, Grady." She looks as dazed as I feel, and it's a beautiful sight.

"Yeah," I agree with a laugh. "Holy shit."

We're quiet again for a little while. As much as I wanted to be with her before, I'm dying to hold her right now. I didn't know it was possible to miss holding someone so much, even when you're looking at them.

"I really do miss you," she says, suddenly sounding so sad it breaks my heart. "So much." She rubs her chest. "It hurts."

"I miss you too, baby. So much. I'll be back soon."

She sighs and starts to slip her hand inside her panties.

"What do you think you're doing?"

"Are we not done?" she asks with a weak laugh.

"Not even close, Little Sweeney. I'm never going to

The Billionaire Is Back

be done with you. And your laundry certainly isn't done yet either."

I tap on Smooth Operator again.

Claire curses under her breath, but when she smiles up at the camera, she can't hide what she's thinking.

That she'll never be done with me either.

Chapter 28

Resting Batch Face

GRADY

"It's about discipline."

I'm sitting at one end of a massive oak conference table on the top floor of the office building owned by Relicteros Inc. Harrison Lynch, the man who is still technically the owner of Relicteros Inc. and the fine oak table, stands at the other end of it, stabbing at it with his index finger while glaring at me. Lynch is making an impassioned speech—well, it's impassioned for him—about what it takes to lead a large company.

"It's about maintaining control."

He's attacking me without attacking me. Very Sun Tzu *The Art of War*, boilerplate passive-aggressive board room tactics. He's an effective speaker—I'll give him that. But all of this talk of "discipline" and "control" has my mind wandering back to Claire. I want to open up that app on my phone. I picture her in a thong, pretending to search for dirty laundry. I imagine her bending over to pick up imaginary laundry outside the high-rise windows on a window-washer platform. She glances over her shoulder to roll her eyes at me. I should not find that sexy, but God damn it, I do.

I have to suppress a grin.

And I have to get my shit under control so I can give my follow-up speech.

Surprisingly, the board members of Fortune 500 companies tend to frown upon executives who address them with even a moderate hard-on.

My stomach drops and a sudden rush of adrenaline courses through my body.

I need to focus.

I can't fuck this up.

But I do want to pull my phone out. Not just for the app but because I want to text Claire, or call her, to see how her opening is going.

This didn't used to be a problem. I don't disagree with Lynch—it does take inhuman amounts of discipline and control to do what we do. I used to have a nearly bottomless well of it.

Now I can't sit in this meeting without risking bursting out into laughter or getting an erection.

Is this why it took me so long to go back home?

Am I bad at my job when I let the people I love back in Beacon Harbor into my world?

"That is why I'm asking you to reconsider this takeover," Lynch says in conclusion. He takes a moment to look around, making eye contact with every single person at this table except me, and then sits back down.

The atmosphere in this room is incredibly tense. To the left is Lynch's board, and behind him, seated on overflow chairs, crammed into the room, are his people. On my right is my executive team. All eyes turn from Lynch as they follow his glare to where I'm sitting. I don't match Lynch's hard stare. This part of it is as much a performance as anything. We're professional wrestlers in bespoke Italian suits. I let that grin I've been suppressing form. I can appear easy and relaxed on the outside, when inside I'm anything but. I stand up, button the front of my jacket. I know that my face will read as confident and relaxed, but I am putting on my armor. I tug at the cuffs of my shirt sleeves for good measure. I look at Lynch, and while keeping the easy grin on my face, I'm thinking *well played.*

But this is over.

I'm Grady fucking Barber. And your company is mine.

It's more of an affirmation for myself than the fundamental fact of the universe it used to be.

But I will myself to believe it.

I pause. I pause for an uncomfortably long time. Most people can't handle being the center of attention for this long without moving or saying something. I think I read somewhere that public speaking is terrifying for most people because it activates the circuits in our brain that make us feel like we're about to be eaten by a predator.

I smile at Lynch.

I'm fine with the silence of the attention.

Right now, I'm not a son or a brother or a best friend.

I am not a boyfriend.

Right now, I am the predator.

"Ladies and gentlemen. You're probably expecting me to dispute what Mr. Lynch has said here today. And while I disagree with many of his statements, the facts that he has presented—that I am in love and that it has changed me...that's all true."

There are some very satisfying murmurs and shifting around in seats.

"But where I disagree with Mr. Lynch is that it's not about me. It never was. This is about the future of your company and mine and what we can accomplish together. I am the leader you chose to bring us into the future. I am not the man I was—I am more. And now I want to show you what we can accomplish together."

And that's my cue to introduce my team and all the work I've gotten them to do over the past couple of weeks. Knockout presentation after knockout presentation. Concise, packed full of drama and data for Aston and his board to digest. If this goes right—and I know it will because I've put my team through relentless preparations—I won't have to do any more talking. I'm not defending myself. I'm on offense, proving that whatever distractions I'm accused of having now aren't affecting my work.

But that's a lie. I look over at my head of marketing, Erickson, who's detailing his strategy for post-acquisition. My face is relaxed in interest. But I want to check my watch so I can imagine what Claire is doing at her bakery right now. I want to text her how much I love her and how proud of her I am. The text I sent her earlier this morning isn't enough. Outwardly, I am a titan of industry, calm and in control as his team unleashes the perfect strategy. Inside I am a concerned boyfriend who's hoping his girlfriend's business is doing just as well as mine is. Wanting desperately to know how she's feeling and what's going on in her head. If there's flour on her face. Wishing I could be there to wipe it away with my thumb.

The lie wasn't that I agreed with Lynch that I've changed.

The lie was that I'm not worried that it will affect how I do business.

The lie was that I'm a better CEO for it.

I need to make sure that I can keep my focus, and I'm having real trouble doing that. Because everything I've built—my empire, the empire that also funds her business, the empire that can give her the kind of life that most of the kings and queens of antiquity could only dream of...that only continues if I'm perfect.

The presentations end, and I stand once more. "Thank you, everyone. I know we've discussed these things over the course of negotiations, but I hope you're as excited as I am to see them fully fleshed out and implemented."

I remove my armor, unbutton my suit jacket, and have to force myself not to collapse into my chair. In my mind, I was right on the edge of screwing this up. It tires me out in a way that is totally unfamiliar to me. I used to eat board meetings for breakfast. Now all I crave is scones and carrot cake muffins.

Aston looks to his left and right at his fellow board members, but there's no question in his eyes. Or theirs. They all agree on the same answer. The one that I want. Aston gets up to shake my hand. "I know I speak for everyone here when we say we can't wait to see you implement that plan."

There's applause from everyone, except for Lynch and the most loyal members of his team.

The meeting is adjourned, and I rise to shake hands and make eye contact with everyone.

Now I can give in and check my phone. I home in on notifications from Claire. I'm about to open and read them, mentally calculating how fast I can get to the airport and what time that will put me down in Maine and then the drive to Beacon Harbor.

"Grady, my boy," I hear behind me.

"Aston," I reply amiably. We're doing the father-son thing, I guess.

He gives me a pat on the back. "That was a fine presentation. Damn fine. But I have to say the way you've successfully parried and counterattacked some of the obstacles thrown in your way these last few weeks, that alone would have sold it for me." He looks back conspiratorially and then moves closer to me, saying in a quiet voice, "I'm glad you're on *our* side."

"I'm glad we can finally, *finally* be on the same side."

"Speaking of that, I'd like to connect you with our head of marketing. Sheila?"

A smart-looking woman in her midforties approaches. She has an angular haircut and square-framed glasses.

"Mr. Barber, this is Sheila Masterson."

"A pleasure, Ms. Masterson," I say, shaking her hand.

"Likewise, Mr. Barber," she says.

Aston places a hand on each of our arms. "You had

some questions about that marketing campaign we abandoned a few years ago. This is the woman to ask about that. Before you can move forward with your own campaign, I think you two need to talk."

"That campaign is central to our plan," I tell him.

"I know," Aston says, concerned. "But before you proceed, I think you need to know the full story."

I'm not one to believe that cell phone signals give you cancer or anything like that. But I can feel my phone radiating in my hand. It has formed its own gravitational field, and it's pulling me away, whispering, *Go to the airport, go into the sky to get to the sea to get to your girl.*

But the faces in front of me anchor me here.

Handle your business.

If you want to give that girl the world, you have to keep conquering it.

I put my phone back into my pocket.

"Of course. You have my full attention."

Chapter 29

Just a Cupcake Looking For Her Stud Muffin

CLAIRE

GRADY: Baby. You are magnificent, and I'm so proud of you. I hope this day feels like the dream it is. A dream you've made real. I'll be thinking about you today—more than you'll ever know. I love you. See you soon.

I READ the text a few more times before putting my phone back into my pocket, as if the more I read it, the truer it will become. It's still the same lovely message I received when I woke up this morning. But it's aging like bread rather than wine, since there hasn't been a follow-up. Several texts from me to Grady have gone without a reply, so I gave up sending them.

But today has felt like a dream. Like a lucid dream that I can control, only with the lingering sense that it isn't real. A sense that at some point, I'm going to wake up.

I stare at myself in the mirror here, in the little public bathroom in my bakery. It has new wallpaper with cupcakes all over it, and it's the cutest, happiest little bathroom I've ever been in. There's a smudge of flour on my forehead, which I consider leaving there for Grady to wipe away when he gets here.

The opening went as well as I could have ever hoped. My baking, decorating, and presentation were all perfect. Vera didn't screw up anything for once. All the wildlife of Beacon Harbor remained outside. The whole town came and cleaned out everything I had to offer. They even paid for it too! And many just hung around because it's such a pleasant, comfortable place to be. Who knew I'd been repelling people by forcing them to pronounce French words?

I got a double thumbs-up from the mayor right after she spurned her juice cleanse to partake in a strawberry–cream cheese Danish. "Claire Sweeney," she said. "This...is the best Danish I have ever had in my entire life. You are a bona fide treasure." Before leaving to run back to her office, she told me that even if Grady hadn't agreed to give a speech at the end of the summer, she would want me to be the official pastry chef for the annual Shellibration. It felt good.

I take a deep breath, possibly the first full one I've managed since before dawn today. I do feel good. Just unsettled.

No, not unsettled—incomplete.

"I own and operate a successful bakery business," I

say out loud, very quietly, to my reflection. It has been ages since I did these affirmations, it seems. "My bakery attracts the perfect clientele." I can hear laughter outside the door, and it makes me smile. It doesn't feel quite right saying these affirmations anymore. Not because they're untrue—just the opposite. They feel like cold, hard facts. I might as well be saying *A day is twenty-four hours long* or *Water freezes at thirty-two degrees Fahrenheit*. I should probably move on to keeping a gratitude journal now.

Just for fun, I say to myself, "I deserve and attract the love of a wonderful, top-notch man who appreciates my talents and supports my aspirations."

It's tough to get a notch topper than the boy you've had a crush on your whole life, who's now a billionaire who fell for you and notches you exclusively. And I wouldn't be saying these things in the perfectly decorated little bathroom of my successful bakery business if he wasn't always ready to place a gentle, supporting hand on my aspirations—or give them a quick little spank if that's what my aspirations were asking for.

It feels like a fact. Mostly. But it's not as cut and dry as the other ones. There's still a little hope and dream left in there to be squeezed out of it.

I wipe the flour from my forehead before rejoining the dwindling party. At this point, it's my parents, Jake, and Vera. They are still here, I know, because they're concerned that if they leave before Grady arrives, he has officially missed the opening. As long as I stay open and there are still people around, there's still a chance. Crabby waited around forever because he was hoping to be my knight in rusting armor if Grady didn't show up, but he finally had to get to the hardware store when his shift started. And I have to wrap up an interview I've been doing with an adorable girl who's working as an intern for the *Beacon Harbor Register*.

I spot Maisy talking to my mom, over by the coffee stand. Maisy is tilting her head and nodding while holding her phone in front of her to record a voice memo, and my mom is gesticulating wildly, probably telling her about the time she found me baking cookies at midnight when I was ten. I join them just as my mom says, "And hopefully Grady will be putting a bun in her oven soon—wouldn't that be wonderful?!" She rubs my belly.

"Please don't put that in the article," I say to Maisy.

"I've got plenty of other anecdotal material," she replies, smiling. "Can I get a quote from you, Mr. Sweeney?" she asks my dad.

"You sure can." He puts his arm around me and says, "The only thing cuter than a puffin is Claire Sweeney's muffin."

"Please don't put that in the article either."

"But it's true!" My dad squeezes my cheeks. "Look at those cheeks. My daughter's got the sweetest cheeks."

"Okay." I step away from him. "Thanks for coming, you guys. You probably need to get back to work..."

"Oh, we wouldn't have missed this for the world," my mom says, hugging me. "Not that it isn't a huge deal if anyone were to miss this for a very good and unavoidable reason."

"Do you think I could get a quote from Mr. Barber via email?" Maisy asks politely.

"I'm sure that can be arranged. I'll give him your information.'

"There you are!" a middle-aged woman calls out to Maisy. "I'm double-parked."

I recognize her as someone who's come in here before.

"Mom!" Maisy mutters. "I told you to text me when you're out front!"

"Well, I wanted to see if there are any s'mores left. I heard from three different people that they're out of this world, but I see I'm out of luck."

"Oh, well, we'll have fresh ones tomorrow."

"Martha!" my mom calls out, even though she's right beside her. "Great to see you! How's the job hunt?"

Maisy's mom frowns. "You'd think more local businesses would be looking for a competent, reliable woman of a certain age who's a fast learner, proficient in QuickBooks, excellent at multitasking and organization, with an MBA in wife and motherhood." She throws her hands up in the air. "I gotta wait for all the kids to go back to school before they'll even bring me in for an interview. Meanwhile I'm trying every recipe on the internet."

"If you find a job before I do, I'll be so mad," Maisy says to her mother. "But at least Dad and I will get a chance to lose some weight if you're out of the house more."

I glance over at Vera, who's glued to her phone. I'm not hiring yet, but I file away this conversation in the back of my mind.

As my parents, Maisy, and her mom leave, Jake comes over to knock my beret off my head and give me yet another noogie. "Not a bad turnout, asshole. Not bad at all."

I swat him away. "Sorry I don't have any leftovers for you to take back to the station today, asshat."

"Aw, no worries, asshole. I do gotta head over there now, though." He wraps a big, beefy arm around my shoulder. "You good?"

"Yeah. I'm good."

He studies my face and sighs—a big-brother sigh. "If I didn't love that guy so much, I'd kick his ass."

I smile, a brave smile. "If I didn't love him so much, I'd love to see that."

"I'm sure he had a good reason."

"For sure. Get outta here."

"I'm gettin'. Congratulations, though. For real."

I wave him off. I can't deal with any more sincerity from my older brother right now, or I will burst into tears.

I sneak up behind Vera, who's still staring at her phone. "Who's texting you? Let me guess—is it time for lobster practice?"

She slips her phone into her pocket. "I don't have to go. You want me to stay, right? I'm staying with you," Vera says. She's trying to sound casual, but she's clearly worried about me.

"Nope. We've already cleaned up for the day—there's nothing else to do here. Go to the beach. Have fun. Train some lobsters. I need to work on the cake design. You know. For when Muhammad Lobbee finally wins."

"Ugh. There's still time to change that name. Are you sure, though?" She gives my hand a squeeze.

I shrug. I shrug so nonchalantly, how can she not see

how there's absolutely no *chalance* here and hence no need to be worried. "Yeah, absolutely. I'll be here working on the designs. No problem."

"*'Okay. You call me if you need me,' she told her best friend, really meaning it because she loves her and is super proud of her for being such a badass,*" Vera says.

I roll my eyes, which helps restrain the tears that are threatening to shoot out at her. "Yeah, yeah. Thanks for everything, bestie." I hug Vera tightly before letting her go.

Returning to the kitchen, I open a cupboard and retrieve the cupcake I saved for myself. I saved a carrot cake muffin for Grady. I just might have to eat it if he doesn't show up soon.

I carry my treat back out to the store, automatically reaching out to flip the **Open** sign to **Closed** and lock the door. But I stop myself. I may not have any fresh treats left to sell, but I am, technically, still open. I take a seat at a small table by the window, glancing out ever so subtly, looking up and down and across the street. No limos pulling up. No billionaires running down the block like Tom Cruise at the end of every movie ever.

Gazing over at the original Sweet Treats sign that hangs on the wall behind the counter, I breathe a sigh of relief and acknowledge that it's done. I've done it. My bakery reopening was a success. Buddy and Ruthie would have been pleased if they'd been able to make it up from Florida.

My store is now empty, and my heart is mostly full. But my stomach is definitely empty, and I'm salivating for this red velvet cupcake. The universally acknowledged snack choice of ladies who eat their feelings.

It's perfect.

Not perfect in the perfectionist sense. It's a perfect cupcake. It's pretty, and it makes me happy to look at and to eat. That's what cupcakes are for.

But I myself am not a cupcake. As sweet as I'm capable of being and as much as I do like to make people happy, I am not consistently perfect or cheerful. And I don't have to be. I don't want to be sad today, but I can't pretend that I'm not. I refuse to use the word *disappointed* because I really hate that word, but the Resignation Plane has been circling overhead for hours and it's about to come in for a landing. I think it's not just Grady that I miss, it's the foolish optimism I had for a little while that we could actually make a relationship work.

I whisper one more affirmation, one more quiet bargain with the future, somewhere between hope and a promise.

"Grady will always come back to me."

Chapter 30

Sir Texts-a-Lot, Grady Got Back

GRADY

I KNOW JUST about every fact there is to know about human psychology. I use this knowledge every day in business. I know that by design we habituate to our surroundings. Things that seemed novel to us, exciting and interesting, become mundane so that we can focus on the next thing we need or the next threat coming toward us. It is a constant battle to not get used to all the abundance that I have, to appreciate it all to the fullest extent that it deserves to be appreciated. I don't want to get used to private jets and personal drivers. I don't want to take them for granted.

Those luxuries are special and hard won, and most people never have the opportunity to experience them even once.

But for how badly I want to get to Claire and how

fast I need to do it, this jet might as well be a fucking donkey.

Since I am a billionaire who is appreciative of what I have, I'm texting her in-flight, updating her minute by minute about where I'm at. I'm able to do that because I have excellent Wi-Fi service and a personal encrypted text relay. I work very, very hard to appreciate these things. While Claire apparently works very, very hard to not text me back.

ME: Baby, we're in the air. Here is the GPS link to track the flight if you want to. You don't have to. I want you to focus on your day.

ME: Babe, we've landed. I'm just getting my stuff and I'm gonna hop in the car. I'm sure it went wonderfully.

ME: I'm driving myself and dictating this. I'm gonna stop at the bakery first.
ME: Unless you're at the house?
ME: Just let me know.

No answer. None. Maybe it's foolish to go to the bakery, but if I go straight to our place, it feels like giving up. I know I'm late. I'm very, very late. Her silence makes it clear that she is aware that I'm very, very, very late.

The sun is going down. But as I drive down Main Street, reaching the block with the Little Sweeney's

Sweet Treats sign, I see that Claire is sitting inside her store. The lights are on, but it looks like she's alone. There is hope. I whip into a parking spot and rush in through the front entrance, which is thankfully still unlocked, opening the door so quickly the bell shrieks my arrival.

"Hey" is all I say.

"Hey," she says. Her voice is thin and far away.

"Baby, I'm so sorry." I lean down to kiss her. She doesn't offer me her lips—or any of her at all, really—but she doesn't move away either. I plant one on her cheekbone. Glancing around the store, I can see that the shelves are all empty. "How'd it go? Did you sell out?"

She gives a little nod. "It went great. You were missed."

Whoa. Even in my most intense alpha meetings with fellow empire builders I have never been hit so hard by six words. She isn't being sarcastic or passive aggressive. She's just sad. And it's a dagger to my heart whether she meant to stab me with those two short sentences or not.

She's staring down at a little plate with an empty baking cup and some crumbs on it. "I saved you a muffin. But then I ate it."

"Okay. Well, I'm glad to hear it went great." I pull out the other chair at this small table so I can sit across from her. Really be here and not look like I'm about to leave again—because I'm not leaving here without her. "I'm very sorry I'm late, Claire." I'm not a guy who apologizes to people, but I've apologized twice since I walked in.

She's quiet for an uncomfortably long time, fiddling

with the empty baking cup and crumbs. "I kept telling myself over and over again that you might be late but you'll come back for me."

"That's true. Here I am. I wish I could have gotten back faster."

"Yeah, here you are." Those words are still thin and far away, no confidence in them whatsoever.

I'm ready to negotiate. "Claire, look—"

"You promised you'd be here."

I hesitate before saying, "No, I didn't."

Claire holds her breath as she studies my expression. If it looks anything like I feel, she sees that I'm being straightforward and honest and open. "Right. Of course you didn't." She sighs and flicks the empty paper muffin cup away. "You're too careful to make promises you can't keep. So very careful and disciplined. If you wanted to be here, if it was the most important thing in the world to you, if *I* was the most important thing in the world to you, you would have been here."

I lean in and take her hand that's resting on the table in mine. "You are the most important thing in the world to me. I couldn't be here. You have no idea how many responsibilities I have."

She pulls her hand from mine. "I don't? I run a business. I have responsibilities. And I still make time for my friends and family. I follow through on being in their lives."

"It's not the same thing," I say, shaking my head.

"That is horseshit!"

"It's not horseshit! It's not even in the same universe, Claire. I run a multibillion-dollar corporation."

"And I just play around with sugar and flour?"

I rub my forehead, sighing. This is it. This is the argument that's been hiding underneath everything, waiting in the wings for its moment to shine. "I believe in your dream. You have a gift, and I want to support that. I have supported that."

"You just don't think it's as important as what you do."

"What I *do* makes all of the problems go away. No one is at risk of losing their business. No one is at risk of losing their house. No one is at risk of going hungry. The plumbing breaks, you can't pay your lease—I solve that. I see what failing businesses do to the people I love. I saw it happen with you. You were stuck in your parents' house."

"Before you saved me?" she says sarcastically, folding her arms in front of her chest. There it is. The sarcasm.

"Where did the money come from to fix this place? Where did the money come from to solve every single problem that came up? It didn't come from marshmallows."

That silences her for a moment. She doesn't have an answer to that. But it certainly doesn't feel like I'm winning this argument. "I'm not ungrateful, Grady. I will always be grateful for your support. But I'm not going to pretend that this is enough for me."

I try to take a calming breath. She just needs to understand where I'm coming from. "Listen...who knows if my father's heart would be giving out right now if he didn't have that stress when we were younger. That fear of losing the house, not being able to feed and clothe kids? That is never going to happen to me. You can't ask me to care less about my work."

"I'm not asking you to do that."

"Yes, you are."

"No, I'm not!"

"I'm just trying to explain who I am."

"That's exactly what I'm saying. I know who you are. I see you. I've understood what drives you since we were teenagers. I'm not asking for clarification. What I'm asking for is for someone to love me and put me first. That means being here. With me. So I can be with the one I love and put him first too. It's that simple. But you will always choose your business over me. Always."

"Choosing my business *is* taking care of you, Claire."

She shakes her head adamantly as she wipes away tears. "No. Your money isn't solving the real problem. The real problem hasn't changed. You are who you are and I am who I am. I would rather lose this business and be stuck in my childhood bedroom in Beacon Harbor. I would rather have a dream that can't come true instead of feeling like half my heart is constantly missing. I don't want to live like that."

"Claire..." I don't know what to say. I don't want to lose her. I don't want this to come between us. "I love you." It's somehow the truest thing I've ever said, the most important feeling I've ever had, and yet it feels completely useless to say it out loud at this moment.

"I love you too. So much it hurts. I was going to keep this place open for as long as I had to so that you wouldn't technically miss reopening day. I would have done that for you. I would have waited for you forever. But as I sat here repeating, 'Grady will always come back to me,' it struck me... If your father hadn't had his heart incident, *would* you have come back for me? Ever? Would you ever have come back at all?" She locks eyes with me.

She has become the most important thing in my life. A dream come true. Something I didn't think I could have, or *we* could have, and now it's real. Or at least I thought it was. But I have no answer for that question. Because would I have?

Claire doesn't look like she's winning this argument either. No one is. My hesitation is obviously the answer she didn't want, but it was what she needed.

"Baby..."

"I'm not asking you to care less about your work. I know that's not possible for you. I'm asking you to go." Her voice cracks at the end, and the tears are pouring down her sad, pretty face now.

"Claire."

"I'll stay at my parents' house. Just go. Please." She stands up and goes to the front door, but it's like she's walking through water. She opens the door and stares at the floor when she says, "We're closed."

Gutted and destroyed, I get up to meet her in the doorway. I didn't win every race I ran in school, I haven't won every business deal, but this is the only time I've felt true defeat. But it can't be over. It can't be. There's no streak of flour on her face, only tears, and I reach out to wipe them away with my thumb, but she pulls back.

She makes a sad little hiccup sound and drags the

back of her hand under her nose, but she still won't look at me.

"I'll go if that's what you really want. But I'm not leaving you, Claire." I step outside. The air is warm, but I get a chill down my spine when I hear her lock the door behind me.

Chapter 31

Un-Bake My Heart

CLAIRE

"Two orders of Sex on the Beach from the guys who look like the kind of idiots my ex-husband used to hang out with," our server mutters as she slides two orange and peach–colored drinks with fruit spears onto our table.

"Oh, that's so sweet. Thank you, Darlene!" I still have my glass of chardonnay in one hand while bringing the cocktail in closer, unsuccessfully trying to guide the wandering big red straw into my gaping mouth. "Thanks, fellas!" I call out to the douchey-looking tourist dudes at the bar.

They raise their glasses and start heading over to our booth. They don't seem at all turned off by the fact that a slice of orange just bonked the end of my nose. Maybe they're actually buying this Living My Best Life bullshit act I've been trying to sell to everyone including myself for the past half hour.

"Oh no," I stage-whisper to Vera. "They're coming over. Hide."

Vera turns to the guys and holds up her hand, stopping them in their tracks. "Hey, what are we—twelve? Do we look like we drink peach schnapps if we don't have to sneak it from our parents' liquor cabinet? Stay where you are. Thank you and good night."

Dejected, they return to their stools. Their butts are flat as pancakes. No one, and I mean no man on earth, has a butt like Grady Barber.

Now I want to cry. "We don't have to give the drinks back, do we?"

"You don't have to do anything you don't want to do, Claire Bear."

I almost burst into tears in response to that. Because what I don't want to do is die alone. Specifically, I don't want to die without Grady. But I also don't want to live without him even though I am quite certain it will be easier to live without him all the time than to live without him some or most of the time. But I really don't want to never see or touch Grady's butt ever again.

"This is so fun, right?!" I exclaim, very convincingly, to my best friend. She is really and truly behaving like the world's best best friend again. "You and me! Out on the town! Yay!"

I'm crying from my nostrils a little, but in a really fun way.

"Sure, honey." Vera slides the second glass of Sex on the Beach over to me and holds up a napkin. I lean in so she can reach my nose. "This is great."

The Hair of the Sea Dog is dead tonight, but that is perfect because I am dead inside.

My lips finally make contact with the stupid straw, and I swallow so much delicious Sex on the Beach. It's delicious, and I hate it because now I'm never going to have sex with Grady on the beach and that is all my fault. "Are we drunk enough? I don't think we're drunk enough. Should we dance?" I think there's music playing over the house speakers, but all I hear is "It Must Have Been Love" by Roxette and the sound of my heart breaking. That dumb, whiny bitch. My heart, not Roxette. I gulp down the rest of my wine and then reach for Vera's hand. "Let's dance!"

She remains seated, giving my hand a squeeze. "Bob Dylan's not my favorite artist to dance to. Let's talk."

"Yeah! Let's talk about your hair. What do you call that color—is that maroon? Burgundy? It's so beautiful. How long has it been like that?"

She exhales loudly. "About a week."

"What? Really?"

"He really hasn't called? He hasn't sent you one text, even?"

Thankfully, I don't have to answer that because our server trudges over with two more drinks on a tray. "Two old-fashioneds from the guy who looks like the guy in the reboot *Star Trek* movies that I never got to see because I was too busy working to support my good-for-nothing ex-husband."

"Yeah, I'll drink to that," Vera says. "Don't make eye contact with him, though," she warns before swallowing half the contents of the glass.

I wave at the guy who looks like Chris Pine's lactose-intolerant frat-boy cousin, who, if I'm being honest, I would probably have gone home with a few years ago. But after Grady Barber, every other man looks like a pile of poo with dumb hair and stupid shoes. "Thank you! We like this kind!" I take a sip through the little straw and give him the thumbs-up. He nods and starts to get up. "Oh, shit, he's coming over. Should we run?"

Vera barely even turns her head in his direction. "Nope. Not happening, Captain."

He salutes us and sits back down.

"So, no text at all since you saw him yesterday?"

I am twenty-eight years old. Grady Barber has been inside of me. We have lived in a house together. And I'm still trying to prove to myself that life without him can be entertaining and fulfilling. I try to laugh, but it sounds like I'm coughing up a hairball. "Men! Can you believe it? Not even to check in."

"What a dick," she says under her breath as she watches me for a reaction.

I glare at her. Actually, I don't think I can make my face move enough to glare at her, but I am not smiling. "Well, it's only been twenty-seven hours. And I mean, I did tell him to give me space. Wait. Did I? Shit. I don't remember. I wish he'd text me so I can tell him to give me space!"

"Yeah. What a dick."

"Ohhhhh, come on...he's not a dick."

"I know that!" She polishes off her old-fashioned and starts chewing on an ice cube. "I'm just not sure how to play this! I want to support you—"

"I know!"

"Because you're my bestest, bestiest, most best friend in the entire world!"

"I know, and you're mine! Forever and ever!" We reach out across the table to hold hands for a second before I go back to double fisting cocktails.

"But it feels like you guys will get back together, so I don't want to be all, *Well, it was obvious you guys would never work out, but hey, at least you gave it a shot!* And then you're back with him and you'll be mad at me for saying that."

"Wait, you never thought we'd work out?"

"What? Noooo, I'm just saying as a hypnothetical." She reaches for the Sex on the Beach that I'm not drinking. "As a hypodermical. A humptydumptical. Why can't I say the word?"

"Because you meant it for real because it's what you believed all along." I slap the tabletop, startling both of us. "You're the one who told me to go for it with him in the first place, Vera!"

"What?! Did I? Yeah, that sounds like me."

"If you hadn't encouraged me to have fun in New York I wouldn't be this miserable right now and for the rest of my entire life!"

"But hey!" She holds her hands up in the air, waiting for me to slap her a high ten. "At least you gave it a shot! Amiright?"

I keep shaking my head at her. Until I have to stop moving because I'm getting dizzy. I hold on to the edge of the table between us. Why do people do this? Come to bars to drink so they can prove to the world that they're not miserable, when they can just stay home and bake things instead? It makes no sense to me. "I have to go. I should get back to the bakery to do a test run for the Shellibration cake."

Vera's face falls. I am certain that is her face falling and not my eyeballs losing the ability to view her face properly. "What? Now? Tonight? Come on, we're having fun! You can't work now." I can tell she's pulling out her phone under the table.

"Baking is exactly what I need to do right now."

"But we haven't even danced yet..." She glances down at her lap. "Right? We should dance!"

"Vera. You didn't order what I asked you to order, did you?"

"I was going to order it in the morning."

I scrub my face with my hand, the way Grady does sometimes, but without the sexy sound of his sexy palm scraping against his sexy facial hair. "I gave you a list and asked you to order everything three days ago. It was supposed to be in my kitchen this afternoon. You said you were there waiting for a delivery."

"I was. I had something else delivered there this afternoon."

"What?"

She mumbles something unintelligible.

"What was that?"

"Lobster food," she says sheepishly.

"Lobster food. For Damien's lobsters?"

She rolls her eyes. "Yes. He usually feeds them pellets, but he wanted to give them shrimp leading up to the race. He asked me to bring it to him at the beach after work. He's the worst—I just hate that he's been wasting his talent lately when I know how amazing he can be. It drives me nuts!" She sighs. "I will go back to pretending he doesn't exist as soon as the Shellibration is over, but enough about me. I'm ordering the ingredients right now, and you will have them in two days. Right? That's enough time. Do I order double what you need for the actual event? Did you text me the list? Never mind—I'll find it. Hang on. I got this."

And now I'm sobbing uncontrollably.

Because I really am going to die alone.

I've pushed away my boyfriend, and now I'm going to have to fire my BFF because she's the worst assistant in the history of bakeries and any other industry, probably.

I cover my face. Everything was going so well, and now my whole entire life is falling apart! I'm a monster! I'm a monster who breaks up with billionaires just because they care more about building empires than being with me and fires besties simply because they don't do what I need them to do even though I'm paying them and can barely afford it.

I feel Vera climbing into the booth next to me, enveloping me in a comforting hug. "Oh, honey, come on. It'll all be okay, I promise. We can pay extra for a rush order. It'll be fine."

I squeeze her tight. "No! It won't!"

She smooths down my hair at the back of my head. "Shhh, shhh, shhhh. I'll take care of it."

"No!" I wail into her neck. "You won't. You're *fiiiiiii-ired*!" I somehow manage to turn *fired* into an epically tragic six-syllable word. "I have to *fiiiiiiiiire* you!"

"What?" She doesn't pull away when she asks, "Did you just say I'm fired?"

After a few attempts at catching my breath through snot-filled weepy hiccups, I continue. "*Yeeeeeesssss*. I'm *sooooo sorryyyyyyy*. But you're *awwwwfullll*! You're a terrible, horrible assistant, and I have to hire someone who can actually help *meeeeeee*!"

She holds me closer. "Oh my God. Claire!"

"I'm *sooorrrrryyyyyy*!!! Please don't hate *meeee*."

"Honey, I don't hate you. I am so proud of you for finally firing me. I'm the worst assistant ever!"

"You are! I love you so much, but you're so bad!"

"Oh, I know! I'm so bad, but I love you so much, I just wanted to help you! I've been waiting for you to nut up and can me for, like, two years!"

I finally pull away from her, wiping my nose with my sleeve. "Huh?"

Vera grabs another napkin and hands it to me. "Here. Blow."

I do. I empty about five gallons of snot into the napkin and then ask again, "What are you saying? You don't want to work for me?"

"Oh, God, no! I mean, I love hanging out with you because you're my Claire Bear and I want you to be successful. But it's not exactly a great fit for me."

"But-but-but-but what'll you do now?"

She waves her hand dismissively. We both face forward, sitting side by side. "I'll figure something out. It's not something you need to worry about. I don't need the money."

"What?"

"Remember when my grandma died?"

I sniffle. "A couple of years ago?"

She nods. "She left me a trust fund. I can't get all the money at once, but I get more than enough to live on every month for the rest of my life. I'll be fine."

"What?" I squeeze my eyes shut and take a somewhat calming breath. "I don't think I'm hearing the words right. Are you saying you haven't really needed this job for two years?"

She shrugs.

"But you've been getting up before dawn five days a week."

She nods.

"But why?"

She squeezes my leg. "Because you needed me, boo."

I hug her tight. "Oh, Vera. I should be so mad at you."

"I know! You could have hired someone who could actually help you. I see that now!"

"I love you," I tell her.

"I love you too."

"Two mugs of virgin not-too-hot hot chocolates from the old guy in the pajamas who's actually pretty cute," Darlene declares.

Vera and I pull apart, both of us cooing as we eye the hot chocolate with whipped cream on top.

"Rockstar move, Old Guy," Vera muses. "Well played."

"This is exactly what I need right now." I pull one of the mugs in closer and wave Crabby over to join us, but he's already shuffling our way.

"There are worse fallback guys, you know," Vera mumbles, laughing.

I nudge her with my elbow.

Vera addresses Clarence with "Hey there, Crumbly Crabshack. What's shakin'?"

"Beat it, Red. I need a minute with the sad one."

"I respect that." She nods and pats my leg. "I'll be back in one minute. You're good, right?"

"Yeah. We're good, right?"

"*'Oh, yeah,' she assured her best friend as she tried not to seem too excited to be free from her employment.*" She kisses me on the cheek. "We're great. I'll show up at the bakery for as long as you need me to until you have a replacement."

I don't tell her that I already have mother-daughter replacements in mind.

Crabby slides into the booth across from me. He's wearing the same pajamas he wore the night I was here with Grady. Clasping his hands together, he fixes me with a hard stare. "How's it goin', kid?"

"Oh, I'm great." I take a sip of hot chocolate to show him how great I'm doing.

"Knock it off. I heard you dumped the suit. It ain't right."

"Wait, what? Why aren't you thrilled?"

"Enh. Yer too young for me anyway. But I'm an alpha male," he explains, shrugging his bony shoulders. "Can't help it if I'm competitive. That fella, though..." He shakes his head. "That guy's a class act. No one else besides me around here who's good enough for ya. What happened? Lose your nerve?"

I mean. I am decades too young for him, obviously, but why do I feel so rejected all of a sudden? "I didn't lose my nerve. It was the opposite, actually. I finally felt confident enough to tell him what I want."

"What's that? The world? From the looks of it he woulda given it to ya."

I shake my head. "I just want him. I want him here. And I can't trust that he will be. If he needs someone who'll move to New York or wherever to be with him, I'll never be that person. I can't give him what he wants." I shrug half-heartedly. I am positive I'm being practical and saving both me and Grady from a lifetime of pain, but the truth is I'm starting to question my own logic. Still, I add, "It's that simple."

"Ayuh..." He flicks at his white stubble. "It's always that simple, ain't it?" He stares down at the table in front of him. "You were too young to remember my Rosie before she passed..."

I lean forward to listen carefully because it's rare for Crabby to talk about his wife.

He has to clear his throat before continuing. "Prettiest damn thing I ever saw. Nothin' but trouble. You know the type." He arches a gray, scraggly eyebrow at me. "I'm no romantic. Neither was she. We couldn't care less about flowers and fancy words. I just wanted her."

"That's nice."

"She just wanted me. And Paris. And Rome. And Tokyo. And Morocco. And Egypt. And the Serengeti. Halifax. Juneau. You name it. If she'd seen pretty pictures of a place in a magazine she wanted to go there. You know where I wanted to go?"

"Anywhere she was?"

He slaps his palm on the table just like I did earlier. "Nowhere. Why would anyone in their right mind want to leave Beacon Harbor?"

I feel like this is a trick question, but I say, "Best place in the world."

"Damn right it is."

I wait for him to tell me about how he knows for a fact that it's the best place in the world because he traveled far and wide with his wife, but he just stares at me, as if he's waiting for me to say something. "So, did you travel with her anyway?"

He wrinkles his nose. "Took her to Paris for our honeymoon. Didn't like it."

"Well, so...did Rosie travel without you, then?"

"Yes, she did. With her sister. Rome. Tokyo. Halifax. Juneau. She always sent postcards. I always secretly begrudged her for leavin'. She always came back. And then one day she was too sick to get out of bed. And then..." The rims of Crabby's eyes get all pink. I guess he's too dehydrated to tear up. But he looks so sad. "Ask me where I wish I'd gone with the love of my life when I had the chance."

There's nothing like seeing someone else's loss to sober you up and put things into perspective. I reach out to give Crabby's hand a squeeze. "I'm so sorry, Clarence."

"Enh. She had no regrets. What she told me, at least. I don't want you to regret anything, kid."

"What are you saying? You think I should go to New York with him?"

"Don't you ever stop making me cookies at that

bakery, you hear me? I'm sayin' yer man'll come around. Believe it or not, he's smarter than me, so it won't take him anywhere near as long. When he does, let's hope you stay focused on the fact that he's come back for you. Instead of mopin' about how he's always leavin'. Matter of fact, I bet he'll be walkin' through that door any minute." Crabby turns his whole body to face the door, and like an idiot, I follow his gaze.

He has a strong point. The one man in town who thought of Grady Barber as a rival is now advocating that I shift my focus from the pain of what's missing to the joy of what I have when Grady and I are together. If I was able to forget how much it hurt when he didn't kiss me twelve years ago because of all the times he's kissed me this summer, then why can't I focus on all the kisses to come instead of the distance between us when we're both being true to who we are? Isn't that what a kiss is? The dream of bridging the distance between two people, if only for a moment?

I stare at the entrance to the Sea Dog. Crabby stares at the entrance to the Sea Dog. There is no chance that the love of his life will walk through that door. But even if the love of my life doesn't walk through it tonight, I want to be able to meet him halfway, with a heart that's full.

Chapter 32

Total E Claire of the Heart

GRADY

I WAS SUPPOSED to spend these past couple of days with Claire before heading back to New York to sign the final paperwork. It feels like the last days of summer vacation before school starts. Only way sadder and a lot more pathetic because everything sucks and I have nothing to live for. But I figured I might as well take advantage of these remaining days in Beacon Harbor—do things that I won't get to do when I have to put my bullshit Armani suit of armor back on and wage corporate battle with a bunch of other assholes in a bunch of other bullshit suits.

For instance, I'm wearing sweatpants.

They're five-hundred-dollar sweatpants, but they're still sweatpants.

And I like them, but it makes me sad to look at them because I brought them so I could wear them at home with Claire. So she could tell me how annoyingly hot I look in sweatpants and then give me a perfect, super casual hand job while smelling like frosting and telling me about her day.

Instead of getting a hand job from the woman I'm in love with, I've been watching a ton of crap on TV. The kinds of shows that make me despise humanity. I've watched even dumber things on my phone, and I've been eating garbage. I haven't gone out for a run because I don't want to run into Claire, even though I really want to run into Claire. But Claire needs space. Or she asked me to go, at least, and I don't know if that meant *Give me space* or not, but I don't want to be the guy who calls and texts her and then she's all: *All I needed was a little space, but you won't even give me that!* So I'm sitting here, all shirtless in my gray sweatpants at my parents' house because being alone in the house I rented for me and Claire is even more depressing than this is.

I check the security-system app every now and then to see if Claire is at the house. She hasn't been. If she were, it would make me a liar because I told her I wouldn't use this app to watch her without her permission first. That would make me a liar *and* an asshole who missed his girlfriend's reopening. But if it meant her being at the house and me being able to see her face in real time again, then I'd rather be a liar at this point.

Which makes me really pathetic.

My family is greatly confused by all of this. My very concerned mother keeps offering activities that would barely interest me under normal circumstances. Does she really think I'd enjoy getting a pedicure with her? Do I look like I want to go to Target to see if they have another pair of those sunglasses she got last week? I don't. Unless Claire is at Target. But I tell my mom that I love her because she's trying because she loves me. At least one woman still loves me. When Alice sent me a text yesterday to ask if there was anything she should send to Claire, I replied that we're spending some time apart and she replied with a thumbs-down emoji.

My brother's way of showing he cares is to leave me the hell alone. Except sometimes when I pass by whatever room he's in, he'll strum "You Give Love a Bad Name" by Bon Jovi because he's an asshole little brother who's been an expert at annoying me all his life who can now do it by shredding power chords on his axe. Or whatever the kids are calling guitars these days. But I'm not the one who gives love a bad name. Rock 'n' roll gives it a bad name. Because rock 'n' roll makes love sound cool. And love is not cool. It's sad.

Like my dad's CD collection.

Which is why I'm listening to sad songs from my dad's old CDs on the old stereo system that he refuses to replace.

What'll I do
When you are far away
And I am blue?
What'll I do?

It's my father who finally breaks, having had quite enough of his old sad music being used for depression. He abruptly turns off the music mid-song. "All right, that's enough of this," he announces to the room, as if we've been having a conversation.

"Enough of what?" I mumble, blowing Cheeto dust off my exposed chest.

My dad claps his hands together and then raises his finger, pointing to the ceiling. "We're taking the boat out. Put a shirt on, come with me to the docks, and then you can take your shirt off again."

It would take more willpower than I currently have to fight him on this.

"Damien, you're coming too!" he calls out. "Let's go."

An hour later, after rigging the vessel from muscle memory alone, we're busy doing nothing, just drifting on the water.

My brother's long, lean body is stretched out on the seats across from me, looking like he doesn't have a care in the world. I mean, he doesn't, really. Aside from his upcoming lobster race and the fact that he's an unemployed grown man with no driver's license who's living with his parents. Aside from the fact that he could be making bank as a global rock star and instead is playing to a bunch of townies in a local dive bar.

But that could be my mood talking.

"Isn't this better?" my father asks. He takes in a lungful of sea air. He gestures at the blue sky.

I shrug.

Marine moping feels no different from land moping.

My dad grabs a few beers from the cooler and offers me one. I take it. Because what else am I gonna do?

"Only silver lining about my heart condition..." He sighs. "I read that having a drink is actually good for it."

"Actually that was debunked. Alcohol doesn't help at all with your heart. Alcohol is just straight up bad for you," I inform him, and then I pour the poison directly down my gullet.

"Figures," my father mumbles before pausing to take a sip. "The one fun scientific fact ever discovered in the last thousand years and they had to take that away too. But Pluto will always be a planet to me, dammit."

We sit for a few minutes, drinking in silence, listening to the waves lapping against the side of the boat.

"Not as nice as your boat back in New York, I suppose."

Sitting here on my family's boat, the one I bought for them, with the familiar breeze caressing my skin, I take a deep breath. I'm still gutted. I'm still a Godforsaken hollowed-out shell because I don't have Claire.

But this is nice.

"No, Dad." I sigh. "This is better."

I watch my father take that in. "What happened with you and the Sweeney girl?"

"They broke up," Damien adds helpfully, his forearm still resting over his face. The big brother in me wants to yell at him for not wearing sunscreen, but I don't have the energy for it.

"I know they broke up. Look at him. He's a Godforsaken hollowed-out shell of a man. You don't think I've heard it all from your mother?"

"Then you know what happened," I remark flatly.

My father shakes his head. "No, I don't. I ran into Jake the other day. According to him, she was just as miserable as you are the last time he saw her. That doesn't sound like two people who should be broken up."

"Jake won't talk to me. Not that I blame him. And it's

not exactly a breakup. I don't think. She just doesn't want to be in a relationship with me when I physically can't be here most of the time. I'm going to be so busy coming up..." I realize, as I say it, how many times I've uttered that exact sentence recently to the people I love the most.

"You miss her this much, and you haven't called her?" my dad asks, genuinely confused. "Or sent her a text message?"

I scrub my face with my hand. I haven't shaved in two and a half days, and the sound of my stubble scraping against my palm probably echoes across the harbor. Maybe Claire will hear it, wherever she is. "She doesn't want me to call her," I groan. "I don't think. I have no idea. She told me to go. If I call her, then I'm the guy who can't even give her space for a day. I don't know. Should I text her just so she can tell me she never wants to hear from me again?"

"She'll be mad no matter what you do at this point," Damien explains with the confidence of a guy who's made many, many girls mad in his life.

I rub the back of my neck, totally confused as to what to do. This is unfamiliar territory for me. The confusion about how to proceed and the uneasy feeling that I can't say the right thing to get what I want. "I have no idea what to do," I say on an exhale. "I don't know how to fix this." Two sentences I have never thought or said out loud before.

"You know, I've always been a little in awe of you," my dad muses.

That snaps my attention to my father. I am absolutely

depressed, but I don't think it gets much better than that level of validation from your father. "Really?"

He nods with a knowing, fatherly grin. "Yeah. I don't know where you got that drive. We don't come from money. We don't have connections. We don't even have good luck. You just manifested all of it through sheer force of will. It's really impressive."

"Thanks, Dad."

"But honestly, I don't know what the point of all that money is if you can't do what you want."

"Money has its limits. I can't move New York City right next to Beacon Harbor. I have too much responsibility to too many people to give Claire the time and energy she deserves."

Damien finally sits up. "I always felt bad for you," he says. Both my father's and my attention snaps to my brother. My younger-brother-is-being-annoying alarm threatens to go off. But Damien doesn't look like he's picking a fight. He actually looks like he legitimately feels bad for me.

"What do you mean?"

He gives me a half grin and shakes his head before looking out over the horizon. "I mean I was in awe of you like everyone else. Like Dad. And also pissed off and scared because you were the golden boy. I could never live up to that. But I saw what it did to you. That drive you can't turn off. You were never really here."

"I know I've missed a lot of holidays and time with you guys—"

Damien shakes his head mechanically, indicating that I'm just not getting it. "No. Even when you were here, living here with us. You were never *here*. Your mind was always on the next thing. I know you've always felt bad for me. Maybe I'm not exactly where I want to be. But I've had fun. I live my life the way I want to live it."

It's my turn to nod and look meaningfully off into the distance. I must really be in a terrible state if Damien of all people is making sense to me. "I can't turn it off."

"Why not?" my dad asks gently.

"I saw what it did to you, Dad. I saw what nearly losing your business and the house did to you." I look over at Damien. He has no idea what I'm talking about. "Damien was too young. But I remember. I more than remember. Maybe all that stress is why your heart is the way it is."

My father looks completely taken aback. I've never told him this, never spoken it aloud with my family. This thing that shaped who I am—I've never talked about it with the people who shaped me.

"Hey, listen," he says when he finally finds the words. "I had no idea you were aware of all that, and I sure as hell wish you weren't. I'm not going to say that time was fun for anyone. But I guess I don't look at it that way. Honestly, these last few weeks, ever since I thought maybe there was a chance I was having a heart attack, I've been thinking the exact opposite."

Now I'm taken aback. "What do you mean?"

"Maybe the stress of trying to provide for my family damaged my heart. Maybe. Who knows? But maybe this old heart of mine keeps on ticking because it has a reason to. You. And your brother. And your mother. Without you guys, I don't know why it would have kept going."

I sit with that for a long time. We all do.

"We've seen what this thing that drives you can do for you," my dad finally continues. "We've seen how it can drive you away. I just hope it doesn't push away the person who finally makes you feel at home. Know what I mean?"

All I can say now is "Yeah. I hope so too. I'm sorry I wasn't here, Dad."

"It's okay, Grady. I get it. But I'm glad you're here now. Because I understand always wanting more. I can never get enough of *this*." He gestures between me and my brother and the boat and the sea.

And I realize that Claire isn't the only one who wants more.

I want every inch of her and every second of her life.

I want so much more with her.

I'm good at getting more.

If I can combine Lynch's empire with mine, then I can figure out how to unite my world with Claire's.

I still just don't know how.

Chapter 33

My Flakey Bakey Heart

GRADY

MY PEN HOVERS a quarter inch from where I'm supposed to sign.

I'm back in the top-floor conference room of Relicteros Inc. to execute the final contract to merge our companies. I chose to do it here instead of my office as a show of good faith to the company that is being absorbed into ours. Like a victorious general allowing the vanquished one to surrender his sword in his own territory.

That vanquished general once again sits on the opposite end of the massive table. Harrison Lynch is stone-faced as usual. He didn't have to be here today. But it says a lot about his character that he is. The room is as packed as it was when I gave my last presentation to hold off Lynch's last play. Fewer of my Beacon Holdings executives are here because I'm not giving any presentations, but they've been supplanted by a small brigade of lawyers to make sure everything is done properly.

I turn my attention back to the arrow on the paper where my name should go. Somehow I still can't get the pen to the paper. I've been a mess since the last time I saw Claire. I've become a twisted, confused mess since my father and brother and I had our talk. I can't stop thinking about what my dad said and what it means for my life. How do I keep going if I know that I'll never be happy without Claire by my side? How can I give Claire myself and the world when I have to sacrifice myself to conquer the world?

I move the pen the final quarter of an inch to the paper. There's uncomfortable shifting and some light coughing in the room. They're wondering what's taking so long. As miserable as I've been, I kept expecting the fire to return once I returned to New York. The burning need to succeed that feeds me. But as I sit here in this room, I don't feel any of it.

In my mind, I hear Claire's quiet voice ask, *But what if it doesn't make you happy?*

The answer is no longer that it does make me happy. Not even for right now. And I know that it never will again.

I look up at the other people in the room. Lynch's board is here, but Aston isn't. I hadn't noticed that in my fog of despair when I first came into the room.

I lean in toward Alice, who's sitting next to me in her lucky black Chanel suit that looks like all of her other black Chanel suits, and whisper, "Where is Mr. Pembroke?"

"His daughter is getting married. They have a rehearsal dinner," she says.

"Why wasn't I told about this?"

Alice looks a little confused. It's so rare that she isn't on top of everything, she doesn't know what it's like for me to question her. "It didn't seem like pertinent information. It has no effect on the agreement or this signing."

Of course not. Why would it? Aston's got his priorities straight. But it does have an effect on me and this signing.

He's made the kind of choice I need to make.

It feels like a light switch has been turned on. A powerful megawatt spotlight that illuminates everything in my life and makes it look completely different. A beacon, one might say. I had no idea I'd been living in the dark for so long.

Becoming rich and successful is a means to an end. I've always known this. But I was so focused on the means that I had lost sight of the end. So much so that I was willing to sacrifice it.

Claire is the end. The end of my story. Or rather, the beginning of the real one.

I've had it all wrong. I didn't need to figure out how to combine our lives—mine in New York and hers in Beacon Harbor. I needed to choose *our* life.

I need to choose her.

I've made my fortune.

Now it's time to go back home to my girl.

I can't sign this document.

I can't. It would mean a life without Claire. A life without love. All means with no end.

But this contract needs to be finalized. These companies need to merge. Everyone in this room is counting on me. Thousands of employees' lives and billions of investor dollars are at stake.

People are starting to shift in their seats more. The coughs are getting louder.

I look up and see Lynch staring at me from across the table. His face is still stone, only hinting at a bit of confusion as to what I'm up to.

Lynch. Beautiful, surly, scowly Lynch. You magnificent misanthrope. In the new light of my realization, Lynch doesn't look like the immovable pain in my ass that he's always been.

Well, he doesn't only look like that.

He looks like my way out.

I've always been careful, dedicated. I'm not impulsive. I chip away at what I want over and over again, like a river running over rock until it creates a canyon.

But now I'm just going to go over the cliff.

Because now I can see that I'm just a fool in love and I have no other choice. And I have never been so happy to be a fool with no other choices.

"Can Mr. Lynch and I have the room, please?"

There are murmurs of confusion, but no one is going to tell me no.

"Me too?" Alice asks. She's not put out. She's a pro. She just wants to make sure.

"Yeah, this needs to be mano a mano."

"Okay, but I'm not cleaning up after any pissing contests," she mutters. Alice waits until everyone is cleared, then exits and shuts the door, giving me a meaningful look just before it closes completely.

When we're alone, Lynch simply continues to stare at me. If I'm going to win him over I'm going to have to be careful. Sure, I'll be giving him exactly what he wants. But I'm living proof that a guy can have everything he has ever wanted right in front of him and he can still find a way to screw it up.

I place my hands on the table. "I've always contended this deal was a win-win for both of our companies. It would increase our market share, of course, but it would also increase our efficiency and vertically integrate our supply chain. You disagreed."

"I did," Lynch says tersely. He's still not going to give up anything easily. If only he knew what he was going to get out of it.

"Do you actually believe that, or was it just a strategy to maintain control of your company?"

Lynch's brow furrows. He sighs, staring me down.

"Please, it's just us. It's over. Man to man, I want...I *need* to know." My body language is open, no bullshit. Or at least I hope he's reading it that way.

"I may have exaggerated the potential negatives of the structure. But I still believe I am the best person to run my company."

I lean forward. "So it's a good deal? This merger?"

"It is," Lynch concedes.

"You just think you're the man to run it?"

"I do."

I grin. I can't help it. He can't stop giving me ways to win. "Well, Lynch, let's say that you were right before. That I've fallen in love and lost my head. And my heart. And everything. And let's say I can't choose something that would keep me from a life with the woman I love for another second. Let's say all of that was true."

"Go on." Lynch now leans forward, mirroring me across the large oak table.

"And let's say I don't want to be CEO of Beacon Holdings any longer."

"You can't mean that." Even with everything going on, it is strangely satisfying turning Lynch's face of stone to one of surprise.

"Let's say that I do. I would still be the major shareholder. But let's say that I want to put you in charge as CEO instead. Say that were true—would you accept the position and lead our merged companies?"

"Let's say that I would. I would want to know what game you're playing before I agree to anything. I won't be anyone's puppet."

"There's no game. It would be your job to manage the company, not mine." It feels strange to admit this to Lynch, but I need him to know I'm serious. "I love Claire. I want to be with her. This is the only thing that's standing in the way of that."

Lynch nods and places his hands on the desk, considering.

"If you agree, I will sign this contract to merge the companies and then step down as CEO. I have no doubt you will be approved as my replacement right away. Particularly because I will be the largest shareholder. Please, Lynch."

He looks up, giving me a lopsided grin. "Even when you're begging it's disgustingly charming."

I match his grin with the original, the vintage, some would say the Pappy Van Winkle of disarming billionaire grins. "We all have our burdens to bear."

"And I guess now mine is figuring out how to lead a company twice as large as Relicteros was."

I feel the weight on my chest lifting. "Where is Miss Lovejoy? I didn't see her by your side at the last meeting either."

Lynch's scowl returns. "What is this—*Sex and the City*? Do you want a CEO or a bestie? That's none of your business."

"Fair enough. One more thing, though. I have a demand to go along with my...surprise." I smile as I picture Claire's smile.

Soon, baby. Soon.

"What is it?"

"Alice Strout. She's an outstanding executive assistant. I don't think she'll want to go with me where I'm going, so I need you to offer her a place here if she wants it."

"Done."

I sign the document.

And now it's time to leave my empire.

I rise and walk toward him, and he does the same.

We tug at the cuffs of our shirt sleeves, button up our suit jackets at the same time, as if this was all choreographed.

I'm the first to extend my hand. "I have complete faith in you. You'll figure it out."

"I will. I have complete faith in myself too. It's about time you got on board." There is no irony in his delivery.

I laugh as we shake hands. "Can you handle things from here? I have to go."

Lynch nods. "I've got it. They'll have a lot of questions. It'll be a little messy. But I'll make sure this train keeps moving."

"Thank you," I say. And I mean it. It does feel good to have Lynch on my side for once.

"You're welcome. Now get out of my building."

I give him a curt nod, and he slaps a big manicured hand on my shoulder.

I leave the room and find everyone waiting anxiously. "Ladies and gentlemen, please go back inside. Mr. Lynch has an announcement to make." I gently place a hand on Alice's arm before she can make her way back inside.

She scans my face like she's trying to speed-read an email. "What the hell happened in there?" she whispers.

I explain as quickly as I can about my change of heart, expecting Alice to tell me that I'm crazy, to take some time to cool off before making any rash decisions. Instead, she turns the table on this conversation and surprises the hell out of me.

"It's about Goddamn time," Alice says, putting her hands on her hips and smirking.

"What?"

"I was married to my late husband Ed for thirty years, God rest his soul. So I know love. And I've been a secretary even longer. So I've seen a lot of rich a-hole types who only care about one thing and not the thing that really matters in this life. You aren't one of those. I saw you with her. I was just waiting for you to figure it all out for yourself. Because like I said, I know rich a-hole types, and nobody can tell you what to believe or what to do. Of course, I can't say I was expecting you to *quit*."

"I'm sorry to leave you, Alice. I made Lynch promise to take care of you in any way that you want."

Alice gets a saucy look on her face that makes her look twenty years younger. "He better be careful what he promised you. I might hold him to that."

I laugh. "Alice!"

She waves a hand at me. "It'll be fine. I know I was the first great secretary of your life, but you are most certainly not the first CEO I've assisted."

I playfully clutch at my heart. "Ouch."

"And you'll be fine. More than fine. You'll be happy! You need me to help you pack up your life and ship it to Beacon Harbor—just give me an address to ship it to. I'll have the jet ready to take off as soon as you get to the airport. Now, go. Go make the merger you really want to make."

"Thank you, Alice." I kiss her on the cheek and rush out of the building.

Now I feel it. Now that I'm on the sidewalk, loosening my tie. The fire is returning. The greed for more. But it isn't about money or power.

It's about my best friend's little sister and wanting every single moment I can take of life together with her.

I have a lot of work ahead of me. I have to mend things with Jake, be there for my parents in a way that I haven't been, and figure out how to help Damien.

Most of all, I have to convince Claire that I'm back for good.

But I'm at my best when the stakes are high. And they can't be any higher than the answer to *What's next?*

My happily ever after with the beautiful baker of Beacon Harbor.

Chapter 34

The Billionaire Is Baking

C*LAIRE*

VERA: You are a wicked bad ass, but you need help. Let me help you!!!
ME: Hey!!! That's so sweet, but I got this!!! Seriously. I just need you to pick up the box truck for me tonight and bring it here in the morning! That's it! I'll remind you later. I'm totally on track to get everything done tonight. All good. Really. Xoxo

I AM SO NOT ALL good, but I do got this. Probably. I am totally wired on caffeine and on track to pass out face first into a bowl of frosting in about three hours. But I'm all good. Really.

I'm making the biggest cake I've ever made, all by myself. I wasn't able to do a trial bake the other night, thanks to Vera. She is still the best friend ever and I'm still very glad I fired her, but I haven't had time to hire her replacements yet. And I can't focus on making everything perfect if my well-meaning yet talkative family is around either. So, I've been in my bakery kitchen ever since the store closed, making seventy-two cups of vanilla cake batter and sixty cups of Italian meringue buttercream by myself while drinking green tea and listening to NPR.

Just kidding, I'm pounding coffee and blasting my Taylor Swift Getaway Carb playlist. And crying. Despite the upbeat soundtrack, I've been crying from every hole in my face for hours. I put on a face mask this afternoon to ensure that no sadness snot would accidentally drip into my cake batter or icing, but things might taste a little salty from the tear drops. I tried wearing goggles, but they fogged up immediately.

I was hoping that throwing myself into work would make me miss Grady less, but it turns out nothing makes me miss him less. All I can do is look forward to seeing him again. And I am looking forward to seeing him at the Shellibration tomorrow. Even if I'm just watching him give a speech from the crowd, like everyone else. But I can't show up at the event without a gigantic cake lobster, so there's no rest for the weary.

Although I'm realizing now that in my frantic rush to make the big base cake that represents the ocean and the template for my lobster cake and the fondant and the batter and getting my cake pans into the oven and setting the timers and then taking them out of the oven and putting them in the fridge so I can carve them, I've forgotten to let Grady know that I am looking forward to seeing him. But I've just started to make the mirror glaze for the base cake so my ocean looks pretty and shiny, so I have to keep an eye on the saucepan to make sure my mixture doesn't boil over.

I think I hear a knock at the back door. If that's Vera, I'm not letting her in. I call out, "Vera, I don't need help and I'm in the middle of something!"

More insistent knocking.

Maybe it's Crabby. That wise old turd is relentless. I haven't been able to turn him away since we bonded at the Sea Dog, but if he brought the raccoon with him, I will knee him in his crumbly old rum balls. "Crabby, I'm busy and I don't have any cookies left!" I call out.

My sugar-glucose water hasn't started to bubble yet, but it will any minute. I set a one-minute timer and then dash over to unlock and open the door.

It's not Vera or Crabby or Mark the raccoon.

It's Grady freaking Barber. In an Armani suit. And an apron with the Beacon Harbor Fire Department logo on it.

I don't understand what's happening. He should be at a fancy celebratory dinner at some fancy restaurant on Madison Avenue or wherever they have fancy dinners in Manhattan. "What are you doing here?" I realize I'm wearing a face mask, so I take it off and repeat myself.

"Hey. I stopped by to talk to Jake on the way, and he told me you fired Vera. So I figured you could use some help." He says it with a little shrug, like it's no big deal. Like he's offering to help carry my books to class because he's big and strong and happens to be heading in the same direction. Not like he's hundreds of miles from where he should be right now.

I just keep staring at him, too overwhelmed to speak because my brain is being flooded with images of Grady coming back to me. That first time I saw him standing in my store to pick up his welcome-home cake. The time he jogged over to my car in the middle of Main Street when I was trying to hide from him. Grady on my parents' doorstep. Grady in the foyer of the house he rented for us here. And I don't even remember how much it hurt to miss him.

He holds up a paper bag that has grease stains on it. "I also brought you a couple of burgers because I figured you forgot to eat dinner."

I have never been so turned on by a greasy brown bag in my life. Tears start squirting out of my eyeballs as I throw my arms around his neck. I never want to let him go, but my timer is going off. "Shit! I have to check my glaze. Come in, come in!"

I run back to the stove and see that my mixture has started to bubble, so I remove it from the heat and stir in the gelatin. Glancing over, I see Grady closing and locking the door. I feel a pang of guilt as I remember the last time he was here I told him to go. "I can't believe you're here."

"Is it okay that I'm here?"

I smile at him. The first genuine smile that has appeared on my face since the evening of the day my bakery reopened. "It could not be okayer." Another timer goes off as I pour in condensed milk. "Shit! Um. Can you help me get my cakes out?"

"I can help you do anything, baby," he says calmly.

And that just sets me off into another round of sobs. "They're in the fridge, not the oven," I explain. "They need to come out now so they don't dry out! Put them on the center table! Thank you!"

"You got it." He puts the bag of burgers on a side table. "I can't believe you were planning to do all of this by yourself, Claire."

And suddenly, it makes no sense to me either. But I can't really think about anything except my mirror glaze because it has to be perfect. When I finally look up from my blue-tinted base color glaze, Grady's placed the stacked cake and the flat cake on the table in the center of my kitchen. He's admiring the base cake on a side counter that I'm about to pour the mirror glaze over. It's covered in a smooth buttercream, so it doesn't look like much yet. "This looks amazing, Claire. This is the design?" He picks up my colored sketch.

"Yeah, I'm going to pour blue-and-aqua-and-white mirror glaze over the base so it looks like glistening sea water, and then I have to carve the upright body of the lobster, and then, see, I have this template for carving out the head and the tail and the claws, and then I soak the cake in simple syrup, and then all the parts get covered with buttercream and crumb coated, back in the fridge, then iced again, back in the fridge, then red fondant to cover the pieces, detail the fondant, sculpt the smaller claws and legs out of red fondant—"

"What about the antenna?"

I sigh. "Yes. Right. The antenna. And then the beady black fondant eyes. Paint the entire surface with gel food coloring. Attach to the body. Lobster gets attached to the base cake so it looks like it's emerging from the sea. Blammo. Done."

"Super simple," he says, hands on his hips, nodding. "Should take, what? Forty minutes?"

"Something like that. Forty minutes plus a couple of hours, give or take another hour or two."

"I have a question."

"Shocker."

He holds up my design sketch. "What about this crown that the lobster is wearing?"

I squeeze my eyes shut. "Fuck me. That's more fondant. I need to make a yellow-gold fondant. Fuck!"

He puts the sketch down and places his hands on my shoulders. "Babe. Claire. We've got this. I'm going to help you."

"But you don't know how—"

"Hey. I helped you bake cupcakes for that bake sale in high school, remember? And since then, I've paid a lot of money for a master class with Buff Goldberg from the Christmas baking show. I know how to work with fondant."

I grin and cross my arms in front of my chest. "Buff Goldberg, huh?" I scoff. "American baking shows are so overproduced."

"No argument there, but he's a great baker and I know my way around fondant." He brushes away flour from my forehead, or maybe he's just touching my forehead—I don't know and I don't care. I just love it. "Just sayin'. Let's get to work."

I shake my head in amazement. "I still can't believe

you're here." I grab him and hug him again. I want to kiss him but I don't have time to kiss him, and if I do kiss him I'll never stop kissing him, and we both need our mouths for other things for the next twenty-four hours, like eating burgers and giving speeches and thanking the mayor after she tells me I've made the greatest cake she has ever seen or tasted and stuff like that.

He rubs my back. "Come on. We've got a crustacean to carve."

"Yup. But I have to pour the mirror glaze first. Back to work."

And we do. We work together. After I pour the glaze over my base cake, Grady Barber forces me to pause to eat, and then he helps me craft a big, magnificent lobster cake. He rolls out fondant for me while I'm sculpting other pieces. He holds things in place for me exactly when I need it without me even having to ask him to. He rolls out the fondant for the creepy lobster legs and then gives them to me to detail. All that famous Grady Barber focus is applied to assisting me, as if we're sculpting some grand work of art instead of a giant dessert lobster. We do all this while listening to classical music. He compliments me and asks questions, but not in that way that makes me think he's questioning the way I do things and all of my life choices. He wants to learn. He wants to know what I know because he respects me.

I have never felt so supported by anyone before. I spent so much of my life being afraid of needing help, like it's a weakness to need another person for anything. But I'm finally realizing how much stronger I feel having Grady by my side, and I like it. I love it, actually.

By one thirty we've completed a giant lobster cake. It's like a scene out of Greek mythology—a lobster emerging from the ocean, victorious, with a crown on its head.

"This is Muhammad Lobbee, right?"

"Don't tell Damien, but it's Clawdia Swiffter. I've never actually seen Lobbee win, no matter what his name is."

"Amazing," he says. "This is gorgeous, Claire. And I bet it tastes fantastic. You're amazing. I love watching you work."

I smile at him. At least, I want to smile at him, but I'm so tired I don't know if I can move my face anymore. "I love working with you."

He gives me a hug, and I relax into it.

And then I close my eyes and melt into him.

When I open my eyes, my head is resting on Grady's lap and I'm lying on the sofa in the store. It's dark. Grady's hand is on my arm and he's fast asleep, but there's still a protective quality in his posture, even when he's unconscious. He is really here for me. And I want to be there for him. I know now that I would go anywhere to be with him. I remember this feeling. I remember having this feeling the night of the grad party. What I don't remember is why I was so afraid of it for so many years later.

I reach up to touch his face. "I'll go anywhere with you," I whisper. It feels good to say it out loud.

I don't think he hears me. But when the sun comes up, he'll know. He'll know I just want to be with him.

Except...

Shit.

I forgot to remind Vera to pick up the box truck and bring it here to the bakery by eight so we can get the lobster to the beach. I carefully reach around to my back pocket and pull out my phone, trying not to disturb Grady.

ME: Remember bringing book true heroes to the battle by either!
VERA: <thumbs-up emoji>

Great. It's fine. She's got this. Everything is fine. I can drift back off to sleep, to a world where Grady and I are always together and everything is enough.

Chapter 35

Rocked Lobster

C<small>LAIRE</small>

I slowly wake, gradually and gracefully, the way you're supposed to, instead of being blasted by cortisol and adrenaline like I usually am. My head is still on Grady's lap. He smells wonderful. His dark spicy wood-tinged scent mixes with a hint of manly sweat and the smell of the cake we worked on together last night. Simply delicious. The deliciousness and warmth is only enhanced by the warm, buttery late summer morning sun glazing our skin. This could be my life. I could wake up like this in Grady's lap or his arms every morning.

Wait.

I can feel the hairs on the back of my neck stand up and scream at me. *That sunlight is way too warm! Way too buttery! Way too golden delicious!*

I bolt upright.

Oh my God!

"What time is it?" I yell out. Grady stirs and fumbles to check his watch, but it doesn't matter what time it is exactly. The fact that I can see the sun at all is a problem. "Vera should be here with the truck."

There's banging on the storefront window. I realize it must have been that banging that woke me from my peaceful slumber. I see Vera on the sidewalk, eyes wide. She has a weird smile on her face as she points to Grady and mouths, *See?! He's your lobster!* She arranges the fingers of both hands into pincher claws, like two old lobsters holding hands, the way Phoebe did on that episode of *Friends*. Normally I would let my BFF in and explain to her that Phoebe was wrong when she said that lobsters fall in love and mate for life, but there is only one thing on my mind right now.

I get up and yell at her through the window. "Tell me you have the box truck!"

"I totally have it!" Vera yells back. "I got it last night!"

I place a calming hand over my heart. All is well. The days of my best friend failing me are over. "Oh, thank God. I love you!"

But Vera's face does not look calm. A person who has actually procured a box truck that could transport a giant cake to the end-of-summer Shellibration would not have that expression on her face.

I clench my hands into fists. "What? Tell me."

"*'I have the truck, but she's still at my place and she won't start,' she said, humbly, silently begging for forgiveness with her doe-like eyes.*"

My fist drops from my heart to my hip. "Why won't the truck start?"

Vera scrunches up her face and rubs the back of her neck. "I left the lights on."

I finally open the door for her, thinking about rehiring her just so I can fire her again.

"Do either of you have jumper cables?" Vera asks as she bursts through.

Despite being the recent owner of a shitbox vehicle, I do not own jumper cables, and Vera knows this. I look to Grady for help.

He shakes his impossibly beautiful, sexy head. "I'd have to drive by my parents' house to get my dad's."

"Dammit, Vera! Why didn't you call roadside assistance?!" When she widens her eyes at me I remember why. Vera boned the only roadside-assistance guy in town a couple of years ago and then ghosted him. I groan. "We're gonna have to pull the cake to the beach on the dolly." I toss my hands up in the air. This is the only solution I can think of, and it makes sense to me. "I can't risk putting it in the back of a pickup truck—it'll be too bumpy and dusty. The dolly is the only way. If we leave now and move very carefully we can get it there in twenty minutes. Half an hour tops."

"Claire. We do not have to drag it there by hand, and we do not have to get it there before nine a.m. I've got this, babe. I'll take care of it," Grady says in his deep morning baritone. "Why don't you make some coffee?" He takes out his cell phone.

"He's got this, babe. Hi!!!! Look what a good friend I am—I brought you an egg sandwich!" Vera holds out a greasy paper bag and gives me a big hug, and I hug my lovable idiot best friend back. Because if there's one thing

I've learned it's that you have no choice but to love the people who give you what they can and not necessarily what you want.

"Jakey, hey," I hear Grady say.

"Why is he calling my brother?" I ask Vera. I turn to Grady. "Why are you calling my brother?"

Grady holds up a finger to silence me. I'm gonna let that slide if he actually solves this problem. "You still work with Robbie?" he asks the phone. "Is he off duty today?" There's some *Charlie Brown* squawking from my brother that I can't make out. "It's parked at his house, right? We need to move the cake. Can you bring it here?" More squawking. "Great. We need it ASAP. Oh, hey, pick up my brother on the way. If I called he probably wouldn't come, but if you just tell him that we need him he will. We'll need the extra set of hands." *Wa-wah wa wa wa wah.* "Great, see you soon."

Grady ends the call. He smiles and winks at me. It doesn't make my heart beat any slower, but instead of fluttering in pure panic, it races because of how he's looking at me. He's back and he has my back and all is well.

"See?!" Vera says, patting my head. "We've got this."

I swipe the egg sandwich from her and stuff my face with it. "Go make coffee," I tell her with my mouth full. This is the last thing I will ever ask her to do for me. If she sets my bakery on fire while doing it, at least I'll get my caffeine hit and dolly my lobster cake out before it all burns to the ground.

After quickly ingesting a sufficient amount of coffee,

Grady claps his hands. "Okay, let's see what we can get outside ourselves."

Vera, Grady, and I work together to move the cake onto the dolly. There are tense moments. I accidentally call Vera a clumsy-ass fucker and threaten to murder her when she trips a little bit, but she doesn't even blink and she forgives me before I even finish apologizing. We manage to wheel the cake through the back door and out to the back alley.

This is a lot of work and stress just to move a dessert shellfish that will end up on hundreds of paper plates by this afternoon. Maybe I'm just tired, but maybe I wouldn't miss owning my own bakery as much as I thought I would.

Once we've got the dolly in a stable location and Vera has ensured that there are no raccoons around, I reach for Grady's arm. "Grady." I have to catch my breath because we exerted a lot of effort just now.

"Yeah, babe?"

"There's something I want to tell you. I've changed my mind."

I hear a siren in the distance.

"If you've decided to move this lobster back inside, I will be very displeased," he says.

It's hot. He's got his shirt sleeves rolled up and he's breathing just a little heavily and I shouldn't be so turned on by the fact that he might be displeased with me, but gosh darn it, I am. "That's not what I'm talking about. I know I said I can't handle only having part of you. That I can't live half a life without..."

Grady looks a little anxious. The siren is now very

loud and headed this way. I can't hear my own voice over it without yelling. "Is there an ambulance coming?"

"I hope no one's hurt," Vera says.

"No one's hurt," Grady says, grinning. "The cavalry has arrived." Instantly forgetting what I just said, he looks over my shoulder and I follow his gaze.

It is indeed an ambulance making its way toward us, and my brother Jake is at the wheel. He looks really pleased with himself, like any ten-year-old boy would when making an excessively loud noise and driving really fast.

Jake parks and turns off the lights and siren.

As he climbs out, I ask him, "Where on earth did you get an ambulance?"

"Robbie. He's a paramedic, remember? He owns it and rents it out to the paramedic company he works with. He's off duty today, so he let me borrow it." He sees the cake on the dolly and his jaw drops. "Holy shit, you made that? Dude, that's amazing." He holds up his hand for a high five.

"Thanks," I say, slapping him five. "Do you think it's gonna fit?"

"Oh yeah," Jake says. "There should be room for three lobsters in there." He opens up the back, and Damien is already in there in the captain's seat, with two large plastic containers that are marked *Clawdia Swiffter* and *Muhammad Lobbee*.

Damien carefully places the lobster containers on the floor of the ambulance and hops out. "I hope you all know I'm giving up precious warm-up time to help with this."

"You shouldn't be warming them up right before the actual race anyway," Vera reminds him.

Damien crosses his arms in front of his chest. "That is your opinion."

"Yeah, based on logic and observation from watching them for the past—"

"Seriously, Damien, thank you for helping us," Grady cuts in. "We couldn't do this without you." Not that it didn't look like Vera and Damien were enjoying arguing with each other, but we don't have time for this.

"No problem," Damien says, matching his brother's deep voice as he flexes his sinewy muscles. "I am a master of crustacean transport, after all." He clocks my cake and says, "Whoa. Nice work, Claire." He furrows his brow as he circles the dolly and studies my design. "Wait a minute—is that Clawdia?"

I have no idea how he can tell, but I don't have time to discuss this with him.

Grady and Jake haul the gurney out from the back of the ambulance.

"Okay, let's get the patient onto the stretcher," Jake says, barely able to get the words out because he's laughing so hard.

"If you drop my lobster because you're laughing, I will break every bone in your body, asshat!"

My brother pretends to speak into a walkie-talkie on his shoulder. "Code *A-S-S*, we have a-hole on the scene. Code eight, backup requested."

Grady makes a walkie-talkie squawking sound. "Ten-four. Code two *ass*-istance squad has been dispatched."

They brace the wheels of the gurney and practically fall over laughing. They will forever be twelve years old when they get together. I would find it adorable if they weren't ruining my life right now. "Okay, everybody, can we get the giggles out of our system and focus? I put a lot of time and effort into this thing!"

"Ten-four. Giggles are GOA, crustacean is on the move." Jake lowers the stretcher. "All hands on deck!"

All five of us bend down to lift my masterpiece onto the stretcher, and I scream at everyone to never let go like it's the end of *Titanic*. My heart is in my throat as we roll the gurney into the ambulance, but it goes in without tipping or toppling and every piece remains intact.

There is a collective sigh of relief, and Jake runs around to the driver's seat. "Let's get this shellfish on the road!"

"You drive slowly, you hear me?! Jake?!"

"Yeah, you need to drive a lot slower than you did on the way here!" Damien shouts at him as he straps himself into the captain's seat again. "Last thing I need is for my champion to get seasick before the race!"

I catch Vera rolling her eyes before she asks me, "Do you want me to hold on to the cake with you back here, or...?"

"No, you ride shotgun," I blurt out without even pretending to consider my answer. She hasn't done anything to fuck anything up in the past half an hour, but I'm not taking any chances.

Grady and I strap ourselves into the seats on either side of the stretcher and hold on to the giant platform that the cake is resting on.

We're off to a rocky start, but once we're on the main road, Jake's speed is appropriate and I can breathe easier.

I look up to find Grady watching me. "What were you saying earlier? About changing your mind?"

I glance over at Damien, who's got his eyes closed and I think he's visualizing the race or something, so it feels private. I lean in a little closer toward Grady and say, "I've decided I want to be with you as much as possible. I'd rather live in your world than live without you in mine."

"Is that from a song?"

"Maybe?"

"'Midnight Train to Georgia,'" Damien says, his eyes still closed. "Sort of."

"I'll sell the bakery," I continue. "And move to New York. I can get a job working at someone else's amazing bakery in Manhattan." I shrug. "That way I'd have more time to be with you."

I don't think I've ever seen Grady look this surprised. Not even that time I did that thing to him on top of the mega yacht. He blinks once and then says, "Is that really what you want?"

I'm tearing up again, but not because I'm sad. Because I finally feel like I have what I want. "What I really want is to be with you."

Chapter 36

A Race against Brine

GRADY

I HAD EXPECTED to be the one to surprise Claire, not the other way around. I've been holding back from telling her that I'm stepping down as CEO because I didn't want her distracted while she made her magnificent cake. But it's been incredibly difficult. I want to hold her and kiss her and make her understand in no uncertain terms that she's mine and I am hers.

When all this time, underneath all the stress and frosting and fondant, she was thinking about our future and choosing us.

Choosing me.

She's willing to give up her life here in Beacon Harbor to be by my side in New York so I can continue my conquest. If there was any doubt in my mind that I had made the right decision in choosing to come back to her—which there wasn't—there wouldn't be now. She has somehow simultaneously promised me what I'd wanted and thrown me completely off-kilter. Only Claire Sweeney could do this to me.

Would it be easier for her in New York?

Does she want a whole new chapter in life?

"What I want is to be with you too, Claire." I reach across the glossy cake sea to hold one of her hands, both of us still gripping the giant cake tray with one hand each. "But there's something that I need to tell you too." Before I can continue, the ambulance comes to an abrupt stop.

Damien mother-seat-belts his lobster containers, and Claire and I steady the lobster cake. Seconds later, Jake and Vera are opening the back doors.

"We're here. Let's move!" Jake yells as he hops up into the back to start moving the gurney.

Claire and I share a look. It's not a sad shared look. Or frustrated. It's bemused. We haven't figured out our future. But now we both know for certain that we have one.

We just don't have time to talk about it right now.

"They're still setting everything up!" Vera yells over her shoulder, pointing at the stage. "We aren't late! I did nothing wrong! Nothing at all!"

"Let's show the town this amazing cake," I say to Claire. "And then we'll figure out the rest of our lives."

Claire smiles a radiant smile, and we help get the cake down and out of the ambulance. Damien follows close behind with Clawdia and Muhammad Lobbee. He looks stressed. My brother never looks stressed. It's actually nice to see. He clearly gives a shit. But what's not okay is that he looks miserable. Without hope. I look over at Claire, who is flanked by Vera and her brother as they get the cake to the award stage.

I'll have to wait to tell Claire everything I need to tell her. But there's another speech that's been burning a hole in my mind. For my brother. And it's now or never.

"Damien, wait!" I call out. He turns back as I jog up to him.

"What? I have to get Muhammad into the race track."

Sugarcoating this like it's one of Claire's donuts will not help matters. So I just say it: "I think you should race Clawdia."

Damien is not accustomed to tough love. Except from Vera, apparently. He looks at me like I just sucker punched him. "What?"

"Clawdia's the one who should race. She's the one who wins."

This evokes a joyless little laugh from my brother. He shakes his head. "You know everything don't you, Grady? You're the winner. You're the racer. You can't even let me have this."

"That's not what I'm saying."

"You're saying you don't think Muhammad Lobbee can do this. You think he's a loser and a fuckup." There's an undertow of emotion in my brother's voice that has nothing to do with lobsters.

"I don't think that at all. He doesn't have to be Clawdia. He shouldn't be. The problem is not that he isn't someone else. The problem is that he's not being who he should be. He's not doing the thing he was born to do."

"What do you mean?" Damien grits out. "Are you saying he should be dinner? A nice bisque, maybe?"

"I'm saying he's not a racer. I'm saying he's the best lobster-racer *trainer* this festival has ever seen. He's trained a champion. Let them both be who they're supposed to be, and stop forcing them to be something they're not."

Damien's face and entire body remain rigid. I don't move. I don't have anything else to say right now. He can tell me to fuck off. He can take a swing at me. But I'm not going anywhere.

And that seems to give Damien the space he needs to hear what I'm trying to tell him. His stance softens. "Yeah," he says quietly with a nod. "Okay."

I place my hand on his shoulder. "And maybe you feel bad for me. But I never felt bad for you. I'm pissed at you." My brother looks up at me. To me. I look him square in the eyes. "After today, when this is all done, I need you to do your music. No more fucking around. It's time to use your gift. I'll support that in whatever way I can."

My brother listens to me. Really listens in a way that he hasn't for a really long time. Maybe ever.

After a few moments of stillness, his easy half grin makes a triumphant comeback. "Yeah. Okay."

I spot my parents waving at us as they approach.

"Hi, honey! Oh, it's so good to see you," my mom cries out, as if it's been more than two days since she last saw me.

I plant a kiss on her cheek. "Hey, Mom. Dad."

"Hey there, son," my dad says as we hug. "You ready, Damien? I mean, is your boy ready?" My dad points at Muhammad.

"We're ready, but there's been a change of plans," my brother says as he gives me a knowing smile.

For both of us. If they only knew.

I make my way over to the stage. Claire, Vera, and Jake are done setting up the cake, and Mayor Stacy is gushing over it. She isn't even jogging in place. "Claire Sweeney—from this year forward, *you* are the official baker of the Shellibration. Of any official town event—my Christmas party included! This. Cake. Is. Magnificent! This cake is the heart and soul of Beacon Harbor and this event—in pastry form!"

Claire grimaces as she points out that technically, this cake is not considered a pastry, but she looks like she's bursting with pride. "Wow. It is literally a dream come true to hear you say that. Thank you, Mayor Stacy. I am so honored. But I'm actually not going to be in Beacon—"

"Claire!" I interrupt. "Babe. Can I talk to you for a second?" I grab Claire's hand and pull her away before she talks herself out of her lifelong dream.

"Grady Barber! Fantastic to see you. You're still giving the keynote speech, yes?" Stacy holds up crossed fingers.

"Absolutely. Big plans for that speech."

"Sensational!" Stacy exclaims, punctuating it with a double thumbs-up.

"*Ladies and gentlemen and racers,*" we hear the announcer say over the loudspeaker, "*start your pincers!*"

"Oh, that's my cue. Gotta go!" Stacy says as a mass of people make their way over to the racetrack for the start of the lobster race. I keep hold of Claire's hand as we follow everyone. All the women in the crowd wear fancy hats like at the Kentucky Derby.

"On your marks. Get set. Crawl!"

The race begins with a huge cheer from the crowd. Claire and I let go of each other's hands so that we can applaud and I add a piercing whistle. My parents and Damien are up front, and I see my dad's hands on Damien's shoulders in support.

"Shellton John's Rocket Lobster takes an early lead, with David Pincher's Fast Club right on his tail!" the announcer calls out.

Now, here's the thing about lobsters. Despite my brother's intense training regimen, they are not greyhounds. They are not horses. They aren't even fish. So while there is a lot of boisterous, joyful community energy to go along with the jaunty lady hats, there is not a lot of action on the racetrack. Because lobsters walk slowly. Even when they're racing. Which is why I finally have a chance to turn to Claire and say, "You said you would come to New York with me."

Claire tears her eyes away from the race to look at me. "I would. I will."

"Lobster?! I Hardly Know'er! has slowly surged ahead!" the announcer intones.

"But is that what you want?" I ask her.

Claire stares at the racetrack. "What I want is a life with you, Grady. I wanted it even when I wouldn't admit it to myself, and I need it more than all the other things I thought were really important to me."

"Claw Me Maybe briefly inches ahead before being overtaken by I Still Haven't Found What I'm Lobster For!

Oh, it's gonna be a tight race, folks. I hope none of these lobsters are claw-strophobic!"

"But let's say that you could have me here. Let's say that we could build a life in Beacon Harbor together. That would be the ideal, right?"

Claire shakes her head. "I would never ask you to—"

"Uh-oh, what's this? Ladies and gentlemen, it looks like we have a fight. Shellfish Bastard, living up to his name, is being separated from Claws and Effect! Both are unharmed, but they have been disqualified! Causing a lot of frust-acean for their owners—that's gotta hurt."

I smooth a strand of Claire's hair behind her ear. "I know. But let's say, oh, I don't know, let's say I didn't need to be in New York all the time anymore. If we could be together here, where we grew up together." I take her hand in mine. "Where our hearts slowly became intertwined over the years, so slowly and organically we didn't even realize what was happening. That would be the ideal. Wouldn't it?"

Claire looks up at me and her eyes well with tears. "That would make me so happy it would hurt a little. In a good way. The best way."

I wrap my arms around her. "Nothing but the best for my girl." Before I get the chance to tell her how everything has changed, we hear, *"Clawdia Swiffter and Dwayne the Rock Lobster are nearing the finish line! Ladies and gentlemen, it's gonna be a close claw!"*

Claire and I break our conversation at the mention of Clawdia Swiffter, and we turn our attention back to the race. Just as the announcer said, our girl and another lobster are crawling antenna and antenna.

"Come on, Clawdia! Move that meaty tail, girl!" Claire yells.

And I know it's crazy, but my beautiful girl yelling at a crustacean makes my heart swell. She's supporting my family. She's supporting me.

And one day, we'll make our own family together, here in Beacon Harbor.

"Finish it!" I call out. I see my brother, my father, and my mother all hugging, and I pull Claire with me as I rush over to them. We watch as Clawdia goes back and forth with Dwayne the Rock Lobster. She's in the lead, then she falls back. Then she takes the lead again. They go back and forth in a somewhat agonizing pattern until Clawdia's antenna crosses the finish line first.

"*Clawdia Swiffter wins! There you have it, ladies and gentlemen—Clawdia wins!*"

My family, Claire, and I are jumping around like crazy people.

"You did it!" I scream at my brother. "You actually did it!" And we hug each other, like when we were little and none of the bullshit of adult life had come between us. My father—my very-alive-and-still-healthy father—joins us, and our mother somehow ends up at the center of the group hug. And then my arm finds Claire because she will always be a part of this family from now on.

The next few minutes are a whirlwind. Clawdia and Damien are presented with the trophy as the mayor tells the crowd that Clawdia, as well as all of today's racers, will get to live in a massive, lush new lobster retirement aquarium that a generous donor has commissioned. It's me. I'm the generous donor who forgot that he donated money for this. I have now ensured that they'll each get their own habitats, of course, so they don't cannibalize each other, the largest tank going to the winner. Nothing but the best saltwater, oxygenation, temperature control, and seafood pellets. Why? I dunno. I didn't want the subjects of my little brother's weird summer obsession to end up on a toasted bun. Now they'll be local shellebrities. Damien asks the mayor if Clawdia's trainer can also be rehomed there, and she says yes, even though she has no idea what he's talking about.

Finally, the mayor reveals Claire's magnificent cake to the crowd, ceremoniously unveiling it to satisfying "awws" and applause from the townsfolk. I can only give Claire a quick kiss before Stacy welcomes me to the stage.

"Shello, Beacon Harbor..." There is some polite laughter, but I really wish I hadn't said that out loud.

"That was pretty funny, Mr. Suit!" I squint as I scan the audience for my nemesis, but I spot him near the stage, smiling up at me. This could be some kind of trap, but it's good to see him smile.

"Thanks, Crabby. Lovely to see you. As Mayor Stacy mentioned, I was born and raised here. Most recently I've been in New York serving as CEO of Beacon Holdings, the company I founded. I named it that because I wanted a piece of what I grew up with with me as I attempted to conquer the world.

"I've been thinking a lot about what I wanted to say in this speech ever since the mayor did me the honor of asking me to give it. And what I want to say is that those of you here, you understand that when you experience

Beacon Harbor and her people, you know that a piece of her isn't enough." I glance over at Claire, who's clasping her hands together and rocking back and forth from her heels to her tiptoes. "Because Beacon Harbor is a place that gets it. This town understands that life isn't about the rat race. It isn't even about winning the lobster race. It's about running the race alongside the people you love. Beacon Harbor is a small town with a huge heart. Personally, I have recently been given a gift. It didn't seem like a gift at first. It was quite terrifying, actually, because it involved my dad's heart. But it offered me the realization that time must be judiciously guarded like any other resource.

"We think of time as something outside of our control. Something that marches on, completely indifferent to us. Like a lobster on a racetrack. But that's not accurate. Early on in my business education, I learned about compound interest. This is the principle that when you give a small amount of money a large amount of time to grow, it will grow at a rate much greater than someone trying to stuff money into a bank account later on in life."

I turn my head to look at Claire, to the side of the stage. Speaking to no one but her.

"Now I know that time is like that too. If you invest your time with the people you love, the moments that come later will compound and every second is richer than the last. You can't wait until you retire to build lives with the people you want to be with. You'd never catch up. I was so busy compounding things that didn't really matter, I nearly lost the thing that matters most."

I look around at my view from this stage—of the

crowd and the beach and the town and the harbor. Taking a deep breath, I turn my attention back to Claire, the center of my stage. "This hasn't become public news yet, but between you and me, I have stepped down as CEO of Beacon Holdings. I'm coming back home to Beacon Harbor. For good."

Chapter 37

Batter Late than Never

GRADY

I REALLY DO LOVE this town and I appreciate the genuinely enthusiastic cheering from the crowd after my announcement—especially from Crabby—but everything fades away when my girl runs out on stage to throw her arms around my neck. I lift her up and swing her around. The cheers grow louder. When I lower her to the ground, Claire asks, "You're really back for good?"

"Yes, I am. You're never getting rid of me." I give her a very PG kiss on the cheek.

She takes my hand in hers as we stroll offstage, where both of our parents have gathered with our brothers and Vera. "Why didn't you tell me?"

"I wanted us to stay focused on you and your cake." There is so much more I want to tell her, with my lips and tongue and hands and another very impatient part of me, but it will have to wait until we're alone.

Like I said, I do love this town. But I'm dying to get back to our house so Claire and I can be alone together. I love the people of the town, and it feels like every single one of them comes over to me and Claire to congratulate us and ask for pictures of us with the lobster cake. I love my parents, who are happier than I even imagined they would be to find out I'm back for good. I love Claire's parents, who give us a ride home, even though Helen Sweeney tells her husband to drive by two open houses just to give us an idea of what else is on the market and Bob pulls over by the side of the road to take a picture of a blue heron.

Finally, I'm unlocking the front door to the five-bedroom house I will be spending the rest of the day and night in with Claire. We wait until her parents' car disappears from view before starting to kiss and undress each other. We pause for three seconds while I punch in the code for the security system and she tears off her T-shirt and then I'm devoting all of my attention to the woman who makes every part of me happy like nothing else ever could.

Claire breathes my name against my lips, over and over. I would sell everything I own if that's what it takes to make her understand that she's the most important thing in the world to me. My tongue finds hers, and we both sigh and groan, begging for forgiveness and giving it in the same frantic, wordless conversation. It turns out my relentless drive and desire to conquer was a bottomless need for this woman. I promise her with the deep-soul kiss of a man who's known her her whole life that I will spend the rest of mine giving her all that I have and taking everything she'll give me.

She tastes like vanilla and butter and sugar and the best decision I've ever made.

"I'm so sorry I told you to go," she tells me between feverish kisses. "All that time we could have spent together."

"I'm here now, baby. I'm not mad about it."

She kicks off her shoes and then jumps up into my arms, wrapping her legs around my waist. "I am! You could have been controlling that remote thing in my panties the whole time you were in New York!"

I carry her to the living room while she finishes unbuttoning my shirt. "Well, not the whole time. You would have had to recharge it at some point." Which reminds me, my tech guy should have that prototype done by now. But more importantly— "Speaking of your panties. Take them off." I drop her onto the sofa, and my mouth waters when I watch her tits bounce under the little cotton camisole.

"Thought you'd never ask," she says, smirking as she unbuttons her jeans.

"That was not a request," I assure her as I step out of my pants. "That was an order."

And there's that eye roll that I look forward to punishing her for for all eternity. "Oh, we're back to that again." Those blue eyes are hooded and begging for me, but she puts on a good show.

"We're back to that." I free my aching erection from the confines of my boxer briefs and sit down beside her. "Again and again and again."

Claire straddles me, gripping my shoulders almost as tight as I'm squeezing her beautiful, round ass. She lowers herself down so, so slowly until her warm, wet pussy kisses the tip of my cock. Holding there, she clenches around me as she stares down at me, kissing me with her eyes open, watching me go mad for her. She moves her hips in tiny circles. I suck in my breath, and the palm of my hand against her taut flesh forces her to release her chokehold on the crown of my cock for a second. She slides down, taking me in as deep as she can, savoring our connection before gently rocking back and forth, softly moaning.

I try to remain still for her, let her control this reunion for as long as I can bear it. "Baby..." I whisper. What I mean is *I am back for good, but now I'm really home.*

"I missed you so much, Grady," she whimpers, leaning back, resting her hands on my knees, keeping the rhythm of our movements nice and slow.

It's poetic and evil, and I am so desperately in love with Claire Sweeney. I want to conquer her and let her conquer me. We will create so much together here, it will make Beacon Holdings look like a lemonade stand.

"I'm gonna fuck you so many times today," I growl. I meant to utter a sweeter sentence, but all the words are coming from the same place now.

Claire giggles and clenches around me again. "Good. I've cleared my schedule."

I pick up the pace, drilling up into her. I can't take this anymore. "We're gonna fill this house with kids, you know that?"

She braces herself against me. "Not if my mom finds us an even bigger house."

"How 'bout you don't talk about your mom while I'm inside you."

"How 'bout you fill me up with your hot billionaire baby batter," she hisses. "That better?"

"Jesus."

That is better.

And I do.

I do, I do.

When I've caught my breath and I'm still inside her, I tell her what I hope my actions have already shown her: "I love you, Little Sweeney. I always will."

Her glistening lips part to whisper, "I've always loved you, Grody Borber."

"One question," I say, grasping her waist because I know she's going to wriggle around and I do not want her to leave me. Ever.

She arches an eyebrow.

"Do you have any dark chocolate?"

The quirk of her lips, the tiny spasm of her hips, and the fire in her hooded eyes is the answer to everything.

The *more* I've been searching for.

I've found it.

And I'll never lose it again.

Epilogue

All's Claire in Love & War, But Give Pizza a Chance

Claire

It's late fall.

Grady is taking me sailing at sunset in his new boat—our new boat, he insists—*The Deal Baker*.

Since Thanksgiving is fast approaching, I've been even busier than I had been throughout September and October. The entire state of Maine had a stunning show of fall foliage this year, but Beacon Harbor's was particularly gorgeous. That meant more tourists than usual, which has meant a lot of customers at the bakery, and I'm down to my last sixteen-ounce container of pumpkin spice. But my days off are real days off now. Outside of the bakery, life has slowed down in the best possible way. We've had time for the people and activities we love.

November, however, has brought in an insane number of orders for pies and pumpkin cheesecake, and I think I've baked half the apples in New England. It's a seasonal thing, and I can handle it. Or rather, *we* can handle it. I've got the cutest, most efficient mother-daughter team working with me at the bakery now. And the most handsome assistant slash manager slash chief operating officer slash stud muffin.

Of course, Grady didn't stay retired for very long. You can't turn off a machine like Grady Barber. You can only idle his engine for a little while before it has to rev back up. He's certainly used a lot of that pent-up energy on me in many creative ways. But now he's also applying his business skills to my bakery.

He's already working on a recipe-book deal and branded store products. It's perfect. I get to focus on my bakery and my bakes and the town and my local brand. He gets to remix those ingredients for use in a new, budding global empire. But this one is thoroughly kneaded into what I do and it won't take him away from me.

I pull up the collar of my coat and gaze out at the choppy water. The leaves have mostly fallen, and winter is gently whispering that she's about to kick our asses. But I'll show her who's lady boss. I'm serving the best hot chocolate in town; my car starts regularly—it's housed in a nice warm, dry garage; and my boyfriend, who sleeps next to me every night, is an absolute furnace.

Unfortunately, I can't get close to Grady right now because he's busy steering the boat. The wind is whipping through me and cutting through to my bones. Why are we doing this right now? Grady made it seem really important. I had to be free at this time on this day when the sun was going down.

As we approach the island, Grady drops anchor and rows us to shore. He is acting strangely. The Grady I know is always so confident and relaxed. Especially when something stresses him out—his freakish billionaire-type-A-alpha response is always to somehow get even calmer and more relaxed.

It would be really annoying if he wasn't so totally mine now. But he is mine and his highly effective personality has rubbed off on me. The small stuff sweats me less.

But that's not the Grady I see before me. He's fidgety. And nervous.

What is going on?

"Grady, are you going to tell me what we're doing here?"

"What? No, we're just gonna have a little picnic. No big deal. What?"

I'm about to ask him why he's being so weird when I get a strange feeling in my gut.

And in all of the other parts of my body that talk to me about Grady.

He's going to murder me.

Finally.

After all these months and years. An underachieving normal dude would have murdered me that first time on the island here. Or over twelve years ago when Robbie nearly ran me over in his wheelbarrow of fire—any other guy would have just let me get squished or burnt like a roasted marshmallow in the middle of my perfect s'more. But not my Grady. He's too strategic and meticulous for that. Of course he would want to plan it all out, make me fall in love with him, every single inch of him. And I have. I thought I was head over heels for him before. But every domestic moment, every new adventure we have together makes my small world of Beacon Harbor as rich and glorious as if I traversed the globe as a queen.

And now the son of a bitch is gonna take that and twist it into a Netflix true-crime special!

All that is a brief half-thought that takes maybe a fraction of a second to flash across my mind. I burst out laughing, and my mildly psychotic laughter pierces the cool night air, echoing across the water. This gives Grady the opportunity to look at me like I'm nuts. And maybe I am.

We know each other so well. He knows he's being weird. I know he's being weird. He knows that I know that he knows he's being weird. He knows my laugh is weird. He knows that I know that my laugh is weird. He knows that I know that he knows that my laugh is weird.

We grew up together. And now we're in love. We've known each other long enough and well enough to accept all of it.

"Come on, baby," he says, holding his hand out to me as he holds up a lantern with the other. My not-at-all-serial-killer-ish Grady has made a return. I interlace my five digits of icicles with his warm fingers, and it feels so good. We make our way through the woods to the beach with the metal fire pit, and he starts building a fire.

"Do you want some help?" I ask, even though I already know the answer.

"Nope. I just want you to relax."

Before I murder you and make you mine forever, my brain adds.

But I'll make intense, passionate love to you before I do! my lady parts chime in.

I hear a fallen branch crack under the weight of something or someone in the woods. "What the hell is that?" I mutter, turning toward the increasingly dark blackness. The sun is now below the horizon. The lantern is basically a beacon that's guiding any land mammal here to stab one or both of us or—who am I kidding—me.

"It's nothing," Grady assures without even giving a cursory glance at the possible second serial killer inhabiting this island.

"You're not even gonna go look?"

"It's probably just teenagers. Or badgers. Or teenage badgers."

Grady is fumbling and stumbling with the kindling. Grady Barber does not fumble or stumble with anything. It's weird.

"Grady, what is going on?"

"Just relax. Relax. Now!" he orders irritably.

"I can't relax! I'm freezing. I'm terrified. You're acting really weird."

Grady stops what he's doing for a second. He silences me with his stare. That look that under any other circumstances would put me in the mood, but right now it makes me feel guilty. "Wait a minute. Are you thinking I'm gonna murder you again?"

"Noooo?" I answer unconvincingly.

He throws down his bundle of sticks. "Dammit. This

is supposed to be romantic. You're supposed to be fully romanced when I do this. Be romanced!"

"Be what?" Now my heart is really racing. Because my brain can't keep up with my heart right now. My heart has figured something out.

"All right, guys. You can come out now," Grady announces to the terrifying darkness.

I hear rustling and jump up, adopting a stance that I imagine karate might look like if you described it to a person who had never seen anyone do karate.

Then my body relaxes from being a not-at-all-deadly weapon when I start to make out who is coming toward us as they turn on their lanterns. "Mom? Dad? Jake! Vera!" I also see Grady's parents and his brother, who are now illuminated. "What are you all doing here? Grady, what are they—"

I turn back to find Grady down on one knee in the sand, holding up a little velvet box. My hands immediately cover my mouth and nose, and my eyes well up with happy tears. *We told you so!* says my still-racing heart and all the other excited lady parts. *Told you he had something planned. Not murder, but still this is a pretty big deal!*

"I had plans to build a fire so I could do this by firelight," Grady explains. "But it doesn't matter as long as I get the answer that I need for the most important offer I've ever made. I know I'm a hard worker, but the thing I want to work on most for the rest of my life is making sure you know you are the most beautiful, wonderful person that I have ever met. My job is to make sure you know how deeply I am in love with you. I want to continue working on building a life with you, Claire. Will you marry me?"

"Yes!" I throw my arms around his neck and scream. Not like someone who's getting murdered or pounded, but like a grown lady who is really and truly getting the thing that she has quietly always wanted. "Yes, yes, yes!"

He rises, putting his strong arms around me and lifting me up off the ground. I cover his not-at-all-murderous cold face with warm kisses, and the cheers from our families echo around the cove and probably all across the harbor. After he sets me down and everyone has congratulated us and opened up a bottle of champagne that magically appeared, he orders Jake to start the fire.

Then he slides a gorgeous diamond ring onto my finger. It's a bezel solitaire engagement ring. "I had it custom designed for you and told them you're a baker. This kind of setting won't snag on your apron or get caught in your equipment, and no food particles will get stuck in there."

That's my Grady. Romantic, extravagant, and totally practical.

"It's perfect, Grady," I tell him as I lovingly stroke his cheekbone, but my brain is already busy designing our wedding cake. "Thank you for not murdering me."

He kisses my forehead and then goes over to unzip a big duffel bag that has appeared out of nowhere. I guess one of those guys must have brought it with them. He removes something from it and hides it behind his back. "Well, Little Sweeney, even though you said yes and have made me the happiest man alive, you are not, in fact, out of danger."

"What is that supposed to mean?"

There's beautiful mischief in that man's eyes as he approaches me.

"We still have some unfinished business, you and I." He tosses me something, and I catch it.

I look down at the object in my hands. "A Nerf gun?" I look up, and he's pointing his own Nerf gun at me.

And he shoots me with a Nerf dart.

It takes me a second to realize that— "You shot me!"

"That's right, Claire. I love you. I respect you. I think you're the best baker in the world, one hell of a business owner, you're going to make an extraordinary wife, and one day I expect you'll be the extraordinary mother of my children."

Well, that certainly take some of the sting out of—

He shoots me again!

"But I will never, ever show you mercy in a Nerf war."

That's when Jake shoots him. "That's for my little sister!" Then Jake shoots me a bunch of times and laughs manically.

Damien shoots Jake. "That's for my older brother!" Then Damien rapid-fires at his beloved older brother's head.

"Just stop it right now, boys!" Mrs. Barber yells out. And then she shoots both of her sons.

Vera blasts Damien three times in the back. "That's for you and your damn lobsters and all the lobster babies Clawdia Swiffter is pregnant with!"

The Billionaire Is Back

The Nerf gun war ensues with the Sweeneys plus Vera on one team and the Barbers on the other. It's pure joyful chaos, and I have no idea who's winning until everyone else is out of ammunition and I tackle Grady. I have him dead to rights. Exactly where I want him. With me. Under me. Smiling up at me.

Then I hear helicopters.

Helicopters?

"What is happening?" I calmly ask as I picture dozens of soldiers parachuting from the sky and descending upon me in a final surprise attack.

"Pizza delivery for after the war," he says, shrugging, like he just put in an order from Uber Eats.

"You arranged to have pizzas delivered here by helicopter?"

"I wanted to make sure the pizzas are hot for you."

I shake my head in amazement.

He will never, ever cease to amaze me.

I will always, always be hot for him.

I gaze lovingly upon the man of my dreams—my fiancé, future husband, and the future father of my children.

And I shoot him with my last Nerf dart.

Then I give him some sugar.

Acknowledgments

Kayley would like to thank all the readers who reached out, and the citizens of Kayleyville who commented with their support for her in 2023, aka the worst year of her life. It really meant a lot. And thanks to Jodi and Beth for keeping things moving.

Connor would like to thank the members of Connor's Corner.

Thanks and apologies to our friend, Avery Maxwell, for sharing the hilarious potential true crime story that led to her IRL HEA.

Thanks to Sara "Hot Dog" McQueen aka McQueen of Sweets, for answering some of Kayley's bake questions.

Thanks to Monica, Jodi M, Chrissy, Yael, Michaela, and Emily S for the beta listens!

And simmer down, Tammy. Simmer. Down.

About Kayley and Connor

Listen to Connor Crais and Samantha Brentmoor narrate The Billionaire Is Back on Audible.

USA Today bestselling author Kayley Loring and narrator/Amazon Top 100 bestselling author Connor Crais have co-authored *The Billionaire Is Back, A Very Vegas St. Patrick's Day* and the Boston Tomcats series.

For more about Kayley and her books,
visit kayleyloring.com.

For more about Connor, his voice, and his books,
visit connorcrais.com.

Made in United States
Orlando, FL
29 January 2024